TV movie 1979

FREEDOM
ROAD

FREEDOM

ROAD

BY HOWARD FAST

DUELL, SLOAN AND PEARCE
Publishers   NEW YORK

61817

11-45

PRINTED IN THE UNITED STATES OF AMERICA
AMERICAN BOOK—STRATFORD PRESS, INC., NEW YORK

*To the men and women, black and white,
yellow and brown, who have laid down
their lives in the struggle against fascism.*

Contents

PART ONE

The Voting

vii

Contents

PART TWO

The Fighting

PART ONE

The Voting

A Prologue

THE WAR WAS DONE—THE LONG AND BLOODY STRUGGLE THAT was, at the time, the greatest people's war the world had ever known—and the men in blue marched home. The men in gray, stunned and hurt, looked about at their land, and saw what war does.

At Appomattox Court House, General Lee laid down his arms, and then it was all finished. And in the warm southland, there were four million black men who were free. A hard-won freedom, a precious thing. A free man counts tomorrow and yesterday, and both of them are his; hunger and there's no master to feed you, but walk with long steps and no master says go slowly. Two hundred thousand of these black men were soldiers of the republic when the struggle finished, and many of them went home with guns in their hands.

Gideon Jackson was one of them. Tall and strong and tired, a gun in his hand and a faded blue uniform on his back, he came home to the Carolina soil and the Carwell Plantation. The big white house stood much as he remembered it, not damaged by the war, but the gardens and fields were weeds and jungle, and the Carwells had gone away— none knew where. The freedmen, as they returned, took up their lives in the old slave quarters, together with those who had never gone away. And as the months passed, more and more of the freedmen returned to the Carwell Plantation, from the cold northland where they had gone to find freedom, from the ranks of the Union Army, and from their hiding places in the piney woods and the lonesome swamps. They took up their lives with the deep wonder that they were free.

How Gideon Jackson Came Home
from the Voting

THE CROWS WOKE RACHEL EARLY THIS COOL NOVEMBER MORN-
ing, and lying in bed, the old cloth pulled up around her
neck, Jenny making a warm spot against her breast, she
listened to their singing. They sang from far off, caw, caw,
caw, a sad sound, but not unpleasant to someone who had
heard it long as Rachel, every morning sun up; a good day
or bad, it was all the same to the crows.

Against her breast, the warm spot of the girl stirred, and
Rachel whispered, "Lie easy, my child, gentle and easy and
listen to them old crows, just listen."

But the day begins—you can't stop it. The straw bag was
warm and crunchy, and there Rachel would like to stay, but
when the sun suddenly broke the mist, it shot the whole
cabin through with light, from where the door sagged and
in between all the warped boards. Jeff stretched and kicked
his heels against the floor. Jenny, pressed against Rachel,
came wide awake, pulled away, and cold slippered over the
warm spot where she had lain. Marcus made noises, whooee,
whooee, and Jeff poked him, and then they rolled over on
the floor, scuffling.

All the sounds that made the morning Rachel knew with
her eyes closed. Why did human beings wake so sudden and
so raucous, she had asked herself a hundred times? She clung
to darkness a moment more, and then came to her feet
brusque and pacifying:

"Jeff, you shut!"

He had his legs twisted around Marcus's belly. He was
fifteen but built like Gideon; the boy was a giant before he

even knew what made a man, six feet tall and chocolate brown, more her color than the prune-skin shining black of Gideon, but handsome and long-faced the way Gideon was, born to make a sinful life for women. Marcus at twelve was skinny and small, and Rachel snapped at Jeff:

"Let go there with your legs, you big fool!"

Jenny was seven. She ran out of the door, first thing, like that every morning, a creature seeking light. The dog met her, barking his fool head off.

Jeff stood up and Marcus pounded him, a woodpecker pecking at a big oak tree. Jeff was easygoing, like Gideon that way, but without the iron inside of him that made Gideon something; Jeff was slow to anger and then the anger came like fire, but Gideon's anger was always inside of him.

"Get out, you both," she told them. "Get on out of here, get out."

She was laughing already. Small herself, it was a constant wonder to her that these masses of dark flesh were hers, out from between her legs, out of a little bundle tied onto her with a cord. Well, she had a big man; and these were Gideon's children, she thought with pride. She stirred about the cabin. It was full of sunlight now, the door swung back. Jeff came in with kindling, his head dripping wet from the rain-water barrel. She went out to the barrel herself, doused head and hands, and called to Jenny:

"Come and get your wetting, come on now!"

Jenny hated water. Five times she had to be called before Rachel caught her and dipped her woolly head into the water, and then screaming as if a little cold water could kill her. When Rachel came back into the cabin, Jeff had the fire burning. She took her wooden bowl and mixed the meal, while Jeff blew the fire up to hot coals. The dog lay in front of the fire—leave that to him on a cold, sharp November morning.

At the time of its greatest glory, almost a decade ago now, the Carwell Plantation covered twenty-two thousand acres of good South Carolina soil. A hundred miles inland from the coast, it lay in that gently rolling country that makes a broad belt of demarcation between the flat tidewater and the high uplands. When cotton was king there, a bale and a half was gathered from the acre, and when the bolls opened, there was a sea of white as far as the eye could reach.

The big plantation house dominated the scene. Four stories, twenty-two rooms, the portico columned like a Greek temple, it stood on a tall hill, almost in the geographical center of the plantation. A line of willows made a fine driveway. Live oaks made a protective wall. If you stood at the slave quarters, half a mile away, and looked up at the big house, its likeness to a temple was increased; and when the white clouds scudded across the sky behind it, it made one of the prettiest sights in that part of the country.

That was in the old times. In this year of 1867, there had been no cotton planting at Carwell. It was said that Dudley Carwell was living in Charleston, but nobody really knew. It was also said that the two Carwell boys had been killed in the war. Debt and unpaid taxes had thrown the plantation into that curious state of suspension that had overtaken so many of the great southern manors. It was said that the government owned it now, and it was also said that every former Carwell slave would be given forty acres of land and a mule. That sort of talk ran like fire, but nobody could put his finger on exactly what was to be done. Several times, white folks had driven out from Columbia, poked around, and gone away.

Meanwhile, the freed slaves lived there. A good many of them had stayed on all through the war, putting in crop after crop and caring for the place. Others, like Gideon, had gone off and joined the Union Army. Still others had run away and hidden themselves. But even when emancipation came, most of them stayed, not so much because they feared the dire punishment set out for runaways as that they had no place in particular to go. This was their home, their land, their country—it had always been so.

For a generation, the Carwells had for the most part lived in Charleston, leaving the plantation to overseers. After the third year of the war, Dudley Carwell visited the place only once, and when he left he closed up the house and took the house servants with him. The last overseer went away in sixty-five, and from there on the slaves were left alone. They no longer planted cotton; that was a cash crop, and they had neither the need nor understanding for cash crops. They put in corn and rice in the lowland part of the plantation. They grew greens in the gardens; they had pigs and chickens, and that way they lived.

They were more fortunate than most freedmen. Three times columns of regulars came by and picked the place clean, but they managed to get through those times of hunger. The bitter, defeated troops had only killed four of their number; that was not as bad as what happened in most places where freedmen lived.

And now, from far away, the thing called Congress had given the order for freedmen to go and vote. It was a time of wonder in the land, you may be sure.

Marcus was the first to see Gideon coming back from the voting, and afterwards he remembered that. He and Axel Christ and a few other boys were playing up toward the plantation house; when they got well up on the hillside, they could see two miles of the road stretching out into the sunny, dusty distance. The road was a door into nowhere. Some said, follow it long enough and you'd come to Columbia, but that was hearsay and the world was full of hearsay. To Marcus and his friends, the road just went off—and why should it have to go anywhere?

Four days before, Gideon and Brother Peter had called together all the men over twenty-one years. A lot of it was a matter of estimation, for how can most men know certainly whether he is twenty, or twenty-one or twenty-two or what? Age isn't a dead reckoning, but something to be set in broader figures. Brother Peter had to search his memory and separate all the multiple small black births, and finally through all the noise and talk, he separated out the cows from the calfs, as he put it. Twenty-seven men in all to go off for the voting.

"Now how about this here voting?" They turned to Gideon for answers.

Marcus recognized it was natural that they should turn to Gideon for questions. Death and God—well, they'd ask Brother Peter, but most everything else, planting and sickness and the rest they'd pile onto Gideon.

And now they were coming back from the voting. Two miles away and down the dusty road, Marcus saw a group of men, walking together and walking slowly for the companionship. Marcus ran screaming down the hillside, "They're a coming! Whooee!"

The other boys piled after him. They set up a screeching that could be heard a mile off, and everyone came tumbling out of the cabins to see what was up. Rachel thought murder had been done, and she had to slap Marcus twice to get some sense into his talk.

"Who's a coming?"

"Pa."

"Gideon?" sister Mary asked, and someone else added, "Lord be praised," expressing the sentiments of most. This was a mystery thing, this voting, it was ominous. All the men went off, and there was a lonesome waiting on the plantation with the menfolk gone, the more so since nobody really knew what the voting was. The women stayed closer than ever before, and from hour to hour the speculation on what a voting was grew wilder.

Now everyone shaded their eyes and looked down the road. Sure enough, the men were coming back—moving slowly, what with all the miles they had walked, but coming back. Everyone who could count counted, and it seemed that all the men were there. Rachel could recognize Gideon already, his big body bulking so large.

Gideon was a quantity of man, built like a bull, heavy in the shoulders, narrow in the waist, lean in the legs; that kind of man, the saying went, would be bull-like, with brains in his hands, but Gideon was not a man for sayings or proverbs. He was himself, and there was a reason why people turned to him; it was true that he moved slowly, both his body and his brain, but if he had a need to, he could move fast. When he had an idea, he turned it over and over, but when he had it at last, it was his.

He came first, and Rachel made him out; that slow, bent walk meant the miles were behind him. He carried his rifle at trail, the way he had learned in the army. He carried a sack on his shoulders, and in that would be something for the children. Alongside of him walked Brother Peter, tall and skinny and unarmed, the way a man of God should be. Then the two Jefferson brothers, both with rifles. Hannibal Washington, the little one. James, Andrew, Ferdinand, Alexander, Harold, Baxter, Trooper—those were men still without family names. By and by, a thought would come to them and they'd take names; but a family name was a thing to ponder on, and most men weren't easily satisfied.

Now Jeff was off, loping down the road to meet the men, a crowd of boys and girls and women following him. Rachel stayed; she held onto Marcus's collar and got him to help her draw cold water out of the well, so that Gideon could quench his thirst. She didn't have to run down to Gideon like a fool child; they understood each other better than that.

It was hot for a late November afternoon. When Gideon and the men plodded in among the cabins, the sweat was running down their dark faces, washing shiny ribbons in the dust.

There was a reward for Rachel for knowing their need, the way they gulped down the clear cold well water, and then held out the wooden mugs for more and more. Everyone had some question to ask, and they came fast and furious as rain:

"What's this voting?"

"How come you don't bring nothing back? Where this voting is?"

"You done bought the voting?"

"Bought and paid for it?"

"How many them voting you find along down by the white folks?"

"How big them are?"

"How many?"

Until Brother Peter declared desperately, "Brethren, sisteren and children, a little peace, a little quiet, and we all will give out them answers."

The men had kissed their wives and children. Gideon had taken Rachel in his arms and kissed her knowingly and gently. They had sweet candy, some of them, and were already handing it around. They opened their sacks; for Jenny, Gideon had a rose made of red gingham, a beautiful thing that was just like real with a perfume smell on it. The talk made a racket, but no one was telling about the voting. The dogs scampered around like mad, because dog-like they felt a need for a large share of affection. Finally, Brother Peter spread his arms and asked for quiet. A sort of quiet, he managed to get; the men squatted on their heels; the children sat and lay on the grass; the women sat down too or stood close together with arms entwined.

"Brother Gideon will tell you," Brother Peter said. "This here voting's like a wedding or Christmas sermon, matter for all. Government puts out a strong right arm, like the angel Gabriel, and says, declare yourself. We done that. Along with maybe five hundred other niggers and white folk, Government says, choose out a delegate. We done that. We pick Gideon."

Gideon stood up slowly, the people watching him with uncertainty. Rachel knew he was frightened; she knew every mood and impulse of Gideon. What did it mean that he was chosen out? What was a delegate?

"We gone and voted," Gideon said. He had a mellow voice, but it came slowly now because he was turning things over and setting them right.

"Voting—" Gideon said.

Gideon remembered how it was only a few days ago when they came into the town for the voting. There was, in their own group, a certain doubt as to just what voting meant; both Gideon and Brother Peter had tried to explain it as a wilful determination of their own destiny. They were free men and they had a voice; when there was a matter in question concerning their lives, they used that voice, and that was voting. But all these things were abstracts, and abstracts bewildered them. They would wait and see just how it turned out.

When they came into town, Gideon thought to himself, every nigger and white man in the world is here. Packed down the main street, packed on the portico of the columned courthouse, packed here and there and everywhere—and all of them talking at the top of their lungs about the voting. Half of them armed, white men and black men with guns in their hands. There was a company of Union troops detailed to keep order. Gideon thanked God for that; there were too many guns, he thought, too many hotheads.

Too many niggers who thought that voting was forty acres and a mule to take home with them, too many who thought voting would make them rich—too many who stared baffled and angry at their empty hands after they had cast the vote.

Now Gideon tried to tell the listeners how it was when his turn came, the dirty, bruised interior of the old courthouse, the registrars sitting around the long table with their huge open books, the stars and stripes prominently displayed behind them, the half-dozen soldiers standing guard, the voting booths and the ballot boxes. How he was given a sheet of paper upon which it said, "For a Constitutional Convention," and under that, "Against a Constitutional Convention," and under that, "Vote one by placing an x in the box indicated." All day long Yankees and Negroes had been talking in the street about how every black man ought to vote for the Convention. That was not hard to realize; the Convention would make a new world, or so they said. As Gideon stared at the paper, a registrar said in tired, bored tones:

"For the Convention or against it. Make your mark. Go into the booth, then fold your ballot."

Another registrar read off, "In the Js, Gideon Jackson." The men at the table ruffled through the pages of their books, and one said:

"Sign here, or make your mark."

Gideon took the pen and wrote painfully and crookedly, "Gideon Jackson," trembling and frightened, but thanking God that he had learned how to write his name and would not have to humiliate himself by making his mark. Then he took his ballot into the booth and tried to read it through before he marked it. He would have said he could read a little, but such words as "Constitutional Convention" might have been Sanskrit. He made the mark where it said "For"; that at least he could read, but his shame was something he'd remember a long while afterwards. He told the listeners now:

"We come like children, ignorant and unknowing. Brother Peter, he pray to God we done right."

"Hallelujah," a few of them said softly.

"A Yankee man, he talk to us," Gideon went on. "He break us down like flocks of sleep, and there was maybe five hundred of us standing unknowing and ignorant. "Pick a delegate," he say to us. Then he hand out more ballots. One nigger speak and then another nigger—then a white man speak. Brother Peter, he speak up and say, "Gideon's the man!"

Gideon couldn't say anymore than that. Everyone understood now how it had come about that Gideon was a delegate, and they felt such pride as they had never known before. As imperfectly as they understood it, they still felt the pride. Brother Peter took over now and told how Gideon would go to Charleston and join in the Convention. Rachel wept. Gideon stared at the ground and scuffed the grass with his feet. Marcus and Jeff threw out their chests; they would be too uppity to condescend for a week to come.

"God be praised," Brother Peter said.

They answered, "Hallelujah."

Then they broke up into little groups; each had his own wonderful story to tell.

Tonight, Rachel had Gideon back with her again; they lay on the straw pallet and listened to the regular breathing of the children; they listened to the frogs croaking in the pond and the nightbirds twittering.

"Cry no more," Gideon begged her.

"Afraid."

"What for you afraid?"

"You go away, and I get me uneasy."

"And I'm back now."

"And you go on off to Charleston," Rachel said, speaking of a legendary place in another world.

"And I come back," Gideon said gently. "Why for a woman should cry in a time of rejoicing? This is the best time there ever was for a black man. This is the hallelujah time, honey child. Nestle close. This here's the sun rising. I'm full of fright, but it ain't fright for my woman and babes."

"What for you're full of fright?"

"I'm a black nigger fool," Gideon said miserably. "I'm a black nigger man. What is there I know—can't read, can't write but my name."

"Brother Peter's no fool."

"How's that?"

"He comes up and says, here's a man to be your delegate. Why you think them niggers pick you?"

"Don't know."

Rachel wept softly and happily. She was prone to tears when there was a good time and good things happening. She told her husband, "Gideon, Gideon honey, you recollect the time when you set off to join the Yankee soldiers? You say to me, when I cry my heart out, here's the way a man has to do, he does it. This ain't no different, Gideon."

"How's that?"

She put her lips close to his ear and hummed, "Nigger in the field picking cotton, picking cotton, thinking about the gal he loves—"

And to that, Gideon fell asleep, to that and tumbled memories, and hope and fear.

CHAPTER TWO

How Gideon Jackson and Brother Peter Talked Together

AT BREAKFAST THE FOLLOWING MORNING, THE WHOLE FAMILY sat together; and Gideon thought with pride that there were few men who had all this, a wife like Rachel, two strong sons, and a pretty little daughter like Jenny. The boys were wild and headstrong, but so had he been in his time; and on his back were the scars of more than a hundred lashes to show just how headstrong he had been.

They had started in on the hot corn pone covered with a gravy of molasses, when Brother Peter put his head through the open doorway and said, "Morning, brother, morning, sister, morning, children."

They didn't have to urge him too much to have him join them at the table. The whole cabin was full of the smell of hot corn baking, and it made a man wet his lips before he even tasted the food. He was lavish in his praise. And after that, he had sugar sweets in his pockets for the children. Rachel always warmed specially to a man who talked up her food; too many of God's men were sour as a vinegar apple.

After the meal, Brother Peter asked Jeff, "Son, could you manage Gideon's chores?"

"I guess," Jeff nodded.

Gideon and Brother Peter walked over to the corncrib and sat down with their backs against the slats, their legs stretched out on the ground. It was a sunny place, and the cool morning wind blew up from the valley. The dog came and laid alongside of them. They pulled sticks of grass and chewed on them.

"When you plan to leave, Gideon?" Brother Peter asked.
"For Charleston?"

"Uh-huh."

When a long moment went by without Gideon answering, Brother Peter said, "Why for you afraid?"

"How come you think I'm frighted?"

"Uh-huh. Look a here, Gideon, you and me, we know each other long time back. Come the Lord's time, you be thirty-six years old. How come I remember that clear? When your mammy had her time come, she lay down on her back with you inside her and screamed, oh Jesus little child, my time's come. Fourteen, I was then. Your daddy say, Peter, run up tell the boss man Sophie's dying. I run up, and old Jim Blake—him the overseer then—say he never remember a nigger woman not dying when it comes her time. Get a doctor? Oh, no. Old mammy Anna, the midwife, she fight the devil three days, then you're born but your mammy's dead. Then old Jim Blake whips the hide off me and swears to God to Mister Carwell I never done told him. So I got a memory of you being born. I got a memory of days we work them hot cotton fields. I got a memory of how we talk, what for a nigger live? When you say, I'll take my life go down to sweet sleep, I'm the nigger, praise God, makes you see the terrible sin. Who you come to when you want to go off fighting with the Yankee men?"

"Come to you," Gideon nodded.

"Say, take care Rachel, take care three little babes. I done that."

"Uh-huh."

"Now you rear up like a mule when I say you afraid."

"Tell me to go down Charleston Town," Gideon muttered. "Nigger can't read, can't write, can't hardly spell his name, you tell me, go down to Charleston Town to Convention. Go down to city full of white houses like that there big house, full of white folks making fun at a damn fool nigger man."

Tracing a pattern on the sand in front of him, Brother Peter asked gently, "How you come to Charleston first time, Gideon?"

"Come in with the Yankee men," Gideon recalled. "Come in with the blue uniform and gun in my hand and ten thousand along side of me, singing a hallelujah song—"

"You wasn't afraid. You is just afraid to go in alone, no blue uniform, no gun in your hand, no hallelujah song, just the hand of the law saying to black nigger man, my child, you is free."

Gideon didn't answer, and Brother Peter said softly, "The Book say of Moses he was a frightened man, but God say, lead my people—"

"I ain't Moses."

"People need a leader, Gideon. I say to myself up at voting place, law say, a nigger man's free, law say, vote, law say, nigger man come out of slavery—make a life. Nigger can't read, can't write, can't think even. Slave got the whip or sold down the river for thinking. Slave got three hundred lashes for learning to read. Nigger's like an old hound dog pushed out of house and set to get his own food. I say to myself, who's going to lead these people? Walk big or talk big, they all frightened. Who's going to lead them?"

"Why you pick me?" Gideon demanded. "Why not you?"

"People picked you," Brother Peter said. "Going to be that way from now on." Brother Peter leaned over and put his boney hand on Gideon's knee, "Look a here, Brother Gideon—say you can't read. Ain't nobody born with reading power. You learn that. You learn to read, you learn to write. Me, I got a little writing knowledge, maybe fifteen, twenty words. Well, I write them down and you study them for a start—"

Gideon shook his head helplessly.

"Take a matter of talking," Brother Peter said. "Words match up, white folks call that grammar. Man with a head on his shoulders, he talks the words right, old nigger like me, he don't. How you going to get that?"

"God knows," Gideon said.

"God, he knows. I know too. You going to listen. You going to listen to white man talk. You going to listen every minute of day. You going to learn yourself. Come a time, maybe, you be able to read a book. Ain't nothing you can't find in books—gospel truth there."

"A man puts his mind to raising a crop," Gideon said. "That's a day's work. Then how come a man's going to fill his head with learning?"

"Cross that bridge when we come to it. Meanwhile, Jeff's able to do chores. Got a fine boy in Marcus. Got the blessings of Jesus all down the line. Going to be a new world, Gideon. Going to be a bright new world." He smiled and motioned to the huddle of windowless slave cabins. "Shake this off." He folded his long, thin arms and bowed his head. "Praise God."

Gideon said, "How you figure this here Convention?"

"Makes out the laws. Constitution's like a Bible book. Can't have a world with niggers running around like wild hogs. White folks hate the nigger—nigger fears the white folks. That ain't the good way."

"How I going to know a good law from a bad law?"

"How you know a good man from a bad man? How you know a good woman from a sinful one?"

"I got a measure to go by."

"Well, you got a measure here," Brother Peter said. "How come you got no reading, no writing. Well, never was a school for niggers—never was a school for poor whites either. There's a start. Make a law for schooling, that's a good law. Here's this Carwell place, maybe twenty thousand acres. Who it belong to? Belong to Mr. Carwell? To Government? To niggers, white folk? Nigger wants land—so does white folk. Well, there's enough for all, plenty for all, but how it going to be divided?"

"How I know that?"

"Patient, Gideon, slow and easy."

"How come you don't go to be a delegate?" Gideon asked.

"How come people don't go and ballot me? Got a way of knowing, Gideon. I'm an old nigger man, just as smart as I'll ever be. Someday, you look at me, Gideon, you say to yourself, how come I ever take comfort from that old nigger man? That old ignorant nigger man."

"I never say that."

"God bless you, maybe you don't, Gideon. But you like a little babe. All ready. Just fill you up, like bucket drawing water from the well. Just wait and see."

Gideon shook his head. "How I wish I believe that—"

"Don't matter, you believe it, you don't believe it, Gideon. All a same, that happen. Like a bucket drawing up cool, clean water."

"Supposing they just laugh and mock this nigger?"

"Sure they going to laugh, Gideon, son. How come we laugh when some poor swamp nigger come out, say where master is? You free, we tell him, and that nigger don't know no more what's free than hound dog. Natural for us to laugh at poor devil. But you going to take laughing, take scorn. First time they give you delegate pay like Yankee man said, maybe dollar a day, you take that dollar buy a book. Maybe you hunger like starving man, but you take that book, buy candle to read by, and you figure out them words."

Gideon nodded. The more Brother Peter spoke, the more terrified Gideon became about the prospect of a Convention at Charleston, but at the same time there was that sickening, wonderful thrill he had felt when he ran off to join the Union Army.

"What kind of book first?"

"Suppose a preaching man ought to say Bible. But Bible ain't easy, Gideon, tie you up in snarls. Get yourself learning book first, spelling book. Then maybe book of sums. Come that time, you know yourself what kind of book you want next."

"Uh-huh," Gideon agreed.

"Ain't all to be found in books," Brother Peter observed, feeling the time had come when he could plant a reservation.

"How that?"

"Ain't no books wrote unless there's something happened. This here thing of a nigger man being free never happen before. Maybe nothing like this since time Moses led the Children out a Egypt. Moses, he don't have book, he turn up face to God. He say, what the good thing to do?"

"How I going to know that?"

"Gideon, fill your heart with love. Fill your heart with understanding."

"I is prone to anger," Gideon admitted.

"And who ain't? Born in sin, we is, brother. Gideon, who you think smartest man in world?"

"Live or dead?" Gideon said thoughtfully.

"One or another."

"Old Abe, I reckon."

"Uh-huh. How come old Abe he got to know all that? How come old Abe, he say to nigger man through the land, you is free?"

"Guess he see that's right."

"Maybe so, Gideon. Maybe more so, he got a heart full of love and mercy. Come right out of the piney woods, they say old Abe was, just no different from you. But got a heart big like that there plantation house."

"Got a big heart, all right," Gideon admitted.

"Now, take a matter of judgment, Gideon. Come two men and bear a witness. One fine, get-up, big-city man, he say, old wind ain't blowing. Other man, dirty, hungry, he say wind blow fine. You got to judge, wind blow or don't blow. How you going to judge?"

"Put up my own hand and see if the wind blows—"

"Uh-huh. Or ask folk, maybe ten, twelve folk. Don't take no man's witness just cause he struts like peacock or talks smooth and fine. Now, Gideon, you going to feel hard about white folk—got the whip lash on your back, got the heart hardened. That just means suffering and misery. Come from here on—color of a man's skin don't matter. There's good men and bad men, black and white."

"I see that," Gideon nodded.

"Ain't no more than that, I guess," Brother Peter reflected. "God's blessing. Let Him walk by your side, Gideon."

"Amen," Gideon said.

CHAPTER THREE

How Gideon Jackson Went to Charleston and the Adventures That Befell Him on the Way

As THE DAYS WENT PAST AND NOTHING HAPPENED, GIDEON'S election to the Convention became of less importance, and sometimes for two or three days he would not think of it at all. Actually, what proof had he that he was the delegate? At first, immediately after Brother Peter had made his long speech at the voting, it had seemed that all the men in their section had been for Gideon; afterwards, no one said that they had voted against Gideon, and he and Brother Peter just naturally concluded that he had been the delegate. But the voting was by secret ballot; they were told that when the ballots were counted, the delegates would be notified and receive the proper credentials. But here it was, two weeks later. Wavering between fear and hope, Gideon often asked himself how long it took a good counter to count up to five or six hundred. Of late, he simply shunted the matter off. No Yankee men in their right senses would call on fool niggers to be delegates.

There were things enough to keep him busy now, with winter coming on. In the summer, living was easy and life was good; men had to be prodded into worrying about the cold weather coming. For a whole week, Gideon had the men cutting wood in the tract they called The Lower Section. In the old days, when the place had an overseer, the wood was just cut back from the cleared section, nothing spared, and a stubble of two foot stumps left to rot through the years. Gideon had been thinking about that, and this year he proposed that they dig at the roots and fell the trees from below ground level.

"Double the work," they said. "What for?"

"Easier to take out the tree with the stump than the stump without the tree," Gideon said.

"Who going to want to take out the stump?"

"That we don't know," Gideon said. "Don't know who the land belong to, but maybe it belong to you and me some day."

"We worry about that when that time come."

They might have argued the question half the day, had not Gideon seized upon an inspiration and suggested that they have a vote. Even as he said it, he was not sure it would work, not certain of the application of so miraculous a principle to a work-a-day occupation like cutting wood. But the idea caught hold, and in the dead silence that followed his suggestion, Gideon applied the yes and no method. Even though the men had voted for the Convention, the mechanics of the thing was new and revolutionary. They had to thrash out the matter of whether a man could vote yes or no only or both yes and no. But in the end, the principle was applied and it worked, and Gideon's proposal for taking out the trees by the roots won with a considerable majority.

Again, when Trooper, big and strong as an ox, protested that he was sawing three times the wood he'd ever use, while a little man like Hannibal Washington didn't contribute half his share of the work, Gideon fell back on the vote. Only this time, a new innovation appeared, for the men laid down their tools and discussed the whole matter of cooperation. In the overseer days, working together had become second nature to them; only now, as they actively awoke to the fact that they were free, did they actually question it. Why shouldn't each man work for himself? If freedom didn't mean that, what did it mean?

The innovation, suggested by Brother Peter, consisted of an appraisal of the many sides of a question, before it was put to a vote. Hannibal Washington, his small, lined face tight with anger, said to Trooper:

"Looka here now, you go off cut your wood single. I say

it won't be no account against equal share this wood we cut together. What for then you come to mock at me, you big hunk of black crow meat?"

Trooper raised his ax. Gideon and others held them apart, and Brother Peter cried, "Shame for men to go as spill blood over something like this!"

For an hour they talked themselves hoarse, and this time the vote won by only a slim margin. Afterwards, Gideon said to Brother Peter:

"We ain't going to be trouble free."

"What man is?"

"Anyway, my head aches—men to scrap and cry like children."

"Gideon, they don't know, work together, work apart. They like children now. How come you expect big things, a nigger's one summer, two summers away from slavery. Time moves slow."

But time brought trouble. The voting was like a bright, sharp sunrise, but afterwards nothing happened, life went on as before. Gideon noticed how often now the people peered through the windows of the big plantation house. It was full of beautiful things, and there was too much talk about those things. In that, there was a certain resentment against Gideon; for, a year past, the disbanded South Carolina troops had come through, broken into the big house, taken what they wanted, and scattered other things about. Gideon, it had been, who ordered the things replaced and the house boarded up once more. When they asked him, "What for?" he said, "They ain't no things of ours." "How they different from the clothes we wear, the houses we sleep in?" "The one is needful, the other ain't," Gideon answered.

And now he found Marcus with a silver spoon that could have come from nowhere but the big house.

How then?—Marcus had broken into the house. A big, rambling house with a hundred entrances and exits, and breaking into it wasn't a difficult thing; but for the first time Gideon felt uncertainty about how to handle his children. Reflecting, it seemed to him that he had known just what to do with a child until now; now he had an immense and frightful sense of his own ignorance. Each night he sat in front of the fire with the list of words Brother Peter had written. Duz, ant, man, wumen, gel, yu, shurnuf, nigru, wide, and so forth and so on, a mountain of fact to confound him and terrify him. Right and wrong became malleable matters instead of great constants, and instead of punishing Marcus firmly, he said to him, uncertainly:

"How you come in that big house, Marcus?"

"Ain't been there."

So Marcus lied. "This is a good boy," Gideon reflected. The puzzles and problems were becoming numberless.

"Where you get that spoon?" Gideon demanded.

"Found it."

"You don't find that spoon, Marcus. You better tell me the truth."

"Found it."

"Then where you find it?"

He caught Marcus unprepared, and the tale came out piece by piece. They had gotten into the house through the kitchen cellar. Other boys had taken things, silk, silver, hidden them. Gideon couldn't whip Marcus; he had never taken a hand to any of his children—his people didn't. Leave the whipping to the white folks; he knew what a whip on his back felt like. He called a meeting of the people, and had Marcus up in front of them, and there, each word like a knife into the boy, he told what had happened. Brother Stephan demanded:

"How long that big house going to stand there, Brother Gideon?"

"Come doomsday, if it got to."

"Nigger live in a dirty little shack, but that damn big house, no one live in it."

"Come doomsday," Gideon said stubbornly.

And that night, Rachel took it to him, sobbingly, "How come you ever done that to the boy, Gideon?"

"Done what I had to do."

"Laying it into him like that in front everybody."

"He done an evil thing."

"Seem like nothing but evil come out of the voting."

"What—?"

"Take you off to Charleston, set the niggers grunting and growling, don't do nothing, don't settle nothing."

Gideon pretended he had fallen asleep. Rachel stopped talking and he heard her crying quietly.

At fifteen, Jeff was chafing and pulling at his bonds. He was headstrong and healthy as a wild beast. To him, Gideon was an old one, Brother Peter was an old one; they drew the world around his neck and tightened it like a noose. He was imprisoned, and he wanted to break the bonds and be free. In this little community, where no one could read or write with any facility, where there was never a newspaper, time became the elastic, primitive thing it had been many thousands of years before. Not even a clock; the sun swung overhead, a big, orange timepiece, and the slow parade of the seasons made an easy calendar. Jeff was fifteen now, and his memory of the time before the war was blurred and uncertain. The constant talk about the difference between freedom and slavery made little impression upon him; as it was, he had been born in chaos, and all his young boyhood had been chaos.

Now he was a young giant, and still just a boy. It made him sick when the men marched away to the voting and he was left behind. Every road sang a song to him, and he felt that some day he would go off down one of them and never come back. Sometimes, Gideon sensed the subdued violence in the boy. For that reason, he let him go off hunting alone, into the swampy lowlands. Jeff could rove the swamps for hours, singing wordless, wild songs. Hunting quelled his impatience as nothing else could. When he came to a cold pool, trodden around, no one had to tell him that here the deer drank. He could lie there, ten hours at a stretch, patient and restful, waiting for a wild horned buck, or a fierce swamp boar. In those long and silent hours, he would dream formlessly and endlessly.

In his dreams were the cities he had never seen, fairylands formed from the words of the men. In his dreams was Father Abraham, shapeless like a God, singing hallelujah songs.

Sometimes, in his dreams, there was a poignant longing, utterly formless, that stretched his heart like rubber.

Once, in the swamp, he had met two white men; this he hadn't told Gideon. They were soldier men, the old gray uniforms torn and stained. They looked at Jeff and swore at him, and when their guns came up, he leaped behind a tree. The two guns went off, and echoed like a battle in the swamp. If they had gotten him, it would have been just another nigger dead, face down in the water, gradually absorbed by the mud and slimy leaves and then forgotten. If anything marked young manhood for Jeff, it was this, for as they ran off through the swamp, he could have shot either of them; yet he didn't—just watched them curiously, quite unafraid, plumbing the mystery of why they should have desired to kill him so immediately and coldly. He never told anyone of that.

This was the first time a letter had come to the Carwell place since the overseer had gone. It was weeks after the voting, and therefore no one made a connection between the two remarkable events. Early one afternoon, a buggy drove up the Columbia Pike, and old Cap Holstien, the postmaster, dismounted in that slow, lazy manner he accentuated in his dealings with the freedmen. All during the war, Cap Holstien had held his job as postmaster, first under the Rebels and then under the Yankees and then under the Rebels and then under the Yankees again.

It wasn't that Cap Holstien was a loyal man; he was a tobacco-chewing, tobacco-spitting, profane enemy of the Constitution, which he cursed from dawn to sunset, nor had he ever saluted the flag. But he was the only man who knew where everyone was through all the chaos of the war and the post-war period; he was the only one who knew who was living and who was dead, who had stayed at home and who had gone off to Charleston, Columbia, Atlanta—or the north. And he was the only man who knew most of the several thousand freed slaves in the countryside. So the military kept him on as postmaster, in spite of the fact that he cursed them out each day and swore that he'd live to see the time when he'd kill a Republican with his own two hands. Now he drove up to the Carwell place and yelled:

"Hey, you nigra black bastards!"

It was a fact that he wasn't afraid of anything that walked. The people, men, women, boys and girls came running. They gathered around him, and he spat tobacco juice in the dust, rubbed his hands, and took out of his pocket a long brown envelope. He squinted at it and then demanded:

"Which one you thieving coons is Gideon Jackson?"

Gideon had been smiling at the little old man. There was something he liked about Cap, just what he didn't know, something summed up by Brother Peter's comment, "There's a man'll sore need praying." Gideon stepped forward, and Cap, who knew him, looked him up and down and asked:

"Gideon Jackson?"

"Uh-huh."

"Sign here."

"Yes, sir."

Holstien held out the stub of a pencil. "Can you write? If not, just make a nigger mark right there."

"I can write," Gideon said. His name anyway. The people hardly gave him room to breath as he shaped it out under Cap's watchful eye. He had never performed the public practice of writing like this before, and the people commented in soft tones upon his skill. Then the old man got back in his buggy, swung it around, and whipped his mule back along the way he had come.

Gideon turned the brown envelope slowly. In the upper left hand corner, there was printed:

> If not delivered in ten days return to
> General E. R. S. Canby, U.S.M.O.F.
> Columbia, S.C. S.M.D.

Most of that, he could read, although he didn't know what the long string of initials stood for. Brother Peter, looking over his shoulder, said:

"General Canby, he the new Yankee man, come to look after things. That there S.C., that mean South Carolina,

S.M.D., maybe that mean second military district, like that time they come tell us go to the voting. The Lord knows what them other letters means."

In the opposite corner it said:

Official Business
Penalty for use to avoid payment of postage $100.00

Neither Brother Peter nor anyone else in the packed group around Gideon could make any sense of that. In the center of the envelope was the address:

Gideon Jackson, esquire,
Carwell Plantation,
Carwell, S.C. S.M.D.

Brother Peter read Gideon's name aloud, but paused at *esquire*. He had never seen the word before, had no idea of its meaning and could not pronounce it. He tried, silently, making motions with his lips. Hannibal Washington, who could read a few words, had a try at it too. So did Marion Jefferson, who had learned to read a few words while in the Union Army—but that completed the literacy of the group, and after that they simply stared at the letter in silence. Finally, Gideon said:

"How you figure that word, Brother Peter?"

Brother Peter shook his head, and Hannibal Washington volunteered, "Could be that like mister or colonel or something."

"Then how come it ain't afore Gideon's name? How come it traipses after it?"

Silence again, until Brother Peter said, "Open her up, Gideon."

Slowly, Gideon opened the envelope. It was full of papers. Around all the others, there was a letter, addressed to Gideon in the same fashion as the envelope. It said:

This will notify you that you have been elected delegate from the Carwell-Sinkerton district, South Carolina, to the State Constitutional Convention, to convene at Charleston S.C. S.M.D. on the Fourteenth of January, 1868. Here inclosed are your instructions and credentials. Major Allen James, at Charleston, has been notified of your election and acceptance, and will receive your credentials. The Government of the United States trusts that you will honorably and conscientiously fulfill your duties, and the Congress of the United States asks that you will truthfully and faithfully play your part in the reconstruction of the State of South Carolina.

signed,
General E. R. S. Canby
U.S.M.O.F S.M.D.

That was what the letter said, but hours went by before they could discern even a part of the meaning. Now, on top of everything else, Gideon's election became, to him, a grotesque, a caricature of a thing that made a mockery of all their fine, new-won freedom. Black, black ignorance covered all, black as his skin, black as the night. It was a trick, like the dreams he had almost every night of the free days, dreams during which he felt the whip on his shoulders, dreams during which he labored in the hot cotton field, dreams so real that he had to crawl out of bed and go to the door and see with his own eyes that the fields were not planted with cotton. Now his waking was a dream. He longed to run away and hide.

And Brother Peter and Hannibal Washington labored over the letter. The people lost interest and the sun set. They went into Gideon's cabin and sat with the papers held in the firelight. Hannibal Washington said:

"We might fetch them to town and let the Yankee man make them out?"

Gideon roared a furious "No!" that brought looks of surprise from everyone. Marcus and Jeff had never seen their father like this, and they sat silent; but for Jeff, this was the beginning of something. He saw three strong men, three men whom the community looked up to, solid and God-fearing, knowing the secret of á good crop, of butchering a cow, a calf or a pig, of many other things, held frustrated and impotent by a scrap of paper. There was strength in that paper. Jeff's way of thinking was in vivid imagery, and now he saw the printed word in its power, in its calm purpose and intention.

He knew he would learn to read, and for the first time he felt superior to Gideon.

Also for the first time, he felt a certain contempt for Gideon—a feeling that he, in Gideon's place, would not have been so enraged and baffled because he lacked the skill to read. Rachel sensed this; she was strung to the emotions of these men like a finely-tuned harp, and she was the most disturbed of any. The night before, she had given a copper coin she had been treasuring to old Mammy Christy, and the old woman made her a luck fetish, a little image that was hidden in the cabin now. If Gideon knew, he would be somberly angry; he hated that sort of thing and stolidly defied bad luck whenever he had an opportunity to; and Brother Peter called such things un-Christian, heathen-like.

In time, the three men unraveled the letter, more or less completely. Words like *reconstruction* and *conscientiously* they could only guess at, and other words they interpreted wrongly, but the gist of it was theirs. Gideon had to go to Charleston; that they knew. The vague shape of a Convention extended into the remote future; it might be a permanent thing, it might not. Gideon was given over; he was one of them no longer. The other papers and cards in the envelope they examined only cursorily; those things Gideon would take with him, and eventually the meaning would emerge.

Gideon asked about the date. A cold wind blew through the cracks in the cabin wall. Could it be January fourteenth already? But Brother Peter thought of the postmark on the envelope:

"Right here, it say January 2."

"Take a long time to walk to Charleston," Hannibal Washington sighed. In a way, the little man envied Gideon.

"Can't go like this," Gideon said, frowning at his ragged cotton trousers, his old blue army shirt, and his ancient army boots.

"Wouldn't be fitting," Brother Peter agreed. "Got my black frock coat. Got a torn sleeve, Rachel can mend. Maybe a little tight, but you can get it on, Gideon."

"Ferdinand's got a pair of pretty pants."

"Get that old stovepipe hat Trooper's been keeping in his cabin. Mighty fine hat, little crushed—but mighty fine hat."

"Gideon, honey, I can wash the shirt and mend it," Rachel said.

Hannibal Washington said generously, "Got that old watch Yankee man give me in the army, Gideon—" It was his most precious possession. Gideon felt a wonderful warmth for these people who loved him so. "You take it, Gideon," Hannibal Washington said. "Got no works and can't keep time, but a mighty nice watch to wear."

"Got to have a hand-kerchief," Brother Peter decided. "Not a nigger sweating kerchief, but one to keep up in breast pocket, the way white folks does. Got a fine piece of red and white calico Rachel can sew into shape."

That was how it came about that Gideon Jackson set off on his long walk to Charleston Town. Two days later, in the bright and early morning, he had left the Carwell place some miles behind him—and now he strode along the dusty road, the stovepipe hat tilted precariously, singing in his rich bass voice the old marching tune of his regiment:

> "There ain't no grass grows under my feet,
>   On freedom road,
> There ain't no grass grows under my feet,
>   On freedom road,
> Old John Brown, grand-daddy,
>   We're coming,
>   We're coming,
> Down freedom road."

A defiant song. Worth a man's life to sing that song on a South Carolina road, but that was the way Gideon felt right now. He had more than a hundred miles to walk to Charleston, a hundred miles of the open road, and he was a walking man. Now the die was cast, and he felt curiously happy and light, like a boy going off to fish in a forbidden stream. Later the old doubts and anxieties would come back; but how could an old slave man feel anything but excited joy at the prospect of such a long walk?

There was some talk before Gideon left as to whether he

should take a musket with him; for all of the danger, he agreed with Brother Peter that it would be the wrong way to come to a Convention, gun in hand.

"Come with peace and love in your heart—and in your hands too," Brother Peter said.

Anyway, he had in his breast pocket the credentials of the United States Government; who would dare to molest him? "Official Business," it said on the brown envelope. Funny, the way his heart and his hopes went up and down, frightened one moment, happy and excited the next. As he strode along, a package of corn bread and cold pork under his arm, singing his song, a cold wind blowing through the piney woods on either side the road, he thought of what would come from this Convention. Strangely, the more he turned it over in his mind, the more clearly he saw the conception of a new state and a new life emerging from the Convention; enough to make a man frightened, and enough to make him proud.

Ahead of him, the pines thinned out. There was the shack and a clearing of some ten acres. Abner Lait's freehold; at least, they still called it a freehold, although Abner Lait had been tenant to the Carwells and so had his father. Lait was a tall, boney, red-headed white man, slow-spoken, regarding the world suspiciously and uncertainly. Hard times were wrapped around him; before the war, he had barely scraped a living out of the land; when he had a good crop, the Carwells took it; when he had a bad one, they put him deeper in debt. When the war came, he went off with Dudley Carwell's regiment. After three and a half years and four wounds and more battles than he wanted to remember, he was taken prisoner, and spent the time between then and the end of the war in a Yankee prison camp. Somehow, while he was gone, his wife and his four children had existed; how, he didn't know—nor did she care to remember. Now he was back, and he had put in two crops. Things were bad, but not as bad as they had been. At least, the Carwells had forgotten him; he raised corn and some pigs and chickens; at least, bellies were reasonably full.

Abner Lait hated black men in the formal way of hatred

he had always known, a thing expected. He hated the planters with reason and precision. Between him and Gideon, there was a respectful animosity. As Gideon came along the road now, Abner stood at his fence line, leaning on a spade.

"Morning, Mr. Lait," Gideon said.

"Now that's a hell of a song for a nigger to be singing."

"When my feet walk the road, there's a song in my mouth," Gideon smiled. "When I marched with the Yankee men, that was the song we sing."

"God damn you to hell," Abner said lazily. It was not a morning to nurse anger. Peter and Jimmy, his two towheaded boys came shyly up to the fence. "I do wish I might of found you in my sights when you was with them damn Yanks," Abner added. "I would of filled you fuller with holes than that there black coat you wearing. How come you all trussed up like a monkey, Gideon?"

"Off to Charleston to the Convention."

"Convention! God damn, if that don't beat it all."

"Got elected at the voting."

Abner whistled and said, "What do you think of that. Nigger at a Convention at Charleston. Reckon they'll damn well lynch you before you open your mouth, Gideon."

"Maybe so," Gideon nodded. "But I got government writing right here in my pocket. You been at the voting?"

"I been, but I don't vote for no nigger."

They stood a while longer, and one of the boys found enough courage to sidle up to Gideon, who stroked his yellow hair gently. Then Gideon said goodby and set off down the road again. Abner Lait stared after him and murmured:

"Off to Charleston. Jesus God, see a nigger walk off to Charleston to sit in a Convention!"

Gideon walked on until the sun was high overhead. Then he stopped by the wayside, built a little fire of brushwood, ate some cornbread and meat, and then lay and rested for about half an hour. It was warmer now than before. The birds sang merrily, and the sound of a brook nearby told Gideon that he would be able to quench his thirst. He was quite happy.

As nightfall came on, Gideon looked about for a place to

sleep. If necessary, he would build a fire in the pines and lie down on a soft bed of brown needles; there were worse places than that to spend a night. But to Gideon it seemed a dreary waste of the evening hours not to hear a human voice or a little laugher; he wasn't one for loneliness. He was tired from the day's walking, and he had come a long way, perhaps twenty-five or thirty miles. He had passed through a town and put it miles behind him. He had walked on a causeway through a cypress swamp, and ahead of him were the flat tidewater lands. The gentle haze of evening had come into the sky, and there was a cold bite in the air.

So when Gideon saw a cabin on a flat, a ribbon of blue smoke fluttering from the chimney, and three chocolate-colored children playing in the sand at the doorway, he felt relief. As he crossed the field, the man of the house came out to meet him, a Negro of sixty-five or seventy, but strong and healthy-looking and smiling.

"Now I bid you good evening," he said.

"And the same to you," Gideon nodded, reflecting how much the same children were everywhere, shy and curious and warmly-excited by the presence of any stranger.

"And what can I do for you?" the old man asked.

"Name's Gideon Jackson, sir. I come down the pike from up a ways, Carwell Plantation—off and down the road to Charleston. I'd mighty appreciate a corner your shed there to spend the night. Ain't like I'm just a footloose nigger asking for bread, got my victuals here in a bundle. Got government papers here in my pocket." The old man was smiling. Gideon stopped, gulped, and swallowed what he was going to say about the Convention at Charleston. The old man said:

"Any stranger is welcome to a place by my fire and a bite of food. The shed is for animals. We can't offer you a bed, but a blanket by the fire, if that will do you. And I ask no man for credentials, sir. My name is James Allenby."

"Thank you kindly, Mr. Allenby," Gideon said, the old man's smile putting him more at ease. Allenby led the way into the shack, an ancient bundle of sticks that might have once been a freehold farm, since it had windows and shutters, a feature lacking in most slave cabins. A girl crouched by the fire, stirring something in a pot; as they entered, she rose, tall, round of limb, brown-skinned, strikingly handsome, her head high and poised, as if she were balancing an urn atop of it. Her eyes were large and lustrous; Gideon realized that even in the dusk; but there was something strange about her eyes, something in the way they never fixed upon his face. Allenby took her by the hand and said:

"My child, we have a guest for the evening. His name is Gideon Jackson. He is journeying through to Charleston, and I have asked him to spend the night with us. He is a good and a gentle man, I think."

Something in what the old man said, in the way the girl continued to stare past him, gave Gideon the clue he had been seeking. The realization that she was blind terrified him for a moment, and he sought reassurance in the children, hanging onto her skirts now, in the good smell coming out of the pot, in the clean if miserable interior of the cabin. Perhaps she was the old man's daughter, certainly not the mother of the children; she was too young for that. He could not ask for explanations now. She said, "I bid you welcome, sir," and then went back to the fire. Gideon sat down on a chair of pine branches, and Allenby set the table with tin dishes and spoons. Night fell outside. Gideon had a way with children; they warmed to him, and soon one was in his arms, the other two bent over his knees.

"They like songs," the old man said.

Gideon sang, "Brother rabbit, he live in the old bramble patch, sky's his roof, he don't want no thatch . . ."

Gideon had finished telling his story, the voting, his being chosen as a delegate; it was late, and the fire was a bed of coals. Ellen Jones, the girl, had climbed the ladder to her bed under the eaves. One of the children slept up there with her; the two boys, Ham and Japet, shared a pallet, and now they were asleep. The old man sat by the fire with Gideon.

"So now you're off to Charleston," the old man said. "The dawn comes after such a long time. How I envy you, Gideon Jackson—God help me, how I envy you. But it's right the way it is—for the young and the strong and the hopeful. For men like you—"

"For all of us," Gideon said.

"Yes?—perhaps. How old do you think I am, Gideon?"

"Maybe sixty-five—"

"Seventy-seven, Gideon. I fought in the 1812 war against the British. Yes, we were allowed to fight then—for this country's freedom. No, I'm not bitter. Then they thought slavery would die its own death. That was before cotton became a great cash crop. Slaves were a liability then, for the most part. They even educated me, turned me into a tutor; they didn't understand then that education was like a disease, that if you educated a man he was no good for slavery and that he would spread his freedom-sickness to others."

"Eat my heart out for a little learning," Gideon said.

"Learning and freedom—patience, Gideon. They come together. Don't I know? When that old British war was over, the master found I was teaching the other slaves to read and write. How could I do that? he wanted to know. How could I not do it? So he sold me down the river. Like a pattern, Gideon. Wherever I was, there was the same hunger for a little learning, to read a passage in the Bible, to spell a word or two, to write a letter to someone they love and who was now gone away. So they sold me, whipped me, threatened me. Can you cure a disease that way? I have read Voltaire, Paine, Jefferson, yes, and Shakespeare. You never heard his name, Gideon, or his golden voice; but you will—you will. Could I be quiet?"

Gideon shook his head dumbly.

"I had three wives, Gideon, and I loved them all—and each time I was sold away from them. I had children, too, but I know where none of them are, Gideon. Four times, I escaped—and each time I was found and brought back, whipped, but permitted to remain alive because I was wealth; a steer is worth something dead, but our flesh was worth nothing unless there was life in it. I don't talk about these things often, Gideon; I tell them to you because it is of utmost importance that you should remember our past, what our people have suffered. In you, Gideon, there is gentleness and strength and fire, too, I can see. You will become a great leader of our people, but you will be worth less than nothing if you ever forget. Now you have been wondering about this blind girl and the three children. I'll tell you—"

"Ain't no call for you to tell me 'less you want to," Gideon said.

"That's why I tell you, Gideon, because I want to. The three children are strays. This poor southland of ours is full of orphans and strays, lost children, black calves who never knew father or mother, cattle abandoned when the cattle market was destroyed. I was in slavery in Alabama when the war began. And when freedom came, I made my way north and east; not to go to the Yankee country—I love this southland—but the deep south I can never love. It lashed me too hard. I thought there might be some place in the Carolinas or in Virginia where a teacher would be needed. And on the way, I picked up the children. How? It happened, Gideon— it would happen to you. I found the girl, too. Ellen is sixteen. Her father was a free Negro in Atlanta, a doctor. That's another story; he's dead; let him rest. After Sherman had gone away, some terrible things happened. I blame no one. Some rebel soldiers—and there are evil men as well as good in every army—killed the girl's father, in her sight, spitted him with their bayonets and cut his eyes out. You see, he had helped the Yankees. I tell you this, Gideon, not to make hatred but understanding. You go to Charleston to make a constitution, a new state, a new world, a new life; then understand how simple people can do devilish things—because they know no better. After they had killed her father, they attacked her. Then she became blind. I don't know about such things, whether a shock can cause blindness or whether she had a sickness in her eyes. But when I found her, she had lost her senses, even the knowledge of who she was; she lived in the woods like a wild animal, and she was as timid as a wild animal. But for some reason, she trusted me, and I added her to my little company." He paused; Gideon was staring at the coals, his hands clenching and unclenching. "Gideon," the old man said softly.

"Sir?"

"Gideon, when you put those government credentials in your pocket, you stopped being a man and became a servant. A man, Gideon, can indulge his hate. He can want to kill and destroy, as you want to at this moment. A servant cannot; he must work for his master. Your people, Gideon, are your master. Now listen to me, and I'll tell you the rest."

"I'm listening," Gideon said.

"I found this shack. God knows where its tenant is—killed in the war, I guess. There are a thousand such lonely shacks in this southland of ours. For two years, I lived here. I raise a small crop, enough for us. I have a few chickens. A litter of wild pigs gave us some livestock. Since we are here, no one has molested us. Ellen is almost normal now—but blind. It's not a bad life for me, to have four young souls to teach. I hired out to work in the village; I am a middling good carpenter, shoemaker, tinker or letter writer, and I made a few pennies at each trade, enough to buy some clothes and some books—"

He left off there and for a long time Gideon said nothing. Then, "and when you die?"

"I've thought of that," Allenby answered. "There is my fear and unhappiness."

"Or suppose you sicken? Or suppose sheriff come along, say, get to blazes out a this shack."

"I've thought of that too, Gideon."

"Now look a here," Gideon said, a note of excitement in his voice. "Man like you, he's a knowing man. Maybe you old—seventy-seven, that's a far along age. But you're brown and tough, like an old nut. Maybe you die tomorrow, old man don't know what God's got in store, maybe you live ten, fifteen year."

"What are you driving at, Gideon?"

"Got a thought. Here's me, black man made free, skinning his heels down the road to Charleston town, proud like a peacock to be a delegate in a Convention. But can't read, can't write, just wrapped in ignorance. Here's maybe four million black men in this southland, just whimpering for a little bit of learning. Got freedom a mile high, like a gracious sweet song, but where that all get a man who bows his head with ignorance? You teach three little ones, that's good. Up at the Carwell place, I got my people—just like you, feeling about, just like every other nigger in this land, don't know what's theirs, don't know what ain't theirs, don't know if land is theirs or old slave shack is theirs. How they ever going to know that when there ain't man on the place can read or write sufficient?"

Gideon paused, swallowed, and then marked his words with a long forefinger. "You go up there—fetch along your little ones. Tell them Gideon, he send you. Talk to Brother Peter, he's our preaching man, tell him you'll teach them, give them learning. They'll take care of you good—"

Allenby shook his head. "I thought so once, Gideon. I'm too old. I'm frightened—I'm content here. There's a Freedman's Bureau that takes care of such things—"

"You wait till doomsday, you wait for Freedman's folks," Gideon said. "What for you frightened? Go along up this road—ask anyone where you find Carwell place. Better some morning those little ones wake up, find you dead, no one to lay you out, no one to shave your beard, no one to shroud you and build a pine coffin? Who going to do it, that poor blind girl?"

Still the old man objected, and Gideon went at him, mercilessly, until at last, when the fire had almost died away, he nodded and said, yes, he would go. He sat in the faint gleam bent over, his head forward, as if he was trying to search the darkness for some assurance. And then he asked:

"Does it seem like a dream to you sometimes, Gideon, this business of freedom?"

"Ain't no dream," Gideon muttered. "I marched along with the Yankee men, made a piece of this with my own two hands. Ain't no dream."

On the next day, many things happened, causing Gideon to reflect, as he had before, that a few hours on the open road can be like a month in the bucolic pace of a country farm. He helped start a stubborn mule for a boy, and rode for two miles in his cart. He spent fifteen minutes talking to an old woman, who was bringing a basket of eggs to the village to sell, and as far as their ways coincided, he carried her basket. A white woman offered him lunch for splitting her cord-wood, and her husband came around from the milking shed and said he had never seen a nigger could make cord-wood fly like that. It was a fine lunch the white woman set out for him, and Gideon, thinking discretion the better part of valor, said never a word about the Convention. Later in the day, he passed by a plantation; there were the black men in the fields with a white overseer, digging a drainage ditch in the hard ground. "Working for wages?" Gideon called. They answered never a word and the overseer yelled, "Get on to hell, you black bastard!"

Late that afternoon, a rainstorm gathered, and Gideon crawled into a haystack while the pelting shower lasted. A cow had already taken shelter there, and Gideon lay against her warm side, humming to himself:

"Gather in the calves, all the little white calves,
    Gather in the calves, oh, mammy."

But that sort of treatment did his black frock coat no good. Gideon picked the pieces of straw off him, but the stovepipe hat was too far on its way to perdition to be saved. The crown fell off, and Gideon debated with himself the question of whether or not to wear it, topless as it was. He sensed that a stovepipe hat without a crown was a redundancy, but he could not bear to just throw it away. Saving it, he traded it later to an old colored man for two juicy apples.

He slept that night under the stars, with a bed of pine boughs between himself and the damp ground. It was not too comfortable, but now his heart was high and the wonder of his mission had taken hold of him.

The next day, Gideon walked through the low country of the coast, and on the fourth day, he saw the roofs of Charleston in front of him.

CHAPTER FOUR

How Gideon Jackson Labored with Both His Hands and His Head

THE FEELING OF PANIC THAT CAME OVER GIDEON JACKSON once he was in Charleston could not be reasoned away. It was terror of the deepest and most threatening unknown, the white man. It was a memory of childhood Gideon called onto the veranda of the big house:—

"Here, boy," flung at him perhaps thirty years ago. Men and women sat on the veranda then, the men in boots and close-fitting breeches and fine coats, and the women's dresses remembered only as beauty. Whoever this woman was, she had mud on her shoe. A man said, "Boy, come here!" Shivering with fright, he wiped the mud off her shoe, and the man flung him a silver coin. He remembered scrambling for it as it rolled in the mud, clenching it in his hand, and then facing them questioningly as they all roared with laughter. He was a small black animal, and he knew it then, and even as a six-year-old child the terror was complete, awful, aching loneliness; hope that should be a part of every living thing was denied him. The white man, thereafter, was in a sense a locked gate, and though he had come very close to that gate since, he had never actually opened it.

Now he had his hand on the gate. Not as it was the last time he came to Charleston, marching shoulder to shoulder with others, a gun on his shoulder; but alone now, and frightened.

Gideon walked through the city. He had no money and no food, and he had not the courage to present himself to the officer of the Convention. He was hungry and tired, and he realized now how shabby and ludicrous his clothes were. Even his checked handkerchief hanging from his breast pocket did not cheer him.

Why, he asked himself, had he ever left home? Why had he allowed Brother Peter to lure him into this trap? Of course, he couldn't present himself to the Convention. What then? Go home? Suppose he went home and they asked him about the Convention—what would he say then? What could he say? Lie? To his own people, to Brother Peter, to Rachel? Face Jeff, who would look at him very coolly and know? And how did he know but that there was some severe punishment for delegates elected to the Convention who did not attend? Suppose he just disappeared? But what kind of a fool notion was that? Leave Rachel, his children, his people —like being sold down the river in the old days? Had he lost his mind?

His feet took him on. He had wandered through the muddy lanes where the Negroes lived, shacks hastily constructed in the time since the war had ended, a few more imposing houses abandoned by the whites. He heard a woman's voice call, "Look at that big buck! Where you going, man?" He didn't know where he was going. He walked through the old part of the city, the fine white houses with their Grecian porticos, the palmettos, the wrought-iron gates and balconies. No kind looks here, no kind word flung at him, a city withdrawn into itself to suffer the terrible indignity of a Convention made by such men as Gideon Jackson—and that Gideon felt, like a quivering wall of frustrated hate.

Once, as evening approached, Gideon glanced up at a handsome building, and there, over the doorway he saw the word, CONVENTION, in great block letters—and painfully he put together the rest of the message, learning that here was the place where the Convention would sit. In front of the building were a guard of a dozen Yankees, leaning lazily on their rifles and chewing tobacco, and nearby were numerous little groups of Negroes and whites, talking and gesticulating and sometimes raising their voices to shout fine words. Gideon noticed with a wave of shame how well some of the men were dressed, one with pearl-gray trousers, a checked coat, and a beautiful green cravat, another in high black boots and white trousers, and still another in plaid from head to foot; such clothes as Gideon would never dream of owning; nor did it cheer him to see that there were a good many dressed no better than himself and some worse, in the shapeless, honest clothes of the field, with no cravats and no hats.

He walked on, down Meeting Street to the Battery, and then over to East Battery. At this time, Charleston, which had suffered so grievously during the war, was in the process of becoming an important port again. There were ships in the harbor, and in the docks at East Bay Street, there was a line of masts like the broken edge of an old comb. It was almost sunset now, and as Gideon walked along the Battery the water shimmered and boiled with red and golden color; old Fort Sumter, hazy out in the harbor, assumed a fairy-like pink shell, and all along the Battery the gulls swooped and screamed.

But all of this served only to deepen Gideon's despondency; he was hungry and cold, he had no money nor any place to sleep. On East Bay Street, there was a yard with cotton bales piled high; three of them made a sort of a cave, and into this Gideon crawled. He could not even sing or hum a song to lift his spirits now. He lay there, awake and miserable for hours and hours before he fell asleep.

Early the next morning, Gideon fell in with a group of black stevedores. He was walking past the dock where they sat and waited for a ship to be warped in, and they picked on his frock coat:

"Now look a there, boy, you a preaching man?"

"He's a deacon, no mistake."

"Look at that coat, must have rolled in cotton!"

Their booming, half-mocking comments had no effect on Gideon; silent and miserable, he stood there and watched them munch a breakfast of cornbread, home-squeezed cheese and onions; and indeed his despair was so obvious and complete that presently they stopped their taunts, and one of them said:

"Have a piece of bread, deacon?"

Gideon shook his head.

"Working?"

Again, Gideon shook his head.

"White boss taking all hands for fifty cents a day."

Gideon nodded; a man worked or he starved; for many things he might be unfit, but he had two strong hands and a back like a bull, fit for lugging a bale, if for nothing else. As things went, fifty cents a day was a good deal of money. Why not?

So all that day he was able to forget, the sweat running down his face, his muscles tensing, bulging, straining until some of the Negroes shouted with respect:

"He's a buck man from way down the river!" "He's a cotton-toting man!"

He had put aside his coat, but the government papers he would not part with. He put them in his pants pocket, and there was a certain comfort in feeling them, stiff and crackling.

For the moment, the future had ceased to exist, and Gideon felt a deep and needful sense of relief. They offered him food at noon, but out of his sense of pride, he refused it. When the day had finished, he was tired and hungry as a bear, but at the same time possessed of fifty cents. With Joe and Harko, two of the stevedores, he went to a place near Cumberland Street where an old colored woman cooked rice and prawns and Jerusalem artichokes, all in one savory mess. For ten cents, she piled a dish high with the stuff and threw in two corn sticks for good measure. Gideon ate his fill. It was a good thing to have money with which to buy food, a full belly, a warm feeling. Joe had a woman, sinful and willing, and he asked Gideon whether he would come; but Gideon shook his head, jolted back suddenly to reality, remembering Rachel, remembering how he and Brother Peter had talked together, wondering where this strange and hopeless road he had embarked on would take him.

Sometime during the course of this evening Gideon recognized the fact of his fear, and the simplicity and naturalness

of his going to Major Allen James and presenting his credentials. Long afterwards, he would try to remember how
the change came in him, whether it was one thing or another that had done it; whether it was his buying a newspaper for five cents and the pride with which he held it
under his arm; whether it was the house where he found a
bed, the residence of Mr. Jacob Carter; whether it was one
or another of the things that had happened to him that evening.

Jacob Carter was a cobbler, a free Negro before and during the war, an industrious and respectable colored man who
had saved pennies for years to buy his freedom. He had a
little four-room house on the edge of Charleston, and he put
a sign out, "Delegates to the Convention boarded." The man
who sold Gideon the newspaper told him about that and how
to find the place; he called Gideon "sir," perhaps only because he had bought a newspaper, but whatever the reason
with good effects upon Gideon's sunken spirits.

It was dark when Gideon came to the Carter house. He
knocked at the door. It opened a crack, letting out a yellow
shaft of light, and a woman's face stared at him suspiciously.

"What you want?"

"Please, ma'am," Gideon said. "I'm looking for a place to
sleep—seen the sign out. Ain't this the Carter place?"

"That's right. Who you?"

Then a man appeared behind her, opening the door a little wider, looking less suspiciously at Gideon.

"Name's Gideon Jackson, sir. Delegate."

"Delegate?"

"Uh-huh." Gideon was wretchedly conscious of his clothes.
"Old clothes," he mumbled. "Ain't had time to buy city
things. Come from up country."

Carter smiled and said, "Come in."

Perhaps it was Gideon's meeting with the Carters, the first
city folk whose home he had ever entered that erased his
fear. They gave him a small but clean room, a bed with a
cotton mattress, the first he had ever slept on, and a real
kerosene lamp. All this and two meals a day for two dollars

a week. When he pointed out that his work at the Convention might not net him two dollars a week, they smiled at his naivete and assured him that the Government would not think of paying a delegate less than five dollars a week, and might even pay them ten.

The Carters had no children and were past middle age; through all the terror of the war years and the two post-war years when the ruthless black codes were in force, they had fought desperately, and in a sense courageously, to sustain the small dignity of their position as free Negroes and home-owners. Yet where other free Negroes had the greatest of contempt for the illiterate, up-country blacks who were delegates, the Carters, in their simplicity, treated people like Gideon much as they would treat their own friends.

That night, in his own room with the yellow light of the lamp to make things bright and clear, Gideon struggled through the newspaper. He had seen newspapers before, but this was the first time he had ever set himself to reading one. The type was small, which made it difficult, forcing him to read even more slowly than was his habit, putting a finger under each word until he had analyzed it and either understood it or guessed at its meaning. Out of most of what he read, he could gain no continuity of thought; there were too many words he did not understand, too many long, blank spaces. Yet he labored through an editorial on the Convention, a mocking thing that compared the Negroes to monkeys, calling the coming assembly a circus, a zoo, a gathering of apes. He found himself fascinated by a story of a ship that had been wrecked, and in a disconnected way he unravelled a statement of Negro outrages throughout the state, all the while wondering why he himself had not seen or heard of any such outrages.

Finally, too tired to keep his eyes open, he took off his clothes and crawled into the soft and comfortable bed. It had metal springs, and experimentally Gideon jounced up and down on them; it was like floating on air. He fell asleep thanking God for all his good fortune and creating a dream world where he and Rachel slept every night on such a bed.

And the next day, without thinking too long or too hard about it, without being too frightened, Gideon presented himself to Major James. Mrs. Carter had cleaned his coat, sewn up the tears, and pressed it. Jacob Carter had put a patch on Gideon's left shoe, where a toe was coming through, and had covered both boots with black grease. Gently as he could, Carter suggested that the checked handkerchief would be more at home in Gideon's pants pocket than hanging from his breast pocket, and after much persuasion talked Gideon into wearing one of his white Sunday shirts. Carter had two of these which he had treasured for years and worn only on the Sabbath, but both he and his wife were charmed with Gideon, and as old people will do, had taken him to their hearts as if he were a young boy.

They brought a basin of hot water into Gideon's room, and Carter sat and listened while Gideon scrubbed off a week's dirt and related patches of his life, to make Carter more at home with him. In return, Carter talked of Charleston, of the Negroes and whites, of the peculiar, ominous tension that had hung over the town since the Convention was announced.

"Seems like they is two nigger delegates for each white," Carter said. "White ones for the most part what they call Scalawags along here, Union men. Making up to a dark time. Seems like there ain't been nothing but dark time a long while now. Maybe you noticed how they's Yankee soldiers everywhere?"

"I noticed."

"Me, I don't take to Yankee soldiers, not one bit," Carter said.

"Why for?"

"Well, you tell me, Gideon, what business they got down here? I say, let them go back to their own land."

"Wouldn't be no free men, excepting for the Yankee soldiers," Gideon said quietly. "Wouldn't be no Convention."

Carter didn't argue the point. Gideon didn't think that Carter went very deeply into anything, but the little cobbler's generosity was complete and unselfish. He was a good churchman, and two thirds of his conversation concerned the church.

Gideon was presentable when he left their house, black coat, white shirt, somewhat tight on him but serviceable nevertheless, black tie. When people turned to glance at him, for his height, his breadth of shoulder, and his clean, large features, he was certain they were admiring the shirt and the black string tie.

Major James was a harried man. Not only was the Constitutional Convention shaping up as a sprawling, unorganized affair; but Charleston was becoming more and more suggestive of a barrel of gunpowder with a lighted fuse.

Major James was attuned to signs and indications; with reason, for in the course of the long and bitter war he had seen some half dozen southern cities occupied by Yankee troops. He knew that a city is a live organism with a heart and a temper, black and sullen moods as well as light and gay ones. A city was dangerous or not dangerous, according to the way it reacted; and like a man who is all on the surface, hot and loud and frequent in anger, a city that bubbled and boiled with fury would not have disconcerted Major Allen James so much as this quiet and ominous Charleston. Too many shutters were bolted; too many of the leading people of the town had not left their homes in days—even weeks. And those who came out of their homes for business or for some other reason, walked the streets quickly, looked straight ahead of them, and said much too little.

All of which was not a good thing, in Major James' lights. Too much could go on behind those bolted shutters. How many guns were there in Charleston? How many loaded pistols? His superior, Colonel Fenton Grace, said unimaginatively, "Let it come, and when it comes we'll put it down, and then we'll know where we stand, and anyway you drink too much and think too much." Which was the answer a military man would give, one who did not, as Major James did, covet a peaceful convention and transition from the military to the civil, and perhaps a promotion and a six-month leave. Major James did not like the south; it was enemy territory. He trusted neither the whites nor the blacks, nor did he understand either group too well. He had no love for "niggers," whom he held at fault for the war; he had no love for Bourbon whites, whom he hated instinctively, out of his Ohio middle-class upbringing; and as for the plain, impoverished southern whites—well, they were the men who had killed his comrades—the god damned rebels.

But as the members of the Convention gathered, came to him and presented their credentials, his hope for a successful outcome waned. What a crew they were! What an ungodly, ignorant, filthy, vulgar crew they were! What sort of an idiotic, mad circus was this that the Yankee radicals, the Sumners and the Stevens and the rest, had imposed upon the south! Field hands that had walked a hundred, two hundred miles, too stupid to know that railroads ran and that as delegates they were entitled to ride the railroads; demobilized Negro soldiers who considered themselves on his level because once they had worn the Union blue and held a gun in their hand; men who couldn't read or write; long-limbed, illiterate white mountaineers who had supported the Union because they hated the slaveholders; black schoolteachers who because they could read and add sums considered themselves scholars;—indeed, was it any wonder that Charleston boiled with suppressed rage?

Major James began to see that there was some justice in the rebel contention that a Negro was a savage with the mind of a child, and his feeling was borne out when a huge Negro in a black frock coat, a white shirt so small that it had begun to split at the seams, and ancient patched pants, presented himself as the delegate from the Carwell-Sinkerton district. The Negro's name was Gideon Jackson; he had walked into Charleston. He could write his name and not much more. Could he read? A little, a proud possessor of perhaps a hundred words of literacy. Did he understand his duties as a delegate? Duties? Well, putting it a little differently, did he realize the significance of the Convention?

Significance? No—of course, he didn't even realize the meaning of the word. One had to walk down a step-ladder to a single syllable language—that this was the reconstruction of a state, to begin with the drafting of a new Constitution; one couldn't; it was impossible. Desperately, James went to Colonel Grace and demanded:

"Sir, do we have to seat that kind?"

"If he was legally elected."

"He has his papers. They all are, if we call this a legal election."

Colonel Grace said frigidly, "I don't question the election. Please remember, sir, that these Negroes were loyal to us in our hour of gravest need." There was no love lost between the two men; Grace had gone into the service willingly and proudly; he came of abolitionist people.

"I warn you, sir, this city will not see a convention of field hands rule over them."

"I tell you, sir," Colonel Grace said quietly, "that this city will damn well do as our Government orders."

"They're proud people."

"The kind of pride that puts a half a million men in their graves," the colonel said.

So Major James went back and countersigned Gideon's right to sit in the Constitutional Convention of the state of South Carolina.

As Gideon was leaving the Military Adjustment Offices, he was stopped by a well-dressed, light-complexioned colored man who introduced himself as Francis L. Cardozo. He said:

"You're a member of the Convention?"

"Uh huh."

"Mind if I walk along with you?"

"Don't know as I mind that," Gideon said uncertainly, troubled somewhat by the ease with which this well-dressed, well-mannered stranger had insinuated himself. They started off down the street, Gideon glancing sidewise at the other again and again, until finally Cardozo, with a slight nod of his head, asked, "And what is your name, sir, if I may inquire?"

"Gideon Jackson."

Cardozo said that he was also a member of the Convention, from the district of Charleston, and would Gideon care to meet with some of the other members? They would be at Cardozo's home that afternoon at about three o'clock, to talk about matters pertaining to the Convention. Had Gideon met any of the delegates?

"Guess I ain't," Gideon said.

"Well, of course you will, once the Convention convenes. This, however, may make some things clear. These are good people, I assure you, Mr. Jackson."

"I'd mighty well like to come," Gideon said.

"Do come then, and I'll write down the address for you."

He wrote it down on a card, which he gave to Gideon. They shook hands, and then Gideon walked away with the salutation ringing in his ears, Mr. Jackson, the nice rounded sound of it and the increasing wonder of it. Like Church singing to glory were all the things that happened to him; and here only a little while ago he was afraid to present his papers. Tomorrow a day, the Convention would begin. The hammering, unnatural pace of Gideon's heart was almost a constant factor now; he walked briskly through the streets, telling himself, "There's a sunshine brightness in the world. Jesus Christ walks. I was born a slave and a slave until maybe yesterday. My little ones, they was born slaves. Look at now—just look at now!"

A white man, walking down the street, facing Gideon and on a line with him, came toward him with the compact assurance that Gideon would give way. Gideon was inside himself, and the world didn't exist. They would have met head on, but at the last moment, the man swerved aside, lashing at Gideon with the cane he carried, catching him full across the back; and Gideon, plucked back to reality by the blow, stood there, surprised, tense, shamed, the welt on his back burning, rage growing inside him; rage and shame and the desire to spring after the white man, but a sense of something that held him back and talked to him until the white man had turned a corner and was out of sight.

Gideon walked on, and the world returned to a place that still needed patching here and there, not perfect yet, Gideon asking himself, "Why for did he had to do that?"

In Gideon's pocket was still twenty-five cents. Money went a long way; money was not like rice or potatoes, crops of the ground that went into a rigid calculation, so much eaten each day and finally the supply exhausted; there was a flexibility to money—one could use it for this or that, or one could not use it at all. The brisk, cool weather had given him an appetite, and he stopped at a stand in the covered market where they were selling rice and onions, five cents for a steaming plate. Then he bought another newspaper, went down to the docks and sat on a bale of cotton, spread the paper, the sting in his back almost gone now, the wonder of print reoccurring and in a certain sense erotic, making his skin tighten and prickle with excitement as he read, "Georgia reports give promise of a more *stabilizing*—" a word his mind underlined for the future, a mystery he moved his lips over, "Stab—stalabl—no, stay-billy—" And as his eyes shifted, "Cotton futures on the New York market—" What was a *future*? The word "market" he could comprehend, a place where they sold things, a homely word; but what sort of a market was this in New York where cotton became cotton futures? His eyes ached and he became drowsy; he dozed a little there in the warming afternoon, coming awake every so often and looking at the newspaper again. Stray words caught his eyes. "Black savages from the Congo—" The stevedores were shouting and singing as they toted their great loads. Was the Congo in Carolina or Georgia? Savages was a familiar word; make a nigger out to be a red, wild Indian. Out in the bay a full-rigged ship tacked back and forth, and all the gulls raced after it. Gideon looked up at the sun and estimated that it was close to three o'clock.

He came to Cardozo's house with his paper folded neatly under his arm, and bowed correctly as he was introduced to Mr. Nash, Mr. Wright, and Mr. Delany, middle-aged Negroes of Charleston, each of them raising a brow at Gideon's clothes, at his soft, slurred back-country slave speech. Gideon was impressed; these were educated men, well-dressed in dark clothes. He was beginning to understand that certain circles preferred dark clothes to the bright, gay colors some of the delegates wore. Mr. Nash said:

"I presume, Mr. Jackson, you come with some instruction from your constituents?"

"We recognize the need of a formulated program," Mr. Delany added.

"I don't know," Gideon muttered.

There was a more gentle understanding in Cardozo. "This is high-falutin' talk, Mr. Jackson," he smiled. "Becoming a legislator, a man leaves half his brain in his pants pocket and tries to operate with an unused half he never knew he possessed."

Gideon nodded, making up his mind to keep his mouth shut and listen. Mr. Wright expressed complete hopelessness about the future. He said to Cardozo:

"But when you come down to it, Francis, there are at least thirty delegates who can neither read nor write!"

Gideon was glad he had the folded newspaper under his arm. What did they think of him, and why had they asked him here?

"So much the better," Cardozo nodded.

"But make sense, please!"

"I'm inclined to agree with Francis," Nash said. "The literate people of this world have worked no wonders."

"That, of course, is sophistry. We're faced with the problem of field-hands participating in the making of a Constitution. Not to mention the anger this is raising among the white population, we're faced with the very real question of the field-hands themselves. What will they do?"

"They can be managed."

Cardozo said lightly, "Do you feel that you can be managed, Mr. Jackson?"

"Sir?" Gideon had the feeling that he was being the butt of something; the bewilderment was changing into anger.

"But don't be angry, Mr. Jackson," Cardozo said. "You were a slave."

"I was."

"A field-hand?"

"That's right."

"How do you see this business of a Constitution? I mean that seriously. What will you want in a Constitution you have a part in making?"

Gideon looked at them, the heavy-set Nash, the slim, almost courtly Cardozo, Wright, round and suave, like a well-fed house servant. And the room they sat in, a room that to Gideon seemed elegant almost beyond belief, upholstered chairs, a stuffed squirrel, even a rug on the floor, and three crayon pictures on the walls. How does a black man come by all this? Where did he fit into it? And the other delegates who had plodded across the state in their shapeless cotton-field boots?

"Don't be offended, Mr. Jackson," Cardozo persisted.

Gideon nodded. "I ain't high. I guess you want an answer. Talk about a man can't read, can't write, just an old nigger come walking out of the cotton fields, that's me. What I want from Constitution? Maybe it ain't what you folks want—want learning, want it for all, black and white. Want a freedom that's sure as an iron fencepost. Want no man should push me off the street. Want a little farm where a nigger can put in a crop and take out a crop all his days. That's what I want."

Then there was a silence, and Gideon felt embarrassed, provocative and high and mighty without reason, a man who said a lot, none of it making sense. A little later, the others made their goodbyes, but when Gideon rose to go, Cardozo plucked at his sleeve and begged him to wait a moment. And when the others had left, said to Gideon:

"Have some tea, please, and we can talk. It wasn't so clever of me bringing you into this, was it?"

"That all right," Gideon nodded, wanting to go, but too unsure of himself to know how to go about his leave-taking. Cardozo's wife came in then, a small, pretty brown woman. Gideon loomed over her like a giant.

"Are they all as big as that in the hills?" she asked, in the way of making conversation, and Gideon, quick to take offense at anything now, answered, "I ain't from the hills, ma'am, but from the middle country."

Cardozo said, "Won't you stay? There's a lot for us to talk about."

Gideon nodded.

"Then look at it this way," Cardozo said. "Here were a few of us who have been free Negroes, maybe not as close to our people as we should have been. Just a few of us, against the four million slaves. But the books were opened to us, and we learned a little; but believe me, in a way we were more slaves than you. Now there comes a situation so strange, so open in its implications, that the world cannot fully realize it. The Union government, backed with a military machine it built during the war, says to the people of the south, white and black, build a new life. From the beginning. A new Constitution, new laws, a new society. The white planters rebel against this, but they are the defeated. Yet they stay away from the voting, and as a result here in this state black men, slaves only yesterday, choose their own people and send them to the Convention. Do you know, Gideon, that we, the blacks, are in the majority, that seventy-six out of one hundred and twenty-four elected delegates are Negroes? That over fifty of these are former slaves? This is the year eighteen sixty-eight; how long have we been out of bondage? The Children of Israel wandered in the wilderness for forty years."

After a moment, Gideon murmured, "I don't quote Scripture when I'm afraid. I'm a God-fearing man, but when the fright was strongest inside of me, I took a gun in my hands and fought for my freedom."

"And what will these field-hands do in the courts of law?"

"What they do? They ain't no black savages, like newspaper say. They got a wife and child and love in their heart. They say what is good for me, for woman, for the child, and they vote that in. They got a hunger for learning, and they vote for that. They know about slavery, and they vote for freedom. They ain't going to be uppity; you lead them by the hand, and by God, they come. But you don't take no lash to their back no more. They know how it taste to be free man."

Thoughtfully, Cardozo said, "That'll take courage from me, Gideon."

"Took courage from me to come to this Convention."

"I suppose so. Tell me something about yourself, Gideon."

The telling came slow and stumblingly from Gideon; it was nightfall when he had finished. He felt dry and used up. But before he left, Cardozo gave him two books, one *Geldon's Basic Speller* and the other *Usage of the English Language* by Fitzroy and James. They were the first real books Gideon ever had; he held them gently in his big hands, as if they were made of eggshell. Plucking a name from his memory, he asked:

"You got the Shakespeare book?"

For a moment, Cardozo hesitated; then, without smiling, he went to his little shelf of books, took *Othello*, and handed it to Gideon.

"Thank you," Gideon said.

And Cardozo nodded, and after Gideon had left, said to his wife, "If I had laughed—if I had! God help me, I almost laughed! What animals we are!"

Gideon asked Carter to tell him something about Cardozo. In a way, a purely social way, that Gideon could not as yet comprehend, Carter was impressed by the fact that Gideon had been to Cardozo's home.

"He's part Jew," Carter said. "That's how he come by the name. He's a proud nigger."

Gideon, who had never seen a Jew before, said, "Looks the same like any black man."

"But uppity," Carter said.

Carter said that Gideon could use the lamp, and then, at the end of the month, by which time surely the delegates would have drawn some wages, pay him for the oil burned. Gideon lay half the night with the speller, writing out the words on the margins of the newspaper, saying the words aloud and trying to hear whether or not they sounded strange. His incessant mumbling brought Carter to the door.

"Ailing?" Carter asked.

"Learning," Gideon apologized.

The speller was a marvelous book, but it fell down on the meaning of words—and Gideon wondered if there was any book that could tell a man what a word meant. He thumbed through the book on usage; a paragraph which caught his eye said:

"While contractions as a whole are to be frowned upon, 'ain't' is certainly the most vulgar. It is an indication of class, as well as a sign of whether or not a person desires to be taken for a gentleman. A gentleman will avoid contractions when possible, and will never, under any circumstances, use 'ain't.' The ambiguity of this contraction twice condemns it, for a person of culture will not use a word which might mean 'is not' or 'am not' or 'are not.' A person of culture will be as precise in his speech as in his thought and his personal habits."

Gideon determined to avoid "ain't" like a plague; the more he read out of usage, the more his fears grew, the more awesome and terrible the matter of learning became. He turned to *Othello* with some small shred of hope, and that was blasted as he read:

IAGO: I am about it; but indeed my invention
   comes from my pate as birdlime does from frize . . .

And he fell asleep finally, his head aching, his despair as complete as ever it had been.

Cardozo lay awake longer than Gideon. Like a gap in his life, like a gap in human history, in the whole aching, crawling stream of human life was that space left on his shelf after he had removed the three books. How did he come to Gideon Jackson? Who was this huge, slow-moving, slow-spoken black man who had come out of the Carolina back country, out of slavery, out of darkness, and why did he make Cardozo feel so small? What was the measure of a man? He, Cardozo, had been born free; in his memories there was an education at the University of Glasgow; there were garden parties outside of London. There was a great meeting where he had addressed three thousand Englishmen, and had been accorded honor and respect. He had crossed oceans and been in homes of the great.

He had been a minister in New Haven, and Abolitionists had met in his house and spun their plots. There was in his veins white blood and black, Negro and Indian, Jew and Gentile spun together. Even the white men of Charleston accorded him respect. He, Cardozo, was closer to a Pringle than Gideon Jackson was to him.

Yet he recognized in Gideon Jackson the salvation, if there was to be any in this dark confusion; the huge, illiterate black man was looking at sunshine which Cardozo did not see. Cardozo, who could not sleep because his fears were so many, his ambitions so hopeless, lay awake and envied a freed slave.

In the way of things, coming finally however long that coming seems, the Convention came, and Gideon Jackson sat among the delegates. It seemed to him that for this moment, time stood still. Thirty-six years he had lived, born a squalling black brat and killing his mother in the birth, cattle from the day he walked, to be pinched and tested and priced —and now he sat among men who were making a world. Still. Quiet. Motionless. The world stood on end. Gideon with his hands clasped in his lap, his knees pressed together, hearing each separate thump of his heart, hardly daring to breathe; well, it was not so easy to breathe, the way the hall was packed, opposing rows of chairs on staged steps, bank after bank of black and white faces, men in country clothes, in city clothes, in fancy clothes and drab clothes, men in stiff black frock coats and men in old army jackets, old men and young men, men born slave and men born free, scalawags and carpet-baggers and tall, blond sunburned Unionists from the mountains, men who had marched with the Rebels sitting knee to knee with those who had marched with the Yankees; no, it was not at all easy to breathe.

And as if that was not enough, the Charleston people had finally come forth from their homes and pressed in to see the circus, to see the "ring-tailed monkeys," and the "black baboons." The press was there too, not only local reporters, but scornful writers from Georgia and Louisiana and Alabama and other southern states, prepared to put the blight once and for all on this insanity, New York reporters, sophisticated, and trying to sort out of the mess just those bits of unique local color the big city readers would properly appreciate; there were reporters from Boston, old Abolitionist editorial writers from New England, and of course the Washington people with a special ear for all that might set the Capital buzzing. Add to that the Yankee soldiers who ringed the hall and you had every single human soul the place would hold.

But for all the apprehension, the anticipation and excitement, the first day of the session went off quietly and in an orderly fashion. A roll was called; Gideon sat sick and terrified until his name came, but after he had spoken "Here!" and the chairman passed on to the next name, it seemed like nothing at all that his voice should be heard by all these people.

After the roll-call, ex-Governor Orr of South Carolina rose to address the Convention. He was there by special invitation, a gesture by the delegates that they were going to work within the body of the public, not outside it. The hall became very still, and Gideon leaned forward that he might not miss a word that was said. He was pleased at first; Orr spoke of the dire need for education on the part of the former slaves. But then, in no uncertain terms, he declared that they did not represent the intelligence of the state, not the wealth, not even the potential. It was a dream that they should talk, as they were talking, of complete suffrage.

Much of this Gideon did not understand. He raged at himself that half-spoken, half-suggested ideas should pass him by, that the meaning of every third or fourth word should escape him. Was Orr laughing at them? Despising them? Attacking them?

There was not a great deal of applause when Orr finished. But there was order. An agenda for the following day was then arranged, after which the Convention was declared adjourned until the next morning.

Gideon listened to a group of delegates who had gathered on the street and were talking hotly. They were country people, heavy-set, muscular field-hands with the shoulders that told of years behind the plough. One of them, an elderly man, black as tar, long-faced and keen-eyed, was saying:

"Education, that we ain't got—who got it in this here state? Whole counties without schools. Boss man, he don't mind that, bring a teacher into his house, send his little ones to Europe. But that ain't what Orr calls intelligence; that learning. How long we been at this—two years freedom, one day Convention. I say, why that man wants to tear us down?"

A tall white man, raw-boned, his speech the slow and stumbling talk of the mountains, elbowed into the crowd and said, "Plenty of reason, uncle."

"How come?"

"Uncle, why don't you niggers open your eyes? This equality thing ain't going to hold water unless you put your shoulders under it. Sure they'll talk you down; they'll talk me down. You're a nigger; I'm white trash. White trash elected me and niggers elected you, and maybe there was a few of your kind in my vote and a few of my kind in yours. I'm no nigger lover, but I like the kind of thinking that makes two and two add up to four. That kind of thinking tells me what we can do if we keep our senses; but it don't tell me they're going to stop calling us animals."

"What you going to do about it, white man?" someone asked.

"Keep my head. Come out of this convention with schools and the right to vote. I know what my enemies are going to say."

"You let them say it?"

"That's right. Then I speak my piece."

"How about land? What good are schools and voting, if you ain't got the means to take out a crop?"

"Land," the white man said, chewing at the word. "Brother, ask them for land and they're going to lick you right down the line. No land's going to come out of this Convention; if we want land, we're going to work and sweat and buy it."

"Ain't we worked that land for maybe a hundred years? Ain't we put in the crop and take it out? Then they go try to smash up the country. Who got a better right to the land?"

"It ain't a question of right, uncle, it's a question of property. I don't shoot for the stars, I aim for the brow of the next hill—"

The argument went on, getting hotter and hotter. When Gideon saw the white man detach himself, he walked along with him and plucked at the other's sleeve.

"Mister?"

The white man paused, looked at Gideon out of a pair of very cool blue eyes, and made as to walk on. Gideon sensed something of the struggle inside the other, a southerner born and bred in the south, hating a slave system that made him a landless scavenger, but hating Negroes too because of the economics that forced him into their class, his white skin the only badge of respect left.

"Please, sir, I'd like to talk to you," Gideon said. "My name's Gideon Jackson."

"Mine's Anderson Clay," the white man nodded grudgingly, walking on then, Gideon alongside of him.

"I don't mean to presume," Gideon said. "It ain't—it not I want to poke uppity, but I hear what you say about the land. That mighty important to me, that my people have land. You figure they won't give us none?"

"They damnwell won't."

"How we going to live?"

"Nigger, that's one for you to figure out."

Walking along in silence for a while, Gideon said finally, "Maybe we can talk this around again?"

"Maybe."

"I'm proud to know you," Gideon said.

Writing to his wife a few days later, writing the first letter he had ever created, feeling the wonder of each word he put down, Gideon said:

"Dear wife Rachel,
I think for you all the time. I make a picture of you to myself. You are pretty I think all the time. Like when I was with

Yankee men in war I feel sad for being away from you. I learn me writing and reading from books and I am delegate in convention to make good law. My pay is very much 3 dollar every day I save most. Before I sleep I see you and children every night and god be good to you I pray. I write so good only with book but learn. I talk at convention once about pay I was so afraid. That is called debate. Be good to Jams Alenb if he come to you god bless you I write again soon.

That was the letter Gideon wrote, hours of labor far into the night, each word checked and copied carefully into the copy book he had bought. It gave him a warm sense of nearness to Rachel, to the people he had left at the plantation. How would they feel when they learned that he had already taken part in a debate on the Convention floor? Not that it was an important matter, nor had he meant to speak; but somehow—exactly how he couldn't recall—he was on his feet and talking. It was the session wherein they took up the question of pay for delegates:

Leading the discussion, a Mr. Langly said that twelve dollars a day would be a round figure. "Certainly, the delegates to his Convention are deserving of that!" The reporters present scribbled furiously. Wright, a Negro, took the floor and said that ten dollars ought to be sufficient. "It will satisfy the basic dignity requisite to a legislator." The gallery hooted and the speaker pounded for order. Parker, a white man, upped the pay to eleven dollars, a fantastic sum to ninety percent of the Convention, men who by and large had always worked with their hands, slaves some of them, tenant farmers some of them, men who had not seen the sparkle of silver in years. Three scalawag delegates joined with two carpet-baggers in earnest seconding when Mr. Leslie, a black delegate, gained the floor and cried:

"I am willing to receive three dollars a day for my services. I want to go on the record for that, as a black man. I think that is all my services are worth. I ask you delegates, if you were called on to pay a similar body of men out of your pockets, how much would you be willing to pay? Wouldn't a dollar fifty be enough? What is this business of eight or nine or ten dollars a day? It looks like fraud!"

A Mr. Melrose spoke through the scattered applause. "—
the damned insult of suggesting one dollar and fifty cents
a day to the members of this Convention!"

That was when Gideon gained the floor and was recognized, forgetting himself in this incredible contradiction, his
deep, rich voice filling the hall.

"I hear all this talk, ten dollars a day, eleven! I read the
newspaper calling us robbers, then I'm mad, angry. We ain't
robbers—but how come this—" At that point, the enormity
of what he had done occurred to him; he felt himself grow
hot and cold, and the next words came falteringly, "I come to
Charleston—just a few years ago in Yankee army—what pay
I got there?—twenty cents a day, maybe, but I fight for freedom. I was a slave, no pay, never. I come along to Charleston
before Convention, got to eat, got to work. Then I go down
on water and tote a bale for fifty cents a day, and good pay.
How come I worth ten dollars now?" Somehow, his terror
had passed; more assured, he said, "Maybe like other man
say, it's dignity. Then three dollar are sure enough for dignity. Makes a difference between delegate and dockhand,
even if that difference is not real. But I is not worth ten
dollars every day."

That was how Gideon spoke for the first time in the Convention hall, carrying a motion.

CHAPTER FIVE

How Gideon Jackson Was a Guest of Honor at a Great Affair

As the days during which the convention was in session became weeks, and the weeks months, Gideon lost the feeling of fear and strangeness he had brought with him to the first sitting. As with other incidents in his life, what had been unnatural became natural, and what had been strange became commonplace. The qualitative change within himself was not completely conscious; there was no point where he paused, observed himself, and saw that he was not the same man he had been a little while ago. The doing of a thing made him practiced in it. Brother Peter had once told him to listen when men spoke, since speech was one of the many things by which men were judged—and for thirty and fifty and ninety days he sat in the Convention Hall and listened. And sometimes he spoke—and it did not seem too curious to him that each time he spoke men listened a little more intently.

Things bore fruit. The three books in his little room at the Carters increased to a dozen and then two dozen. Each night, as soon as he had finished dinner, he went in there, closed the door, and spread his books on the little table under the lamp. He rarely worked less than three hours, sometimes five, sometimes all night through—as was the case when he first opened *Uncle Tom's Cabin*. It was his first novel, and when one of the members of the Convention, a colored man called DeLarge, offered it to him, Gideon objected that he had no time for story books.

"This," DeLarge said, "is one of the factors that made it possible for you to be here, at the Convention."

"A book?"

"When old Abe Lincoln met Mrs. Stowe, who wrote this book, he said to her, 'Is this the little lady who plunged a great nation into war?' "

Smiling, Gideon said, "I reckon maybe one or two other things contributed."

"But take the book and read it."

Gideon took the book home, but it was weeks before he came around to reading it; then a world opened up, and the Carters pleaded with him that unless he slept he would surely break down. There were parts of the book he copied —keys to matters that had puzzled and disturbed him and which were now apparently plain, such as the following passage:

"Now, an aristocrat, you know, the world over, has no human sympathies, beyond a certain line in society. In England the line is in one place, in Burmah in another, and in America in another; but the aristocrat of these countries never goes over it. What would be hardship and distress and injustice in his own class, is a cool matter of course in another one. My father's dividing line was that of color. *Among his equals,* never was a man more just and generous; but he considered the Negro, through all possible gradations of color, as an intermediate link between man and animals, and graded all his ideas of justice and generosity on this hypothesis . . ."

And this piece.

"Alfred, who is as determined a despot as ever walked, does not pretend to this kind of defense; no, he stands, high and haughty, on that good old respectable ground, *the right of the strongest;* and he says, and I think quite sensibly, that the American planter is 'only doing in another form what the English aristocracy and capitalists are doing by the lower classes'; that is I take it, *appropriating* them, body and bone, soul and spirit, to their use and convenience. He defends both—and I think at least, *consistently.* He says there can be no high civilization without enslavement of the masses, either nominal or real. There must, he says, be a lower class, given up to physical toil and confined to an animal nature;

and a higher one thereby acquires leisure and wealth for a more expanded intelligence and improvement, and becomes the directing soul of the lower. So he reasons, because as I said, he is born an aristocrat; so I don't believe, because I was born a democrat."

That, Gideon copied and studied, and when he saw De-Large again, said, "I've been reading the book."

"And learning?"

"I always learn a little," Gideon smiled. "Tell me, was the book printed in England too?"

"Yes, and translated into German, Russian, Hungarian, French, Spanish and a dozen more tongues. In Europe, working men call it their Bible."

"A book about a black slave?"

"Or just slaves, Gideon."

The work told; for the first time in his life, Gideon's eyes ached. He had lost weight, become leaner, and more tired than he had ever been with his two hands on a plough or marching thirty miles a day in the army. Heretofore, all his life, it had seemed to him that there would be time for everything, days coming and going as the sun rose and set, the slow, bucolic rhythm of the cotton fields, things that had always been, the piney wastes, the dark swamps, the slow and mournful melody of the work songs; but here was a world of flux that would not wait; each day counted, each hour. A dictionary he bought had fifty thousand words in it, and words were the tools he worked with now. Knowledge was never-ending, and always he had the despairing realization that he was only scratching the surface. A whole week given to learning addition and subtraction, basic multiplication; a whole night spent wakefully on a single-page speech he would deliver the next day on the subject of education. The presumption of it—the presumption of Gideon Jackson rising in the hall and stating:

"I have heard, these past days, my fellow delegates argue about education which is enforced, like a law. I have heard gentlemen say that it was beyond reason or the right thing to hope to enforce education. I disagree. Maybe people would go naked if it wasn't law that they must wear clothes. They must wear clothes because it is law, and they become soon used to it. I think that in five or ten years soon people would become used to the fact that they must go to school if they want to or not. Why it was that slave owners would sell a slave so soon they found he could read or write? I tell you only because ignorant people can be slaves. Democracy and Equality cannot understand themselves to men and women who have no knowledge to learn about these things. No people can be free without learning about it."

A whole night to write that little bit; and afterwards a feeling of how completely inadequate it had been, badly phrased, not saying the things he had hoped to say and wanted to say. Yet for all of that, Cardozo came to him and wanted to know:

"Where have you been hiding, Gideon?"

"Hiding?"

"I mean you disappear after each session."

"I study," Gideon said.

"Every night?"

"Every night."

"No rest, no play," Cardozo said thoughtfully. "You meet no one, do you? That isn't the best thing either."

"I come to the sessions."

"Yes—but I want you to meet some people, white as well as black. It's important that you should know white people, know what they are thinking, saying, doing. We are going to have to work closer and closer with the white folks, Gideon."

"I guess so," Gideon nodded.

"Will you come and dine with us tomorrow?"

"Dine?" Gideon hesitated, but Cardozo pressed him, "Please come, do come."

"All right."

"But that wasn't what I wanted to speak about. I was impressed with what you said about compulsory education. It's something I'm extremely interested in, and I think if we fail in that point, we fail in the whole of the Constitution. It goes to committee next week. Will you serve on the committee?"

Gideon stared at Cardozo, but there was no trace of humor in the man's eyes. Gideon agreed.

"I'm glad," Cardozo said.

Some time before this, Gideon had decided that he must have a suit of clothes. For all of Mrs. Carter's patching, the trousers he wore were in a process of deterioration that would soon end in ruin. Hardly a day went by when the frock coat, which had been too small for him all along, did not split at one seam or the other. For two dollars, Jacob Carter had made Gideon a fine pair of shoes, but the suit situation was definitely at a crisis. Mrs. Carter said that it was a shame for him, a delegate, to come to the Convention day after day in those old rags.

"Clothes," Gideon said, "cost money. I got better ways to spend it."

"Clothes go along with the man who's inside them," Mrs. Carter said. So Gideon took the bit in his teeth and went to old Uncle Baddy, who had a shack behind the Henry place on Rutledge Avenue. The Henry place was a huge, white Georgian town house and Uncle Baddy had been one of the Henry slaves during and before the war—for as long as anyone could remember. He was seventy-five, possibly eighty years old; the Henrys had trained him as a tailor, and for two generations he had sat on the table in his shack, legs crossed, stitching away at ballroom dresses, brocade gowns, and gentlemen's suits of fine brown and gray and black worsted and broadcloth. When emancipation came, he just stayed in the same place; the Henrys let him have the shack for the family sewing he did, and of late he had been doing a little cutting and sewing for hire.

Carter sent Gideon there. The old man looked Gideon up and down, blinked his eyes, and said, "Ain't no end to you, sure enough. How I'm going to find cloth enough to cover a nigger your size?"

"Don't have to be much of a suit," Gideon said. "Just so long as I can wear it."

"What you mean, ain't much of a suit? Made suits for the Henrys these forty, fifty year. Don't go telling me how to make a suit."

Gideon apologized, and two weeks later the suit was finished, the price ten dollars for a fine set of beautifully-tailored black broadcloth clothes. Gideon wrote to Rachel:

"Dear wife Rachel,
I had to buy a suit of clothes, for my old ones were done and gone. It cost ten dollars, mostly for the cloth, and so much money I know it is a shame but everything is a lot of money here in Charleston. I am happy to hear that things are quiet and good with you and Mister James Allenby is learning the children and happy. It was sad for me to hear from Mister Allenby's letter about the murder of four Negro people in Sinkerton by lawless men who hate us and use terror but such badness will stop when the Constitution is framed and a Civil Government makes our pretty Carolina a good land. I meet good men and I think it will all be good but be patient. Kiss the children for me God bless you and them."

He put a dollar bill in the letter; he did that each day, and each day he managed to write something to Rachel. And Gideon wore the new suit to dinner at the Cardozos.

Dinner at the Cardozos then, in 1868, was in the manner of a pause in history, even as the whole incident of the Convention was in the way of being a pause, a gap, a hole scooped in the developing stream of America by Union bayonets. Charleston, the beautiful, fairylike, palmetto-fringed city, the crown and glory of the south, lay exhausted. The war had torn the guts out of the town. There was hardly one of the great white Georgian houses that had not felt its portion of death and economic ruin. The mighty fortunes that built this cluster of white and wonderful houses, unequaled anywhere in America, were founded upon one thing, the broad back of the black slave. Not only was labor, the source of all wealth, tied up in the slaves, but the slaves themselves had been capital, the most important capital the south owned, in a sense primitive machine tools, bought and bred and sold, and in their fluid state the bottom rock of southern economy. Then, in the course of a ruinous war, a war that wrecked the monitary system of the south, blockaded its ports, Charleston among them, and sent armies marching and counter-marching across its lands for four years, the slaves were liberated: liberated by an edict signed by the great, tired man in the White House, a liberation enforced by the strength and guns of the Union Army.

In the immediate post-war period, the south lay stunned and sick. Two hundred thousand black slaves had taken up the arms and uniform of the north and fought in the last fierce struggle for their freedom. The southern armies had dissolved; the southern leaders sat back in exhaustion, staring wonderingly at the dissolution—a house of sugar which upon being thoroughly saturated suddenly collapses. And the plantation kings, the men behind the war, the men who had engineered it, made it, and plunged their hands elbow-deep in blood that their great empires of cotton, rice and sugar and tobacco might endure, saw the impossible happen, the slaves emancipated, millions and millions and millions of dollars of capital they once owned taken from them and overnight dissolved into thin air.

Perhaps never before in human history had a whole class, a ruling class of a nation been so stunningly and quickly deprived of its property. The first reaction of the planters was silence, a sick and bewildered silence during which time they contemplated the ruin that had been accomplished. They could not rebel, because they possessed no means of rebellion; they could not plan because they had never envisioned a future without slaves. Some of them had counterbalanced their wealth of slaves with large loans, and when the collateral of slavery disappeared, their empires went with it. Great plantations stood empty and abandoned, or worked in a desultory way by the Negroes who stayed upon the soil because they had no place in particular to go; other plantations were put up to auction, sold for debt or taxes. Fields lay fallow; cotton planting dwindled and in many sections disappeared.

When the first paralyzing shock passed, the planters bestirred themselves. This farce of Emancipation, they thought, would not be played through; the slaves could be kept slaves; a nigger was a nigger; that was the beginning, it would also be the end; what went on in Washington was one thing, practical needs of the south were another. With almost hysterical haste, they set about inaugurating a set of laws called "Black Codes." Laws that returned the Negro legally to precisely the position he was in before the war; it was simple at first. There was a president in the White House who played along with them, who generously supported the terror they were establishing. They smiled to each other, "Tennessee Johnson is useful," despising the man and using him at one and the same time. Once more, the planters saw a future, the same future they had always seen, propped on the backs of four million black slaves.

And then their house of cards fell down. A bitter, wrathful, revolutionary Congress that had fought one of the most terrible wars known to mankind, decided that the blood spilt should not be in vain. In their anger, they almost impeached the president; they sent troops into the south and smashed the incipient terror. They legally nullified the rebellious states, established military districts, and called upon the whole population to vote for delegates to state Conventions, Conventions which would frame new state constitutions and create a new democracy in the south, one in which the black man and the white man stood side by side, building together.

In South Carolina, the black population outnumbered the white. Under this second stunning blow, the planters could see only one course of action, one device—to show their contempt by remaining away from the polls. Let the illiterate niggers and white trash vote, and the result would destroy this incredible and monstrous plan of Congress. The result, much as they had planned, gave the Negroes an overwhelming majority of delegates to the Convention; yet where the result went askew was that instead of making a circus, the black and white Convention was slowly, painfully but certainly nevertheless, beginning to operate as a sound legislative body. A constitution was emerging.

And in Charleston, while that happened, the white aristocrats locked their doors, barred their shutters, and waited.

Yankee bayonets in the street made them impotent for the time. There was no future and no past in this moment. In the deep strange hole that had been violently scooped in the stream of history, something was happening. In that hole a dinner was given at Francis Cardozo's house; in that hole, Gideon Jackson dressed himself in his new suit of black broadcloth.

And the planters waited.

The curious part of this dinner was the way in which it led to the other, the great affair at which Gideon was the guest of honor; for one of the guests at the Cardozo home this night was Stephan Holms, delegate to the Convention and former slave owner. Technically Holms was a Scalawag, the term for a southern white who collaborated with the freed slaves and the Yankees; actually, he was not of them. The Scalawags were poor whites for the most part; Holms had been and still was wealthy. Singularly, he had defied the rule that planters should sit back and have no part of this incredible revolution; he was elected to the Convention on the votes of his former slaves; he sat in the Convention as a spectator. He watched and listened; he said nothing. He was courteous to white and colored alike, and he became an enigma that Cardozo determined to solve.

On the surface, he had no secrets. He was the last male of a good South Carolina family; a brother and a son had died in the war. Holms had been a Major, had fought with Jackson and Lee, and had gained neither distinction nor fame. It was known that he disapproved of the war, that he thought the Secession unutterably stupid and hopeless from the very beginning. He had once owned a plantation on the Congaree River not far from Columbia, but he now lived with his mother in their Charleston house, and it was taken for granted that the country place had been lost, either through debt or taxes; in any case, he did not speak of it.

He was handsome, in a pale, self-effacing manner; stomach-trouble jaundiced his skin, gave it a yellow tinge; he was dark, longfaced, with a full head of hair, taller than the average, delicate in his movements, consciously a gentleman, quiet in his speech. He had singled out Cardozo, talked with him several times, indicated an interest in education and land, and graciously accepted Cardozo's uncertain invitation to dinner.

It was an invitation and an acceptance that troubled Cardozo. When white men dined with black in the city of Charleston, the world stood on end and shivered, and that was a part of what Cardozo felt as he introduced Gideon Jackson, former slave to Stephan Holms, former slave-holder. And Holms said:

"I am honored to meet you, Mr. Jackson," pleasantly and quietly, as if this were the most everyday thing, looking at Gideon appraisingly. Gideon was a matter for appraisal, tailored well, his great chest and shoulders set off by the black coat, a plain white shirt and a black string tie. His woolly hair was cropped close to his head; clean-shaven with big features to hold the flesh, but leaner than he had ever been before—recalling to Holms that once such a man on the auction block would have created a near-riot, the bidding mounting in dizzy spirals, the auctioneer screaming, "My friends and gentlemen, you who know and value breed, here's a bull stallion such as you never laid eyes on before!"

"I am pleased to meet you, sir," Gideon said.

Dr. Randolph, a small, quick-speaking, brown-skinned man, also a delegate, was the fourth for dinner; he was more nervous than Gideon, more nervous than Cardozo at the presence of Holms; he stuttered as his speech spilled out. Mrs. Cardozo was the only woman at the table, and she tried to put people at their ease; Holms joined with her, and they were gracious back and forth. Gideon asked himself, bewildered, "What is the man? Why and how and who?" It was the first time in his life he ever took the hand of a man of Holms' class, first time he had ever spoken to one, man to man, first time he had ever sat down to eat with a white man. Obviously, it was not the case with Cardozo, but wasn't it with Randolph? Randolph was frightened. Gideon stared behind his hostess to the buffet, where a stuffed partridge stood under a bell of glass. There was patterned wallpaper and prints on the walls. Cardozo knew the world, but Gideon could not help but be aware how carefully he was treading with Holms, saying, "Education, sir, you see, is a necessity."

"A necessity?" Holms asked. Holms neutralized himself completely, never stating but always asking, his constant withdrawal being a most effective blandishment.

"Simply by a statement of the fact. Four million illiterate slaves are possible. Four million illiterate free Negroes are obviously impossible."

"That's a curious way to look at it," Holms admitted. "What do you think, Mr. Jackson?"

"I think education is like a gun," Gideon said.

"Like a gun?"

Cardozo frowned and Randolph played with his fork. "Go on, please," Holms smiled.

In Holms' smile, there was something Gideon reached for and almost found, a balance of qualitative changes, part in himself, part in Holms, a play of forces. Bluntly, he stopped the process of attempting to understand Stephan Holms; he would not understand Holms, ever. "Like a gun," Gideon said. "Maybe better. Take a man who got a gun, you want to enslave him, you got to take that gun away. You got to take your chances, maybe he kill you, maybe he don't. But you got to take the gun away. Why?"

"Isn't it obvious?"

"It ain't obvious," Gideon said slowly. He groped for the words he wanted, struggled with his thoughts, his hands gripping the edge of the table. "A man who's got no gun is a slave or not a slave; that depends on many things. A man with a gun is not a slave, depending on one thing, his gun. Before he come like other men, you got to take away gun. Now with education—that you cannot take away from a man who has learned, and I believe a man who has learned truly cannot be a slave. In one way, it like a gun, in other way, it is better than the gun."

"I wouldn't put it quite that way," Cardozo smiled.

"Of course you wouldn't," Holms said easily. "Nevertheless, Mr. Jackson's analysis is most interesting, since he looks at education in terms of two things, freedom versus slavery.

I think that is understandable. You were a slave, weren't you, Mr. Jackson?"

"I was."

"But slavery has been abolished."

Gideon nodded slowly.

"But you think it will return?" Holms asked gently.

"It could return," Gideon said, happening to glance at Mrs. Cardozo at that moment, seeing in her eyes complete, animal-like terror . . .

The dinner broke up early, but it led to something else. A week later, coming out of the Convention, Holms stopped Gideon and said:

"I am having some people at my home, Mr. Jackson. Would you come?"

Gideon hesitated, and Holms said winningly, "I want you to come, I assure you. After all, if we are to work together—"

Gideon agreed to come.

The Convention made progress. Out of the initial confusion, slowly, measure after measure appeared, small things at first, then larger things. The small things made agreement possible. Duelling was abolished. Imprisonment for debt was abolished by a large majority. The very naivete of the majority of the delegates gave them a fresh and curious approach to legislation; there was behind them no awesome, imposing tower of law, mores, habits, customs and deceptions; the insoluble became obvious, and very often the obvious became insoluble. So when these men approached the relationship of women to men in society, they broke walls that had stood for ages. A white swamp delegate said:

"Four years I fought the Yankees, and all that time my wife carried the house. Fed the kids, clothed them, broke ground, put in a crop, took it out. Now I ask these gentlemen, do they propose to give me the vote and deny it to my wife?"

Gideon took the floor and said, "I took my wife in slavery. We married in secret because my master did not approve marriage for slaves. We was equal beasts in his eyes. We was equal in the work we did; we was equal when we nearly fainted in the cotton fields. Sure enough, we suffered equal. Then I say, my wife is equal to me in the eyes of this Convention."

· They came as close to universal suffrage as man had come yet, and only the realization of the radical nature of the measure kept it from being passed, a fear that they might abuse the power given to them by a Congress in far-off Washington. However, out of their argument came the first divorce law in the history of South Carolina, a sane and simple divorce law that sent the southern newspapers to screaming that the black savages had already given the land over to infamy and degradation. Out of their argument came a law which said that the property of a wife could not be sold to pay her husband's debts—and that too was a beginning in South Carolina. Out of their argument came a long and curiously sane debate on the whole matter of suffrage, a debate that led Gideon to read the Constitution of the United States over and over, until he almost knew it by heart. He fought, along with others, for absolute equality of black and white at the polls—a forceful prevention of discrimination. And the motion won.

It was March already, and spring was coming to the land. The sky over Charleston was bluer than anywhere else in the world. The gulls swooped and shrieked over the bay and the rain fell fine as mist and cleared and left the sky brighter. A delegate offered from the floor that this should be known as the "Glory Year," but his motion was laughingly rejected. Yet men knew that this was a year like no other year, and a reporter of the New York *Herald* wrote:

"Here in Charleston is being enacted the most incredible, hopeful, and yet unbelievable experiment in all the history of mankind."

Charles Cavour, an aged colored delegate was attacked and badly beaten by three former soldiers, but the threatened explosion in Charleston did not come. The palmettos sent forth green shoots, and Gideon, enjoying the fine sea breeze, stood on the Battery and watched the ships cross the bay with white sails spread. He had found a book called *Leaves of Grass,* and in it were these lines:

> Earth! you seem to look for something at my hands,
> Say, old top-knot, what do you want?

"What do you want" echoed back and forth in his head; he wanted the whole world, and it was here at hand. Even the stevedores, singing as they went about their work, knew that this was a hallelujah year. Gideon was not alone in his study now; eight of the delegates had joined in a class which met three times a week at Cardozo's home to study American history and economics, and two of the members of that class were white. And Gideon, leaving the Convention one day, had been joined by Anderson Clay, who said:

"Wait a minute there, Jackson!"

Gideon paused, and then they walked along together, Clay even taller than Gideon, his blond hair loose and long and bright as brass in the sunlight.

"What I'm thinking these days," Clay said bluntly, "is that you're going to work with us, not against us."

"How's that?"

"I've eaten more crow sitting in a houseful of niggers these past weeks then anytime before in my life. I figured in the beginning I could just as well go home, live in a nigger land, and maybe raise some hell about it."

"You shouldn't feel that way," Gideon said softly.

"All right. I'm beginning to think maybe a black man and a white man can live together—I don't know. Do you want to talk about it?"

"I'd like to talk about it," Gideon said.

For some time, they walked in silence, neither able fully to break a wall that was so high and old between them. They walked through the narrow Charleston streets and under the whitewashed walls that split the world off from the houses, through the rich splashes of sunshine, and finally Clay said:

"What do you do when a new world comes? You make a piece of it, or you smash it. And I don't like the folks who are getting ready to do the smashing."

Gideon slept little these days; work on the committee for education drew him closer to Cardozo, nor did Gideon resent the fact that the sharp, cultured Negro was using him as a sounding board. The one was a product of education, the other a person who having just tasted it was already drunk upon it. Together, they set their shoulders for a single object, in a sense the basis for the whole new state Constitution—universal compulsory education. They had good support; they had opposition, on the other hand, that pleaded with them:

"Compromise—conciliate! You cannot force education on a whole population of illiterates."

"Why?"

"They won't stand for it."

"Then we make it law."

"Where will you find field-hands if you educate a population to be lawyers?"

"Not all men are lawyers, even in New England where literacy is so high. An educated man can work as well in the field as an uneducated man."

"The whites won't go to school with the colored."

"Then we'll build separate schools for those who want them. But all children, black and white, must go to school."

"This in insanity. There has never been such a law before in this country."

"Then we will begin. It has to begin somewhere."

"And can Carolina niggers do what the smartest folk in the world haven't done?"

"We can try."

Finally, the committee brought their bill to the floor, and for hours the debate raged hotly and stridently. Gideon noticed that they found support where they had least expected it, from white southern delegates, the poor white trash that the newspapers raged at even more fiercely than they condemned the Negroes, the despised Scalawags, the tall, lean, slow-spoken, straw-haired men elected by that shadow-race of the poor and landless, men from the swamps and the lonely piney woods. Anderson Clay, who rose and yelled, "Damn it, yes! If the only way is schools where black and white go together, then sure enough, I'm for schools! If I can sit in a Convention hall with niggers, then my son can sit in a schoolhouse with them!"

And Clair Boone, from the Pee Dee Swamp, "I fought in this war. I fought three years before I got enough learning to read a newspaper, or a book. Two brothers of mine, they're dead—for what? A war to keep a few damned slave operators in power! We didn't know, by God, we couldn't! Damn it, I say educate—educate and to hell with the consequences! We sit here, the elected representatives of the people of this state, and we chew our fingernails about the consequences of every word we say."

Gideon spoke shortly. "No man stays free," he said. "I know a little history, and the little I know makes it a fight for freedom, all along. There's one big gun for freedom—education. I say, arm ourselves."

Summing up the following day, Cardozo said, "It was argued by some yesterday with some considerable weight that we should do everything in our power to incorporate in the Constitution all possible measures that will conciliate those opposed to us. No one would go further in conciliating others than I would; but we should be most careful of what we do to conciliate. In the first place, there is an element that is opposed to us no matter what we do, which will never be conciliated. It is not that they are opposed so much to the Constitution we may frame, but they are opposed to us sitting in the Convention. Their objection is of so fundamental a nature, that any attempt to frame a Constitution to please them would be abortive. Next, there are those who ask us to frame a Constitution to please our enemies, promising us that if we do, they will come over to us. Then, there is a third class who honestly question our capacity to frame a Constitution. I respect them, and believe that if we can do justice to them, laying our Constitution on a sure foundation of republican government and liberal principles, the intelligence of that class will be conciliated.

"Before I proceed to discuss the question, I want to divest it of all the false issue of the imaginary consequences that some gentlemen have illogically thought would result from the adoption of this section with the word 'compulsory.' They say that it compels the attendance of both white and colored children in the same schools. There is nothing of the kind in the section. It simply says that all children should be educated; but how, it is left with the parents to decide. It is left to the parent to say whether the child should be sent to a public or private school. There can be separate schools for white and colored. It is left so that if any colored child wishes to go to a white school, it shall have the privilege of doing so. I have no doubt that in most localities colored people will prefer separate schools, particularly until some of the present prejudice against their race is removed."

Looking around the hall, Gideon noticed the rows of intent faces, black and white making a pattern, faces such as had not filled a legislative gallery since so long ago when the farmers and the artisans met to vote in a revolution, faces that unconsciously nodded to Cardozo's words. Warmth and strength and brotherhood; Gideon felt like laying his head on his arms and crying; he thought to himself, a black man is like a lost child, he has no country or piece of soil he can call his own: but they were making a land now; the speaker's platform was draped in red, white and blue, and behind it were two big flags of the Union. Gideon stared at them and heard Randolph, in his wavering voice, say:

"We, the undersigned, people of South Carolina, in Convention assembled, do hereby recommend that the Bureau of Refugees, Freedmen and Abandoned Lands be continued until the restoration of civil authority; that then a Bureau of Education be established, in order that an efficient system of schools be established . . ."

Nearby Gideon, an old black man sat and wept, nodding his head to a slow and ancient rhythm as applause filled the hall, as newspaper men dashed for the exits to write stories such as the one that appeared in the next day's *Observer:*

THE INCREDIBLE MOVE OF RECKLESS BLACKS

Yesterday, abandoning all scruples, the circus that calls itself a Convention set in motion a proposition that will complete the ruin and bankruptcy of this state. Black and white children of all classes are to be herded together in the same schools. Southern womanhood is to be degraded and debauched even before the teen age is past, and honest citizens will be starved and ruined to support a corrupt school structure . . .

And so forth and so on, stuff that Gideon was used to now, that he had come to expect as the result of each day's session, as the structure of the Constitution became more and more plain, as the judicial system was reformed, judges to be elected instead of appointed as all discriminations of race and color were abolished, as free speech was guarded and enforced, as a motion was passed to petition the Government to buy and subdivide great land holdings. The last was a great uncertainty; that the Federal Government would destroy the plantation system was more than could be expected, yet the proposition was adopted out of principle . . .

It seemed now an eternity ago that Gideon had first come to the Carters. Sitting at their dinner table, painting the future for these two old people, he became in their eyes sufficient reason why they might boast to their friends that Gideon Jackson, the delegate, lived with them.

Stephan Holms told his mother, "At dinner, tomorrow night, there will be a nigger."

And she, thinking he referred to the servants, said, "Naturally, Stephan."

"I don't think you understood me, my dear. At the dinner table, I mean—a guest of mine."

She began, "I wish you wouldn't, Stephan. You say things—"

"I'm serious, mother. Understand me, I invited a nigger to dinner tomorrow, as the guest of honor, you might say."

She sat down in a chair and stared at him, and he, looking over her head and through the window, studied the vague outline of Fort Sumter. Looking at him, she realized that he had gone into himself; she might argue with him for a while, but in the end, he would have his way. His strength was complete, beyond her understanding, intellectual, and to a degree very frightening. If people said this or that of Stephan, approved him or disapproved of him, she could say in his defense, and always did, "You don't understand, my dear. Stephan does things—"

Martha Holms was close to sixty, tired; she was ready to accept the fact that part of a world had disappeared in the great blood bath and cling to what was left; Stephan would not accept the fact that any had been irretrievably lost nor would he cling to what was left. When he told her, "My dear, I am going into the Convention because the only way to fight this monstrous thing that has happened is to understand it, and the only way to understand it is to become a part of it," she attempted to understand but could not. Nor could she now when Stephan told her.

"Mother, it is necessary for me to have a nigger at dinner. Please take it for granted that if I say it is necessary, it is."

"But why? What earthly reason—?"

"Several earthly reasons, very sound ones. I would gladly explain to you—"

"Stephan, I can't."

"But you can, and you will."

"Stephan, if you must make a clown of yourself, a Scalawag and a buffoon, can't you at least respect my feelings?"

"My dear," Holms said, "there is no one whose feelings I respect more highly."

"And what will people say?"

"They will say nothing. Colonel Fenton will be here, Mrs. Fenton, Santel, Robert and Jane Dupre, Carwell and General Ganfret and his wife."

"And they know a nigger will be at dinner?"

"They know."

"And who is this person, if I may ask, Stephan?"

"A former slave of Carwell's," Holms said. "His name is Gideon Jackson—"

In the end, the wall reared up against Gideon, the wall of childhood, youth, young manhood, the wall of a thousand memories when these people bred Negroes like cattle, and he would not have gone had not Cardozo said:

"Go, Gideon. It's important that you go. Holms asked you

for one of three reasons; firstly, because he may sincerely wish
to work with and understand us, and that I doubt. He's a
clever man and an old slave holder. Secondly, because he desires to make a fool of you, and that too I doubt. I don't
think that you will be easily made a fool of, and I don't
think Holms is childish enough to indulge in that sort of
thing. The third reason, and the only reason I can put credit
in is that, suspecting some mysterious Negro plot, Holms
wishes to get at it, get at what he may think goes on behind
his back. If that is the case, certainly you have nothing to
hide."

Gideon had nothing to hide but his fears, all the old,
ancient fears that rose like a sick feeling in his stomach. A
man can tell himself this and that, freedom has come and
black men and white men are working together to create a
new world, the old chains are broken, slavery is only a bitter
memory—all that a man can tell himself, yet fears and memories are burned like brands on the skin, beatings, flight, old
songs, let my people go, let my people go, scorn and hatred—

He walked slowly along the Battery, came finally to the
proud white house that fronted on the Bay, rang the bell
next to the gate, shivered at the clang it made, and was let in
by an old Negro servant who eyed him curiously but had
evidently been warned beforehand. He went up the walk
and mounted the stairs to the veranda, his legs so weak that
they would hardly hold him, and then the door of the house
was held open to him and he entered.

It was the first time that Gideon had ever been in such a
house, a house like this, lit, alive, hostile, and beautiful beyond words. As a child, he had been in and out of the kitchen
wing of the Carwell house, never in the main rooms; later,
as a man, he had walked through the Carwell house, empty,
dead. This house was not empty, not dead. Light blazed from
lamps and candles, dazzling him. The woodwork in the hall-
way was snow white, the furniture twisting in all the gracious
curves of a generation before. The stairway spiraled up into
misty distance; the drawing room beyond yawned like a
devil's mouth. He felt sick, hopeless, and his feelings were

not bettered much by Holms' warm and pleasant greeting, "So glad you came, Jackson."

Gideon nodded; he couldn't speak. Holms led him into the brightly lit drawing room, and Gideon had an impression of people carved from ice in all this warmth, the women in their fine gowns, the men in black and snowy white for dinner, glitter and dazzle from the great chandelier, rich mahogany furniture that made Cardozo's furniture pathetically poor by contrast, silver and glass. One by one, Holms introduced the people there to Gideon, but no one rose and no one offered their hand, and when Gideon faced Dudley Carwell, who had once been his master, the white man gave no sign of recognition—which was reasonable enough, since Gideon had been a field-hand and no more. They had been talking when Gideon entered, and they went on talking after the introductions were over, leaving Gideon to Holms, who, smiling thinly, said:

"Forgive them, Jackson. Sometimes our so-called courtesy does not rise to the occasion. What will you drink?"

Black servants moved through the room like shadows; in fact, for Gideon everything was blurred and nightmarish, nothing that afterwards made a clear, cohesive picture in his memory. He shook his head now. Nothing. Nothing at all? Nothing. He stood as still as stone, his skin prickling all over, conscious of the way the servants' eyes moved sidewise to glance at him. He was an animal trapped; he was a runaway slave brought to bay; he was a man roped to a stake and beaten there—and worst of all, bitterest of all, most terrible of all, he was afraid.

And it seemed like an eternity to him before they finally went in to dinner.

He had seen how people eat; his people at the plantation ate one way; the Carters ate in another way; the Cardozos in still a third way: but none of it was like this, nowhere the array of plates and silver so large and confusing. It was hard for him to hold a fork or spoon the way they held it; he was clumsy; he dropped things; he had to wait and watch them, and they knew he was watching. Why had he ever allowed himself to be trapped like this? Thirty times thirty he had been a fool; his thoughts raced like squirrels in a cage; what did Holms mean? What was all this? Why? What did it profit Holms?

Presently, he realized that they were talking to him, and after a fashion he was answering. Holms forced the conversation; Holms was driving at something—something that Gideon could not put his hands on. Gideon's head cleared; now he was angry, seeing these people for the first time in his thirty-six years, listening to them for the first time. They spoke words, and the words were the same words he used. He drove words back at them. He listened carefully, and what they said was not too clever; all in an instant, he had to fling a century over his head and come whirling through a readjustment that left him reeling. Anderson Clay, the poor white, could think more coldly to the marrow of a thing than they could; they thought they were baiting him, but his deep voice answered slowly; he wouldn't permit himself to be baited. Holms was his equal, but not the others, Holms smiling slightly as Colonel Fenton said:

"I imagine, Jackson, that you find lawmaking a diversion. As a change from other things?"

"It's more profitable than picking cotton," Gideon answered. "We are paid three dollars a day."

"More than many an honest man lays hands on these days."

"What can a nigra do with that much money?" Jane Dupre wondered. She was slim and blond and fragile, and her husband frowned as she spoke. The extra consonant was a concession to Gideon's social place at the table.

"He could spend it on clothes and food," Gideon said. "But mostly he just drinks it up."

He seemed simple enough, and they too were uncertain as to what all this meant. If anything, their position was more difficult than his, for they realized that Holms was enjoying the situation. Afterwards, Jane Dupre said that she almost retched at the table, watching that black eat, using his fork like a shovel.

General Ganfret said, "I would presume, Jackson, that education might be accepted as a prerequisite for legislation. Don't you find it difficult at the Convention?"

"I find it hard," Gideon agreed.

"The more so since I understand you were one of Carwell's field-hands only a few years ago."

"I was," Gideon smiled.

Santel, a man of fifty, owner of one of the largest plantations in the state, long-faced, hard, small-eyed, remarked that Gideon had come up in the world. Gideon said, yes, he thought so, but the world was changing. For the worse, someone said.

"That," Gideon nodded, "depends on how you look at it."

"You do read," one of the women remarked.

"I learned to read a little when I was in the army."

"When you were in the army?" the general asked.

"I was with the Yankee troops that marched into Charleston—you remember the colored brigades?"

There was a fuse lit in the room, a barrel of gunpowder sitting under it. Holms chuckled, but the general and most of the others sat frozen; Gideon likened them to ice again, the old strain running through his mind, nought ain't nothing, three's a figure, all for the white boss, none for the nigger: he realized this couldn't go on; something would explode. Mrs. Holms excused herself and left the table. The sound of her tears followed her from the room; Holms, who had followed her, returned and said, "Forgive my mother—she is slightly indisposed."

The general retreated into grim silence; Fenton, to break the general unhappiness, said to Gideon, "You bear a fine southern name, Jackson. But I understand that niggers take their master's name."

"Some do," Gideon said. "I went without a family name until they made me a sergeant in the army. Yankee captain tells me, you got to have a name, Gideon, got to have a family name. Who owned you?" Gideon paused, nodded at Carwell, half-believing that at that moment, were it not for the women present, they would have killed him. "I tell him," Gideon continued, "that man who own me for a slave, his name I never take. What about Jackson—"

Gideon did not finish his story. Carwell rose and said, "Get out of here, you black swine!"

As Gideon walked home, he felt strangely light-hearted. How many mysteries there were that had evaporated into nothing! How many fears there had been that were groundless! All the world was part of a great unknown until you examined it. The dark and silvery bay, so ghost-like now, would become a placid sheet of sunlit water tomorrow. The chains that bound his people would never be forged again; there was no place for those chains in the sunlight. The rule of the many by the few, the darkest, heaviest evil man had born in all man's memory, could be pricked like a water-filled bladder, and the content would ooze out the same way. Gideon sang softly, "When Israel was in Egypt land—let my people go—oppressed so hard she could not stand—let my people go!"

At the Holms house, the women had retired and the men were left at the table with their cigars, the general saying, "This, Holms, is unforgivable."

"Hardly."

"You said you had a reason," Santel put in, his voice hard and cold. "You said there was reason enough, Stephan, for us to sit at dinner with a nigger. You've always had your reasons—and we've humored you. You were dark and mysterious when you went into the Convention, licking enough niggers' asses to put you there, and you said you had a reason for that. I, for one, am sick to death of your god damned reasons."

"Reason," Holms said lightly, "is nevertheless at a premium. There was little enough of it tonight, and if I may say so, that nigger made fools of all of you."

From the general, "I think you've said enough, Stephan."

"I don't," Colonel Fenton put in. "Whatever you think of Stephan he's right in this case. The nigger made fools of us. Accept that, gentlemen."

"I'll accept an explanation from Stephan, or—"

Holms broke in, "For Christ's sake, Dupre, you're not going to challenge me to a duel! That would be too much. Are we infants? Babes? Idiotic fools? I asked you gentlemen here tonight because I considered you, in one fashion or another, persons of character. Permit me to retain a few of my illusions—"

"Holms!"

"All right! Let me do the talking for a while! I staged a circus here tonight, granted. I took that nigger and I put him and you into an impossible situation. Granted. I guessed what would follow; but I did not think that you would be so completely demoralized by the presence of a single nigger sitting across the table from you. Let us analyze the situation —I begged you, as a favor to me, a favor that was of extreme importance to each and every one of us, to spend a social evening with a black member of this Constitutional Convention. I made it a social evening, because only in that way could I make my point; I did not tell you the point in advance because the point did not exist at that stage. Am I not clear? Then bear with me a little longer.

"What is your attitude, the attitude of the whole class to which I belong? Faced with the federal order of reconstruction, you refused to accept it. You sulked—yes, all over the south, men of our kind sulked, refused to register, to vote, to campaign. You called the niggers and the white trash savages and said that this whole thing would overnight dissolve of its own accord. Did you believe that, gentlemen? Did you really believe that? Have you, after fighting this damned bloody war, so infantile a conception of power? Have you been watching the progress of this Convention? Watching it, I mean, not reading about it in our stupidly partisan newspapers?"

"Isn't this enough—" Dupre began, and Colonel Fenton cut him short with a savage, "Shut up, Dupre! Go on, Stephan." Dupre, spluttering, bewildered, looked from face to face. Holms bit off the end of a fresh cigar, lit it with a candle from the table, poured himself a splash of brandy, and continued:

"What is our situation at this point, gentlemen? Do you remember our world, the world that existed for us only eight years ago? That isn't so long; I was twenty-six then, I am thirty-four now, still young—young enough to have a taste for life, gentlemen, as I think you all have. I remember our world then—and what is our situation at this point? One thing we all have in common, we were or are plantation owners; we are the base, the rock upon which this south of ours exists. Another thing we have in common—we all face the same destiny, ruin, complete, unequivocal ruin. I have lost a plantation which has been in our family one hundred and thirty years. Dupre has lost his, so has Carwell—debt, taxes, war, emancipation. The others cling to what is left. When we went into this senseless war, I predicted the outcome—and fools accused me of being disloyal. Disloyal! Do we have to lie to ourselves? Can I be disloyal to what has made me, to what I am, blood and body? I say to you earnestly, gentlemen, we have to understand this situation in which we find ourselves. There is our only salvation."

The general, trailing smoke from his cigar, said, "Stephan, do you propose that we go into this circus of baboons?"

And Santel added, "How? We've tried to buy the niggers, wheedle them, threaten them—they remember only one thing, we owned them."

"Why did you bring that nigger here tonight?" Fenton asked.

"That, gentlemen, is the key to it. I object to the general's terminology—circus of baboons. When we think that way, gentlemen, we defeat ourselves. This Convention is not a circus of baboons, it is a gathering of determined and intelligent men who, for the most part, are honest according to their own lights."

"You're talking nonsense," the general objected.

"Am I? Have you been to one session?"

"I read the papers."

"And the papers lie! Believe me, I have been at almost every session—and the papers lie! I brought that nigger here for only one reason; two or three years ago, he was completely illiterate. A few years before that, he was Carwell's slave. Did you see him tonight? Was he a baboon? What is the potential of these black people we've bought and sold for two hundred years? We don't know, gentlemen, and we don't dare to guess. Will such men as this Gideon Jackson easily give up what they have? And they are not alone; they are learning to work with the white trash we despised until we needed them to fight a war. And these whites who fought the war for us are beginning to think. Gentlemen, when you gave the Convention over to these niggers and these whites, you made the second greatest blunder in these times; the first was the war itself. You said that the Convention would fall to pieces, it did not; it has been sitting for more than ninety days and it has framed a Constitution. You said that the nation would rise indignantly and crush this monster; the nation has not risen indignantly; instead, Yankee reporters are spreading the truth about this Convention all over the country. When we inaugurated our stupid reign of terror after the war, our fanciful Black Codes, we thought that we were bold enough and strong enough to snatch victory from a nation that just defeated us in battle; we used that fool Johnson, thinking that the people would follow him, and instead Congress crushed him. Now the niggers are winning the sympathy we sacrificed, and that too, gentlemen, is our fault."

Dupre said, "You don't have a high opinion of us, Holms."

"Frankly, I don't. In a sense, I have a higher opinion of that nigger I brought here."

"And I haven't—"

Fenton said, "For Christ's sake, Dupre!" And to Holms, "What do you propose, Stephan? Stop moralizing. We saw the nigger and you made your point. Now what do you propose?"

"All right," Holms nodded. "You saw the nigger—you must accept him for what he is, a representative example of the potential of four million people here in the south."

"Very well, go on!"

"Let's look at this Convention—and what it's done. Firstly, education; it has made it universal and compulsory throughout the state. Which means that niggers and white trash will be fighting us on equal terms—"

"They'll still be niggers and white trash!"

"God help me, can't I get you to look at reality? One generation of such education, and we'll be a vague memory— I assure you. Now another point, the Convention has moved and petitioned for a subdivision of the land, a breaking down of the plantations to small farms. Combine that with education, and you have the death-knell of the plantation. The Convention has legalized equality of race and color everywhere—contemplate that, gentlemen. The Convention has assured us that black men will sit with white men on juries, that black judges will sit on the bench; let that soak in, my friends. The Convention has safeguarded the ballot—and there goes whatever legalized dream of power you might have had. And last of all, gentlemen, the Convention has consistently made its appeal to black and white together; in every law, in every edict, every proposal, the poor white has been bracketed with the nigger. Does that awake a response, gentlemen?"

A long moment of silence was broken by the general, who said, "They can't carry it through, Holms. It'll break down. The finances of this state will not carry it. At the elections—"

"At the elections, they will move into the Government, just as they moved into the Convention."

"And where do we stand, Stephan?" Carwell asked.

"Precisely nowhere."

"Why not play their game?"

"And offer the voters what? Twenty cents a day wages? A return to slavery? No small farms? Ignorance?"

"There are ways."

"Yes, but not that way. We've had power; we lost it; we propose to regain it: that is all, simply. You saw that nigger here tonight. Can you wheedle him, coddle him, deceive him?"

"No—" Fenton said thoughtfully. "But you could hang him."

The general observed, "We tried terror and failed, Stephan. You pointed that out."

"Yes, we failed—because it was stupid terror, and because terror with only terror as the end is predestined to fail. We pitted mobs against Yankee bayonets; we indulged in adolescent outrages, prodding ex-soldiers to bludgeon and lynch and steal. And we had no plan, no goal—and this most of all, no organization."

Fenton lit a fresh cigar. One of the women opened the door and asked, "Are you going to sit here forever?" A colored servant came in with whisky, and Holms said to him, "When you go, I want no one else to interrupt us." The ash on Stephan's cigar was long; he touched it with his finger and it fell to the cloth; then he blew it away.

"An organization," he said, "a plan, and a destination."

Fenton said, "You've thought of the Klan, Stephan."

"Yes, I've given some thought to that. Their record in the two years or so they've existed doesn't make for brilliance or cohesion, but at least there is an organization. And rather than split our forces and organize counter to them, we would be wiser to take what they have and work with it. If we decide to, it must be done quickly, before they destroy their usefulness."

"They are officered by army people," the general said.

"That's a point—and it will help. Dupre here is already a member of the Klan; he can help us on that score. This business of white nightshirts and burning crosses is tomfoolery, but it has its use. The weasel type, the timid, the frightened—they become bolder when they hide their faces."

"I don't like that kind of talk."

"Don't you, Dupre? Do *you* intend to put a white napkin on your head and go scampering through the night? No—this is a tool, let's understand that. And to operate it, we'll need men, thousands. Where will they come from? Some army men, not too many; whatever you say about our troops, they had courage, yes, and honor, the kind of honor we talk about; they won't take kindly to nightshirts, terror, hanging, murdering."

"I don't like the way you put that, Stephan," the general said.

"How else shall I put it? We can tell ourselves the truth, can't we? But there'll be men enough, the scum that we used for overseers, the trash that bought and sold slaves and bred them, the kind who were men with bullwhip and filth without one, the kind who have only one virtue, a white skin. Gentlemen, we'll play a symphony on that white skin, we'll make it a badge of honor. We'll put a premium on that white skin. We'll dredge the sewers and the swamps for candidates, and we'll give them their white skin—and in return, gentlemen, they will give us back what we lost through this insane war, yes, all of it."

"But how, Stephan?" Fenton wanted to know. "When we tried before—"

"Yes, but this time, we know. We start slowly—organization and nothing but organization to begin. We enter the Klan, we subsidize it, gentlemen, yes, with what little we have left, we subsidize it. While the occupation troops are here, we do nothing—that is, nothing they could counter. A few acts, a nigger put in his place, a rape scare, a lynching —those will come about naturally; and when they come, the Klan can ride. As a matter of advertisement, you might say, romantic hooded figures dashing through the night; but only as a matter of advertisement. We wait; we organize; we do nothing premature. Concurrent with that, those of us who can enter politics, not as an opposition, but as men who wish to work with the reconstructionists. I propose to do that; others must join me. We move step by step, and we wait—"

"And how long do we wait?" the general demanded.

"I don't know—certainly two or three years, possibly five. But we wait until we are certain of success, until a reconstructed south becomes a matter of importance in national politics, until every Yankee soldier is withdrawn. And while we wait, we are not idle. We suffer, not hysterically, but patiently and manfully—and we let the North know the extent of our sufferings. We do not scream stupidly, but rather declare with dignity that we have been wronged, and when we have said it enough, we will be believed. We win sympathizers and adherents in the North, where there are thousands who have always envied us, envied those very things they fought against, our plantation system, our slaves, our pomp, our way of life—envied these to an extent which will not be covered by their false and filmsy moral scruples. Yes, and more than that—the nigger was pitied, the slave, the bondman; but what will become of that pity when we show the world that he is the oppressor, the black savages are taking all that is worthy, human, good, decent from gentlemen, from ladies?"

"As they are," the general said softly.

"Very well. We win adherents. We cultivate northern capital. The center of manufacture is shifting from England to the North; they will be screaming for cotton; we will give them some, but not enough. But we cultivate them, we invite their industry South, and we give them a stake in our future, a stake that will matter once they forget the moralistic frenzy that drove them to war, once they begin to realize that their war was unjust, that we were a freedom-loving people who fought to retain our American freedom."

"As we were," the general said.

"And then, when that time comes, whether in two years or five years, we strike—with force, force and terror; because force and terror are the only two things that can decide the issue. But by then, we will have achieved our goal; the North will not know, and what little they hear, they will not believe. The Klan will be an army by then, and the Klan will smash this thing that has arisen, smash it so completely that it will never again rear its head. Gentlemen, the nigger will be a slave, again, as he has been, as he is destined to be. Yes, he will fight—but he will not be organized for terror, for force, and we will be. Some white men will fight on his side; most, I assure you, will not; fear and the badge of a white skin will take care of that. And gentlemen, when that time comes, we will win!"

As he spoke, Stephan Holms showed fire and passion, a dynamic strength that impressed even the general, perhaps the least sensitive person there. But when he had finished, the flare died; the passion resolved into the pale and composed figure of civilization complete. He lit another cigar, and when the others had talked enough about his plan, pro and con, he suggested, "Shall we join the ladies now?"

CHAPTER SIX

How Gideon Jackson Went Home to His People

NOW IT WAS FINISHED, A CONSTITUTION MADE, LAWS ONE AFTER another set down, a definition of freedom, life, liberty and the pursuit of happiness as presented by the people of a state of this Union, the United States of America. It was the spring of the year 1868, a bright, fresh new year, a new era, as the chaplain said:

"Lord God of mercy, understanding, forgiveness, we ask thy blessing for our efforts. Our mistakes were not willful, but rather because we are mortal men, subject to the evils, the sins, the transgressions that all mortal men make . . ."

Then the whole Convention stood and sang, their voices rich and proud, "My country, 'tis of thee, sweet land of liberty, of thee I sing!"

"What are your plans?" Cardozo asked Gideon.

"To go home."

"It's been a long time, hasn't it?"

"Too long," Gideon smiled. "Funny thing about black folk, Francis, they got a homesick heart. Back in the bad old times, sell a nigger down the river, and that was worse than if you killed him. I got a hunger to go home."

"And then what?"

"I been thinking," Gideon said reflectively. "My people, they know the soil, they know how to coax up a little cotton, a little corn, and not much more. Where they live now, it's the old Carwell plantation—but that won't last forever. I been to the land office, tracing the place; Carwell lost it for debt, then the debtors for taxes. One of these fine days, it's going to be knocked down from the auction block, and where will my people be then?"

"Where so many colored folk are, landless, footloose, starving. That's a problem, Gideon, the biggest problem we face."

"Maybe I can do something about it, not much, but at least show my people how they can buy a little land. Even that I'm not certain of; there might be a way, there might not. I don't know—at least I can go home and try."

"Which might help a few, Gideon, but wouldn't solve the problem in any real way."

"I know."

"Gideon, have you ever thought of politics?"

"How's that?"

Cardozo, smiling somewhat uncertainly, recalled to Gideon the first time they had met. "I began to realize then," he said, "that I would have to put my trust in people like you."

"Why people like me?"

"Because this whole state, in fact this whole southland, except for a tiny minority who oppose us, has only one future, to pull itself up by its bootstraps. You've done it, so have hundreds of others. We don't agree, Gideon; we're an ocean apart on many things; you're a man of violence, for all of your gentleness, and I don't think that way. But there's much in you that I lack, much of great strength, great value. How will you use that?"

"If it's there," Gideon smiled. "It may be, and maybe it ain't; I sure enough don't know. I want to think about it; I want to learn. I'm an ignorant man, Francis; if I had known, three months ago, how ignorant, I would have given up then."

"Gideon, before you decide to go back, just think a little. In a few days, the Republican delegates from this state are going to meet. I'm one of them. Think of that, Gideon; Abe Lincoln's party is going to come in here, and it's going to carry the state; we know that, we've seen the results in the Convention vote. It means a state legislature, a whole governmental structure, congressmen, senators, everything from the bottom up. You've been in at the beginning of this, Gideon, a piece, no matter how small, of our Constitution came from your hands. Well, you have a chance to follow it, to implement the laws—"

"How's that?" Gideon said slowly.

"Some of us want you to sit in the State Senate, to be a candidate—"

Gideon shook his head.

"Why not?"

"It wouldn't work," Gideon said.

"Are you afraid?"

"I'm not afraid anymore," Gideon smiled. "It just wouldn't work—I know what I am. Maybe in a year or five years, not now. I'm not fit, Francis."

"You're fitter than most of the men who'll go in."

"Maybe," Gideon shrugged.

"You'll think about it?"

"No. I'm going home."

"And if I said you were wrong, Gideon?"

"I have to do what I think best."

"It's no use to argue with you is it?" Cardozo realized.

"No use, I'm afraid."

"I'm sorry," Cardozo said, sincerely.

He and Gideon shook hands, and Cardozo said, after a moment, "Knowing you, Gideon, was a good thing to happen to me."

"How is that, sir?"

"Maybe I'll be able to go home sometime."

When the time came for Gideon to go, Mrs. Carter wept frankly and unashamedly, held Gideon in her arms and kissed him on the mouth. "If you come back to Charleston, you stay with us, Gideon." They fussed over him, made up a box of things to eat; there was a pair of shoes Carter had made for Rachel, black shoes, high and button-up. Gideon wanted to pay him. "This is just a little gift thing, Gideon, son." Another gift was a Bible. "For comfort," Carter said. "You're a good boy, Gideon, but turn your face to God." Gideon had a sense of how desolate they would be after he left. They made a big and festive meal, fried chicken, fried prawns, hot cornbread, pots of greens, and their neighbors came in until the little house was packed full. Gideon hadn't known it was like this; they all wanted to shake his hands, and there were more tears than at a burying: for Gideon, in a sense, the Convention and the Constitution had existed alone, not in relation to people, weeping and laughter and pride . . .

He spent an hour with Anderson Clay, who said to him, "Gideon, I'm not like some who are crazy with joy and hallelujahs. This is a beginning. Suppose it smashes; then we begin again. There'll always be some of us here and there; we'll know each other."

"We'll know each other," Gideon nodded, holding the hand of the tall, lean, red-faced man.

But already things were moving out past him and beyond him. He had stepped away, but the little world he had occupied these past fifteen weeks was in a flux of change and excitement. For all his eagerness to see his people, he was lonely as he packed his books, a good-sized pile of them now, as he filled a small carpet bag with his clothes. He had his ticket on the railroad already; no, he was not walking back to Carwell. To a degree he envied that black man who, with long strides, had walked a hundred miles and more from the back country to Charleston town.

And had nothing changed at Carwell? The old colored man who drove him the last twenty miles in a mule-hitched ancient surrey was completely unaware of the Convention, of the earth shaking at Charleston, of all the great events that Gideon had been a part of. "Convention, I ain't heard—" And as he told Gideon the news of the country-side all about, it was the same news as ever, births, deaths, bucolic tides of peace and violent outrages to erupt like little, hidden volcanoes. "Missy Buller's boy done ambling to town, just ambling, and five white folk take hold of him, beat him with sticks and then hang him up on the cotton-wood tree." "What did he do?" "Ain't done nothing, so far I know, just ambling." The old man told Gideon that the railroad was coming through, over by the big swamp, and that they were going to build an embanked causeway clear through the swamp. "Taking on men, they is. Dollar a day." "A dollar a day for colored men?" Gideon wanted to know. "Dollar a day. Yankee men building this here road." And how was it at Carwell, Gideon asked him. He said he didn't get up to Carwell much, not this past year. "What do you hear?" "What all you expect to happen, younger?" the old man said testily. "What for you all so impatience? You just wait and see. Ain't no kingdom come, tell you that. Old cow calves and old nigger woman gets a belly. What else you expect?" So Gideon held it inside of him and heard how the weather had been, six weeks back and week by week; now it was spring and lovely, and the crops were in the ground. The crows flew along, caw-cawing, as they always had, and there was a man out hunting, his shotgun in the crook of his arm, his setter dog splashing through the meadow grass in front of him.

And then, in late afternoon, the shadows long and tired, Gideon was back at Carwell, the great and stately plantation house showing first on its high perch, caught in the rays of the sun, shadowed white on one side, pink and golden on the other. The mule was tired and stepped slowly. "Come a long ways," the old man complained. "Going to drive back in the almighty dark."

As always, it was the children who came running first, screaming at the top of their lungs, children springing out from everywhere, like a meadow of quail flushed; Marcus was among them; Gideon hadn't remembered him as so tall. Jeff was manly and far behind, walking and not running, a dignity there. And finally, Gideon was standing with Rachel in his arms, his eyes wet, and ashamed of that in front of his children.

Rachel had him back now; for her, too, time had become a flexible thing, like an instrument of rubber that can be pulled taut and far apart, or allowed to relax and tie itself together into a tight and small knot. These three months were an eternity; and Rachel had known, in her own way of knowing, that the same Gideon would not be coming back.

Her fears were formless, changing, shadow-things; their substance was the unknown, which began over the brow of the hill on the horizon and extended on to include all of the world. The beginning and the end of everything was Carwell, because she had not known any other place. Her mother, brought down from Virginia and auctioned on the block at Charleston, had a suckling babe in her arms that added forty-two dollars to her price; that was Rachel, with a memory that began at Carwell and included no other place. Even the war, which eddied all over the South, never laid its stamp very hard on this place. Once a young man, with red cheeks, blue eyes and golden-brown whiskers, dressed in a dirty blue uniform and riding a tired black horse, led a long column of tired men in blue uniforms over the lawns of Carwell—those were her first Yankees, the young man calling out to her, "Lassie, when've you seen your last reb?"

She could hardly understand his nasal, clipped New England speech; Marcus hid behind her skirts, and the dreadful thought occurred to her that they might take Marcus, sell him down the river or something, so she ran away: and when she came back, the Yankee men were gone. As time passed, there were other Yankees, rebel troops too, the surf of the war washing first at one side of Carwell, then at the other. In one part of that surf, Gideon and Hannibal Washington and others disappeared—going off to take up the Yankee gun and fight for their freedom. The maw of the great and mysterious and yawning outside world swallowed them, and Rachel left with two children had to find faith in their return. But Gideon was vast and certain as the rising and setting of the sun; if the other women wept, Rachel kept her eyes dry and told herself, "Gideon say he come back." That might make for faith, but it didn't quiet her fears. If she lost Gideon, the whole world ceased to be. Other women weren't like that; take sinfulness—some women might give their body in a sinful way; understanding that and even the desires and loneliness that prompted it, Rachel would sometimes project a situation where she was unfaithful to Gideon, and the whole vague shape of that situation would make her smile; for she was Gideon, Gideon was she. Even as their marriage had been, going in the night to Brother Peter for the secret ceremony, whereas so many men and women simply gave their bodies to each other, knowing that for them marriage was for a day, a month, a year, not a bond before God but a flickering happiness before they were sold, traded, debauched. Yet she and Gideon married and swore an oath to each other.

She had been happy in a way that made an expression, "Like Rachel." If a lark sang well, it sang like Rachel. She knew her man; God was smiling when he gave her Gideon; she knew that. When he went away, it increased her suffering, but that too was a part of having Gideon which she recognized and understood. Her understanding was different from Gideon's: as a child, she accepted with the other children the fact that the moving branches of the trees made the wind; when Gideon pointed out that it was quite the other way, she accepted that because Gideon said so. Gideon had to know why, always; for him nothing existed without a reason: but inside of her the warm tides of her blood made for reason enough. The deep, strong feelings inside of her could know things, and sometimes the knowledge was strangely exact. She did not have to know about Charleston, the Convention, the new world created, to realize that the man who went away would not be the man who returned. "Let my people go," had meant to her having Gideon, having her children always; yet she sensed the sunlit horizons the phrase held for her husband. The first letters Gideon ever wrote came to her from Charleston, and at the beginning they had to be read to her, by Brother Peter, by James Allenby. The shame of that made her learn to read, sitting at night with the other men and women, crowded into a little cabin, while Allenby taught them as he taught the children in the daytime; but she learned slowly; her head ached. Gideon was moving away, farther and farther . . .

And then he came back and held her in his arms again, and she knew better than ever before the meaning of the phrase, "Freedom is a hard won thing."

The day after Gideon came back was Sunday, and Brother Peter held meeting on the lawn in the sunshine. In their strong voices, the people sang, "Take me by the hand, oh

Lord, take me by the hand." Brother Peter opened the Book
and read from Isaiah: "Behold, the Lord God will come
with a strong hand, and his arm shall rule for him: behold,
his reward is with him and his work before him. He shall
feed his flock like a shepherd: he shall gather his lambs with
his arm, and carry them in his bosom, and shall gently lead
those that are with young." "Amen," the people nodded.
The children shifted and twisted, and pulled each other's
hair and clucked at the dogs. Gideon sat with Rachel, Jeff,
Marcus and Jenny; but Rachel would not let him be on
the grass in his fine Charleston clothes and had spread a
piece of cloth underneath him—they were all so proud of
the way he looked. "Say ye Amen," the people nodded. Jeff's
eyes went again and again to where Ellen Jones, the blind
girl, sat with old Mr. Allenby, and Gideon, noticing it,
frowned. Marion Jefferson's little girl began to cry, and he
leaned over her, "Hush you, hush you now." "Hallelujah,"
the people nodded, rocking back and forth. Brother Peter
said:

"I will make no sermon today on account of Brother
Gideon is here with us again, praise God. The good God
seen fit to give us our freedom, he hear our prayer; he seen
fit to reward us here with the blessing of the land, rich as
milk and honey, when other black folk, they don't eat, they
don't have a place to lay the head. The good Lord God seen
fit to give us a voting and been along with Brother Gideon
far off there in Charleston Town. How that was? Brother
Gideon he sat there in Convention Hall with the high and
mighty folk—the good Lord exalted him like he done with
young King David, praise God!"

"Amen," the people said.

"Brother Gideon he come back, he going to talk to us in
place my usual sermon. He going to tell us how that was.
Stand up, Brother Gideon. Come up here where the whole
congregation can face you."

So Gideon spoke to them. As plainly as he could, he told
them all that had happened, how he walked to Charleston,
his fears, how he had worked as a stevedore, how he had
come to live with the Carters, and how finally he had taken

his seat in the Convention. For the first time, he was able to make plain to them just what the voting had meant, what lay behind the whole policy of reconstruction as ordained by the Congress and how the process of reconstruction would proceed, now that a new State Constitution had been created. One by one, he outlined the measures included in the Constitution, explaining them, but making clear what a great gap lay between a measure written into the Constitution and the practical application of that measure. The Constitution said there would be universal education in the State of South Carolina, but money would have to be found, teachers trained, school buildings erected—and until that time they must learn in whatever way was possible. He pointed out that a measure abolishing racial discrimination did not do away with it; that would take years and years.

"And what about us, us people here?" Gideon said. "How do we fit in with the future? Well, I done gone and poked around and found out something. Dudley Carwell lost this here place to another man, who let it go for taxes. That means, sooner or later it come up on the auction block and knock down to the highest bidder. That time come, out we go, less we do something first. I don't know what we going to do; I thought about it—give it a lot of thought, and whatever we do, we need money. Where we going to get that money, I don't know yet. But it ain't no reason for despair. Reason for despair is dead and gone; it's a bright new time we can see in front of us, bright new time coming up."

There was not the same haste here, the same press of time that Gideon had felt in Charleston. The sun set and the sun rose; his fine clothes put away, he wore his old jeans and his old shirt. A sick sow trying to give birth to a litter kept him all night in the barn. Contrasts were not so startling now, and the slave shacks that had seemed so dreadful on his return gradually became what they were before, an old and familiar sight.

Nights, he read by candle-light, mostly aloud. Marcus, Jeff, Jenny and Rachel sat and listened. Often, Allenby would come in with Ellen Jones, sometimes Brother Peter, sometimes some of the others. He read them from Whitman and Emerson, the ringing last words of old John Brown, the poems of John Greenleaf Whittier. Poetry caught their imagination, and Gideon read well; they rocked with the rhythm and softly clapped their hands. Jeff would watch him as he read, and Gideon thought that sometime soon he would talk with the boy and discover what was behind the dark eyes and the stolid black face Marcus took life easily, impressing Allenby by his agility at learning. This, altogether, was a pause, an interval, a time when Gideon found himself disturbed by a growing impatience. Brother Peter said to him, "Recall you, Gideon, I say you would fill up, like drawing cold, clean water out of the well."

"I remember," Gideon nodded.

"You done go off to Charleston where the Lord exalted you—and you come back and feel no bond with your people."

"That isn't true," Gideon said.

"Turn your face from God, Gideon, and God turns his from you." Brother Peter added thoughtfully, somewhat sorrowfully, "You done that, Gideon—"

"No—no, that's not it, more than that. I looked at things, Brother Peter, in the only way I can, in the way of my understanding. I seen men in bondage, and not God broke the bonds but men. I seen bad men and I seen indifferent men take up guns in a good cause, because good men had their way, and out of the blood and the suffering there came something."

"And salvation, Gideon?"

"Maybe I can only see salvation my way, in the truth of something, in schools, in good laws, in good houses instead of these shacks we live in—"

And Rachel, at night, would whisper to him desperately, "Gideon?"

"What is it?"

"Tell me you loving me, Gideon."

"Who else am I going to love?"

"Then what happen, Gideon, the change come over you,

talk different, act different—what going to come of you and me?"

"Nothing, darling, nothing."

"Soon enough, you going off, you going off, Gideon—"

"No."

"Mouth say one thing, heart say another."

"No, no," Gideon reassured her.

And Cap Holstein brought a letter from Cardozo, which said, "Have you thought about it, Gideon? You can't vegetate there while the earth is shaking."

One late afternoon, they sat down with their backs to the corncrib, their feet stretched out, as in the old days, Gideon, Brother Peter, Hannibal Washington, Allenby, Andrew and Ferdinand who had both taken the name of Lincoln, chewing on pieces of straw, kicking at the dust—

"Look like rain."

"Maybe it do, just a wee bit."

"Old dirt can use a little rain."

"Old dirt can."

"Coming up from the west."

"Coming up mighty strong."

Gideon said, "I almost wish you'd put in a few acres of cotton."

"Be happy if I never see a cotton boll break again."

"A sorrow crop."

"It's the crop of this land," Gideon said. "It's a cash crop, and we need cash."

"You keep saying that," Allenby observed.

"Yes—nothing's ours. Not the land, not even the shacks we live in. Nothing. Until now, everything was confused, no one to straighten out the records, no one to ask, what are them niggers doing there? Comes the first election, we're going to have civil administration, and then there won't be an acre unaccounted for."

"Who going to put us off the land, Gideon?"

"Whoever buys it."

"Ain't a white man going to work the land alone. Man'll need niggers."

"Yes, he'll need niggers, work it on shares the way white folks did before the war. Put every acre in cotton, and have the nigger come a begging for a little piece of fatback to feed his children. Like Brother Peter say, this is a land of milk and honey now. But why? Because we put the land into corn, into feed, because we do without cash. Just a little candle to read a book by cost cash, just a lesson book for the children cost cash."

"Gideon, won't the Government buy land for the niggers?" Hannibal Washington asked.

"Maybe—but suppose the Government does that. Government's a thousand folk moving slow. Might be a year or two years or not at all. Government might say, here's a piece of land down Georgia way, move over to it. That ain't good. Here we lived; here is our place, right here. We got to have this land."

"How?"

"Buy it," Gideon said. "Work and get money, and buy the land."

Allenby said, "That would take a lot of money, Gideon."

"Sure, but things can be started. Banks lend money—yes, even to niggers if they see something sound, see our intention, see a little cash of our own. Railroad's putting a causeway through the swamp, asking for men at a dollar a day, nigger and white. Suppose we go down, work six or eight weeks on the railroad—"

"And the crops?"

"Come back and take out the crops."

There was a long silence until Brother Peter said, "It's a sad thing, Gideon, to take the men away from the women."

But Hannibal Washington said, "Gideon's right."

"We'll have a meeting," Gideon told them.

But for the women it was a sad thing. Washing in the brook, they looked at Rachel, who pounded and scrubbed her clothes in silence. Change was a troublesome thing, and from now on there would be change, which though it was a part of freedom was a troublesome thing. All right to be like the children, who splashed naked in the water, shouting and laughing and screaming, feeling no shame; but they weren't like children. The swamp was heavy with malaria and men would sicken and die; the swamp was a bewitched place. Rachel pounded and wrung the clothes in silence, when she saw Jenny fall, cried, "Jenny, Jenny, come on out," and then said nothing when the other women looked at her so strangely . . .

And Allenby asked Gideon, "Are you going to take Jeff with you?"

"Yes—he's strong as a man."

"I wouldn't, Gideon."

"Why?"

They were in the part of the barn Allenby used as a schoolhouse, his desk a feed-box, light pouring down in broad shaft from the open loft. There was a pile of cheap paper, sharpened sticks of charcoal, a sense of children that Gideon could not define, hunger and longing in the air even though the children had gone. Gideon had been at one of the lessons and watched the old man's incredible patience. "They are like little animals," he had said then. "Of course, what did you expect? But they learn." Their eagerness was apparent enough, and Allenby was a good teacher, patient.

"Why?" Gideon asked him, wondering that he had never gotten around to that talk he intended to have with Jeff.

"That's hard to say. Perhaps because he's like a fire. Do you know what goes on inside of him, Gideon?"

Embarrassed, Gideon did not answer.

"He can read and write already. He's like a sponge, soaking things in. He's trying to soak the whole world in—so quickly that it makes me afraid. He knows what he wants to do, Gideon; he wants to be a doctor."

"How do you know?"

"He told me."

"He never told me," Gideon said.

"Did you ever ask him?"

Gideon shook his head, and Allenby went on, "Did you ever look at yourself and ask things, Gideon? Do you remember the man walking down the road to Charleston? That wasn't so long ago, but you're not he. Do you ever ask yourself what's happening to you, what's happening to all of us, this world we live in? When you sat in the Convention and planned the change, did it ever occur to you that the change would be like birth agonies?"

"What about Jeff?" Gideon said slowly.

"What about him? He's your son. Take him into the swamp and he'll earn a dollar a day, and I'm not saying that would be wrong. But we have to make a beginning; there are no schools here yet, but he could go to a school in the north; there are schools there, in Massachusetts, that will take a colored boy, educate him, train him—"

"I don't know how," Gideon said bewilderedly.

"You have friends in Charleston. This Cardozo could tell you."

"Just send him away?" Gideon said.

Jeff took her into the piney woods; he told her about the many things, small and large, that surrounded her. "There's a hop toad crossing over in front your feet." The setting sun he told her about, "Coming like an old rose through them branches." She could feel the wind herself, "Like someone's hand," she said to him. At first her fears were wrapped all around her, and it was only by some miracle, knowing why and how instinctively, that Jeff gently broke through; she lived in a deep, dark cave and there was no color, no light in there. Jeff never made a move, a step, or spoke a word to frighten this blind girl who was, for him, the most beautiful creature that had ever existed. He took her into the meadows and let her feel the texture of the meadow flowers, the meadow grass, and once he crushed a wild strawberry in her hand. Allenby lived in a shack the men fixed up for him, and he didn't mind if Jeff came there and read from his books to Ellen while she did the work in the house. From old Uncle Sexton, who had died the year before, Jeff had the swamp tales, the birds and the beasts and the reptiles who spoke to each other, living their own wonderous lives; those too he told Ellen Jones. Rachel knew he was in love and understood his lumbering tenderness, so like Gideon's, whacking Marcus across the knuckles when he laughed at Jeff. Yet it made her sad, a blind girl; a blind girl had to be cared for; a blind girl was a burden on a man, no matter how you looked at it, and here was Jeff already almost as old as Gideon had been when he married her. A man needs a woman and a woman a man, but an equal thing, like the two halves of a scale pulling together.

Allenby told her, "It will be all right Rachel, believe me."

Through the woods, half a mile from where the south fields ended, there was an acre of space that had been lumbered out, and lay open and stump-filled in the hot sun. The buzzards came there, perched on the rotting stumps and nodded at one another, and coiled garden snakes sunned themselves there. There Jeff took Ellen; there was a place on the hot sand where they could sit with their backs against a fallen tree, and there they were wonderfully alone. For hours Jeff could sit and make the world with words for the girl who couldn't see, a cloud winding across the sky, a bluejay, and in time his own dreams built up into pictures for her.

Slowly, slowly and gently, something happened to her; part of it was being in a community of friendly, warm people, the sound of voices all day, children laughing and people calling to each other across a distance; part of it was Jeff, who said to her one time, "I love you sweetly, Ellen." Another time, when he took her in his arms, she said to him, "Don't hurt me, Jeff, please." And he began to realize what life was and had been to this girl. This was strange and special; he had to know and there was no one to ask—and the other boys his age were hiding in the shrubbery of the creek to watch the girls when they bathed, or running after them and dragging them down to the grass—

"What will you do?" she asked him once.

"Whatever I want to do, I feel that way."

"But what?"

"Like your father," he said; he was the first one able to talk to her about her father.

"A doctor?" she said. He said, "That's right." His thoughts made pictures; the doctor in the village was a profane, whisky-drinking man with a tobacco-stained beard; once, when one of the women lay dying, he had heard folks talk-

ing wildly and aimlessly about doctors. He thought of talking to Gideon; his father would know, yet he couldn't talk
with Gideon about that, for all that he worshipped his
father. He asked Allenby:

"A doctor—what is it just?"

"A man who heals sick people."

"Sure enough?" There was a poor old woman who lived
in the brush a few miles off, practiced a sort of voodoo, made
charms and sold them. "Like that?" he wanted to know.

"Not like that, with science, with a knowledge of what
makes men sick."

"What make them sick?"

So, that way, it had begun, and now, leading Ellen by
the hand into the pines, he told her, "They going to send
me off."

"Send you off? Where?"

"North, maybe. Study and be a doctor."

That was incredible; she asked him, pleadingly, who
would be here when he left, and he was able to see how
the darkness would close in. It was as if the thought had
not occurred to him before. "I love you," he said. "You, I
love, only you."

"But you want to go?"

"I want to go," he said, miserable. "Come someday, I'll
come back, sure enough, I swear I come back . . ."

Gideon told Rachel only after he had received an answer
from Cardozo. Cardozo said, yes, it could be arranged. Jeff
should come to him in Charleston; he would write to Frederick Douglass and some other friends of his in the north.
Twenty-five dollars would be enough for a time, and Cardozo would arrange for Jeff to go by sea to Boston. Then
Gideon told Rachel.

"How far this place, Boston?"

"A thousand miles, I guess," Gideon said. "But do you
understand what it means, Rachel, a son of ours, a child
born in slavery, going to Boston to study doctoring?"

Rachel nodded.

"Don't you think I wanted him with me?" Gideon demanded.

Again, Rachel nodded. Gideon took her in his arms, "Look, baby, little baby, going to be proud of that son, going to be almighty proud of him, going to see him walking with long, glory steps."

"I know," Rachel said.

The Yankee boss, a tall, bearded man, leather-booted, mud-stained in his dank clothes, just out of a malarial bout, said to Gideon, "You talking for these men?" "That's right." "How many?" "Twenty-two," said Gideon. "Shovel, ax and pick. One dollar a day. Seven days a week—sunup to sundown. We pay on Tuesdays." "That's right," Gideon nodded. The boss said, nodding at the pay shack, "Have them sign or make their mark."

Gideon, Trooper, and Ferdinand Lincoln were with the cutting gang. They went into the six- and eight-inch second growth, standing knee-deep in mud and water, and all day long their double-bladed axes cracked and gouged at the wood. For most of the black men who made up the gangs, this work on the railroad was the first free labor they had ever performed. When the Yankee company set up employment offices in the nearby towns to recruit gangs for construction, the local merchants shook their heads and decided, "A waste of time. Nigger won't work without a whip at his back or a master to own him." It was scandalous, they said, to pay niggers a dollar a day; spoil them and ruin them—who ever heard of such a wage? The Yankee gang bosses and engineers shrugged their shoulders and went on with the hiring. "Anyway," the local people said, "you can't put a causeway through that swamp, and serve the goddam Yankees right." But strangely enough, the causeway was going through. When the crisscross corduroy of logs and branches sank out of sight, the engineers filled with gravel and started over. When the rains came and made the swamp a tar-like sea of mud and glue, men stood in the ooze waist deep and sank their logs by feel. When the mosquitoes bred and malaria sent the shivering, fever-ridden men out to be hospitalized, the hiring signs went up again. The first casual enthusiasm that the countryside had indulged in when they heard that the railroad was breaking south soon passed; to the former plantation owners, overseers and slave drivers, there was something ominous, foreign and inevitable about this New England formed, New England owned company that was driving a railroad through in the same heedless, incredible manner that Sherman had driven through to the sea.

But for the black men, it was something else. For the first time, Gideon had an inkling of the relationship of labor to the whole of life and civilization. As slaves, he and his people had worked, year in and year out, having nothing, gaining nothing, the way the mule or the ox works. Now the railroad had advertised for a product they wanted to buy; the product was labor; Gideon and his people came and sold their labor for a dollar a day, and out of their labor was coming a conception and a dream, a causeway, shining steel rails, a train screaming in the night. They would go away free men, men with some money, and they in turn would buy. And they would leave behind them what their strength and sweat had built.

Whether or not this right of way could have been built with slave labor, Gideon didn't know; he did know that slaves had never worked like this, even with the lash crossing their backs. His gang cut and trimmed logs for the corduroy. Facing, two men would attack a tree, one low, one high, eight cuts on the young second growth, and then, boomed out and echoing, "Timber, timber!" The slopping crash of the log as it hit the water, the trimming down the line, blow for blow, and then eight men lifting and tossing it onto the mule sledge. The men worked bare to the waist, their black bodies gleaming, muscles rippling. First they sang the old slave work songs; but that was no good; rhythms didn't fit, the pace had changed, and this was no lament. So first without words, the new songs came; they had to sing, and the first words were the simplest threads of thought—"Old wood don't like my ax, old wood don't like my ax—" the words came and the music came . . .

Gideon had grown soft. With the night, his whole body ached, and he had no desire, no thought except to throw himself down on the stiff barracks cot and sleep. Sleep and work and food, and that was all; and he began to ask himself, "Where is learning, rest, books, anything at all but work in a life like this?" The step from slavery bridged a whole era in civilization, but did men stop here?

The food was stew three times a day, meat, potatoes, rice, good enough if unvarying in its sameness. The men stood in line and it was ladled onto tin dishes, the only breaks in a fourteen-hour work day. The men slept in long, wooden barracks, hastily thrown up, and old army tents. Kelly, boss of number four gang, told Chief Engineer Rhead, "Give me ten gangs like mine and I'll build you a road to hell." And Rhead, who had been with the engineers during the war, answered, "Hold your water, and you'll find the equivalent right here." Malaria came in one of its recurrent waves, and Rhead's words were borne out; the swamp turned into a pest-ridden oven; day and night the mosquito swarms twisted and hummed. George Rider, one of Gideon's people, came down with the fever, and in four days he was dead. Hannibal Washington and Brother Peter went home with the body, so that the women might see the burying and weep and take some comfort from that. No matter how it was, you paid the price. Gideon went into the gravelling gang, and then he shaved hickory for ties. And one night they heard the scream of a whistle as the work train poked forward. The swamp water sank; the mud dried and cracked; the heat increased but in spite of that conditions were better for work. An apron of gravel and crushed rock dressed up the crisscross corduroy, and steel rails laid a path for the work train. Gideon's head ached from attempting an understanding of this; Hannibal Washington asked him once:

"Gideon, up north, do white folk work like this?"

"Maybe some do."

"No rest, no play, no time with a woman?"

"Maybe."

"You figure it's right, Gideon?"

"I don't know—maybe I'll find out."

The thing happened while the men were gone. Trooper had a daughter called Jessie. who was fourteen years old, and it happened to her. She could reconstruct the tale only brokenly, incoherently, how she had wandered out onto the old tobacco road, just walking along and daydreaming to herself, when two white men came along driving a mule cart. They had yelled at her, "Hey, you—you come here." She ran across the fields and they chased her. She ran into a patch of bramble, fell, and they pulled her out of there, tore off her clothes, and raped her. They talked about killing her or not killing her, but finally let her go, and she ran home naked and half insane with fear.

When Trooper heard about it, he went half mad himself; his main reaction was violent, he wanted to kill. He said sure as hell itself, he would kill a white man. Gideon and Brother Peter reasoned with him and pleaded with him, "You going to get yourself hanged, sure as God." "Then I will." "What good that going to do?" "Do some good." Gideon said finally, with cold anger, "You're talking like a fool—you'll not do that. Seven weeks we worked in that swamp—what for? Ask yourself what for, Trooper? A man died of malaria and they took him back and buried him. We never lay back and saw the blue sky, never saw a woman, what for, ask yourself that?"

"What for?" Trooper said dully.

"For a new life, damn you, understand that!"

"Sure enough, you talk big, Gideon. Talk mighty big and loud. Go off to Charleston, high and mighty. Eat the fat of the land. Sit with fancy nigger and white folk—"

"You fool! I went to Charleston because I was forced to go to Charleston—I went afraid, small, because there was so much to be feared. There still is, yes—" He put his arm around Trooper and said, "Look a here, man. This is a terrible thing that happened, a sad and terrible thing, a little girl with a wound cut deep into her. But that wound going to heal, Trooper; wounds heal. She'll forget. Give a what-for and a how-come to our own; you got a wife, you got other children. We come back from the swamp work with near a thousand dollars—hear me, Trooper near a thousand dollars, never was that much money together in the world for a nigger. Enough money to get drunk on, enough money to go a whoring on; sinful things to be bought high and wide and handsome for that money, calico dresses, sweet candy, Lord knows, I could go on, Trooper. That's a temptation, but I spoke to the men and they say, All right, Gideon, put that money away, buy the land. Why for they do that, these old ignorant nigger slave men? Why they got such a hope, such a trust in the future?"

Trooper shook his head miserably.

"Let me tell you why. Future shapes up, slow, like tomorrow, like when that old sun goes down and a man can't sleep. Then he say to himself, never be tomorrow, never come another sunrise, going to be night forever and ever, just twisting and turning and counting all that long, lonesome time when he can't sleep. Well, that time's almost gone; tomorrow's going to be here real soon, sure enough. All the old, evil bad things, they fade out slowly, a nigger is lynched, a poor little nigger girl is mistreated. But they fade out."

Reading to Rachel, Gideon described the school where Jeff was studying. It seemed astonishing to him that the round, careful script should be the only projection of his son; he tried to bridge the gap for himself, more so for Rachel and Jenny and Marcus. When Jenny and Marcus asked to know precisely where Massachusetts was, Gideon could only tell them it was a long distance, a great distance. It was a place where Yankees lived. "Only Yankees?" "Only Yankees, I guess." Gideon said, "Here he tells about the town, listen: 'Worcester is pretty and with many people, a city such a place is called. At first it is frightening but you soon are used to be living here in a city.'"

"Like Charleston?" Marcus asked, though he had only the haziest notion of what Charleston could be like. "Yes, like Charleston, I guess," Gideon replied uncertainly, reading then:

"There are fourteen students here at the Prebyterian Free Academy, all of them colored boys like me only most of them orphans who have no mother and father not like me. The Reverend Charles Smith and the Reverend Claude

Southwick who is a Unitarian not a Presbyterian teaches us Reading, Writing, Sums, Latin, History and Geography—"

"What is a Unitarian?"

Gideon didn't know; but he could tell them what geography was and that Latin was a language spoken hundreds of years ago by people who lived in another country. "Do they talk it now?" Gideon wasn't sure, nor could he say whether they planned to send Jeff to that country. He read:

" 'We learn and sleep in a room behind the manse called the annex. The ladys committee do our meals and they have clothes for us to wear. These are clean and good clothes that were worn only a short time. We do work in return. We mow grass, wash windows and do sweeping and keeping the church clean which we get 10 cents a week for spending. I am lonely for you but happy here. Ellen tell her I miss her too . . .' "

Rachel wiped her eyes, but Marcus and Jenny lived life in the north with Jeff, arguing the fascinating points he brought up. "You see," Gideon said, "how good this is for him—" Gideon could walk with Jeff's dreams. In letters, he became closer to Jeff than he ever had been in life; in one of them, he said, "Read the books Charles Dickens writes. They will teach you much of brotherhood and of good and bad men."

Before beginning his negotiations over the land, Gideon went to see Abner Lait. Walking down the road to Abner's place one morning, he leaned on the gate and waited for the white man to notice him. Mrs. Lait came to the door of the house, glanced at Gideon and then went back inside. Jimmy scuffled up and informed Gideon that Abner was feeding the hogs.

"What's your name, nigger?" the boy said.

"Gideon Jackson."

"I seen you before."

"That's right," Gideon nodded. "I guess maybe you remember how I came along here last fall."

"Uh-huh."

"How old are you, boy?" Gideon asked.

"Ten summer."

"Got any schooling?"

The boy grinned and shook his head. "Don't want any neither."

Abner came around from the hog pen and nodded at Gideon. "Morning."

"Morning, Mr. Abner," Gideon said. "Got a mighty nice corn stand, I see. Got a few acres of cotton, too. That's going to be a paying crop, a good, solid cash crop, come this year."

"If I get the picking done," Abner said.

"You will."

"Well, that's mighty nice of you to be that optimistic," Abner said. "Maybe you'd like to come down and help?"

"Maybe I would."

Abner hitched his pants, spat, and rubbed his hands up and down his pants seat. "Hear you been working on the railroad, Gideon," he observed. Peter came up now and Abner's little six-year-old girl, hanging onto her father's belt and staring at Gideon from a circle of red hair.

"That right."

"Seems a sure enough come down for an uppity nigger who sat on the Convention."

"Maybe it is, maybe it's not, depending on how you look at it," Gideon smiled.

"Seems like the niggers are going to run the state."

"I wouldn't say that, Mr. Abner."

"You wouldn't?"

Gideon said, "Might I come on in, Mr. Abner? I'm sure enough dry and I'd appreciate a glass of cold water."

"I'll get it," Peter cried, and ran for the well.

"Come in," Abner said shortly, and led the way over to a broad shade tree. He squatted and Gideon let down beside him. Peter brought a tin cup of water, and Gideon drank gratefully. "Got a fine well," he nodded. Abner said, "It stays cool. I keep it shaded." "Nothing like fine cool water." Abner's wife came out on the porch again, stared at them for a moment, and then went inside. Gideon said, "Good times don't come so often you can turn a cold shoulder on them."

"Just how you figure it."

"I figure this is going to be a better time than before the war," Gideon answered, slowly. "Maybe it's going to be hard hoeing for plantation people, but the small farmer'll have a chance. Never did have a chance before."

"Uh-huh."

"Still and all," Gideon said, plucking a stem of dry grass and chewing on it thoughtfully, "good times are one thing, fool's heaven's another." Abner remained silent; he cast an eye at the sun, as if estimating the time Gideon had stayed already. His hound dog came up, sniffed at Gideon, and then stretched out. The children drifted away. Abner's wife called from the house, "Peter—you come here, you!"

"Look at it this way," Gideon said. "Bygones are bygones, but there ain't no man here the war didn't make it almighty hard and sorrowful for. Women at home worked and suffered and hoped; you and me, we came back, rolled up our sleeves, and say, make something out of all this grief. Got a little seed, got an animal or two. Put in some feed and greens. Sure enough, that's a mighty big ploughing you did for one man, corn and cotton; just about broke your back over it, I reckon. Well, you got a crop in, crop for a man to be proud of. But who owns that land you're ploughing, Mr. Abner?"

"Who owns it?" Abner stared at Gideon. "Damned if I know—damned if I care. Belonged to Dudley Carwell one time, seems he lost it to Ferguson White. They say White's moved over to Texas."

"That's right. The land's gone for taxes, every foot and acre Carwell owned."

"All right, let it go. God knows, I ain't got cash for taxes."

"This is the point," Gideon said quietly. "The Carwell place is going to be sold at auction in Columbia sometime during October. I got that from the Federal Commissioner. It will probably go in thousand acre lots, not in smaller parcels. When it goes, where are we going to be, Mr. Abner—where're you going to be?"

"Right where I am," Abner said stolidly. "Ain't no god-damn Yankee going to tell me to get off of here, ain't no goddamn nigger-owner going to tell me that. I fought this war through—and what in hell did I get from it? No sir. I'm sitting right here on my ass, and ain't nobody going to tell me to move!"

"Begging your pardon, Mr. Abner, just look at what you're saying. Nobody going to tell you to get off, that's fine, but that's not practical. Sheriff come along, what are you going to do? Fight the law? You going to fight a planta-tion man with law and order behind him? How can you do that?"

"I don't need a nigger to tell me how."

"All right, but wait a minute, Mr. Abner. How you feel about niggers, that's your business and don't come into the argument nohow. But let me say, what ever you feel, nigger is not your enemy."

Abner told Gideon coldly, "You can damnwell get to hell out of here."

"Sure I can," Gideon said, his mouth tightening. "I can get out of here. Carwell place is knocked down on the auc-tion block, and then you going to hate the whole world, but what are you going to do? I'll tell you something, Mr. Abner, whether you want to hear it or not. Me and my people went down to work in that swamp to get money to buy land. A man without land in this here country is no better than a slave, and it don't make much difference, Mr. Abner, if a slave's a nigger or a white man. We got near a thousand dollars now, and if we can get a banker to give us a draft against a mortgage, we can go in there and bid for a few thousand acre lots. Mighty nice feeling that would be, going in there and bidding for your own piece of land."

Abner Lait rocked slowly on his haunches, stared at the ground, and traced curious patterns with his fingers. Minutes went by, the white man saying nothing, just staring at his large, angular hands, at the orange-colored hairs that stood out from the skin, curling like stiff wire, at the scar across his wrist that a Yankee bayonet had made. Watching him, Gideon tried to understand something of the struggle he was having with himself, with a lifetime of heartbreaking contradictions: whom did he hate? what had he fought? for what? A man isn't the same after years of killing, marching, and trying to keep from being killed. A man can come back and get behind his plough again and feed his pigs again, but he isn't the same.

"I got no money," Abner said finally, tiredly, the edge gone from his voice. "Four dollars, sixty cents inside the house, Gideon. That's all."

"You don't need money," Gideon told him. "Takers is what I want, families. Money we got is enough to make things go, or else they'll never go. On this here Carwell place there's twenty-seven colored families and seven white—all of them living on the old acreage, all of them going to get off or be share tenants when the land is sold. Suppose we say eighty, ninety acres of land to a family, more or less, just depending. That includes a piece of scrub for burning, a piece of pasture, a piece of ploughland. Three thousand-acre lots would make out for us, give every man his piece."

"Why do you want me?" Abner asked. "What've I ever done for you? I ain't no nigger lover or goddamn Scalawag that you got to come here licking my ass."

"That's right," Gideon agreed.

"How come, then?"

"All right," Gideon said. "Look at it this way—this here South of ours got four million niggers, eight million white folk. Right here in South Carolina, the black man's got a little edge in population. Things ain't ever going to be again the way they was; the war killed the old way. Out of the Convention and the elections is coming a new life for this southland. What's that going to be, Mr. Abner, that new life? Don't look like much from here, same rotten old shacks folks lived in before the war, same bad feeling, same hate, same dark ignorance. Where's that new life? Well, it don't happen, can't just happen of its own wishing; nothing does. Everything's made. Got a railroad causeway through the swamp because men went in there and worked—talking didn't do it. Well, same thing here. This is a good land, this country here, a sweet land, full of milk and honey if you work it right. Ain't cold, like in the Yankee country, ain't full of sickness, like down in the river country. Got good people in it too, good white folks, good black folks—"

"Until the goddamn Yankees ruined it," Abner said.

"Did they now? War's a sad thing, sad and wasteful. You took up a gun, I took up a gun, and in a way of speaking you and me fought against each other. Why for? Sure the Yankees come in here, freed the niggers and maybe half the plantation owners see themselves ruined. But how many plantations are there? Just look around you—everywhere the eyes rest, there's the same old Carwell place. Me, I'm a free man instead of just a nigger slave; you got the same as before the war, maybe better. Never had no hope of owning your own piece before the war. Every inch of good land was part of some plantation—poor white could have some swamp or patch of pines to raise a crop. The Yankees left us the land, and maybe a little more hope than before."

Abner stirred the dirt with his fingers. "Go on," he said.

"All right. What's this future going to be except what we make it? And it won't be no good unless we make it for black and white the same. Ain't no end of hate here unless the future belongs to both of us. We're stronger to buy the land if you come in, if Max Bromly comes in, if the Carson brothers come in, if Fred McHugh comes in."

"They won't."

"Maybe they will, Mr. Abner. This here world's changing. Now we got a little school up among my people. No reason why your children shouldn't come to school there. Some day, Government'll come in and build a real fine school hereabouts. Nothing stopping your children going to school with mine excepting one's white, the other's black."

Abner shook his head.

"That's something to think about, Mr. Abner. Takes time, I'll admit that. But there's no reason you shouldn't come in on this land thing."

"I don't need no goddamn nigger charity," Abner said stubbornly.

"It ain't no charity to strengthen my hand. If I come to

the banker and say white folks are in this with me, then I got a so much stronger hand."

"Maybe so." After a moment, Abner said, "How do you know they'll sell us the land?"

"I spoke to the Yankee land agent. He says it'll be a fair auction, gone off to the highest bidder."

"Suppose you're lying?"

"Suppose I am," Gideon said, and then they looked at each other, and for the first time Abner smiled.

"Who's going to do the buying?"

"My people want me to talk for them. That's not set. We could discuss the matter."

"I'd settle on you."

"Then you'll come in with us?" Gideon asked.

"I'll come in."

"I'd be pleased and proud, Mr. Abner," Gideon said, "to shake hands with you on that."

Abner Lait shook hands with a Negro for the first time in his life.

After two hours of talk with the Carson brothers, they came in and gave Gideon sixty-five dollars to add to the fund. Max Bromly shook his head to all Gideon's arguments; he'd have nothing to do with niggers, and that was the end of it. Fred McHugh came in, and so did his brother-in-law, Jake Sutter. It took three days and pleading enough with Gideon's own people. "What for we need white folks?" they demanded. The money was theirs. Hadn't one of them died in the swamp?

Gideon told them. He repeated it over and over. At least half of them were on his side to begin, and finally the rest were persuaded. Gideon was triumphant, vibrantly triumphant for the first time in months. Now, holding Rachel in his arms, it was like old times, so long ago.

And then, four mornings after Gideon had been to see him, Abner Lait came walking up the hill with his two boys. He told Gideon, "I talked it over with Helen, and she thinks they ought to have some spelling."

The boys twisted, squealed and kicked. Abner clouted

them and said they'd damnwell mind, or he'd know why. His own shame at coming this way to niggers was something he had to stand up to, and Gideon, recognizing that, made it as easy as possible. He said, "Thank you, Mr. Abner. This is a beginning."

Abner nodded, stood around a while without saying anything, and then turned and left.

CHAPTER SEVEN

How Gideon Jackson Journeyed Far Afield and How He Made Both a Bargain and a Choice

CARL ROBBINS, VICE PRESIDENT OF THE FIRST NATIONAL BANK of Columbia, shook his head and told Gideon, no, he was not interested. Hardly. No, completely uninterested, smiling slightly to convey his opinion of such an affair. He had a heavy bald head, Mr. Robbins, sandy fringes of hair, tiny blue eyes, a roll of flesh in the back of his neck that seemed to support his skull. He said to Gideon, patiently:

"You see, Jackson, things are not done so simply; if they were, we should have chaos. You come to me with a thousand dollars, tell me that you represent some motley lot of niggers and white trash, squatters on the Carwell place, and suggest that I give you a draft on this bank to buy with at the public auction. That is completely fantastic."

"Not just a draft," Gideon argued. "The same sum you advance will be a mortgage—"

"Come now, Jackson," Robbins interrupted. "Be sensible. These are bad times; one hesitates about taking any mortgages, much less a mortgage on land that doesn't exist. What kind of security are a few footloose niggers?"

"Please, sir, Mr. Robbins," Gideon said, "we are not footloose. We have been on the land, this land, all our lives, most of us, worked it, took out three crops on our own. If you would only come over and see the Carwell place you would think differently, I am sure."

"I'm not used to having niggers tell me how to think," Robbins said.

"Mr. Robbins, sir, I didn't mean that. I am acting in good faith and honestly, believe me, sir. Our only hope is to own a few acres of land."

"I don't see that at all," Mr. Robbins said impatiently, looking at his watch, and nodding at the guard who was standing a little distance away, outside of the enclosure. "If you show good faith and a desire to work, whoever buys the land will keep you on to work it. As a matter of fact, I don't approve of niggers owning land; spoils them. I'm sorry, Jackson, but I'm a busy man—" And at that moment the guard came, took Gideon's arm, and led him out.

Rachel said to him, "It'll be all right, Gideon, mind me—sure enough it'll come out all right," and Gideon heard her with part of his mind, wondering how many of his people thought that way, always today and not tomorrow, the bone and marrow of slavery not being a thing that is shed overnight, like chains. He had come back miserable and beaten, and Rachel was only glad to have him home. He began, almost fiercely, "Don't you see—" but broke off when Rachel said, "It'll come out all right, you setting your mind to it, Gideon honey."

Then he began to smile, looking at her, the roundness of her, the woman of her, the flat cheeks, the small turned-up nose, the skin with just enough sheen on it to catch the light of the fire, the note in her voice as she asked, "What for you laughing at me, Gideon?"

"Not laughing, honey child," and thinking to himself how strange were links and reasons and the simple way of life becoming so incredibly complex—the fact of this woman here, his wife, whom he loved so warmly and completely at this moment, the fact of her in relation to a poor black man snatched from the African coast once so long ago, the fact of her in relation to Jeff, to himself—to a continuing, pulsating stream that made up humanfolk, climbing and reaching, joyous and tired . . .

"What you thinking, Gideon?" she said. Jenny climbed into his arms. Marcus lay in front of the fire. Rachel said, "Time you got bedded, Jenny."

Gideon asked Jenny, "What for now, pigeon?"

"Brother Fox." "Old Brother Fox—I told you all I know, honest to May," Gideon said. Jenny wanted to know, "How come he never have to do with Brother Tortoise." "Mind as he did," Gideon said. "Brother Fox being mighty smart, smartest old man in the piney woods, he wouldn't consider Brother Tortoise. Old Tortoise got a shell so thick no one ever credit him with smartness—" Rachel watched Gideon, half listening to the story, as Marcus listened with half an ear, an old tale being that way, not asking too much attention, but being good for the sure and specific qualities it always contained. There was a knock at the door and Rachel let James Allenby in. He sat down and said nothing until Gideon finished the story, it being a flexible thing he adjusted to Jenny's falling asleep. The child clung to his neck as he set her down on the pallet. Marcus dozed by the fire, a comfortable, half-grown animal. Allenby said finally, after commenting on the weather outside and on how fine Rachel looked:

"What happened in Columbia was to be expected, Gideon."

"I suppose so."

"Have you considered what to do now?"

"Charleston, I guess."

"They won't be more receptive."

Gideon said, "There's Boston, New York, Philadelphia—"

"Onto the other side of nowhere," Rachel thought, and Allenby reflected, "You'll have that land, won't you, Gideon?"

"I'll try."

"I think you will, Gideon," the old man said. "In the way of things, after you spent that night with me in my cabin, I was sure you would go your way fully. What's going to stop you, Gideon? I think nothing. Only don't do the thing for doing it; power's no good as of itself. Keep coming home."

"How do you mean that?"

Allenby shrugged and smiled. "I'm an old man talking, Gideon, and maybe I talk too much. If you go up north and see Yankees, remember this—they aren't cut of a cloth. Some of them hate a black man worse than any southerner, and to those people we are alien, strange creatures with black skins. Even to southern folk who hate us, we are never alien, but as much a part of this land as the piney woods and the cotton and tobacco. Also, you will meet Yankees, a few, who have turned themselves into something strange and wonderful; they will sit at a table with you and take your hand and the color of your skin will no longer matter. Trust those people, Gideon; accept them for what they are. For two generations they fought to make us free because they believed in the brotherhood of man; don't credit the lies that you will hear about them."

Gideon nodded; the old man leaned over, put a hand on Gideon's knee, and said, "Don't be too proud to take, Gideon. If there were none who took and none who gave, we would be like savages. You will go for more important things, but if some books should come your way, some paper, some slates and chalk—we need them so much, Gideon."

"I'll remember," Gideon said.

Gideon's learning continued. In Columbia he found a copy of Blackstone's *Commentaries on the Laws of England*. Old and battered, he bought it for sixty cents. Anderson Clay sent him a dog-eared edition of Paine's *Rights of Man,* a book which for all its vagueness, for all its being out of context with Gideon's knowledge and experience, became for him a constant wonder, a pool of astonishment that never dried up. Allenby had some poems of Poe which he gave to Gideon, but Gideon reading them was troubled and confused. "No one is alive," he said. He was happier with Emerson, and Allenby said, "If you could meet him, Gideon—"

It was in early fall that Gideon came back to Charleston, came back to the Carters, who welcomed him so gladly, and then walked into the house of Francis Cardozo, who took his hand, smiling rather strangely, and said, "So you're back again, Gideon."

"I'm back."

"A little older and a little wiser?"

"Some of each," Gideon agreed. In Cardozo's parlor he sat stiffly, his hands between his knees. He had a glass of wine and a few sweet cakes; the room seemed smaller than as he remembered it, Cardozo seemed smaller too. Gideon talked slowly and carefully, and Cardozo said nothing until Gideon came to the incident of the Columbia banker.

"Were you surprised, Gideon?"

"No, I wasn't too surprised. I half expected that to happen."

"And probably," Cardozo reflected, "the same thing would happen here. You know, Gideon, according to his lights, Robbins was not too unfair. What can you present? A few dollars of cash, your own word, the supposed backing of a few penniless colored and poor white families and a very vague and dream-like future."

"All futures are dreams," Gideon said.

"More or less, I'll grant that. But can't you see, Gideon, that this problem of land exists everywhere in the south, that it's the single great problem upon which our future rests. How is it solved? A year ago this past March, Thaddeus Stevens introduced his Land-Division bill into Congress. What was his proposal? To take the great rebel plantations, break them down, and give each freedman forty acres and fifty dollars for a homestead. Wait a moment, I want to read you precisely what Stevens himself said on the subject—" Cardozo went to his desk, shuffled among some papers, and then turned back to Gideon and read:

"This plan would, no doubt, work a radical reorganization in Southern institutions, habits and manners. It is intended to revolutionize their principles and feelings. This may startle feeble minds and shake weak nerves. So do all great improvements in the political and moral world. The Southern States have been despotisms, not governments of the people. It is impossible that any practical equality of rights can exist where a few thousand men monopolize the whole landed property. How can republican institutions, free schools, free churches, free social intercourse, exist in a mingled community of nabobs and serfs, of the owners of twenty-thousand-acre manors with lordly palaces, and the occupants of narrow huts?"

Cardozo crossed back to Gideon now and spread his hands, "All right, there it is. As Stevens puts it, we, with our Convention and our new Constitution created a contradiction, for unless there is a free basis for all our fine proposals, what good are they? And that basis means free, land-owning farmers instead of landless serfs and peons."

"And what do you propose?" Gideon demanded. "I, at least, have a plan for a few of these people, a practical plan that can be made to work."

"And I have a plan for twelve million of them," Cardozo smiled, leaning back against a chair, his hands behind him. "When Thaddeus Stevens died last month, we lost a great, good fighter and friend. But he pointed out the way—make it plain to the people, enforce their power to vote, educate them, give them honest representatives, and legally in the halls of this state's legislature and this country's Congress, fight for legal, universal land division."

"And meanwhile the people suffer," Gideon said.

"Meanwhile, they suffer. That's right. We alleviate their suffering all we can, but in the large overall picture of the thing, there is not much we can do."

"Still and all," Gideon said, "I intend to buy land. If I can't find the money here, I'll find it in Boston, or in New York."

For a while, Cardozo just looked at Gideon, bending back over the chair; then he sat down; then he said, "I'll make a bargain with you, Gideon. I know Isaac Went, a Boston banker, an old abolitionist, and a man who doesn't put a silk thread on every dollar he lets go of. I'll give you a letter to him, and, I think, a letter that will carry some weight. I'll also give you a letter to Frederick Douglass, who might be able to help you with this if other things fail. In return, I want your promise that you'll stand for the state legislature at the next election."

"Suppose I let you know tomorrow," Gideon said.

"All right. Come for dinner tomorrow."

The next day, Gideon saw two Charleston bankers; one of

them was Colonel Fenton, whom he had met at the dinner Stephen Holms gave. When he saw Cardozo again, Gideon expected the question:

"What happened?"

"What you thought would happen," Gideon said, smiling a little.

"At least maintain the nigger reputation for mirth. He's happy poor and he's happy rich."

"I'm doing that," Gideon said sourly. "I'm not unhappy."

"And about the legislature?"

"If anyone wants me," Gideon agreed, "I'll go in. I'll try not to realize what I was a year ago or five years ago," and then added, "Considering what I've read of laws and law-making, I can't do very much worse."

"I'm glad, Gideon," Cardozo said.

"And I ain't—you see, I still talk like a swamp nigger. If I can, I'd like to leave for the north mighty soon—to-morrow?"

"I suppose you could, tomorrow."

The train that carried Gideon Jackson through the night, north from Washington, D. C., roared into a new world. That was in the exact sense of the word. All that had happened to him until now, in his thirty-seven years of life, storm and eruption, had been within the world he knew, the southland that had borne him, bred him and fed him, whipped him and gouged and cut at him; yet that land was one and the same; he knew that land, the erosion, the darkness and ignorance, the wasted soil and life, the great feudal homes looming over the sub-strata of white peons and black slaves. And knowing that, there had been a warmth and goodness wherever he went in the south, a sameness. In this new world, there was no sameness; Washington, the city of giant white palaces and muddy streets, was like nothing he had ever experienced; now he sat in a railroad car among white people who read their newspaper, spoke to one another, and neither minded nor cared that a black man was among them. In early fall, it was cold here. When it rained, the rain whipped angrily and savagely. When people spoke, they talked in hard, clipped, hurrying tones.

"Grant, that's a general, not a statesman." "And what, mister, is wrong with a general being president." "I don't like it." "No, maybe you'd like another term of Johnson?" "Don't put words in my mouth, mister, I do my own thinking." "Not much of it." "Wheat—wheat's at sixty-two." "Is that your *Herald*, mister? Mind if I read it?" "I got two sons in Chicago, believe me, they're doing all right."

Gideon dozed off to the sound of those voices. Later, he woke when a conductor came through, blinking off the smelly kerosene lamps. The plush seat was hard and uncomfortable; the train stopped every few miles, jolting, starting again. People sat down next to him, then rose and left the train, a white man, a white woman, a young girl . . . And the next day, there were the Jersey flats, the sprawling, ugly city of Newark, and finally a disgorging at Jersey City with New York just across the river. On the ferry, Gideon gripped the rail and stared; boats on the river like dry sticks on a pond, ferries, steamers laying their lush black smoke on the river, like charcoal marks on shiny white paper, sailing craft of all sizes, angry little tugs, strings of barges, and across the river the mass of houses—just pluck out a handful, and there was Charleston, another handful and there Columbia, not the queen of cities but a great, nursing mother. This was what Whitman meant; this was the meat and blood of countless thousands.

Staring, Gideon thought of the dogged, slogging, uninspired Yankee armies that had pushed their way into the south, cut to pieces a hundred times and closing their ranks each time, clumsily, foolishly, painfully learning the art of war, and finally rocking and splitting the whole southland with their battle hymn of freedom. This was it, these small, colorless folk who crowded the ferry, the crowds on the streets, hurrying, minding their own business, the jumble, confusion, rush, roar, clatter, the goods piled high on the wharves, the dirty streets, the strings of pushcarts and sidewalk stands, the carriages, carts, wagons, vans pushing past each other in the streets, the pall of smoke over the red brick buildings, the clatter of tongues. The nations were here, and no one minded or noticed the tall black man. Gideon had two and a half hours between trains; he walked from the river to the financial district; he passed through acres of hastily erected tenements. The day was as blisteringly hot as the day before had been unnaturally cool; this was weather to keep pace with the city, the blustering, cocky, dirty, miserable, confident metropolis that was already becoming one of the wonders of the world. It rained and it cleared; the streets ran with water and dirt where they were paved and became sluices of mud where they were not. Olive-skinned children sailed bits of wood in the gutters; other children sold newspapers, running and shrieking along the sidewalks. Gideon tried to understand; this was the city where a hundred Negroes were murdered in insane mob rage. This was also the city where working men, by the thousands, laid down their tools, gave their own money to buy uniforms and guns, and knowing nothing of war, nothing of death and slaughter, marched hundreds of miles to the south so that black men might be free. This was the city that had spawned regiment after regiment, year after year, to fight in the war—yet here too were the worst draft riots, the worst anti-war riots that the country had ever known. Gideon looked, wondered, and saw too much . . .

Boston was more simple, more what he was used to in the way of a city. The quiet bay street where Isaac Went lived might have been a street in Charleston; there were green trees shading it. The houses were old, and being old, unaggressive; under the clean white paint, the woodwork was cracked and worm-eaten. In response to Gideon's uncertain tap with the knocker, a starched maid came to the door and said politely, who would he see? Mr. Isaac Went, if he might. "Won't you come in, please, sir," the maid said, a blue-eyed girl with corn-colored hair and Vermont in her voice.

His hat in his hands, Gideon entered the house. Just beyond the door was a small vestibule, two facing oval-framed mahogany mirrors, four prim mahogany chairs and two small black tables, covered with Chinese lacquer and design. Walnut doors, opened by the maid, disclosed a fine old staircase that divided the parlor from the dining room. The rooms were large, but low-ceilinged, in contrast to the great, high ceilings of the south. Here was, Gideon saw, as clear an evidence of wealth as in Stephan Holms' house; yet there was a division, a split; he was expected here, for all that they had not known of his coming. The maid said to him:

"Won't you sit down, please, sir, and I'll tell Mr. Went you're here—what did you say your name was?"

"Gideon Jackson."

"Just Mr. Gideon Jackson?"

"With a letter from Mr. Francis Cardozo?"

"Uh-huh," the maid said. "Just sit down." Her politeness was blunt, taking him for granted. She made no effort to put him at ease, yet he was more at ease than ever before in the house of a white man. He glanced around the room, noticed the two large, comfortable wing chairs that flanked the fireplace, rejected them, took a step toward the couch that backed on the other wall, caught himself, tested a broad-bottomed Chippendale chair, and then rose quickly to his feet as he heard footsteps. It was about five o'clock in the afternoon now, and he wondered whether he had been right to call at such an hour. He stood stiffly and awkwardly as Isaac Went came into the room.

Isaac Went was a small man; standing against Gideon, the top of his bald head would just touch Gideon's string tie. He had a sandy little mustache, a thin mouth and a pointed chin. Now he wore a smoking jacket over black pants, silk slippers, and a stiff white collar with a black tie. His walk was nervous; birdlike, striking toward Gideon, he thrust out his hand and said:

"What is your name? Jackson? Gideon Jackson? The girl said you have a letter from somebody, couldn't remember who. It's a wonder she remembers her head's on her shoulders."

"The letter, sir, is from Francis Cardozo," Gideon said.

"Cardozo? You from the south?"

"South Carolina," Gideon said.

"Well, what is Cardozo doing? Making a bigwig out of himself in politics? Where's the letter?"

Gideon gave it to him. Tearing it open, he read it quickly, and then looked at Gideon again. "Cardozo thinks a lot of you," he said. "Why don't you sit down? Do you want a drink?" He nodded toward one of the wing chairs, meanwhile taking a decanter and two glasses. Gideon sat down. "This is sherry," Went said. "Do you like sherry?"

Gideon nodded.

"Yes or no," Went shrugged. "Most black people don't give two damns about liquor, you know. Never had a chance to get a taste for it. That's all it is, a taste; I used to drink whisky, now sherry. I still miss the whisky, I'm not in good health. Will you have a cigar?"

Gideon shook his head.

"All right. You don't mind if I smoke? No—I don't give a damn if you do mind. When my wife was alive, I saved these damn things for after dinner." He took out a long, black cigar and lit it, stretched out in the wing chair, and blew smoke at the mantle. "It says here—" he referred to the letter—"that you sat in the Convention. You must tell me about that. I couldn't make anything out of the newspaper stories. First tell me about this land scheme of yours—no, save that for dinner. I want Doc Emery to hear that, he'll be here, he's just stupid enough to swing the balance. Tell me about the Convention now—"

Gideon told him. With the little man, Gideon was on flat, unruffled ground. Went spat, argued, disagreed, lost his temper and yelled at Gideon; but always as one man to another. Gideon was not a black man; for the first time in his life, whether with colored people or white people, Gideon completely forgot the color of his skin; for the first time in his life he was talking to a man who by a long and studied psychological process, a period of training that must have begun in his earliest childhood, had conditioned himself to racial democracy in clean and simple terms. For Went, subjectively, Gideon was a man; he could not think otherwise, willingly or unwillingly, anymore than the average American could think in Latin. When he yelled at him, in relation to the land question in debate at the Convention:

"You were a fool, Jackson, you and all the rest! Stevens was alive then; did you consult him? Did you ask for support from Washington? No, all by yourself you were going to remake civilization! That's Cardozo! That's all your narrow, cultured imbeciles! Well, you missed a historic opportunity! You could have destroyed the plantations then and there—you didn't—"

When he yelled at Gideon that way, he was screaming at his equal, not at a black man, not at a white man, no courtesy here, no barriers. Later, he gave Gideon a hint as to the background of this, telling him, "I come of Abolitionist people, Mr. Jackson. Maybe I'm not the best product they've produced. I sat on my behind when others were in there, fighting and dying. But I did a little; my money was useful. Did you know that old Osawatomie Brown sat right there where you're sitting, pleading for money, for guns, for powder, for men—yes, he was going to march through the south to glory and sweep away slavery like the wrath of the Lord. And I gave him money and guns. That seems like a thousand years ago, doesn't it, when men spoke so glibly of doing away with that rotten disease? And then we bled ourselves dry for four years. Right there, old Brown sat, with his beard, his eyes burning—would you like to hear his words? I remember his words—'The Lord God has not deserted us, Mr. Went,' he said. 'But we, Mr. Went, we pitiful, small, frightened, crawling creatures have deserted the Lord God of Hosts, the God of our fathers who led the children of Israel from the land of Egypt.' Those were his words as nearly as I can remember them, Jackson. He was sitting where you are sitting; Emerson was sitting here; I was standing. Waldo looked at me and I looked at him. You understand, Jackson, that old John Brown was a great man, a great and misunderstood man. The old man could give people the power of belief. I am not a believer; I pride myself on my atheism even more than Doc Emery prides himself on his; but right here, at that time, with old Osawatomie talking, I believed. God was at my right hand, my great-grandfather's God, the grand and ter-

rible old man of a God who came over to this land with
the Pilgrims. Have I offended you, Mr. Jackson? I don't
know if you're a believer. So many black people are—"

"You haven't offended me," Gideon said slowly.

They talked a while longer; then Went suggested that both
he and Gideon lie down for a while before dinner. "I have
the habit—I'm getting old. You, you're a young man, Jackson, but you might enjoy a nap." Gideon pointed out that as
yet he had no place to stay in Boston, that Went might suggest a hotel for colored people. "Of course you'll stay here,"
Went said. Gideon objected weakly, but Went brushed his
objections aside. "Douglass stays with me," he said. "It ought
to be damn well good enough for you." Then the maid came
and led Gideon upstairs to his room.

"The effect," Gideon said, "of the two years right after the
war was to wake us up. The bad black codes were made to
drive us straight back to slavery. You see, the planters felt
they could just push away the Union victory, and they were
almost right. But it won't happen a second time. We made a
good and an honest alliance with the poor whites; we're
united now, and we got our eyes open. We got the power,
and we mean to hold onto it."

There were three of them at the dinner table, Isaac Went,
the banker; Dr. Norman Emery, who had made a name for
himself and Boston with his pioneering in the field of ab-
dominal surgery; and Gideon. Emery was a tall, lean, dark-
eyed man; he wore a pointed beard and pince-nez on a black
ribbon; his appearance was deceptive, aloof, disinterested; by
blood and marriage he was related to the Lowells, the Emer-
sons, the Lodges. He had an incisive mind, a knife-like subtle
humor with which he cut at Went constantly. As Gideon
noticed soon enough, he was a humane man, though par-
simonious and watchful of his humanity. Between him and
Went, both widowers, there was a warm yet wary bond. Now
Emery asked Gideon:

"But by what means, Mr. Jackson, do you intend to hold
onto the power?"

"In three ways," Gideon said. "First, by the ballot. There

on every count we got the planters beat, twenty votes to every one they can find. Second, we are going to educate. All we need is ten years and in that time we raise up a whole generation of educated children. That, Dr. Emery is going to be our biggest gun. The planters taught us that way back, when they made it a crime for a slave to want education, even to learn himself. Third way is the land, like I said, like I told you. We're a planting people down there, all of us; we ain't —have not got the mills you got here. Folk live off the soil; man with a plough in his hands has bread and shortening in his mouth. When we get the land, when we parcel it out, when we set up a nation of free farmers down there, like you got here, then we stand on our own feet and talk loud and sure. Once that land's our own, we are not going to give it up, never."

"All right," Went said. "Granted your utopian conception of a new south, granted all your fine dreams of schools. Do you want a tot of brandy, Emery?"

"I told you it's bad for your heart. I'm sick of telling you that."

"All right. I have little enough heart. Granted all you say, Jackson, it adds up to a legalistic projection of the future. Business is another matter. If you were to come to me asking for charity, I might help you, I might not, depending on many things. Understand, I'm not a soft-hearted man, not a sentimentalist."

Emery said, "I think he realizes that, Isaac."

"But you come with a fantastic scheme. Your people earned a little money; with that money you intend to undertake a staggering land venture, a venture that would require at least fifteen dollars of mortage money for every dollar you propose to invest. And what have I to go by, a handful of former slaves, a few poor whites, men who were recently members of the rebel army, and some good intentions. You ask me to invest money in an unknown quantity and quality. Is that reasonable, Jackson? I put it up to you." He lit a cigar; Emery leaned back and watched Gideon, smiling a little. Hopelessness made a hot, heavy load inside of Gideon; he had come this far; he had spent part of the money. A dollar was something you broke your heart for. A man died for a dollar. A railroad ticket cost so many dollars. How far he had gone by now—and how much farther could he go? Was Cardozo right, completely? Was all progress born out of suffering, endless suffering, a mighty burden carried by the poor for ever and ever?

"Maybe it is not reasonable," Gideon said. "I know very little, nothing, I guess, about business. But I know cotton and I know rice. All my life I seen the cotton plant grow, seen the bolls burst, seen the black man out in the field doing the picking. Show me a cotton seed, and I'll tell you quality. Show me rice and I'll tell you where it growed, high-land or lowland. I know that, believe me. I know something else; here you Yankees got a way of making cotton cloth. All over this New England of yours, the mills are building. How you going to spin that cotton if no one's growing the bolls? Want the planters to grow it? That'll take time; they'll have to break us before they grow cotton the old way. And what's the price going to be with a few planters controlling it? You ask what security you got from my people—just this. This is a cotton-hungry land, a cotton-hungry world. There ain't been a real good cotton crop in four years now. It's a seller's market. Give my people the land; let them set an example; let them show Carolina it can be done, the way the black man showed it with rice on the sea islands before the Government turned its back on them and took away the land, the same land they seized fighting rebels who wanted to destroy this Union. If you do it, if you not afraid, then others not afraid. Give us five years of our own land, and we'll break our backs putting in the cotton; we'll break our backs picking it. We'll pay you off, every cent and with a profit. You ever seen niggers work? If you been down the south in the old slave days, then you seen how niggers could work with a lash on their back. Well, I tell you this, I tell you a free nigger on his own land can work twice as hard. I know. Believe me, Mr. Went, I don't come asking for charity. I ain't too proud. Old teacher, learning the children down among my people, he said to me, Gideon, don't be proud. The children need books, paper, if they give, take

and don't be proud. But this is different; this is not charity.
I pledge you that, with all my word of honor."

Gideon finished; he had never spoken so heatedly before
to white men, never at such length; embarrassed and uneasy,
he sat and stared at the tablecloth. Dr. Emery studied his
fingernails. The long while of silence was punctuated by the
ticking of the tall grandfather clock in the corner. Then
Went tapped the ash from his cigar and said:

"How big is this Carwell place, Jackson?"

"Twenty-two thousand acres and some little more."

Emery whistled. Went nodded slowly. "You don't know,"
he said. "If you know, you forget. This whole god damned
war is forgotten."

"In the old country," Emery remarked, "that would be a
dukedom, a nice-sized dukedom."

"What kind of land?"

"At least half is good acreage," Gideon answered. "The
rest is brushwood, piney woods, some pasturage and a piece
of swamp."

"There's a house on it, isn't there?"

"The big plantation house. The Carwells lived in it only
on and off; mostly they lived in Charleston."

"Do you think anyone would buy the house, buy it as a
serviceable plantation house?"

Gideon shook his head. "It's too big—planters who hold
their land are just holding on. I don't guess there's that
much free money in the state."

"Do you know the evaluation on the place, land and house
and all?"

"The Federal agent put the prewar valuation, less slaves,
at four hundred and fifty thousand dollars. At auction, they
reckon it to bring five dollars an acre. They're going to break
it into twenty-two thousand-acre sections, and some will go
for more and some for less."

"You say you have some thirty-odd families. Three thousand acres is a good deal. I've known Massachusetts men
to run a good farm with twenty or thirty acres and put
money in the bank to boot. And this isn't the best soil in
the world."

"That's right, sir," Gideon agreed. "We got good soil. But the sections'll be only about half working land. Men'll clear, but that's slow work. Then we do different kind of farming from you folks up here. You got dairy land here; aside from the corn and greens we eat, aside from a hog or two, we got to raise a cash crop. You can't make money out of cotton unless you put in fifteen, twenty acres."

"How would you market it?"

"Buy an old gin, old baler, plenty of them. The railroad's coming through, and there'll be loading with a ten-mile haul."

"Got mules?"

"Got a few. We can buy more."

Went turned to Emery and asked, "What do you think, doc?"

"I've seen you lose your money on worse things."

"Will you go in for a third?"

"I'm not a banker," Emery smiled.

"You have more money than I—and you can't take it with you when you go."

"But it's nice having now."

"Will you go in for a third if I guarantee?"

"If you guarantee, why do you want my third?"

"I want companionship," Went said resignedly. "This is the most damnfool thing I ever indulged in."

"You can't take it with you either," Emery said.

"That's right. Look, Jackson, you're costing me just three times what old Osawatomie did—and I don't know if you're half the man he was. All right; I'll give you a draft for fifteen thousand dollars. Don't thank me. Tell us something about yourself for a change, now that's done."

Went was more things than one man. After Emery left, he sat until far into the morning talking with Gideon; he smoked his long black cigars, he drank too much brandy. Huddled in his dressing gown, the little man told Gideon:

"I'm sixty-seven years old, son, and alone. So I look back most of the time. When I was your age, Gideon, there were still soldiers of the revolution alive; we were a vigorous breed

here in New England then. Think about that. We came here
with the word of God and the law of God, a staff in our
hands and unsmiling lips, and we scratched a living from
this inhospitable and rocky land. And we did great things,
Gideon; in our meeting houses, democracy became a thing
that lived and breathed. The old prophets walked with us,
and in the revolution our farmers and fishermen fought with
a living, just God peering over their shoulders. That's all
forgotten now, isn't it? I'll die soon, Emery soon, Waldo
growing old, Thoreau a recluse, Whittier hidden away, Long-
fellow drooling inanities—where is all our glory? This
Brooklyn man, Whitman, roars like a savage, but loud and
clear enough; there are others while we begin to sit and
contemplate our navels. We have just a little spark left,
Gideon; old Thad Stevens was right when he left New England and went to Pennsylvania. But don't forget that while
we lived we did great things. It was our song, 'Mine eyes have
seen the glory of the coming of the Lord.' Well, come upstairs with me—"

Gideon followed him; Went walked slowly and tiredly,
pausing on the landing to catch his breath. They went into
a boy's room, and Gideon saw that it had been a long time
unused. There were stacks of books, notebooks, a mineral
collection, two stuffed owls, a pencil drawing of a young girl,
a pair of lacrosse sticks, Indian moccasins, a cleverly carved
schooner model. Went said:

"He died in the Wilderness, Gideon, on the second day
of the battle. Afterwards, I spoke to his captain and he told
me about it. The boy was wounded three times, twice in one
arm, once in the head, and he stayed in the battle. Gideon,
maybe five hundred times I've sat downstairs in front of the
fire, trying to understand, trying to reach the boy, put myself inside of him, and see why he should stay in a battle, cut
all to pieces, bleeding, dying on his feet. Gideon, you're a
young man, but you've got something inside you. You'll
be a leader of your people; Gideon, understand us, don't cut
yourself off from us—whatever happens."

"Whatever happens," Gideon nodded.

"All right. Now I'm going to have these books crated,

everything here crated. His toys and childhood books are in the attic, you can have those too—"

"I don't feel right about taking—," Gideon began.

"That's nonsense. I haven't been in here for a year. I keep my part of the boy inside of me, I don't need this trash. You can make some use of it, and that's as it should be. If I'm in for fifteen thousand dollars, I'll be in for twenty slates and a bin of chalk. Just tell me where to have it sent, and I'll take care of the rest."

Gideon tried to thank him, but it was not easy. Falling asleep in the ancient four-poster bed, the roof eaves cutting down over his head to a moonlit window, Gideon thought long and wonderingly of the many things that had happened, the many faces men may have, notwithstanding the color of their skins, and the many directions in which they went. The hallelujah song was not something that roared up; it came quietly and slowly. In logical and scientific analysis, all things were answerable but one, that being why at least a few men should find their only happiness and sustenance in a dream of brotherhood.

The next day, before going on to Worcester to see Jeff, Gideon paid a visit to Dr. Emery's dispensary. There, the suave and polished gentleman had vanished; a white-gowned, efficient scientist with two young assistants were waiting on a room and corridor packed full of patients. This was a part of Boston that reminded Gideon of New York, shacks, crumbling houses, dirty streets, poverty, poor Irish and poor Poles and poor Italians. Emery's dispensary was an old house, repaired, painted a clean cream throughout. Gideon sat in the examination room and watched the doctor. A boy with a sunken chest and misshapen bones—

"You see this, Jackson?" The boy naked, eight years old, standing there with his arms crossed, shivering. "We don't know what it is; I have a dozen cases every week, only among the poor. I have my own name for it—Maleficio Paupertatis, sufficiently descriptive."

He ran his hand over the boy's skin. "All right, son, put on your clothes. You see, Jackson, the ills of society have their different faces. We fought and died to free your people while our own cesspool was bred right here. It is not pretty, is it, when we who call ourselves civilized cannot provide free medicine, no, cannot even provide a little adequate research so that we may understand this black art called medicine. Here, in this rich land, people sicken and die of starvation, of the lack of fresh air, sunlight. Charity, which is what I dispense, Jackson, is a nauseous, fungus growth, and sometimes I think my illustrious neighbors here in this town are right when they keep their pockets sewn tight."

Afterwards, Emery asked Gideon about Jeff. "You're sure he wants to be a doctor?"

"How sure can a boy of sixteen be?" Gideon said. "He's a smart boy, I don't say that just because he's my son."

"Well, to get an education in this country is practically impossible. Our medical schools do not admit that a black man can either be sick or heal the sick. In time, when you've created your utopia down there in Carolina, I presume you'll take care of that. However, that's still in the future. If he passes the examination, he can be admitted to the university at Edinburgh in Scotland."

"Scotland?" Gideon shook his head uncertainly. "That's a long way, isn't it?"

"A good long way. Fortunately, in the old countries, they have not yet realized that a black skin makes a man subhuman."

"I don't know," Gideon said. "He's just a boy—send him off all that distance by himself. Maybe a year—"

"At least three years," Emery nodded, watching curiously the expression of pain on the Negro's face. Gideon, falteringly seeking a way out, said, "Not like I couldn't see what's best, but Rachel, his mother—"

"Then I would suggest," Emery shrugged, "that you give up the notion of his being a doctor."

"That's what he wanted," Gideon said.

"It will cost some money."

Gideon said, "Come back south, I plan to stand in the elections, go to the legislature." He hesitated. "When I sat in the convention, pay was three dollars a day. I could save maybe a dollar and fifty cents of that—would it be enough?"

Emery turned away. "It would be enough," he replied quietly. He walked over to a window and stared out, then turned back to Gideon. "Look, Jackson, where is that boy of yours now?"

"At the Presbyterian school at Worcester."

"I know the place—he'll learn to read and write and not much more. How long has he been there?"

"Four months."

"Let him stay there for six. You say he's sixteen. He can come here in two months, and I'll teach him more in a year than they could in ten. Mind you, he'll have to earn his keep; I can use a boy to sweep out, wash the lab, clean the instruments and vessels. I'm not a half baked Abolitionist like Went. If the boy is bright enough, if he shows any aptitude at all, if he's willing to work, I can train him sufficiently in two years for him to pass the Edinburgh examinations. If he isn't—"

Seated in the study of Reverend Charles Smith, in Worcester, Gideon repeated what Dr. Emery had said. Smith, a timid, gentle, uncertain man, said, yes, Jeff was a good boy, very good, very earnest, gave them no trouble; but Gideon should understand that education was a slow process, a tedious process; Gideon should remember that only a short time ago the boy could not read or write. It was true that he showed great imitative ability, that he absorbed things quickly, but medicine was a profession that required scholarship of the highest degree. Wasn't it presumptuous of Emery to say that in two years he could prepare the boy for Edinburgh? Gideon didn't know. And should one conclude that medicine was the only way in which a young man could serve his people? What of the pulpit? There was a spiritual side to the boy that might almost be recognized as a sign.

"It's not that I am ungrateful for all you have done," Gideon said. Could he tell Smith what it would do to him, to Rachel not to see Jeff for five years? Did white people understand what a child meant to a black man? "But I want the boy to do what he has to do."

"Naturally, insofar as a boy knows."

"I'll talk to him," Gideon said.

Jeff was taller than Gideon remembered him as being, taller and more like his father. Now they had been strangers for a while, they could see the resemblance in one another more easily. Gideon found himself able to talk; he had not been able to talk to Jeff before. Now, this afternoon, they walked together. Jeff knew many people in the town, and he would introduce Gideon with pride. "This is my father." Gideon was used to change in people; he lived in a world of change; he could estimate the change in Jeff without being too puzzled by it.

They left the town and walked down a country road. The maples were red; the fields were parceled out, neat and square, and the land seemed to be old and thoughtful, the red barns, the clean white houses, the rock-speckled pastures.

"You like it here?" Gideon asked.

Jeff said, yes, he liked it here. Not just that the people were good to him; it went deeper than that. The people weren't saints; some of them called him a dirty nigger. A large number of people in town hated black men and always had. But all in all, the feeling was so different here than in the south.

Gideon nodded. That he could understand, although for him it would have been exile to live here. In a way he couldn't describe, this was a cold land.

"I study hard," Jeff said.

"That's good." And then, a while later, Gideon asked him, "Have you thought much about what you want to do—afterward?"

"I still want to be a doctor," Jeff said.

They came over the brow of a hill, and the sun was setting beneath them. A farmer was nudging his cows out of pasture, his dog yapping excitedly.

"We'd better turn back," Gideon said.

They walked slowly and Jeff tried to put things into words. Gideon stayed silent. "We're new people," Jeff said. "You know what I mean?" Gideon nodded. "I mean, white boy does what he wants to or what's set out for him; he don't have to reckon careful with service—"

Again, Gideon nodded.

"I get to thinking," Jeff went on, "here I am up here, how come? Marcus, Carry Lincoln, all the others, they don't come up here. In a way, I got special luck. So I figure it to be some service, something I go back with and say, See here, I got all this, I bring it back. Man's sick, I can make him better, maybe."

Gideon said, "Reverend Smith, he'd like you to be a preacher. That could be likened to a service."

"Maybe," Jeff agreed. "But Brother Peter, he's a mighty fine preacher, I think. Preaching ain't a science. Reverend Smith, he's a good man, a fine man, but that's not for me."

Gideon told him about Emery, about the dispensary, about Emery's offer and how a colored man might become a doctor at the University of Edinburgh. Jeff listened, tight, eager, anxious. Gideon painted both sides of the picture. Emery might change his mind. Two years might not be long enough to educate Jeff, and Emery might grow weary of the whole thing.

"Two years'll be enough," Jeff said. "I swear it will, I'll do any work he wants me to—just work myself down, anything. I'll sweep and clean that place of his out so fine it'll shine like gold, sure enough, father, I swear I will. It ain't no trouble for me. They say I'm the strongest boy here in town. Old Mr. Jarvis' cart was in the ditch, I lifted it out all myself, sure enough. That white doctor won't wear me down; I'll work all day long for him, he just lets me come there. I'll learn, too."

They walked on; already, Gideon was wondering how he'd tell Rachel. He wanted to put his arm around Jeff and hold him close and warm, but he couldn't. He felt a great and unreasonable pride. He felt—if only he could sit down with Jeff, talk out all the things there were to talk about, tell him all he might tell him. Jeff said, suddenly:

"You'll let me do it, won't you, please?"

"I'll let you do it," Gideon agreed.

It was almost dark now, and they hurried back to the manse. Jeff was buoyant, exhuberant; Gideon had to take long strides to keep by his side.

Before Gideon left, he said to his son, "Jeff, boy, you and me, both of us coming out of the dark old days and remembering, we got an idea about distance being a lonely thing, calculating how far a man can walk in a day. But that's not right; a few days, Jeff, and you're here or down there in Carolina. If you want me to come to you, I'll come—you want to go home, just don't fear, write to me and I'll send you money to go home."

He gave Jeff the few presents he had for him. They shook hands—and then Gideon kissed his son, the first time in years.

When Gideon came home to Carwell, a man who had accomplished a great deal, the impossible in one sense, this was the first thing he heard about. They told him about it even as he was saying his hellos, lifting Jenny up in his arms, and then seeing beyond her the few blackened sticks that were left of the barns, and among the homes two gaunt chimneys that were left of shacks. They were silent and unsmiling and troubled, and Rachel clung to him.

"Where's Marcus?" he cried.

But Marcus was all right, crowding through to him. "Well, what is it?" he demanded. "When did it happen? How?" He had that strange, almost mystical sensation of death, and he looked around to see whether a face was missing. Marion Jefferson's arm was bandaged. Hannibal Washington's wife, Ada, held her new baby, born while he was gone in her arms. Life and death went on together.

"Well, what happened?" he demanded.

Then Andrew Sherman's wife, Lucy, began to cry, Andrew calming her, petting her, "There, Lucy, now—" and Gideon realized that her son, Jackey, nine years old, such a pride to her for his light brown skin, his unearthly beauty that was a product of the blood of two of South Carolina's "best families," was gone. He looked at Brother Peter who said quietly, "The Lord givith, the Lord takith away."

"How was it?" Gideon asked.

Brother Peter told him; sometimes, the others filled in.

One saw one part of it; others saw another part of it. It happened four days after he had gone—something they had heard about but never seen before in the vicinity of Carwell. About nine o'clock in the evening, they were coming from the vespers, which Brother Peter had held in the barn, there being a chill in the air. That night, his text had been from *Psalms*, 100, he couldn't forget, "Make a joyful noise unto the Lord, all ye lands. Serve the Lord with gladness." They came out of the barn and didn't go home immediately, but stood around in little clusters for a while, as people do after church services. Then they saw it, on the hillock beyond the west pastures, a giant burning cross, something that flared into light all in a moment, one of the women screaming out and attracting the attention of the others.

Others of the women screamed and some of the children became sick with terror. Yes, Gideon could understand that, there being nothing but the soft peace of sunset first and then the grim sudden outline of the burning cross. Yet the men managed to calm the women and children soon enough. Brother Peter said, very matter of factly, that the sign of the holy cross, whether in blood or fire, could work evil to no man. Some of them took comfort from that; others, having heard of a thing called the Ku Klux Klan, tightened their lips but kept their knowledge inside their heads. The people stood around until the cross had burned itself out, and then went home to their houses, many of them still considerably upset.

"Then," Hannibal Washington told Gideon, "I figured that something to look about, crosses don't burn in air without someone to light them up, no sir. Seem there something mighty strange, and I tell Trooper, you and me, we going to look at that piece of hill."

Taking their rifles, he and Trooper circled the pasture and cut up in back of the hill. No one was there, but as they had expected, there was a charred cross made of two pieces of blackjack pine. A strong smell of kerosene filled the air and there were wisps of hay on the ground. It was not difficult for them to surmise what had happened. Someone had set up the cross, bound it up and down with hay, soaked it with kerosene, and then set flame to it. It was the sort of childish, terroristic, imbecilic thing they had heard rumors of; and being that, it puzzled and disturbed them more than any real menace would have.

When they came back, the men were waiting up for them. Hannibal Washington reported what they had found. Allenby said, "We haven't had our share of the scum and trash of the south here at Carwell." About that time, Abner Lait arrived with the Carson brothers, Frank and Leslie, all of them armed, calling out, "Hello—hello, there," as they came through the darkness. They had seen the cross from their places and had come over to find out just what it was about.

"Probably ain't nothing," Hannibal Washington said.

"Or maybe that Klan. Or maybe some fool folks here in the neighborhood."

"Don't know that any folks round about here would do a damnfool thing like that," Abner Lait said. After that, there was much talk and much discussion about what should be done. Actually, there was nothing to be done. They wanted to know whether Gideon could see that, telling him the tale. What could be done in the face of such nonsense? Someone suggested a guard, and someone else, quite rightly, said that they were law-abiding folk living in a civilized land. They couldn't be setting guards every night.

"You can see that, Gideon?" Brother Peter said uncertainly now.

"You were right," Gideon nodded. "What happened then?"

Well, they went to bed, later than usual, but finally all of them slept. When the thing happened, it must have been long after midnight. Each had the same story to tell now, of being awakened by the thunder of hoofs. Some of the women, screaming, woke out of nightmares; some of the men, frightened, stayed in bed. Hannibal Washington, Andrew Sherman, Ferdinand Lincoln, and Trooper had all left loaded rifles near their beds, and when they heard the hoofs they seized the guns and ran outside. So did Brother Peter, Allenby, and a dozen more of the men, but none of those were armed. All of them reported the same sequence of events—mounted men in white shrouds, twelve of them, armed, although they did not notice that at first. At least half of the men carried pitch-soaked torches, and by the time the men emerged the old, dry barn was already on fire, the hay hissing and giving out long tongues of flame. The cows and the mules were screaming with terror. Trooper admitted to firing first; he said that when he heard the mules screaming, he shot at one of the white-shrouded men without thinking, but he was certain, and so were the others, that he hit nothing—he had just fired in red anger. At that point, perhaps because of the shot, the white-shrouded men wheeled their horses, tossed the torches they had left at the shacks, fired a volley of shots at the people, and rode off.

"You must understand, Gideon," Allenby said now, "the sort of cowardly scum they were. The one shot sent them away. With all their white shirts, their dirty night raiding, their burning crosses, they were afraid once they knew we were armed. They scampered off like rabbits, and it wasn't until a while later that we noticed Jackey Sherman stretched out in the dark with a bullet between his eyes. One of the wild shots they fired—we were trying to put out the fire, save the stock, and the child didn't make a sound, he couldn't, poor thing."

Lucy Sherman began to sob again. Brother Peter told Gideon what was left to tell. The dead child took the heart out of their fire fighting; they saved the stock, but the barns and two of the shacks burned to the ground. The fire brought Abner Lait, Fred McHugh, his son, Jake Sutter, and the Carson brothers. Hannibal told how Abner Lait looked at the dead child and cursed the way they had never heard a man curse before. "You see, Gideon," he explained, "that take away what we been thinking, God help us, we been thinking any white men, maybe them. Then they come and we know it ain't them. Can't bring back child's life, but that help."

"And what have you done about it?" Gideon demanded, his voice so even and bitter that it seemed like another man speaking.

Allenby said, "What was there to do, Gideon? The next day, Abner Lait took his mule and rode off to town. We heard afterwards that he demanded something from the sheriff—and the sheriff just laughed at him. You know a man called Jason Hugar, he used to run slaves in the old days?"

"I know him."

"Well, Abner heard talk that he was the local Klan leader. Abner accused him, and they say he called Abner a dirty nigger lover. They had a fight, and the story goes that Abner half killed him. There was a mob, and Abner pulled his gun and said, yes, who would be first? Charley Kent, who was in Abner's company in the war stood by him, and then Abner got on his mule and came back. The next day, Hannibal hitched up the cart, and we both went to Columbia and spoke to Major Shelton there."

"And what did Shelton say?"

"He said that measures would be taken. That's an expression, Gideon—measures will be taken."

In Columbia, Major Shelton said the same to Gideon, "You can rest assured that proper measures are being taken." Shelton was a tall, hard, narrow-eyed man, nine years out of West Point, young enough to feel resentful of a fate that kept him here in the south, miles from anywhere, a police command that earned him bitterness from the people he respected and sympathy only from those he despised.

"What are those proper measures?" Gideon demanded.

"Military measures which I am neither inclined nor obliged to discuss with you. Your complaint was filed; action is being taken."

"And meanwhile, a dead child stays dead, and it ends there."

"No, of course it doesn't end there," Shelton said impatiently. "Don't try to put words in my mouth, Mr. Jackson. As I understand the case, it was purely accidental that the child was killed. Nevertheless, we are doing all we can to apprehend the criminals."

"Accidental!" Gideon said. "Accidental that those white-robed bandits burned the cross, raided our village, set the barns on fire, barns which are not ours, Major Shelton, but at that moment the property of the Government of the United States. What kind of an accident was that?"

"I'm sorry—"

"Mighty sorry, I guess. Have you looked into Klan organization hereabout? Investigated and questioned men like Jason Hugar? Have you done that?"

"Don't shout at me, Jackson? I'm not going to run in circles for every nigger who comes in here, screaming for protection!"

Gideon said evenly, "Look, sir. I am not losing my temper, I will not. I am not asking for anything, I talk about our right. Congress of this here country provided military protection for this district until civil law established. Either you provide that protection, or we will. I fought in the war too; I was master sergeant with the Black Fifty-Fourth Massachusetts—no, we was not a ditch-digging, wall-building nigger work battalion; we was free niggers and escaped slaves from this state and we fought nine separate battles, and eight of every ten men in our regiment was a casualty. Do you remember how we attacked Fort Wagner, leaving on the works four hundred dead from our regiment and our Colonel Shaw among them, and the rebels cut up his body and threw him in a mass grave with the niggers, because he, a white gentleman, a saintly white gentleman led a regiment of niggers? And do you remember our song—if you fought in this state, you heard men sing, *The gates of heaven opened wide for Colonel Shaw*. I don't like to talk about them things; they gone and in the past, the bad past. But I say, if you don't provide that protection, we will provide it ourselves."

His voice hard, Major Shelton said, "I will put down any disturbance, whether originated by whites or blacks."

"And we will protect ourselves," Gideon said.

Afterwards, back at Carwell, Gideon called a meeting of all the men, black and white together, and told them:

"You know what came of my trip to the north. Isaac Went, a Boston banker, gave me a draft of fifteen thousand dollars on him. We are going to buy the land—and we are going to keep the land. This evil thing rising up here will oppose us. I propose that we stand for our rights, that we organize our own militia, that we drill once each week until the need for that goes."

There was a good deal of discussion. Frank Carson said, matter-of-factly, that he did not like the idea of drilling under a nigger. He had ridden with Stuart, and he was uneasy about this whole business. Gideon proposed Fred McHugh, who had been a non-commissioned officer through the war, as drill-master. It was voted, and he accepted. In turn, he chose Hannibal Washington and Abner Lait to help him. Allenby questioned the legality of the matter, but Gideon pointed out that they were merely exercising their Constitutional right to bear arms; that they had borne arms, all of them since the war, and that their organized drilling would merely serve notice to night-shirted gangs that they were not fair picking. To a degree, he was right, for after that a long time passed before the Klan again rode in the vicinity of Carwell.

Ellen Jones, the blind girl, asked Gideon about Jeff, and Gideon told her how it would be, the time with Dr. Emery, the chance that Jeff would go to Edinburgh. Edinburgh, across the world and at the beginning of nowhere. Gideon realized now that the girl loved Jeff; why was he shut to so many things? She said, "Maybe five years," and there was a tone in her voice that made an end of everything. "Maybe," Gideon agreed, and then tried to make it as gentle for her as he could, but thinking to himself all the time, why did Jeff let it go on? He thought so much and often of Jeff now, when he saw the way the other boys skylarked with the girls, when he saw Marcus shooting up like a reed.

Ellen would come and sit with Rachel. They had a lot to talk about. Rachel had said little to Gideon about Jeff. "It is best for him, no doubting it," Gideon had said. Then Rachel accepted that. Sometimes Gideon would take hold of himself, realized that a tide of things was carrying him farther and farther from Rachel, and try to be extra gentle, extra sweet, show her many little attentions. She would say, "Gideon, Gideon, don't pay no worry to me."

"I love you, Rachel honey."

But he even said it differently now; the change in him was with his speech, his bearing, his thoughts, his actions. When Rachel realized that some of the other women were talking about her and Gideon, she made more of a point than ever of Gideon's accomplishments. She could tell the other women that there was no one in the world like Gideon, fan their jealousy, their admiration or envy; but she couldn't tell it to herself in the same terms. She would wake at night and lie stiff and still by Gideon's side for hours. Once, something told him she was up, and he asked her:

"What is it, honey child?"

"Nothing."

"Then sleep."

After a while, she said, "Jeff's gone. God, I want another baby."

"We got two fine boys and a girl," Gideon said.

"I want a baby. I'm empty inside."

"Just like the good God plans it," Gideon whispered. "Child comes or it doesn't—you can't help that."

"You don't believe in God," Rachel said.

"Honey—honey."

"Child comes to them that have love."

Gideon said, "I love you, baby, believe me, with all my heart."

"Jeff's gone," Rachel said miserably. "He gone, that's all."

It was decided that Abner Lait, Gideon, and James Allenby would appear at the auction to buy the land. The men delegated to Gideon their power of attorney, and Daniel Greene, a Yankee lawyer who had recently set up in Columbia procured Gideon a tracing of the land holding. During all the time that was left, they went over the tracing, dividing it and subdividing it. They had no clear idea about how the government surveyors would apportion the land into thousand-acre lots, but they tried to provide for all eventualities. For a whole week, Gideon, together with Abner and Frank Carson, roamed over the twenty-two thousand acres of Carwell land. They found places they had not known the existence of. Frank Carson pointed out that in one spot, where the creek dropped a full seven feet, a waterwheel could be cheaply built and they could grind their own hominy. They found a fine stand of sycamore, high and leafy, a good place for living. When Abner Lait, pointing to a seven-hundred-acre stretch of swamp, said that was something they would do well to stay away from, Gideon asked closer investigation. The swamp trees were second growth and would make easy clearing; the ground was black muck, wonderfully fertile, oozing decay. "Two fine crops of rice a year," Gideon said. "No man'll ever starve if he has a piece of rice paddy." Gideon, full of dreams now, showed how a causeway through the swamp would bring them within four miles of the railroad. Frank Carson, straining the muck through his fingers, grinned and said, "Going to build me a fine house, right up there on the sycamore hillock. Set in rice and get me a clean cash crop instead of that goddamn cotton. Goddamn, I never seen a man to get no happiness out of cotton." "I'll plant cotton," Gideon said. "This is going to be a hungry country for cotton. I'm going to watch the bolls break and say, they're my own." "Never seen lowland without malaria," Abner said.

They went on; they walked through miles of piney woods. They emerged on hillocks, with land sweeping below them like a never-ending ocean. Frank Carson, regarding it strangely, said in a quiet voice, "I seen the land before, but never like this. I'm seeing it the way my granddaddy must have done, just coming out here slow and easy, a gun over one shoulder and a fry over the other."

That way, in the time that was left, they saw all the land they could pace over. The crops were being harvested; it was a good year that was ebbing out in this fall of 1868. The yellow ears of corn were stacked in the temporary cribs that had been built; a rough shed housed their fodder and stock. There was a market for the cotton the white men put in, and one night the people heard the shrill whistle of the first through freight train.

On the twenty-second of October, Gideon, Abner Lait, and James Allenby stabled their cart in Columbia and joined the crowd for the big public auction. Daniel Greene, who had been hired to handle their bids, waved to Gideon as he darted in and out of the crowd; he wore a checked suit, a white straw hat, and a fat black cigar poked from a corner of his mouth. "See you, Jackson, see you!" His pockets were full of tracings and titles.

People had come in from all over the state for the auction. Recently, it had rained, and the muddy streets of the state capital were crowded with carts, carriages, and saddle-horses. The auctioneer's pulpit had been set up on the steps of the Capitol, a huge, half-completed stone pile that stood on a hilltop and overlooked the countryside for miles in every direction. On improvised billboards, maps of the tax-for-feited holdings were posted, with the section-cuttings marked out in bright crayon lines. In the packed crowds around them were people of every description, Charleston gentlemen, Negro fieldhands, Yankee speculators, up-country farmers, plantation owners from as far as New Orleans and Texas; there were representatives of Morgan and representatives of the Unitarian Church, and there were representatives of two English land companies. One hundred and sixteen thousand acres were going on sale.

Gideon, his sleeve plucked, turned and looking into the level, slightly-smiling eyes of Stephan Holms. Casual, at his ease, gently-polite, Holms was gracious as Gideon introduced Abner Lait and James Allenby.

"Here to buy, Gideon?" Holms asked him.

"That's right."

"Then we're both on the same mission. I'm representing Dudley Carwell, Colonel Fenton, and to a degree, myself."

"Are you interested in the Carwell place?" Gideon asked, as offhandedly as he could.

"Possibly—or any other piece as good. Dudley doesn't want the house, it always has been a white elephant. I heard you were negotiating a loan in Charleston?"

"I made the loan in Boston," Gideon said.

"Did you? Well, let's try not to bid against one an-other—enough strangers for that. Wasn't it your folks, Gideon, that had some trouble recently with—"

"With the Klan," Gideon said.

"Scum and damn white trash," Holms said. "Glad to have met you, Gideon—and you, sir, and you."

When he had walked on, Lait remarked, "That kind I know, Gideon. Was he an officer?"

"I think so."

"A mighty fine man. How many niggers did he have in the old days? I reckon he'd put a knife in his mother's back."

A little while later, the auction started, and from there on, for Gideon and his two friends as well as for most of the others in the crowd, all was hopeless confusion, two auctioneers spelling each other, screaming out, "Block four, Chipden, twenty-two, north and south, two dollars government minimum, eight hundred, two dollars, two dollars, two dollars, going, going, going, up to three, three dollars ten cents, I got fifteen cents, fifteen cents—" Greene, breathless, his cigar bent and lifeless, found Gideon and said, "Look at this tracing! I got the section breakdown, twenty-three blocks, slightly less than a thousand acres each! The house goes separate with two hundred acres! Government minimum is dollar an acre!"

Gideon, Lait, and Allenby pulled out of the crowd and peered at the tracing. "Pick three," Greene said, "and then successive alternates through the rest."

"How do you mean?"

"Well, the best land first. I mark that A1." They pointed out the three most desirable sections. "Now from there on, in case we lose out at first—" Gideon and Abner, weighing pros and cons quickly, numbered the remaining twenty blocks. "Top price five dollars?"

"Five dollars," Gideon nodded. "But get it cheaper if you can."

"The best," Greene nodded, plunging back into the crowd. The voice of the auctioneer droned on. From all over, men shouted their bids. Land agents fought their way to the platform. The bidding had started at nine o'clock in the morning; by noon, it was still going on, and the Carwell place had not yet come up. Then, at two o'clock, the first Carwell section was put on the block. Gideon saw Greene close to the pulpit, shouting his bids, but Gideon could not keep pace with what was going on. But by five, it was over; the lawyer, exhausted, crumpled but a triumphant grin on his face, pushed out of the crowd, "Got them!"

"Which ones?"

"Two of them A1." The lawyer spread the battered tracing on the board walk, knelt down, Gideon, Abner, and Allenby grouped over him. "These two, four dollars straight." Lait whooped with joy, leaping up and down, slapping his thighs. "God damn, God damn, Gideon! Look at that! That's the hill with the sycamores! That's them flats, meaty, like a gal's ass!" Gideon got down on his knees next to Greene, grinning happily. "Where's the third?"

"Your number four alternate—funny, the bidding on that went up to five. You sure you know these places?"

"Hell, yes, we know them!" Abner said. "All right—that's good piece, damn good piece."

"Seven thousand three hundred for the first two pieces— that's a bargain, Gideon, a damn good bargain, that's giving away the land. Four thousand, seven hundred and fifty dollars for number three. You got land there. Near three thousand acres—"

They came home triumphantly, Old James Allenby driving the mules, Gideon and Abner singing drunkenly, "Green grow the lilacs, so wet with the dew, I'm lonely, my darling, and thinking of you." Abner had invested two dollars in a jug of corn, and he and Gideon had polished it down over the whole long ride from Columbia. Gideon wasn't a good drinker; he drank rarely and gingerly. Three quarters of the jug had gone into Abner, the rest into Gideon, and they had achieved the same state of glory. Gideon roared out to the people, "We are tomorrow, we are, sure enough!" Allenby told the story of what had happened. Rachel, laughing at Gideon, put him to bed; he dragged her down with him, while she protested, "Gideon, have some shame." But it was like old times, Gideon laughing and singing out in his deep bass voice, until at last he fell asleep.

The next day, Brother Peter held a special meeting. As he told Gideon, "Forget the Lord God, brother, be not humble but brazen and loud, then sure enough the Lord God he going to forget you." And his voice more gentle, "Gideon, you going to lead the people, then you got a dispensation, and you got to know that. Know it humbly, Gideon. When you do good, you do good on account the people put their trust in you. Long time back, I put my trust in you. Don't disappoint me, Gideon. You a knowing man, climbing high up a ladder. Look down, Gideon, just look down."

"I'm sorry," Gideon said. "Believe me, Brother Peter, I'm sorry."

"Sure, Gideon, you sorry, you got a big heart. But hear me, Gideon, look inside yourself and find God. Find God and give him your trust."

"Your way is your way," Gideon said softly. "Mine is mine. Brother Peter, there's no man in this world I reverence more than you, believe me."

"I got to believe you, Gideon," Brother Peter said softly. At the meeting, he said, "My text is from Numbers, We came into the land whither Thou sentest us, and surely it flowed with milk and honey; and this is the fruit of it." He preached his sermon slowly and pointedly; in a place of the landless, they had land. Theirs was the mercy and a sign too, for wherever a black man bought a piece of land, a thousand eyes would be upon him. "Use it well," Brother Peter said.

After the meeting, the dividing of the land began. It had to be done immediately if they were to move from here, take over their pieces, and build some sort of shelter against the winter. Gideon had thought it would be difficult, but not so difficult as this, men fighting, arguing, protesting, weighing each one's piece against the others', jealous, name-calling, the white hunching together against the black, the black instinctively putting shoulder to shoulder against the white, until at last Gideon roared:

"Stop it—damn you all for fools! We've come this far already and now you're ready to cut each other's throats. We going to pick one man, vote for him, and let him portion out the land. Now who's it going to be?"

They wanted Gideon, but he refused. They nominated Allenby and Brother Peter, and in the voting, Brother Peter won by three votes. Trooper asked him, "Who going to pick your land?" and Brother Peter answered, "Whatever's left—it don't matter." Then they looked at each other shame-facedly, grinning sheepishly. It went better after that.

In the way of things, it was natural and easy that this should be the time for voting again and that they should not contemplate the thousand matters that had wrought a change in them. A year ago, they had walked in to the voting with their guns, but things were different now. The land had changed; the people had changed; the future overtook them, and they were part of it now. They went into town together early on the first Tuesday in November, black men and white men together. There was a nip of coming winter in the air. Dead leaves scurried across the dusty road. The black men were going to vote Republican, solid, but Abner Lait said that when all was said and done, he thought he'd vote Democrat. His daddy had; his granddaddy had; he didn't like to upset a thing like that. Yet all of them, together, walked into town for the voting.

PART TWO

The Fighting

CHAPTER EIGHT

How Gideon Jackson Went to See a Tired Man

GIDEON TOOK OUT HIS WATCH AND LOOKED AT IT. IT WAS twenty minutes to three, and he had been waiting since two o'clock. He had hoped to have his appointment and be at the station by five-sixteen, to meet Jeff, who was coming down from New York. Well, likely enough, he would still make the station in time to meet Jeff. Actually, he had very little to say here and now, and what he said, he was sure, would not be to too much effect.

Outside, on this bleak February day, it was snowing, Washington snow, large wet flakes that folded against the window panes and then dissolved into globs of cold moisture that wriggled down the glass. Gideon relaxed into the leather chair and folded his hands in his lap. At this moment, he felt, he would like to sleep, a long, long sleep such as he had not known for many months—just to sleep and be free of thinking for a time, and then to wake up, fresh and eager. But how eager could a man be at forty-five? Gideon shook his head and smiled and began to think about Jeff; it was better to think of Jeff than to think about other things; Jeff was reality. Jeff would swing off the train and come striding toward him. Or would he? Perhaps he would just stand, uncertainly, and look at Gideon, and perhaps there would be nothing at all between them. But that was impossible. Seven years do not make such a difference. But seven years in Edinburgh, seven years during which a frightened black boy becomes a doctor of medicine; seven such years are something to be considered.

Gideon, recalling that day when Dr. Emery put the matter up to him, smiled wryly. What had Emery been thinking?

What, indeed, had he said to Dr. Emery? Something about money—did it cost much money? That was so long ago—eight years? Nine years? He would have liked to have known Emery better, to have known Went better; now they were both of them dead. He recreated the picture of himself standing in the dispensary, talking with Emery, watching the shivering, naked rickets-stricken child, and that way memory after memory came back, until the flow of pictures was dissolved by the striking of a tall grandfather clock in the corner, one, two, three. He must have been sleeping. The secretary, standing in front of him, said:

"The president will see you now, Mr. Jackson."

Gideon rose, blinked his eyes, and followed the secretary to the office. Grant was sitting behind his desk, hunched, tired, red-eyed, a man defeated and lost and regarding the long, empty years before him without hope and without pleasure. He nodded and said:

"Sit down, Gideon," and then told his secretary, "I don't want to be interrupted."

"If Senator Gordon—"

"Tell him to go to hell! I won't talk to him, do you understand? I don't want to be interrupted!" The door closed behind the secretary. The president said to Gideon, "Do you want a cigar? No—I forgot, you don't smoke. You don't mind if I do?" He bit off the end of his cigar, struck a match, puffed long and deeply. Gideon watched him, but the president avoided his look. Age had come suddenly and ruthlessly on Ulysses Simpson Grant; his eyes were sunken, his beard streaked with gray. Even his smoking was in short, jagged, nervous motions. When he spoke, he barked at Gideon:

"I know what you're going to say."

"Then why did you let me come here and say it?" Gideon asked gently.

"Why?" Grant looked at him with sudden bewilderment, and Gideon felt a complete and understanding pity for this beaten, helpless man, this man who was understood by so few, loved by so few, used by so many, hated by so many, despised by so many, this man who by fate and circumstance had been elevated to a remote and hopeless glory.

"Why come here?" Grant said dully.

"Because you are still president of these United States," Gideon answered carefully. "Because you are my friend and I am yours—"

"So I have friends?"

"And because," Gideon went on, "when all is said and done, this is your country and you love it as few men I know do. You love it in a way that I understand, in a manner that is beyond the conception of the cheating, lying, small men who have done their best to wreck it. Do you remember Everett Hale's story, *The Man Without a Country?* Do you remember how Philip Nolan came to love and understand his native land?"

Grant smiled ruefully. "Are you going to preach me a sermon, Gideon?"

"No—I'm going to talk to you about this land. I'm going to talk because it's the last chance I'll have to talk to a president of the United States. I've tried for two weeks to see you—"

"I was busy, Gideon."

"You were busy, Mr. President," Gideon said. "That is all, you were busy. God help us, we have so many pat phrases, busy, occupied, a thousand things to do. Why aren't our enemies busy? Why?"

"I've heard all that," Grant said coldly.

"And you don't want to hear it again. At this time, you'd like me to go. Well, perhaps I can put it differently. Leaving aside what the newspapers have said and what the histories will say of the eight years during which you were president, what is the truth?"

"Say it—I was used!" Grant growled.

"I won't say that. My God, Mr. President, this is—well it's our country; let's use the schoolboy phrases, nothing else will do now. This is our native land. We fought for this. We lived for this, what men died at Gettysburg for. We don't exist apart from it, or from each other. It is all bound together, making one. What is a country?" Gideon hesitated, then went on, "What is the United States of America? Is it a dream, an ideal, a piece of paper called the Constitution, a coalition? Promoters? Grafters? Robber barons? Is it Morgan or Jay Gould or Senator Gordon? Or is it a man standing out in the street and looking at the White House?" Now Gideon spoke more haltingly, "Is it the Episcopal Church or the Congregational Church? Is it a prayer or a fool's fancy or fifty million men? It it Congress? All the years I sat in Congress I thought of that, watching small men or great men, listening to fools like Peterson and heroes like Sumner. Or is it you and me, and bound into us, and inseparable from us—because what we are is America, what we have, what we've done, what we have dreamed!"

Grant's cigar had gone out. Clenched between his stubby fingers, it made a focus for his eyes. Slowly, automatically, he shook his head. "I'm through, Gideon."

"You're president."

"For a few more days—"

"For long enough to hit them!"

Grant said wearily, "But I don't know, Gideon. I'm tired. I'm finished. I want to go home and rest. I've been dragged through sewers. I want to go home and forget."

"You won't forget," Gideon said.

"Maybe. I'm no Solomon; I'm no God of judgment. I didn't ask for this. I won battles because I wasn't afraid to pay the price. Did that make me a president? Did that fit me to play their dirty, rotten game of politics?"

"There are still battles," Gideon said.

"When you don't know the enemy? When you don't know who fights on your own side?"

"And when Hayes slides into that chair where you're sitting, his legs knee-deep in blood, will you rest easy?"

"God damn it, Gideon, where are your facts? Hayes is a Republican; so am I; so are you. He was legally elected president. I am sick of the calamity howlers. Life will go on; so will this country—"

"All right," Gideon said, and rose.

"Are you going?"

"Yes."

"What were you going to say?"

"Why bother? It won't matter."

"God damn you, say it!" Grant growled. "Say it and get it done!"

"Do you want to hear it?"

"Stop being a prima donna and say it."

"All right," Gideon nodded. "There was a deal."

"Where is your proof?"

"I have the proof, sir," Gideon said quietly. "Will you listen to me for a while?"

"I've been listening." Grant lit his cigar. Gideon sat down again. The clock on Grant's desk showed a quarter of four. "I'll start a while back," Gideon began. Outside, it still snowed, fat, lazy white flakes that melted on the window panes. It was growing dark in the president's office. The single lamp on his desk threw a circle of yellow light, and as the darkness increased his face became more tired, more indistinguishable. The smoke from his cigar drifted into the light, twisting, turning, running up the chimney of the lamp.

"You remember the South Carolina Convention?" Gideon said. "That was nine years ago."

"I remember."

"In a way of speaking, that began the reconstruction. I served on the Convention. Two years later, I served a term in the State Senate, and five years ago I came to Congress. In the light of that, I think I can speak with some knowledge of what happened. The word *reconstruction*, which they use for all that happened in the south since 1868, is too pat. It is meaningless. It was not essentially a problem of reconstruction, not even a problem of readmission of the rebel states into the Union. All this I have said in the House; I have said it over and over, these five years past. I am saying it now, I suppose, for the record—for I think that this is the last time for a long while to come that a Negro representative of his people will sit in the office of the president of the United States."

Grant knocked the ashes off his cigar; now his face was lost in the shadow.

"What is reconstruction? What has it been? What has it meant? Why has it been destroyed? I ask you because you're the only man in the country who can bring it back to life—

and doing so, save this country untold suffering and misery in the future."

"Go on, Gideon," Grant said.

"Reconstruction was the beginning of the new and the death of the old. The plantation slave system, a feudal thing, abhorrent to the nature of this country, only a few years ago set out to rule and conquer this nation. It had to be destroyed or it would destroy democracy. It was destroyed, and in the course of that destruction my people were freed. Do you want me to go on?"

"Go on," Grant said.

"Very well. Out of that terrible war came reconstruction—essentially a test for democracy, a test of whether freed Negroes and freed whites—for the poor white was as much a slave before the war as the black—could live and work and build together. I say that test was taken and proven, that democracy worked in the south—with all its faults, its blunders, its boasting extravagances, its fools and loud-mouths—with all that, it worked! For the first time in the history of this nation, black men and white men together built a democracy in the south. You have the proof, the schools, the farms, the just courts, a whole literate, eager generation. But this was not done easily and never done completely; the planters organized their army, white-shirted scum by the thousands. They haven't given up. You yourself, Mr. President, said that only the presence of Union troops in the south preserves order. I tell you, the day Rutherford B. Hayes takes office, those troops will be withdrawn—and the Klan will strike. In one form or another, it will strike everywhere, and there will be terror such as this land never knew, murder and destruction and burning and looting, until every vestige of that democracy we built is destroyed. We will be put back a hundred years, and for generations to come men will suffer and die—"

Grant's voice came wearily, as from a great distance. "Even if I accepted what you say, Gideon, and I don't accept it, what is the alternative? To keep troops in the south forever?"

"Not forever. But for ten years more—to give us a chance to bring to manhood a whole new generation, black men and white men who have learned to work together, to stand together. Then no force on earth will take away from us what we have built."

"I don't accept that, Gideon. I don't accept your accusation of Hayes. I don't accept your fanciful notion of the power of the Klan. This is 1877."

"You wanted proof," Gideon said. "I have the proof." He took some papers out of his pocket, spread them on the desk in the lamplight. "Here are the statistics of the election. The popular vote for Tilden is 4,300,000, and Hayes' popular vote is 4,036,000. That is the first lie; I say that half a million Negroes and whites in the south who voted the Republican ticket had their votes destroyed, miscounted, tampered with. No, I can't prove that; I'll prove other things later. Actually, it does not matter; these two men, Tilden and Hayes, are both corrupt, sad commentaries on what our presidency has sunk to. They are Tweedlededum and Tweedledee, cut out of the same cloth."

"So far," Grant said, "you are making groundless accusations. I won't listen to much more of that, Gideon."

"You said you would listen. I'll give you the proof; first let me establish my facts. Even our Congress, which fears democracy and the people more than anything on earth, will let me establish my facts when I rise to speak. I'll be quick with it. My boy, whom I haven't seen for a long while, is coming in on the five-sixteen train from New York; I assure you I'll be through before then."

The room was quite dark now outside of the circle of yellow light. "Go on," Grant said.

"We come to the electoral votes, 184 for Tilden, the Democrat, for Hayes, the Republican 166 undisputed votes. With one more vote, Tilden could be president, but Hayes claimed South Carolina, Louisiana and Florida, enough to give him the 185 that would make him president. And Hayes was right—those votes belonged to him; as I said, they were tampered with, destroyed. What was the situation? A Democratic House, a Republican Senate, one to give the election to Tilden, the other to Hayes, and the whole country screaming of the second Civil War, of a southern march on Washington. Mr. President, did you believe that? Did you believe there was a difference between these two corrupt men?'

Grant said, "God damn you, Gideon, I've listened to enough!"

"I come to the proof now, Mr. President. Let me give you the proof, and then I'll go. I think we are both through. As you said, you have only a few days to be president, and I have not too much time either."

"Go on," Grant muttered.

"Yes—evidently our southern Democrats knew that the two men were of a stripe. They threw Tilden aside; he would be too much trouble; they had risked a civil war once and they had failed; they were not prepared to risk it again. They made their deal with Hayes. He could have South Carolina, Florida, Louisiana—and to make the deal certain, Oregon, too. In return, he would give them a very small and inconsequential thing, control of South Carolina and Louisiana, and withdrawal of Union troops from the south. Such a small matter to stand between a man and the presidency, between the Republican party, Lincoln's party and power! Here is the proof, a record made by two of Mr. Hayes' friends, Stanley Matthews and Charles Foster. It gives the gist of certain talks they had with Senator John B. Gordon of Georgia and the Kentucky Congressman, Mr. J. Young Brown. This is an exact copy, made and brought to me by a colored servant of Mr. Foster; I will swear to that. I'll read it:

* " 'Referring to the conversation we had with you yesterday in which Governor Hayes' policy as to the status of certain southern states was discussed, we desire to say that we can assure you in the strongest possible manner of our great desire to have him adopt such a policy as will give the people of the States of South Carolina and Louisiana the right to control their own affairs in their own way, subject only to the Constitution of the United States and the laws made in pursuance thereof, and to say further that from an acquaintance with and knowledge of Governor Hayes and his views,

* This document may be found in Williams' *Life of Rutherford B. Hayes*, Vol. I, p. 533.

we have the most complete confidence that such will be the policy of his administration.'

"There it is, Mr. President."

A long silence then; and finally Grant asked tonelessly, "Why don't you bring it before the House?"

"Because I haven't the original, because while I am prepared to swear on a stack of Bibles that this is the truth, I cannot bring evidence; I cannot set the word of a poor old colored servant against that of the president elect of the United States. If I were to stand up in the House and say to them what I just said to you, ten of our cultured Bourbon members would be screaming that this damned, insolent, lying nigger be lynched."

"Why should I believe you?"

"Because the whole future of this country is at stake. Because when we fought our revolution, when we fought our civil war, we were moving down a proud and shining road, what my people call a hallelujah road. We were moving with all the good men who lived behind us, and we had our faces turned to God. Do you hear me, Mr. President? Now we're going to leave that road; from here on, we turn our face to darkness. For how long, Mr. President? How many shall have to die before we can call this a government of the people, by them and for them?"

"It's not as bad as that—" Grant began.

"But it is!"

Grant stood up, lifting himself from his chair with both hands, leaning over into the lamplight, staring at Gideon, and then pushing away from the table and striding angrily across the room.

"That's all?" Gideon asked.

"What can I do?" Grant demanded, whirling on him. "Even if your insane, fairy-tale of a story were true, what in God's name could I do?"

"Everything. You're still president. Give this to the people. Hold a press conference tomorrow; there are papers with guts enough to print this. Let Hayes prove the accusation false. Throw this whole rotten thing open and let the people look at it. They'll know what to do. We're not a bad people, here in America; we're not an ignorant people. We've moved the world before; we've done bad things, but we've done more good things. Go before Congress and demand the truth—"

Grant shook his head. "Gideon—"

"Are you afraid?" Gideon cried. "What have you to lose? Those who remember the days when you led them to victory, they'll support you. And the others—" Gideon's voice trailed away.

He gathered up the papers and put them in his pocket. "All right. I'll go now."

After Gideon had left, long after, Grant sat at his desk, face sunk in his hands, staring at the closed door.

It was late when Gideon got to the station. The train had already pulled in. On the station platform, he saw Jeff, a tall young man, broad, like a mirror of himself, standing between two carpet-bags with his hands in his pockets. It was not a question of memory, not a question of change; the two of them looked at each other and knew each other, and though each was many years older, each was more like the other. They approached and shook hands. Gideon swallowed; Jeff smiled slowly, letting one hand grasp his father's arm.

"You're bigger than I remember," he said.

"And you too," Gideon nodded.

"You recognized me."

"Yes, I'm glad you're back, Jeff."

"I'm glad to be back," Jeff said. Gideon bent for the bags. "I'll carry them," Jeff said.

"One apiece."

"All right," Jeff smiled, looking curiously at Gideon, measuring him from top to bottom, casually, but in such a way as to make Gideon feel that he was being appraised. They stood shoulder to shoulder, two large men, moving slowly, uncertainly, each trying after this long time to adjust his movements, his thoughts, his desires to the other. They walked down the length of the platform, through the station, and Jeff said, with a sense of guilt and omission, "How is mother?" "Fine," Gideon said. "We all get older." "You look no older," Jeff said. Gideon had a cab waiting for them; they climbed into it, filling the tight space with their long-limbed bodies. Snow flurried around like a white fisherman's net. "I thought of Washington as a warm place," Jeff said. "I've never been here before—" "No, you haven't," Gideon realized, thinking of all the years this sprawling, boastful city on the Potomac had been a part of his life. The horse set off with an easy clack, clack of shod hoofs. "I've had a small house here these past two years," Gideon said.

"Mother—"

"She tried it last year," Gideon said. "I think she's happier at Carwell."

"You still call it that, Carwell?"

"Carwell?" Gideon seemed a little puzzled. "Yes, we never thought of calling it anything else. Have you room?" The bags were tight against their knees.

"It's quite comfortable," Jeff said.

"You must be hungry?"

"I am, a little."

"We'll have dinner at home, just the two of us. I didn't ask anyone else."

Jeff wondered why his father said that.

The house Gideon had was a small, white-frame five-room building. A withered old Negro woman kept it clean and prepared his meals. Gideon called her Mother Joan. "Mother Joan," he said, "This is my son, Jeff." "That's a fine big boy, Mr. Jackson. You a proud man." "Mighty proud," Gideon said. They had a simple dinner, hot bean soup, and then chops, greens, and buttered grits. "These are the first grits in how long—?" Jeff smiled.

"You wouldn't have them in Scotland," Gideon remembered. Of course, he couldn't expect it all to come flooding out at once, the moment the two of them met; it would come bit by bit, as they broke down all the things between them. Seven years was a long time; they even spoke differently, Jeff's speech harder than Gideon's, with a curious foreign sound.

Jeff said, "I worked for a year with Dr. Kendrick. He had a grant dispensary at the mines. It was good experience— bad accidents, crushed arms or legs, burns, lacerations, and the household things too—croup, mumps, little things that are so difficult to get onto."

"White people?"

"I was the only Negro in the county. That makes a difference."

"There was no feeling?"

"Not the way it is here. I was a curiosity. They're not a complicated people, and their fears and suspicions were basic things. You could put your finger on them and clear them away."

They went into Gideon's study, a small, book-filled room that he also used as an office. They sat with their feet stretched out to the glowing coal grate, and they talked of many things. It was easier now; Jeff was able to say:

"You know, I'm terribly proud."

"Of what?"

"Your being in Congress. I don't know how to say it, but that's a wonderful thing."

Gideon's eyes were thoughtful. "It's a matter of circumstance. People are made. The things were present to make me into this or that, and those things operated."

Jeff asked him about the election, and slowly at first, and then with more passion, Gideon told him, traced the whole sequence of events in the last eight years, told how he had gone today to see the president. "And I've failed," Gideon said.

"Are you sure? Can a thing come to an end that way, suddenly, the way a bomb explodes? Do things happen that way?"

"Not suddenly," Gideon said. "This has been going on for a long time. More than eight years ago, the Klan raided our people at Carwell. That was a clumsy thing, a frightened thing. They burned the barns and killed one little boy. But they were beginning then, as far back as that. From the very first, they planned to destroy us. The war was hardly over before the same people who made it set about planning for the next war, a different one this time, armies that ride in the night, underground organization, intimidation, threats, terror. Now their preparation has been completed; they're ready."

"I can't believe it."

"If I could only think that I was wrong," Gideon said. "But I'm not wrong—"

"What are you going to do?"

"I don't know yet; I want to think about it. In any case, I'm going home. I want to be with them." Jeff nodded. "That's right for me, I think," Gideon pointed out. "But what is right for me is not necessarily right for you. Do you see, Jeff?"

"What are you driving at?"

"I'll be leaving in the next few days," Gideon said. "I don't want you to go back with me. There is no reason for you to come with me. If things are all right in the spring—"

"What on earth are you talking about?" Jeff wanted to know.

Gideon shook his head. "Easy, Jeff. Now you listen to me. There was a time when you'd listen to me." He stood up for a moment, rubbed his long-fingered hands together, leaned toward his son, and then sat back in his chair abruptly. He sat there silent, staring ahead of him, the glow from the fire picking out highlights on his long, high-ridged face. Jeff looked at him, noticing how the large, full mouth was set, how weary and red-rimmed the deep-sunk eyes were. The man was older, older than forty-five years, older than logic and reason. The broad shoulders that Jeff had so often seen as a child, bared to the hot sun, sweat-covered, immensely powerful, bound over as they were with layer upon layer of flat, hard muscle, were now bent and slack. The short, kinky hair that covered his head like a tight cap, was streaked through with grey. Jeff didn't know him; Jeff had never known him; a boy of fifteen is malleable clay. Nine years had stretched Jeff but broken nothing; he had learned, grown, expanded, been hurt and healed his hurt; he had found a God in science, and under a microscope a man's skin is not of a color but of many cells, wonderfully placed together.

All the world was reason. A man called Darwin had cleared away the haze that covered the uncounted ages beyond man. A broken leg was set in such and such a fashion, whether the skin that enveloped it was black or white. In a lonely cabin on the moors, he had delivered a child of a white woman, slapped it, and watched it scream with the wonderful agony of birth. The world was an understandable place, a planet twisting through nothingness, gently enveloped with a protective skin of atmosphere. Men were evil because they did not know, but a man who dedicated his life to knowing, in the scientific nature of the word, could have no fears. That was how it had been with him; but what had been with his father? He remembered the tall field-hand who set off for Charleston, a delegate walking to a convention, a crushed stovepipe hat on his head, a bright checked handkerchief hanging out of his pocket. Another man had come back, but what sort of twisting agony had made that second man? And what convulsions within Gideon Jackson made the third man, the fourth man?—the man of whom Dr. Emery had said, "That is greatness in the essential of the word, Jeff, remember. There are no scientific definitions. When you come to the end of logic, think about him." Jeff thought about him now, the man who sat in the State Senate of South Carolina, the man who served in the Congress of the United States and in answer to a Georgia representative made that statement that every child in the country knew:

"Yes, as the gentlemen from Georgia says, I was a slave only a short while past. And today, as a free man, I answer him in the Congress of this nation. That, gentlemen, is the American testament, my American testament. I need not indulge in patriotic sentiments. The fact that I stand here defines the country I serve better than any words a man could speak or write."

That statement Jeff saw reprinted in Scottish magazines; a member of parliament spoke it in Commons; over that statement, a fierce debate raged in the French Chamber for three hours; and in Germany, Hungary and Russia, underground revolutionary groups of workingmen had translated that statement, printed and circulated thousands of copies of it.

Now, looking at Gideon, Jeff felt a complex of pity, of pride and longing, a desire to come close to this man, his father, to understand him and be understood by him; yet a sense of himself as an individual, a man beyond Gideon, ahead of Gideon.

"I'll listen to you," he said. "Whatever I have to do, I'll still listen to you."

"I'm going back," Gideon explained, speaking slowly, softly, "because I belong there. The nature of all I am, Jeff, son, all I have been, is in my people. I come from them; I have my strength from them. It took me a long time to learn that; I have a gift; I could learn, I could talk, I could soak in things, but there was nothing in me that wasn't a part of them. I want to go back to them because that will give me the greatest happiness, and the nature of a man, Jeff, is to seek his happiness, whether in the small things he does or in the large ones.

"With you, it is different. You have been away for a long time. You have been schooled and trained, and today you are a doctor. A doctor is like a fine book; it has a use outside of the toil and effort that went into creating it. I have no use outside of the things that went into me; you have. No matter how bad things are, when the need comes, my people will find other Gideon Jacksons. With you, it is different. I can talk to you as a man; that makes me proud and happy. When I told President Grant today that I thought this was the last time in many years a black man would talk to the president, I was saying something I believed. I also believe there will be few black men trained as you are in the years to come. Stay here; you can live in this house. There will be enough broken bodies to heal. It would be waste if you came back with me."

When Gideon finished talking, they sat in silence for several minutes. Jeff knocked out his pipe, filled it again, took a coal from the fire with the tongs and dropped it onto the soft, fragrant tobacco. Gideon poured some wine. Looking about the room finally, Jeff said, "This is a nice room, a warm room. I should like to read some of the books."

Gideon nodded.

"I always think of reading books tomorrow, when there's time. Somehow, there's never time today."

"There's time," Gideon said.

"Tell me," Jeff asked him. "If it happens, the way you think it might happen, would you fight?"

"I don't know," Gideon said.

"Marcus wrote me that when someone is sick, you call old Doc Leed. Sometimes he comes, sometimes he doesn't."

"Mostly, he comes."

"He won't come anymore now," Jeff said. "If what you tell me is true, he won't come anymore now." Jeff rose and walked to the window, wiping away the moisture that had gathered inside the pane. "It's still snowing," he remarked. "It's funny, being away so long, I never learned to love any other place. Did Allenby ever show you any of the letters I sent him, to read to Ellen?"

Gideon shook his head. "The old man died last month. I thought you knew."

"I didn't know," Jeff said. "I'm going back with you, father."

In the last few things Gideon did in Washington, there was a sort of compromise between an attitude of leaving for good and a half-formed hope that he might be back for the spring session. He would find himself thinking that Jeff was right, that a world simply could not explode like a bomb-shell. He left the house as it was, telling Mother Joan to keep things in order. He attended a meeting of the Ways and Means Committee, and found himself hotly engaged in the discussion of a law pertaining to railroad land grants. Well, a man was so constituted; he went ahead with habitual things; he dressed and ate and shaved and slept. And one day, soon after Jeff came home, he was told by his secretary that Senator Stephan Holms would like to see him.

"You may tell Senator Holms," Gideon said, "that I am completely engaged. I have only a few days before I leave Washington, and I am making no appointments."

The secretary came back and said that Senator Holms was quite insistent.

"All right," Gideon nodded. "Let him come in." Holms entered; Gideon made no effort to rise, no offer of his hand. Smiling, Holms smoothed the nap of his hat, took off his coat carefully, set his stick and gloves on a corner of Gideon's desk, and seated himself.

"What do you want?" Gideon said.

"I wanted to see you, Gideon, because we are both civilized human beings, because on that basis we can discuss things, because in a world full of fools, idiots, small men, and little minds, you and I can certainly discuss the truth, recognize it, and make our peace with it without passion."

"You believe that, don't you?" Gideon asked, watching the slim, delicate man who sat so completely at his ease, so immaculate in his clothes, so unruffled in his demeanor, the smooth, shiny, faintly-yellow skin untouched by the years, the ascetic face both an enigma and an invitation, reacting to Gideon's every mood and word. Certainly, this was a product of civilization; after a fashion, too, this was a truthful man, a strangely truthful and direct man in a strangely untruthful and indirect world. Yet at this moment, Gideon felt for him a loathing such as he had never felt for a living being, loathing, disgust, hatred; Gideon Jackson, who in all his life, as a slave and as a free man, had reacted from hatred, who had tried to understand what makes one man good and another bad, what makes one man gentle and another hard, who with a whip on his back had tried to feel and comprehend reason, logic and truth, who had fought and killed without hating what he was fighting and killing; this man, Gideon Jackson, would have quickly and surely killed Stephan Holms and felt no regret for it. And now, Gideon repeated, "You believe that, don't you?"

"I believe it, Gideon," Holms said quietly. And added with complete sincerity, "I assure you, Gideon, that I am one of the few people of my class who does not draw back in horror from the color of a man's skin. You see, I am essentially a reasonable and logical human being: so are you. We recognize that certain shibboleths have been set up. I can afford to smile at them, at the brainless, empty idiots—my friends, I admit—who look upon all creatures of your race, and so many of mine, as being inferior. God knows, I recognize their caliber. But my lot is with them, Gideon, partially by birth, partially by choice. Let us face the facts; my people lost a great deal by the war, not only power—which is no small thing in itself—but material things that result from power, a way of life. I wanted those things back, and I fought for them sensibly."

"And now you have them."

"To a degree," Holms admitted. "There are still matters to be arranged, but to a degree we have succeeded. I need not pretend; you know why Rutherford Hayes is our next president, and you know that he is at least gentleman enough to keep his word. At any rate, the Republican party has made its peace with us, and certain things will be done."

"You are a truthful and a reasonable man," Gideon said, staring at Holms with real curiosity. "You pride yourself on that, don't you?"

"After a fashion, yes."

"And you didn't come here to gloat. You are much too civilized for that."

"Much too civilized, Gideon. Too civilized to be impressed by a black man's irony. And you, I think, are too civilized to throw me out of here."

"I want to hear what you have to say," Gideon answered quietly.

"I thought you would. Let's dispense with innuendoes. I admire you, Gideon. I watched you during the Convention, during the years that followed; there was an amazing development. You are a man of great ability and profound talent. You have a mind. The mere fact that a former slave, whose speech was back-country gibberish, should be the cultured man I speak with now, is in itself incredible. I have listened to you in Congress, often with admiration. Your delivery, which has that rare combination of being both rational and emotional, is most effective in moving men."

"You are flattering," Gideon said. "Go on."

"I think that if you had the original of that amazing and stupid document you showed to President Grant, you might have gone to Congress with it and changed history. Or perhaps not. Our party has a majority in the House, and it is doubtful whether one man in one act can appreciably change history."

"So you know about that too. At least, you are thorough."

"We have had to be thorough, Gideon. We were the conquered. Our country was an occupied country——"

"You think of it as your country?"

"Essentially, yes. The country of a few select men, men who are fit to rule. You should recognize that, Gideon. Neither the degenerate white trash that we have used in the Klan, nor the debased and childlike nigger field-hand is capable of rule. You are an exception. I am an exception. That is why I appeal to you, both with sincerity and logic. There are other ways, but how much simpler it would be if you were with us, if some of your colleagues joined us. The nigger will follow you; he has before; he will continue to. In the long run, our way is best. I dislike force and I dislike violence, believe me; I will use them if necessary, but how much better it would be to achieve our ends without resorting to wholesale violence. A land where prosperity and order is combined for the good of all, where the man in the field has enough to eat and can sleep without worry as to his next day's bread."

"And you propose this to me?" Gideon asked incredulously.

"Will you accept?"

"That I should lead my people back to slavery?"

"If you would put it that way."

"You are incredible," Gideon said softly. "I should have recognized that the first time, when I went to your house. But I looked upon you as human. I looked upon all men as human. I failed to realize that a disease could enter a man's mind, a disease beyond cure. I didn't understand that some men are sick, and with their sickness they could contaminate the earth. We all make mistakes, don't we? I think that was the greatest mistake that the men on my side made. When the earth ran with blood during the war, they thought that the evil had been stamped out. But the blood of the sick, the diseased, the debased beyond reason—that blood never ran

at all, only the blood of good men, men who had been led
and lied to. We let your kind live—"

Gideon had not seen Senator Holms angry before, a tightening of the lips, a few vertical lines on the high, smooth
brow. Senator Holms rose, put on his coat and hat, picked up
his gloves and stick from the desk.

"I take it that is your answer," he said.

"You may take it as such," Gideon agreed.

Gideon and Jeff took the three o'clock train for the South
the following day. There was not much that Gideon took
with him, a small bag and a briefcase which contained his
old copy of Whitman's poems, a signed photograph of Charles
Sumner, which had been given to him just before that man's
death, and a notebook. He intended to write a report of the
whole Hayes-Tilden affair, and he thought he might start
it on the train, to pass the hours away.

With Jeff, he walked down the platform, the length of the
train. "The last car," he said.

"Why?"

"You don't know, do you?" Gideon realized, looking at his
son. "You remember, I told you it did not come like a bomb
bursting. You see, it's been going on."

They came to the last car, an old and venerable veteran
of the road. The windows were dirty; two of them had been
replaced by boarding. Over the door, a sign said simply,
"Colored." Jeff read it and turned on his father.

"No—no, it's impossible! It's rotten, do you hear me,
rotten! You—a member of Congress—"

"Get in, Jeff," Gideon said. "This isn't a new thing. It
grows in popularity. One gets accustomed."

They got in and sat together on the old wooden bench.
Other colored people filed in. And in time, the train started.
Gideon said:

"After all, it's only for a while. Soon we'll be back at Carwell."

CHAPTER NINE

How Gideon Jackson and His Son Came Once More to Carwell

MARCUS WAS WAITING FOR THEM AT THE STATION, AND TO Jeff, this was a stranger, actually and completely, this slim, handsome Negro boy, lighter-skinned than any other Jackson, reaching only to Gideon's shoulder, but well-proportioned, small in the hips, broad at the shoulders, moving so easily, so gracefully that Jeff's first thought was of a wild animal, unafraid, possessed of itself, and completely integrated. Dressed in blue jeans and a brown leather jacket, he stood casually by a one horse chaise, grinned at Gideon, waved a hand, and then engaged in a frankly curious study of his brother.

"Hello, son," Gideon said, and then began to toss the bags into the freight box. There was a way between them, a warm regard that Jeff recognized in the offhand manner they shook hands.

"Picked a fine day to come back," Marcus remarked, and then, "Hello, Jeff. Don't know me, do you?"

"You've grown," Jeff admitted. He put his bags in with Gideon's. Then he shook hands with his brother; then they stood there, facing each other, Marcus grinning a little. Gideon came around the chaise, watching the two of them, feeling the wonderful achievement of having them both with him, together like that, the massive, earnest pile of Jeff facing the grinning, handsome boy. "I'll drive," Gideon said. "Get in." "Dr. Jackson?" Marcus smiled. Jeff said, "That's right. My God, how old are you?"

"You've forgotten that too—twenty."

"Twenty," Jeff repeated.

"Get in," Gideon said. Marcus told Jeff, "You first, doctor," bowing and extending a hand. "All right," Gideon told them. The three crowded onto the single seat, and Jeff put an arm around Marcus. "How was Scotland?" "Lonely," Jeff said. Marcus said aloofly, "You talk like a foreigner; You back to stay now?" "Maybe." "You'll find it changed," Marcus said. "We haven't sat still."

Gideon listened to them; it was good to be in the old chaise with his sons, to have the reins in his hand, and to be guiding the little black mare down the road. It was a fine, clear March day, not too cool, not too warm, the sort of a day just before the spring that can be more wonderful in South Carolina than anywhere else in the world. The mare was a five-year-old that he had bought two summers before, a small, alert animal with a smooth trot. He liked to drive; all during the long winter months in Washington, he had been thinking of this, of sitting behind the mare, listening to the steady thud of its hoofs. When they turned off the dirt road onto a corduroy causeway through a neck of cypress swamp, he told Jeff proudly:

"We built this four years ago. It cuts the distance to the railroad in half."

"We built other things," Marcus remarked, unable to keep a smug note of satisfaction out of his voice. Jeff had been away; he had done the things Marcus wanted to do. Gideon glanced sidewise at them. "Jeff's home to stay," he said.

"Is he? He'll find it mighty lonely at Carwell."

Gideon told Jeff how they had built the causeway. Most of them had worked on the railroad right of way, and knew the mechanics behind the principle. They had laid out the line of the road themselves, straight as an arrow, without an engineer, a mile and a half of it. "When I mentioned it in the house," Gideon said, "the only comment came from one of my colleagues, who wanted to know how we came by the right to build on government property."

Marcus looked at his father. Jeff sang softly, "My daddy went a hunting, Lord, Lord, Lord, my daddy went a hunting, Lord, Lord, Lord . . ."

"You remember that?"

"I remember a good deal," Jeff said.

Jenny was grown, a woman, her full breasts high under her smock; Jeff held her and his mother in his arms. "You're so big, so big." "I'm no bigger," Jeff smiled. Rachel wept with complete happiness; she had grown old more markedly than Gideon; she kept touching Jeff's face, running her hand across his woolly hair.

Gideon and Marcus stood apart from them. Marcus said to his father, "I read in the papers—"

"Yes."

"How was it? Does it mean—?"

"I'm not sure what it means," Gideon said. "We'll talk about it later."

Marcus said, "They don't know us if they think, up there in Washington, that they can wipe us off with the stroke of a pen."

"We'll talk about it later."

"They don't know us," Marcus said.

They led Jeff around and showed him things. Suddenly, everything had become new again. They showed him the house, a simple frame structure of five rooms, painted white outside. The chimney was red brick. "Kiln brick," Jenny said. Rachel showed the kitchen; they had tin pans, bright and shiny, a whole set of them in graduated sizes hanging from the wall; there was an iron spider. And more wonderful than anything, there was an inside pump. Rachel pumped fresh, cold well water. "Here, just you try it, Jeff." He had to try it, drink a glass and say what fine water it was. Jeff said, "Are the other places like this, the other people? I mean, you being a Congressman—"

"A person's house is like himself, different in one man than in another. We haven't had to complain. This is a good land for a man who loves it and understands it." Jeff wanted to know what became of the old slave cabins, and Gideon said they were still there, untenanted. "No one lives there now?" "No one," Gideon said. "No one bought the house, no one wanted it." There was a note in his voice that made

Jeff look at him curiously. Marcus said that afterwards, if the doctor had time, they could walk over to the big house.

Rachel was torn between a desire to serve the hot bread and chicken she had prepared and show Jeff the rest of the house. She would say nothing about the real beds with metal springs; he would have to see them for himself. She led him into the bedrooms.

"Where does Ellen live?" he asked.

"With Brother Peter. All of Allenby's children with Brother Peter."

"Was it bad for her when the old man died?"

"She came here," Marcus said. "She wanted to be here."

"But she went back?"

"Yes, she went back."

"She knew I was coming?"

"Yes, she knew. All the people know. They'll come later."

Rachel spread her hands on the bed and pushed up and down. "Soft and sweet, like a baby in a cradle. Feel here, Jeff." He pressed on the mattress. "Just set on it." He sat down, smiling at her. "Go ahead, go ahead and move up and down, up and down." He jounced up and down, then rose and put his arms around Rachel. She couldn't resist the kitchen now, whirled him through the other bedroom and then into and out of the parlor, a small room packed close with overstuffed Victorian furniture, a table, and Gideon's books. Then they sat at the kitchen table and Jeff told her how wonderful the bread was. "There ain't no corn bread in Scotland?" Jeff answered, no, none, none anywhere in that whole land. To please Rachel, he ate more than he could hold, just ate and ate, and then she began to cry again, looking at him and touching his hands. "All right, mother, now everything's all right." But she kept on crying.

Gideon and Marcus went out to the porch. "She shouldn't take on so," Gideon said uneasily. The need, the aching hunger in Rachel had never been so apparent as now. "I'll unhitch the mare," Marcus said.

"He'll want to go to Ellen."

"Will he?"

"I guess he will."

"Well, they're going to come over here, all of them, they are. He can just as well wait here. I'll unhitch the mare."

Gideon nodded. Marcus led the horse away, and Gideon stood on the porch, leaning against one of the posts, somewhat sad, somewhat lonely. This should be a beginning; instead it was an end. He shook his head savagely; only a fool would think that way. Washington was one thing, unhealthy, full of small, hungry, frustrated, ambitious men; this was something else, this was his home. Washington was not America; this, multiplied over a million times, was—this small frame house, the homely furniture that filled it, the live oaks and the locusts that covered it over and shaded it from the sun, the sweeping hillsides, the fields where cotton and corn and tobacco would grow soon, the plough that Marcus had left out there, a few hundred yards from the house, tilted, the stiff, wet March soil clinging to its blade—all this was his, his own. This he had fought for, slaved for, worked for, planned for; a man is not parted from the ground that has tasted his blood, his free footsteps. A man has his feet in the soil, and there he stands.

Marcus went into the house and told Jeff, "She's coming now," nodding over his shoulder. Jeff went outside alone. Brother Peter came walking through the slanting shadows toward the house, holding Ellen's arm. Brother Peter had grown a beard since Jeff last saw him; close to sixty years, his thin, tall figure had a patriarchal dignity. The beard was white, and he walked with a limp. Gideon said that he had been ailing. When an old field slave passed forty-five, he was hardly ever much good for anything; rheumatism crept into all his bones; malarial fever wracked him, and an enlarged heart recorded the endless hours of toil behind him. But the girl by his side was as she had always been, as Jeff remembered her, more mature, rounder, more full in body, but much as Jeff remembered her, the head held high, the glossy black hair braided behind her shoulders.

Jeff walked toward them, and Brother Peter and the girl stopped. Jeff saw the old man bend toward her and say something. Then the girl stood without moving. Brother Peter smiled at Jeff and said:

"Welcome home, my son."

Jeff halted a few paces from them. Ellen's face was turned toward him. Then he went over to her and took her hand and said, "Hello, Ellen. Do you remember?" She nodded, just slightly.

"I'll go up to the house and pay my respects to Brother Gideon," Brother Peter said. "And you two just come along when it pleases you."

Jeff nodded. The old man walked away. Jeff remained there, holding her hand, and she didn't move, standing straight and still. She wore a green calico frock, a blue cape thrown over her shoulders, black stockings and black shoes. And finally she said, "Jeff, do I look the same—do I look the way you wanted me to look?"

"Just that way."

"No difference, Jeff?"

"There's always a difference. But you look the way I wanted you to look."

"I'm older, Jeff."

"We're both of us older."

He took her arm and they began to walk. Jeff led her along the slope, toward the field Marcus had been ploughing. As it was in the old times, he told her how the sun was setting. He was full of Carwell, choking with it, feeling all the sensuous rush of discovery that comes with a return to youth. The smoky, mist-filled, fog-corroded Scottish skies were already part of an only dimly-recalled past; here the sky was a glaze of March blue, streaked with the sunset colors of gold and orange and pink. Here the land was warm and lush and soft; he and his kind were not made for rocky, treeless hillsides. He had finally come home, and as with Gideon, that in itself was sustenance and comfort. He told Ellen how the sky was, but not how it had been in Scotland. He bent over the plough and crushed the strong-smelling dirt in his hands, and then pressed it against hers. "How far is Scotland?" she wanted to know, and he told her that it was at least four thousand miles from here. But that was distance beyond her conception, just distance and distance, gathering on without end. "It's good you're back. But you're different now, Jeff. You're a man. You're a doctor. My father was a doctor. Did you know, Jeff?"

"Of course I knew."

They climbed the hillside toward the house, stopping to rest where Marcus had built a bench. The house stood like a small, squat box in the gathering dusk above them. People were coming; the sound of voices drifted down. There was a steady thud-thud of horses' hoofs on the other cheek of the hill, on the little road that led to the house. Someone up there called:

"Jeff—oh, where are you?"

"They're calling us," Ellen said.

"We'll go up in a little while."

They sat there, and it grew dark. A dog barked and barked. Jeff said finally, "Have you thought that you would marry me when I came back?"

"Do you want to marry me?"

"I want to," Jeff said.

"A blind woman."

"Some day," Jeff said, "I'll learn how to give you back your eyes."

"They're calling us," she told him.

He took her hand and led her up to the house.

Everyone at Carwell had come. Horses and mules were hobbled all the length of the barnyard. The women had brought their children, new children whom Jeff had never seen before. The house was full; the porch was full. People crowded around him, the older people, flinging more questions at him than he could answer. The young men, who were children when he had gone away, stood apart. The girls stared at him. The women cried with Rachel. It surprised Jeff to see how many white folks there were, the casual, easy way they mingled with the Negroes. Some of them he knew, the lanky, red-headed Abner Lait, squat, small-eyed Frank Carson; others, he didn't know. There were young men his age, tow-headed sunburnt boys who watched him curiously

but without malice. The new schoolmaster was there, a
Rhode Island Yankee called Benjamin Winthrope. He said,
"The benefit to the community of having you here, Dr. Jackson, is inestimable. I presume you'll stay." "I hope to," Jeff
nodded. There was a white man, a worn, small man, Fred
McHugh by name, who said to Jeff, "The way my woman's
ailing—you couldn't come along and see her?" "I could, tomorrow," Jeff agreed. McHugh said, "There's a pain in her
belly like a snake eating her." "I'll come," Jeff said.

Marcus had an accordion. He sat on the edge of the porch,
playing, "My mammy chased me home to Atlanta, to Atlanta,
to Atlanta." The young people around him kept time, beat-
ing their feet on the ground, clapping their hands. Gideon
opened three jugs of corn, and everybody had to drink.
Rachel and the women stood over the stove with frying pans
and pots. The strong sound of voices singing ran over the
dark fields, "My mammy chased me home to Atlanta—"

Brother Peter said to Gideon, "We have our rewards, we
taste of happiness." And some of the people standing by
nodded, "Amen."

Jeff said to Marcus the next day, "Come along."

"Some men can play, others got to work."

"There's time for work."

"Go with him," Gideon said. "I'll pick up your plough."
He was back in his old and shapeless shoes, jeans, a brown
shirt. "Go with him," Gideon said. Marcus harnessed the
mare, and they drove the chaise to the schoolhouse. It was a
single-room, white-painted frame building with a short
steeple on the farther end, and that way served the dual
purpose of meeting house and school. Some thirty boys and
girls of varying ages sat in the pews; Winthrope's was the
complex problem of teaching all subjects for all ages and
preserving order at the same time. A harried man, he was
flustered and flattered that Jeff had come so soon. The visit
broke down discipline, and he alternated between imposing
order on the class and explaining his methods to Jeff. One
age group would study while he gave oral instruction to
another.

"It's difficult," he admitted. "Two teachers and two rooms would be so much better. I've found, however, that certain things break down. If I speak on literature for the oldest, it does not harm the youngest to listen."

"Naturally not," Jeff admitted.

"Of course, I am comparatively new here. Old Mr. Allenby, who preceded me, had his own methods. They were not the most modern, you understand."

"Still, when I remember that even a schoolhouse was once a dream . . ."

They drove on. Jeff said, "I want to stop at McHugh's house. You know where that is?"

"I know. Because his wife's sick?"

"He wants me to look at her."

"So we have a doctor now."

"Worse things could happen," Jeff said.

"Maybe so."

Jeff looked at him, but Marcus said nothing more. McHugh's place was in sight of the old plantation house, a small building, but set off with care. He had planted shrubs around it, an unusual thing in that section. He lived with his wife, a good deal alone, mixing hardly with anyone; he had no children. When Jeff came in and saw the neglect, he asked McHugh, "How long has she been sick?"

"Ailing on and off a year now. She stays to bed now. Last night she didn't scream none, just moaning and whimpering. He led Jeff into the bedroom, where a colorless, thin woman of forty lay. "This is Gideon's boy, Jeff. He's a doctor man from studying in the old country. He's a fine boy, Sally. He going to look at you, please, Sally."

She said nothing, just lay there, staring at the ceiling. "Would you go out?" Jeff asked McHugh. After he left, the woman didn't move. Jeff said, "Please, ma'am, I'm a doctor. Maybe I can help you."

"If you can, you can."

Jeff touched her abdomen, and she twisted and groaned with pain. When he came out, McHugh was waiting for him. "Did you have Dr. Leed up from town?"

"I had him."

"What did he say?"

"He say she's going to die," McHugh muttered.

"Did he know what it was?"

"Can't ask Doc Leed no questions," McHugh said. "He don't take to Carwell folks. He say she going to die, that's all."

Marcus, standing there, asked, "Do you know what it is, Jeff?"

"I think I know. I think it's what they call typhlitis—that's an inflammation of a part of the intestines, a small, finger-like projection. Often, for some reason we don't understand, an inflammation sets in, and if uncontrolled, becomes gangrenous. At a certain stage, it responds to ice treatments. At this stage, it doesn't."

"You mean she's going to die?" McHugh asked.

Jeff nodded.

"You can't do nothing? Jesus Christ, you can't do nothing?"

Jeff said, "I remember, when I was with Dr. Emery, I saw a surgeon cut out the part. The patient recovered. That surgeon operated. I never saw another operation of the sort. In Edinburgh, they admitted it fatal."

"Could you operate?" Marcus asked.

"I don't know—"

"Well, God damn it, you can try, can't you? If she's going to die anyway!"

"I don't know how," Jeff said. "You can't try something when you don't know how."

"Why not?"

Jeff stared at Marcus. McHugh was watching them both, his upper lip trembling. He said, "Look a here, Jeff. I know Gideon—way back, I know Gideon. Time was, they said to me, God damn you, McHugh, stay away from that nigger. You know how it was, send me a note with blood on it, stay away from that nigger. Then Gideon come to me and talk about buying the land; I go along with him. I go along with him every time. I go off to Aiken to be a vote watcher, after they tar and feather a white man for voting niggers.

You ask Gideon? Just ask him if I held back. Just ask him how I told that son of a bitch Jason Hugar—"

"All right," Jeff nodded. "If I leave her alone, she hasn't more than a few days to live, and she'd be in pain all the time, terrible pain. Marcus, drive back to the house. Bring my small bag; bring some clean sheets and towels. Tell mother to come back with you. Have you any corn whisky?" he asked McHugh. The man nodded. "All right, go in and ease her and begin to feed her whisky, just a little at a time; try not to make her sick; don't give her enough to make her drunk, no more than half a cupful all told. Wait a minute, put a fire in your stove first and set some water to boil. Who does she trust, among the women?"

Pale, frightened, McHugh said, "Helen Lait."

"Fetch her, Marcus. Can she stand up? Do you understand what I'm going to do, McHugh? I'm going to cut open your wife's stomach and cut out that diseased portion. It's going to hurt her. It's going to be a bad thing to watch. And I have to do it right away."

McHugh nodded.

"I want your permission. I want you to say that you're willing."

"I'm willing," McHugh whispered.

"Understand—this is something I never did before. I don't even know how to do it. If I make a mistake, your wife is going to die. Even if I do it right, the gangrene may set in and she may die. That's a risk you take in any operation, and here, with these primitive facilities, it's worse."

"I'm willing," McHugh said.

Gideon was on the porch, waiting, when Jeff came back to the house. It was almost sunrise. Jeff said tiredly, "Didn't you sleep?"

"No—I had a lot to think about. Is she still alive?"

Jeff nodded. "She sleeping now, quietly. She's all right, I think—no, I know it. She's all right."

"Try to get some sleep yourself."

Jeff smiled and shook his head. He sat down on the edge of the porch, next to Gideon. The world grew lighter. Presently, the first edge of the sun showed. A cock crowed some-where. Softly, Jeff said, "My God, when I think about it—when I think that only two men in the whole world have done it before. When I think of how simple it is, once you know. When I think that I did it here, with nothing, do you understand, with nothing."

"I've been thinking that," Gideon said.

"Do you know how many people die every year of typh-litis? Thousands, perhaps. A country doctor calls it acute in-digestion, or poisoning, or a tumor. But it's typhlitis—"

Gideon nodded, put a hand on Jeff's shoulder.

"You didn't want me to come here."

"I didn't want you to come," Gideon admitted. "I had reason, Jeff."

"There are no reasons," Jeff said. "Do you know that when I was just a boy, I used to envy you. You were pos-sessed; you were building a new world. Well, I don't envy you now; I think I know you. I'm going to go on building, here—I'm going to build—"

"Try to get some sleep."

"I can't sleep now," Jeff smiled. "My God, how can I sleep now?"

A week later, Jeff and Ellen were married. All of Carwell packed the little schoolhouse. Brother Peter, in his new black deacon coat, said, "Do you, Jeff Jackson, take this woman—?" Gideon watched, thinking how strangely, how surely and slowly time moved. He felt old; in a sense, he felt used up. He stood with his arm around Rachel, and he listened to Brother Peter's voice, that voice which had been with him all his life, that sure, confident, resonant voice . . .

Jeff had picked for his home a small plot of land near the schoolhouse, a piece that was owned by the people in community. They had set this section aside for a school and a cemetery, and as Jeff said lightly, it might well do for him to be near both. Gideon arranged for the building; they were old hands at it by now. The timber was their own, two by fours, sweet-smelling pine siding, three-quarter inch plank for the flooring, dovetail oak to do the inside properly. All of it was cut at the mill and carted over. Hannibal Washington, a fine bricklayer, set in the hearths and chimneys. Jeff spent hours drawing plans: a sunlit examination room, a space for two beds, a large section that would someday be an operating room. He said to Gideon, finally, "It comes out the largest house at Carwell."

"Which is fitting," Gideon agreed.

"Where will the money come from?"

"I have enough money for that, I think," Gideon smiled.

"I can't take any more from you. I've been taking all these years."

"I wouldn't worry about it, Jeff. You'll want equipment, won't you, furniture, beds? Other things?"

"They cost a lot."

"We'll manage. I suppose you could find some of it in Columbia, but I think we'd do better in Charleston. We'll go there soon." He had other reasons for wanting to go to Charleston, but he thought it would be nice if the two of them, he and Jeff, could go together. For the time being, Jeff and Ellen lived with Gideon. There was a deep trust and close communion between Ellen and Rachel, something Gideon did not share. Once Jeff said to his father, "Do you hold it against me, my marrying Ellen?"

"A man should marry the woman he loves," Gideon replied. And he tried to tell that to himself, to make himself believe that along with many other things. As he realized later, much of the world he lived in that March of 1877 was a fool's world; for Gideon Jackson to believe that the sun stood still and that time stood still was strange: stranger even than that was the fact that he had so much real happiness in those few weeks, happiness marred by many small things— but real happiness. For the first time in almost a decade, Gideon laid aside his books; he didn't want to read, to study, to think. Giving Jeff his parlor-study to take care of the increasing number of patients, he spent the whole of every day working with Marcus.

For people so far apart, so different in basic matters, he and Marcus understood each other well. Marcus lacked the driving pain that was a part of Gideon and Jeff; for them there was the whole of the puzzling world, for Marcus the world was constrained and understandable, and in a sense more complete. Marcus was a sinner; Brother Peter admitted that sadly yet comprehendingly; Marcus loved the fact of women, body, breast and thigh, without shame yet without lust—and animal health and freedom filled him like a cup brimming over with life liquid. Small and slim as he was, he could outwork Gideon; he drank with the white men, the way they drank, matching Leslie Carson's son, Joe, drink for drink, down a half-gallon jug of raw corn. He loved to dance. His accordion made the old music new; all the old swamp songs, the tired, pleading songs of slavery, he played, but under his fingers they became something new. He gave them new rhythms, new life—

He worshipped Gideon. He knew cotton, but Gideon knew it better; he knew the soil and bowed to Gideon there. They worked at the forge in the barn and put a new tire on a cartwheel. Stripped to the waist, Gideon drove his hammer like a smith. Forty-five years hadn't taken the strength out of his arms, and as the hammer came down again and again, it filled the world with its sound. "Mark it," the boy sang, turning the iron, "mark it, mark it, mark it!" And Gideon piled on, sweat streaming down his face. They shifted all the remaining fodder into a new bin, working together in smooth rhythm with their forks, singing together, "I got a crick in my back, I'm old and tired." They cleared swamp growth for planting, swinging two-edged axes in short, stinging blows, and came tramping back to the house, laughing with pleasure, filthy but delighted with themselves. Jeff told Gideon, "At your age, that isn't the wisest thing—"

"At my age," Gideon smiled.

"It's not as if you did it all the time. When you live a sedentary life most of the year—"

Gideon and Marcus took a day off hunting, Gideon with a rifle in hope of raising a deer, Marcus with a shotgun, saying he would be satisfied with rabbits. They whistled their two speckled pointers, filled their pockets with bread, and set off across the fields one cold, crisp morning. They sang their own song, softly and happily, "Daddy went a hunting, Lord, Lord, Lord, yes, Daddy went a hunting, Lord, Lord, Lord . . ." The dogs fanned out and cut back and forth across the meadows. The two men didn't talk much; somehow, it never mattered that Gideon and Marcus had so little to say to each other; they fitted.

It was almost nightfall when they came home. Not hide nor hair of a deer had Gideon seen, but Marcus's pouch held a brace of fat rabbits. He took them to the barn to skin and dress them and give the dogs their reward of the gizzards; Gideon went to the house. Jeff was waiting for him, his face like a piece of granite, his eyes hard, the way Gideon had never seen them before. He led his father into the parlor; Abner Lait sat there, his big red hands tight on his knees.

"What is it?" Gideon wanted to know.

Abner Lait looked at him strangely, and Gideon said, "For God's sake, what happened?" Jeff motioned him into the bedroom; Rachel sat there, her face blank of expression. A man on the bed moaned a little, twisted a little; his whole body was wrapped in bandages. "McHugh," Gideon whispered. Jeff said, "That's right."

Gideon went to the bed and said, "Fred—hello, Fred." McHugh lay there as before, twisting a little, moaning a little. Gideon took his hand, "Fred—it's Gideon."

Back in the parlor, they were joined by Marcus. "He was whipped?" Gideon asked.

"You could say it that way, whipped."

"His wife?"

"She's dead," Abner Lait said quietly. "Those sons of bitches murdered her. Those filthy bastards took her out of her bed and killed her."

"Who?" Gideon whispered.

Jeff told him as much as they could get from the tortured, half insane McHugh. Six men in the white robes of the Klan had come to his house last night. They dragged him and his wife from bed, in spite of his pleading that his wife was sick, that it would kill her. They dragged them into the barn, tied their crossed wrists to a rafter, and whipped them.

"I don't think his wife suffered much," Jeff said. "I think she fainted almost immediately. The wound opened, and she died. But Fred had to hang there and watch her, until almost three o'clock when we found them."

"Will he live?" Gideon said.

Smiling strangely, Jeff answered, "That's an academic question. He's out of his mind and his arms are no good. He'll never be able to work again."

Abner Lait said, "You know what I want to do, Gideon. I'd like to know what you're going to do."

"It's time you told them, isn't it?" Jeff said.

"I didn't see any use in telling them."

"It's time you told them, I think," Jeff said.

"All right, tomorrow," Gideon nodded. "We'll have a meeting tomorrow."

Jeff was waiting for Marcus on the porch. He caught him by the arm and stopped him. "Marcus?"

"Yes?"

"What are you holding against me?" Jeff asked.

"Holding against you? I ain't holding a thing against you."

"Do we go on like this?"

"We're going on all right," Marcus said.

"What have I done?" Jeff said.

"It's nothing you done."

"Is it because I've been away and you stayed here? Is that it?"

"No—"

"What then?"

"Nothing," Marcus said. "How many times I got to tell you that? Nothing."

"All right—don't be angry."

"I ain't angry."

"You remember, when we were children, it was different.'

"Everything's different for children."

"You think I'm against—Gideon?"

Marcus kept silent.

"You think that, don't you?"

Still, Marcus kept silent.

"Do you know what's coming? Did he tell you what's coming? What he thinks is coming?"

"I didn't ask him, he didn't tell me," Marcus said.

"He thinks it's the end of all this—did you know that?" Marcus nodded.

"What are you going to do?"

"He knows what to do," Marcus replied.

The men filled the schoolhouse, black men and white men in their work clothes, blue jeans and blue overalls, heavy leather shoes, brown and red shirts. With the white men, the sun line ended at the neck and wrists; the skin was windblown and sun-tanned. The black men ranged in color from plum to ivory. Counting Winthrope, the school teacher, counting the eighteen- and nineteen-year-olds, there were more than fifty men in the room. One was a doctor, one was a preacher, one was a schoolteacher, one was a congressman; the main trade of the rest was farming. Principally, they grew cotton, but they grew tobacco too, some rice, corn; they held cattle and hogs and horses. They made up a community called Carwell, and what they made had not existed a decade before, nor did it have its exact counterpart anywhere outside of the south. War, ruin, death, emancipation, and peonage had thrown them together; they had built from nothing in the strictest sense of the word, and they could look about them and say that this or that or everything had come from their hands. They had created everything among them, schools, houses, mills, ideas, because there had been nothing before. All the long centuries between feudalism and democracy, they had crossed over in one long step.

As Gideon Jackson stood before them now, looking at them, weighing them, remembering faces, remembering the different lives each man there had lived, he thought of that. Jeff wanted to build—and Gideon had a sudden despairing vision of how men could build. He said to the people:

"All of you know me. I have talked to you before."

They knew him; they had voted for him; they had driven

their wagons twenty miles in every direction, telling people that a vote for Gideon Jackson meant something.

"You know what happened to Fred McHugh. We buried his wife this morning. In our little graveyard, outside of here, four people lie who have died through violence, who have been murdered at Carwell in the past eight years. That is a terrible thing. To take a human life in any cause is a terrible thing. But men become beasts when they murder to impose terror on free men. You know why Fred McHugh was whipped, why his wife was tortured to death—only for one reason, to tell the white men here at Carwell that they can no longer live together or work together with black men.

"Why is that so important? Why is it so necessary here that the white man should learn to hate the Negro, to despise him, to humiliate him, and that the Negro in turn should learn to fear the white man, avoid him, mistrust him? Is it because the two, the black and the white, are incompatible, that they cannot work or live together? But Carwell, a thousand Carwells all through the southland have proven differently. Is it because the blood will mix, the white being debauched by the black, as the Klan has screamed all through the South? But we have lived here for almost a decade, and that has not happened. Our children have set in this schoolhouse together, and that has not happened. Then what is the reason? What is this great sin that we have committed here at Carwell, that black men and white men have committed everywhere in the South when they put their good right arms together? It is important for us to know, not only for the black people here, but for the white people.

"I don't want to frighten you, my friends. God knows, I had reason enough to be frightened in Washington, but when I came back to Carwell, all seemed different. It reassured me; this is my home; these people are my friends. They knew me when I was a slave, when I ran away from Dudley Carwell, my master, when I came back, as so many of you came back, to a great domain which had lost its master, its overseers, its whips and its compulsions. I looked around me, and here was reason, here were the good things of life; so I said to myself, all the evil things I dreamed of cannot be, not here, not where we have built. I lived for a little while in my fool's paradise.

"That is gone, my friends. I want to tell you the truth now, I want you to understand why Fred McHugh lies in my house, his arms twisted from their sockets and useless to him, his wife dead, his mind gone. I want to tell you why, when my son and I came down here from Washington, we were forced to ride in a separate car marked, 'Colored.' I want to tell you why, all over the South, from Texas to Virginia, cries of suffering fill the air. And most of all, I want you to know why, from here on, the white man will be set against the black like a dog against a sheep; why, if they succeed, it will be a dream that there had ever been such a place as Carwell.

"How is it that no one here at Carwell belongs to the Klan? How is it that all over the South honest, hardworking farmers till their land and do not belong to the Klan? Who belongs to the Klan, if it is, as our newspapers tell us, the honest protest of an indignant and suffering and prostrate South? Where does it come from? Who organized it? If it wishes to save the South from the savage nigger, why does it strike down two white men for every black man, why did it come here to Carwell and kill Fred McHugh's sick wife?

"It took me a long time to realize what the Klan is, how it operates, why it was organized. I know now, just as you know. The Klan has only one purpose, to destroy democracy in the South, to kill off the independent farmer, to split, in so doing, the black man from the white man. The black man will become a peon, not too different from the slave he was before the war. And because he is that, a slave in effect if not in fact, the white man will be drawn down with him. A few will become great and mighty, as before the war. But only a few. For the rest of us, poverty, hunger, hatred—such hatred as will become a sickness for this nation.

"That is the sin Fred McHugh committed at Carwell. He was tortured so that Abner Lait, Jake Sutter, Frank Carson, Leslie Carson, Will Boone—every white man here would take heed and play his correct part in the day of reckoning.

That is up to you; there is a way out that is no way out. Join the Klan, cooperate with the Klan, don't resist—and destroy yourselves. You know those men, the dirty, diseased, degenerate louts who were the slave runners, the overseers, the whip men, the hangers on, the toughs, the gamblers, the cheats, the sheriffs, the men who became brave with a gun in their hands but not brave enough to be seen at the front, not brave enough to die, the way thousands of southern men died because they loved their land. I don't have to describe them; when they dragged Sally McHugh out of her bed, hanged her up by her hands, and whipped her to death, they described themselves. They are the scum, the dregs of this land. For every one of them, there are a hundred decent, good men in this South; but the scum are organized; the decent, good men are not. They have money; they have hirelings to plead their cause at Washington; they have rich planters to lead them and direct them. We have none of those things—and I, for one, say thank God.

"What are we to do? I know what my friend Abner Lait wanted to do, to take his gun and kill Jason Hugar. That's not the way. To lose our heads, to murder the way they murder—that's not the way."

"Then what is the way, Gideon?" Abner Lait shouted. "Why don't you tell us what happened at Washington?"

"I'll tell you. At Washington, we were sold. We were sold by the Republican Party, my party, Abe Lincoln's party—and the price was the presidency. The planters paid that price. In return, when Hayes takes office, the troops will be withdrawn, from Columbia, from Charleston—from everywhere. The Klan will become the law—"

"Then you admit it!"

"I admit it. I told you I would give you the truth. But what are we going to do? Lose our heads? Murder? Rip ourselves to pieces? Do their work for them before they're ready to do it themselves? Is that what you want?" Gideon paused and stared at them. "Is that what you want?" he repeated. "If that's what you want, I'm no use here—I'll go."

There was a long moment of silence, and then Frank Carson said, "Go on, Gideon, tell us what you think."

"All right. Remember that we're still strong. Here in this room are fifty of us; we have arms; we have ammunition; we have drilled together and worked together. I think we can defend ourselves if we don't lose our heads. On the other hand, defense will not help us; to lose gloriously will not help us. We have to organize with others; all over the South are thousands like us. I've arranged to go to Charleston and meet with Francis Cardozo and other Negro leaders. Anderson Clay and Arnold Murphy, white leaders, will be there. Perhaps together, we can find some way of forestalling them. I'm not promising you anything; I'm not hopeful. I don't know—But let me try. After that, there will be time for other things. Let me try; let Jason Hugar live; it won't change things to kill him. If you'll give me a chance—"

The men sat there, and then a few heads nodded. "All right," Abner Lait said softly. "Try."

Ellen couldn't sleep; all night long she heard, through the wall, the soft, animal-like moans of Fred McHugh. It was the body and the sound and the memory of terror; she remembered the things she didn't want to remember; she remembered hiding in the woods; she remembered death and screaming. She lay there shivering and listening until, unable to stand it any more, she woke Jeff. He said, "What is it, what is it, darling?"

"I'm afraid."

"There's nothing to be afraid of."

"I'm afraid—" His body shaped itself under her hands, his strong, narrow thighs, his great barrel of a chest, the slabs of loose, relaxed muscle that lay all over him, his neck, his chin, eyes, mouth. In the night, in the darkness, he and she were the same; she clung to him, whispering, "Jeff, Jeff, Jeff."

"You see I'm here, Ellen. I'll always be here."

But she couldn't stop being afraid; she lay there, listening to the moans of the hurt man, short, sharp moans that came through his sleep. Suddenly, the full deeps of darkness encompassed her; a well of darkness that people moved into and went out of, all those shadowy figures, Allenby and the others, coming and going. She clung to Jeff with all her strength, but it was no use.

Cardozo said to Gideon, "I'm not denying the essential truth of your conclusions; I deny the dramatic form in which you present them."

"I'm not concerned with abstracts, but with the form itself. It's with the form I have to live."

Anderson Clay said, "There, I go along with Gideon."

Eight of them, five colored men and three white, sat together in Cardozo's parlor. Four of them were from South Carolina, one from Georgia, two from Louisiana, and one from Florida. They had been talking for almost three hours now, and had come to no conclusion. Some of them were militant, others were frightened; at least half of them seized upon the momentary opportunity of taking refuge in words. They talked in circles; they recounted their achievements, what they had won, gained, done—until Gideon snapped at them:

"That's over now, I tell you. That's in the past, finished. It has no meaning for today."

"But the record, dozens of Negroes and poor whites in the House, in the Senate, in the state governments, governors too—"

"I tell you it's done," Gideon said.

"By virtue of what?" Cardozo asked calmly, his judicial, quiet voice making reason where there was no reason. "Nobody, Gideon—and you know this—respects you more highly than I do. But aren't your conclusions empirical, to give them the most credit?"

"Because a man has been lynched here, tortured there, threatened, because Senator Holms confided in me, I must not anticipate results? Is that what you infer? Am I an alarmist?"

"To a degree, yes."

"Yet you, Francis, were state treasurer a year ago, and today you are not. What were the forces that operated? If I say that I will not be permitted to sit in the House again, must that be tested? Can I see no farther than my nose? If that were so, Francis, I would be a slave today, and four million other black men would be slaves."

Capra, a small, aging colored man, one time representative from Florida, interposed, "Nobody, Gideon, is denying your personal integrity."

"I don't give two damns about my personal integrity!"

"But Gideon, you tell us that the Republican Party sold the reconstruction for the election. We are the party; our lives have been dedicated to the party; the party fought for us, gave us our freedom. You have no proof. You say that the troops will be withdrawn from the South in ten days—but you have no proof. You say that there will be terror, that all we have built will be destroyed. Where is your proof?"

"It is being destroyed," Gideon said tiredly. "Look around you. No niggers on this train, no niggers on the bench, white only, white only—no niggers in this school; we built the school, but no niggers now, no niggers on this jury, the lawyer for the defense objects. Last year the Judge was a black man, a poor white—today a planter or a planter's lacky supports the lawyer's objection. A nigger is on trial, but no niggers on the jury."

"I concede that," Cardozo nodded. "Essentially, we have been forced to compromise—"

"Is that compromise?" Anderson Clay smiled. "Do you compromise with the air you breathe, Francis? With the food you eat? These things are the blood and bone and muscle of our lives! You can't compromise with a son of a bitch who wants your blood!"

"You talk as a white man. Ask a black man—"

"God damn it, I'm sick of hearing that! Whatever we have we've gotten because black men and white men stood together. Gideon's right, think the way you do and we go down separately—we go down to hell."

Ables, who three years ago was a secretary of state, asked Gideon, "But why, precisely, should the Party have sold us, as you put it? For what end?"

"Because we've served our purpose, we've broken the planters' backs. In the last eight years, this has become an industrial nation, the greatest industrial machine on earth. The north has the west and the southwest; even here in the South mills are beginning to open. Let the planters have their serfs back—the North is safe."

"And the people's party—"

"There is no people's party today," Clay growled.

Cardozo answered wearily, "Still, what you ask cannot be done, Gideon. To reinaugurate the Negro and poor white militia after it has been abolished—how? In defiance of the law?"

"The people are the law."

"That, Gideon, is a more primitive conception than I would expect from you. The people are the law only through due process."

"A process that wrote into the Constitution the right of the people to bear arms, to have a militia!"

"We could carry the matter to the Supreme Court, that would take months. You suggest a convention to unite every pro-reconstruction force in the South—that, indeed, Gideon, would produce violence."

"I see. If we raise a voice in our defense, we promote violence."

"Yes."

Gideon said, "And if there should be violence regardless? As, indeed, there has been."

Abels shook his head. "What's the use, Jackson? We have been over this and over this, again and again."

"Do you all feel that way?" Gideon asked. He was used up now; you got to the end of a thing, and that was the end. "Is that the end, gentlemen? Well—it is one thing to have every newspaper in the country scream its lies, the golden cuspidors we spit into, the millions that go to walling our legislative hall with mirrors and gilt, the thousands in graft we have squeezed from a defenseless land, the way we have debauched southern manhood and womanhood, the carpet-baggers, the evil, money-mad Yankees who pull the strings—all that I read in my newspaper. That is one thing, gentlemen. It is another thing to sit here and have you tell me that we must not raise our voices in defense, that we must not try to bring unity to this twice damned southland of ours. I love my country, gentlemen; I didn't want to talk like this—but I have to. I love this country because it is my own, because it has been good to me, because it gave me dignity, courage, hope. Am I alone in that, gentlemen?"

They sat silent; some of them stared at the floor; some of them watched Gideon uncertainly. Anderson Clay smiled a little.

"Then you all agree with Mr. Abels?"

Still silence.

"And the curious part is," Gideon said quietly, "that even those things which you cling to will be forgotten. The black men who sat in the House, in the Senate; they will be forgotten, the black men who built schools and justice—all of it, my friends. We will not be men any more. They will grind us down until we lose our humanity, until we hate the white men as truly as they hate us. They will make of us a tortured, debased people, unlike any other people on earth. And how long, my friends, before we see a little sunlight again? How long? Ask yourselves that."

Gideon asked Anderson Clay to come with him and meet Jeff. They walked together through the sunlit, still, white-walled streets of Charleston. It was such a spring day as Gideon remembered from long ago, here in this same city. The palmettos wore the clean green of the new season high on their spreading tops. The birds sang and flashed their bright plumage. The sky was a gentle blue, traced through with streaks of mist. The things that Gideon had seen on and off for so many years were familiar, and the familiarity gave the lie to his gloom. The city was so staid, so beautiful, so gently civilized that it made its reassurance without protest or pressure, but simply and matter of factly.

Anderson Clay said, "I thought I'd like to live here some day."

"It's a nice place to live."

Clay said, after a while, "You know, in a way, Gideon, you were wrong and they were right. They'll live on, but you—"

"They'll live on and they'll change slowly," Gideon answered thoughtfully. "Each year a little more pressure, a little more of this and that taken away. They won't know. Is that best?"

"I don't say if it's best."

"But you thought it was hopeless, from the beginning?"

"You see, Gideon, we didn't know. We started from nothing, groping around in the dark. We had only one idea, to build—schools, courts, hospitals, roads, people too. Maybe you could say that all of us, your people, mine, went a little insane when they saw there was freedom stretching ahead, maybe forever. All they thought was to build. The others wanted to destroy, and they organized for that. Ten days isn't long enough for us to organize, Gideon—a year isn't long enough."

"Then what?"

"Well, we'll fight," Clay shrugged. "We'll fight because we've fought before, because we're trained to fight. But they've taken that into consideration. We'll be fighting alone."

Jeff was waiting for them by the Battery. Gideon said, "My son, Dr. Jackson. Jeff, this is Anderson Clay, a good old friend of mine." Jeff shook hands with the tall white man.

"I hear you've come to Charleston, doctor, to buy supplies."

"We're building a hospital at Carwell, a small one."

Clay said, "I intend to come to Carwell next year."

"You've said that for nine years," Gideon smiled. "Each year, it's next year."

"That's right. Next year, Gideon." They crossed to the water-front and walked along slowly. Clay and Jeff talked about Scotland, about medicine, about the lack of any sort of adequate hospital facilities in the state. "Give us time, son," Clay said.

"Some of those great old plantation houses, like the Carwell place," Jeff said. "They just stand, empty, useless— that's what a hospital should be, in the country, big, clean."

Gideon looked at Anderson Clay.

"A statesman could do worse things," Jeff said.

"He could," Clay nodded. "I hear you were just married. Congratulations."

"Thank you," Jeff said. And after a moment, "It's strange, I don't know what came of your meeting—I don't know that I care a great deal. You see, we're going on. A man who sells his soul to live in the White House can't change that."

They walked slowly. The setting sun gave the water of the bay a turning sheen of color. The gulls dropped down to the water and rose triumphantly. A small sign on the rail, unobtrusive, said, "White only." A steamer, trailing its smoke, was being piloted into the harbor. A laughing group of boys lay on the deck of a sailing gig on close tack. A carriage clattered down the street, and two children, in a grassy, iron-railed enclosure across the street, skipped rope.

At Carwell, for the first time in so many years, suddenly and desolately for Gideon, things stood still. Brother Peter, coming over to his house the day after Gideon returned, saw him sitting on the edge of the porch, elbows on knees, chin in hands. "Like that for hours," Marcus said, "low—" Gideon answered, "Evening, Brother Peter."

Brother Peter said, "Tired, Gideon?"

"Uh-huh."

Brother Peter sat down beside him, first spreading the skirts of his black deacon coat. He leaned his cane, which he had been using of late, on the porch next to him, and he sat down his high black hat alongside of it. Then, sighing, he stretched his legs and remarked, "A long walk. Ain't as spry as I used to be."

"No."

"Not near as spry, Gideon."

Gideon didn't answer. Rachel came out on the porch, and Brother Peter started to rise. "No, you just sit there. Mighty glad to see you."

"Thank you, sister."

"Stay for supper?"

"Now, I don't mind if I do, thanking you kindly," Brother Peter said. Rachel glanced at Gideon, who had not turned around, and Brother Peter shook his head. Rachel stood a moment and then went back into the house. Brother Peter sat down on the edge of the porch again. "Fine woman, Sister Rachel. A pleasure to eat her food, a pleasure to sit at her table. There's something I sure miss, you up there in Washington, Gideon."

"Yes."

Brother Peter went on, after a moment, "Do you good to talk, Gideon—do any man good to talk. Let the bile out from inside him, believe me. Was it that bad in Charleston, that awful bad?"

"Just about."

"How come then, Gideon? How awful bad is something? The good Lord gives and the good Lord takes away, measure for measure. You got no faith, Gideon."

Smiling a little, Gideon said, "I wish it were faith."

"How come then? Man comes in this world just a naked little babe, goes out naked. There's the judgment and the proof, Gideon. I ain't talking about God—long time ago I give up you ever being a believer. You got a mighty store of strength, Gideon, but maybe it would have been more, you just had faith. All right, then I talk to you about men. Just leave God aside, Gideon, He don't mind that, just leave him aside and talk about men. You believe in men, Gideon?"

"Believe in men?"

"That's right, Gideon."

Gideon looked at the old man thoughtfully. Brother Peter brushed a speck of dust off his tall black hat. It was a gift from his congregation; four years, day in and day out now he had worn it, excepting rain, and it looked as good and new as ever.

"I think I believe in men," Gideon said. "I don't know—"

"How come you don't know that? Maybe man got a load of sin on his shoulder, but how come nigger's a slave one day, free man the next?"

"And a slave again," Gideon said.

"You think that? Suppose we all die off, Gideon, everyone hereabouts. You don't think there's a little speck of something left on, little speck more than there was before. You think there ain't no hallelujah songs going to go on ringing?"

Gideon said nothing; the evening wore on, the sun sank. Marcus came up, glanced at them, and entered the house. Finally, Gideon said, "Supper soon, Brother Peter."

"Sure enough. Tell you, I got a good appetite too for an old gentleman my age. Walking does that. You just go in and I'll join you, brother."

Gideon rose and went into the house. Jeff had just finished washing his hands at the kitchen pump. Rachel said, "Going to have Brother Peter for supper, Gideon."

"I know."

Jeff left the kitchen. Rachel turned to Gideon, looked at him for a moment, and then went over to him.

"Gideon?"

"Yes."

Rachel went over and touched his shirt, ran her hand down his arm. "I can stand near anything, Gideon," she said softly. "But I can't stand to see you with misery. I been less and less use, but I can't stand to see you with misery."

Gideon took her in his arms and the pressure drove the breath from her. He held her to him in a bearlike, desperate grasp, and her words came jaggedly, "Can't stand it, Gideon, can't—"

"Rachel, Rachel, baby."

"You going to smile, Gideon?"

He smiled at her, and she lay against him, inertly, her fingers plucking at his shirt.

The next morning, as Gideon stood with Jeff and Ellen, watching Hannibal Washington lay the bricks for the chimney of the new house, Abner Lait stopped on his way in from town. Dropping his reins, he climbed out of his wagon and joined Gideon.

"Where'd you learn to slap that mortar?" he asked Hannibal Washington.

"Learned from my pappy—he gone and built them seven stacks up there at the big house."

"Don't tell?"

"Sure enough," Hannibal Washington said. "That a long time ago, though."

"When'd they build that old house?"

"Fifty years ago, sure enough."

"Seems like it been there forever," Abner said, plucking at Gideon's sleeve. Gideon walked over behind the wagon with him, and the white man said, "I just come from town, Gideon. Seems you were right, President made his deal with that damned old son of a bitch, Wade Hampton. The troops at Columbia got their marching orders—come April tenth, they're going to entrain for the North."

"Who said that?"

"Well, look a here at this newspaper," Abner told him, reaching into the wagon, pulling out a newspaper, and pointing to the headline: SOUTH WINS SECOND EMANCIPATION. "There it is, the whole story. The town's full of talk. Jason Hugar's strutting around in an army uniform, going to march in the victory parade at Columbia. You said make no trouble; well, I made no trouble, just watched that son of a bitch, Hugar. Where'd he fight? I been on a hell of a lot of fields, but never saw no man called Hugar."

Gideon was reading the story, scanning the lines quickly and nervously—"in amiable agreement with the governor, President Hayes set his signature to an order which finally establishes democracy and home rule in the south. The last Federal troops will be withdrawn on the tenth of April—"

"It's going to be a picnic," Abner Lait muttered.

"What?"

"You know, Gideon, my grandpappy should have gone west. Old Dan Boone come down here and just beg him to go over into Kentuck. Hell no, my smart grandpappy said. Jesus God, I wish he'd gone—I wish he'd gone into Kentuck and into Illinois and right across the whole God damned country and out of here. I wish he'd gone out of here to that blue Pacific Ocean, I wish—"

"Shut up," Gideon said, nodding at where Ellen stood. Hannibal Washington and Jeff were looking at them.

"What are you going to do, Gideon?"

"Today's the sixth, isn't it? We've got four days. I'm going to Columbia. I don't know what I'll do there; I'll try to do something."

When Gideon finished writing out the telegram in the Western Union office, on Sumter Street in Columbia, he handed it across the counter to the clerk. The clerk was a pimply-faced boy of nineteen. "Read it back to me, please," Gideon said. The boy looked at him and made no move.

"I said, read it, please."

The boy read:

"RUTHERFORD B HAYES
THE WHITE HOUSE
WASHINGTON DC
MR PRESIDENT I BESEECH YOU TO DELAY YOUR
ACTION WITHDRAWING FEDERAL TROOPS FROM
COLUMBIA STOP ABOLITION OF NEGRO AND POOR
WHITE MILITIA LEAVES PRO RECONSTRUCTION
FORCES DEPENDENT ON FEDERAL PROTECTION
STOP FEAR RIOTING AND TERROR STOP LOYAL
REPUBLICANS HERE CANNOT COMPREHEND ABAN-
DONMENT OF ALL UNION ELEMENTS IN SOUTH
WE PLEAD YOUR HELP AND SYMPATHY
GIDEON JACKSON
REPRESENTATIVE FOR SOUTH CAROLINA"

"How much is it?" Gideon asked.

The boy hesitated, then said, "Ten dollars."

Gideon looked at him a moment, paid him and left. The boy walked back to the operator and boasted, "Never seen a nigger yet knew what a telegram cost."

"God damn you if I don't have you fired for that! How much he give you?"

"Ten."

"Well, you going to split, God damn well. Give it here." The boy handed over the telegram and the operator glanced at it. He whistled and read it more carefully. "Who gave you this?"

"Some big nigger."

"Well, look. You take this over to Judge Clayton. Tell him

I want to know if I should send it. And keep your big mouth shut!"

In about twenty minutes, the boy was back. "The judge kept the telegram and give me a dollar."

"You split!"

"The judge said we'd better damnwell keep shut, or he'd know the reason why."

From the telegraph office, Gideon went to see Colonel J. L. Williams, in command of the Federal troops. The colonel was a busy man that day; it was an hour and a half before Gideon was shown in. Then he said, "Representative, I'm sorry. Every one in the South wants to talk to me today."

'I know," Gideon nodded. "I don't know how different my case is. Here is a copy of a telegram I sent to the president. An answer may come in a day or in ten days—until it comes, I beg of you not to let all your troops entrain."

The colonel read the telegram and then shook his head. "My orders—"

"I know you have orders, Colonel," Gideon said. "I'm not asking a personal favor. This is a matter of life and death to a great many people."

"I can't," the colonel said. "I'm sorry."

"Do you know what will follow when your troops leave?"

"Whatever I may think will follow," the colonel said, "I have to obey my orders. "If you took this up with General Hampton, in command of the district—"

"That would be useless," Gideon said. "He would not. I know what orders mean. I've been in the army, Colonel."

"It's no use."

"Don't you see that the president cannot ignore the telegram."

"I could be court martialed."

"I have some influence in Washington."

"I can't do it!" the colonel said, raising his voice. "Believe me, sir, however much I might want to, I can't do it. Don't you think I have eyes to see? I'm a soldier, I'm not a politician!"

For a moment, Gideon stood there, tense, sick, terrified; then he nodded. "I'm sorry."

"So am I," the colonel said.

Then Gideon left.

He remained in Columbia until the tenth of the month, making frequent visits to the telegraph office. On the ninth, he sent a second wire. On the tenth, he watched the troops march to the waiting train, and then he went back to Carwell.

On the afternoon of the fifteenth of April, the people of Carwell heard a woman shrieking. Her loud, shrill screams echoed across the place, bringing people running from many directions. A terror-stricken boy, pushing through the woods, whimpered, "The horse came back, he came back." The people followed this boy, Juddy Hale, to his father's farm. His father, Zeke Hale, was a stolid colored man, a quiet family man who farmed well and turned over a larger net cash cotton profit than almost anyone on the place. There they found Franny Hale, his wife, screaming loudly and insanely. There they found a wagon with a horse harnessed to it, and when they saw what was inside it, they turned away.

They pieced the story together. Zeke Hale had gone to town to buy some new shoes and a present for his boy, who had just turned ten. Evidently, he had been driving back slowly and enjoying the fine spring afternoon. Anyway, he was a man who liked to walk his horse whenever possible, especially if the weather showed any signs of turning hot.

At some point, on the way back from town, someone had stepped up to the slow-moving wagon and fired both barrels of a shotgun at Zeke Hale's head. The noise of the gun had caused the horse to bolt forward, pitching Zeke back into the wagon. The horse had run all the way back to the place, and Franny Hale had looked into the wagon and seen what a shotgun fired at close range can do to a man.

They buried Zeke Hale, and after that, for the first time in nine years, the men who lived at Carwell went to their work with guns slung over their shoulders.

CHAPTER TEN

How Gideon Jackson Fought the Good Fight

IT WAS THE MORNING OF THE EIGHTEENTH OF APRIL, 1877, AT Carwell. The mist lay in the valleys and ran like white milk through the cypress groves. Four pointers, out hunting most of the night, loped wearily home through the pines. The high-pitched call of the roosters met them, and crows winged overhead crying, caw, caw, caw to the dawning. Then men at the various farms, milking and doing the other pre-dawn chores, thought all the thoughts that had always, from time out of memory, been a part of such morning work, would it be a fair day or a muggy day, would Nelly try to kick the bucket over, she always tried, would that fool dog across the valley get tired of his hollow belling, how fine and simple and good the voice of the crows is, just the same and just as nostalgically pleasing morning after morning, would there be bacon or fried chicken with the grits this morning, would the sick calf go on vomiting like that, would the rheumatism down near the small of the back start acting up again—none of these thoughts very complicated, none of them very important, yet none of them entirely unimportant. The sun raised over the brow of a hill, and light came with a sudden and glorious rush. In hilly country, the light splashes on one side of a slope while the other stays in shadow. The mists in the valleys churn and vanish, except where they cling to the watery bottom of a swamp hole. The snakes, copperhead, blacks, and others crawled gratefully toward the warmth; the fat terrapins came out into the sunlight. The rabbits crawled deep into the bramble patches, and the squirrels raced up and down the fine old hickories. The deer moved away to the thickets to bed down and rest.

Morning at Carwell, after the chores were done, found the men sitting down to breakfast, hot cakes, pan bread, molasses, white, cold butter with little drops of water standing stiff on the surface, bacon, grits, eggs, sometimes fried chicken or fried fresh fish, buttermilk heavy with clods of turning, milk, fried potatoes, yellow cornmeal mush cut in slices from the pan where it had set since the night before, fried in the bacon grease—all of those foods in some combination were breakfast at Carwell, and not too much for men who had already worked two or three hours. The schoolbell called for the children; they took shortcuts, no roads for them. They were filled with life at eight o'clock, pushing ankle deep through the ploughing, whooping to each other, shouting as they raced up a hillside, chucking cones at each other as they cut through a neck of piney woods. Their incredible, violent, unpredictable energy made each day a rather awesome adventure for Benjamin Winthrope. He tugged the schoolbell to give himself courage, and philosophized that anyone could teach well-behaved, gentle students. He thought of Frank Carson's daughter, sixteen years old, staring at him boldly all day with those round, clear-blue eyes of hers, and he thought of all the things that went on inside of himself. The Congregational Educational Service that had dispatched him to Carwell spoke of it as God's work, and after only a few months here he could understand why God had relegated the duty. He took comfort in his few prize students, Hannibal Washington's son, Jamie, Abner Lait's daughter, two or three more. Today, he would introduce the upper levels to Emerson. "Emerson," he repeated to himself, standing in front of the school. listening to the children's shouting, and letting his eyes roam over the sundrenched fields and woods. "Emerson," he told himself firmly.

At the breakfast table, talking to Marcus, Gideon thought vagrantly of how adaptable the human mechanism is, how easily the bizarre can become the normal, and how complete is the adjustment to almost any condition. He was saying to Marcus:

"I would add an acre of tobacco, not cotton," talking like that, matter of factly, with the two rifles leaning against the door jamb, waiting for the men to leave.

"This ain't tobacco country."

"Still," Gideon said, "we grow a good leaf. Not as fine as Piedmont or Virginia, I admit that, but it's marketable. These new things they call cigarettes are going to increase smoking."

"It's bad for soil."

"So is cotton. You sicken your soil in either case unless you rotate or leave the fields fallow. I've been preaching that for years."

Rachel said, "If it was my doing, I'd plant corn."

"We're not stock farmers."

"Got to go on doing what your grandpappy did?"

"I want to go for buying this afternoon," Jenny said.

"To town?"

"Uh-huh."

Marcus shook his head.

"Why?"

"There'll be some folks going in later on in the week," Gideon told her.

"This is a fine day."

"You stay here," Marcus told her.

"Well I don't take orders from you. I don't have to stay anywhere for you telling me."

"You stay here!"

Jenny began to sob. Ellen, who had been sitting next to her, fondled her hand. Gideon rose, then Marcus. As he started from the room, Gideon glanced toward the rifles, hesitated, then picked one up and went out with it.

At ten o'clock, Jeff was at the home of Marion Jefferson. His wife, Louise, had broken out with boils all over her hands; they were nothing serious, but they were painful and itchy and kept her awake nights. Jeff told her how to mix a soothing paste, and then he lingered on the porch to pass the time of the day with Marion. As a boy, Jeff had been one of Marion's favorites; now, as a doctor, he was like a God in

Marion's eyes. As they stood there, talking about one thing and another, Trooper came running across from his place. He stopped, panting, took a deep swallow, and said:

"Jeff, I just seen Jason Hugar and Sheriff Bentley headed for your pappy's place. I been standing on the rise, and sure as God I couldn't miss the sheriff's gig. The other man's Jason Hugar, I swear."

"Well, it's nothing to be alarmed about," Jeff told him.

"Maybe it is, maybe it ain't," Marion said. "Just suppose we ride up there in your chaise." He went inside the house for his rifle. His wife, frightened, asked, "What is it? What you going to do?"

"It ain't a thing, not near," he smiled. "Just the sheriff riding over to Gideon's. We going up there to make sure."

"Don't make no trouble, Marion. We had enough of trouble."

"We sure enough did," he told her quietly. "This ain't going to be no trouble, not at all. All the same, I guess you better walk over and tell Abner Lait the sheriff's up at Gideon's."

Cutting a tall pine out by its roots, digging around it, and then chopping at the fat, moist tendrils, had employed Gideon and Marcus since they left the breakfast table. It was good work for the cool morning; it let a man give himself to the ax, taking his anger out in the best way, on inanimate objects that in no way resented it. When the pine fell, they would leave it lie all through the spring and summer, and when the leaves were turning it would be fine and crisp for cutting, ready to be marked off into four-foot logs that burned like paper. Now it had begun to totter, its long stem vibrating ever so slightly, when Marcus spied the sheriff's little gig, wheeling up from the swamp and taking the climb to the Jackson house. He dropped his ax and pointed.

"The sheriff?" Gideon asked.

"Looks enough like his gig. I'm going up to see."

Gideon nodded; they picked up their guns and walked quickly toward the house. When the shoulder of the hill hid them from the road, they broke into a run, and, panting, reached the house just a moment or two after the gig got there. Jason Hugar and the sheriff sat together, their sleeves rolled up, both of them wearing leather vests, each of them with a double barreled shotgun across his knees. Rachel was on the porch, tense, worried, breathing a sigh of relief when she saw Gideon and Marcus.

"Morning, sheriff," Gideon said. Jenny and Ellen came out on the porch and stood behind Rachel. Fracus, their spotted pointer, made a fool of himself over Marcus until he saw that he was neither noticed nor wanted, and then he lay down and watched. Marcus stood with his gun hanging through the crook of his arm, tight, bent, and only Rachel there knew that he was like a charge of gunpowder, stable yet ready to explode. Nodding at Gideon's rifle, the sheriff said:

"Going hunting, Gideon?"

"Maybe so!" Marcus snapped. "And when you talk to my father, call him mister, understand?"

"Mister," Jason Hugar drawled. "Mister."

"That's right."

"All right, mister," Hugar smiled.

"What can I do for you, sheriff?" Gideon asked softly.

"There you are," Bentley nodded. "For my money, you're a reasonable man, Gideon, and my God, if that ain't a virtue these days, I don't know what is. No use losing our heads. I got a job to do and come up here on a small matter of business—and find you menacing the law with guns. Jesus Christ, Gideon, that ain't a way for niggers, it leads to trouble—"

Marcus said, "Shut your God damned mouth!"

"Now look, son," Hugar said. "Now look, you nigger bastard," his finger curled across both triggers of the shotgun. "If you make one move with that bird gun of yours, I'm going to rip the God damn guts out of you—"

Rachel cried out, half a whimper; Gideon gripped Marcus' shoulder so that the boy felt the fingers sink in, like iron claws. "Just take it easy, Mr. Hugar," Gideon said. "There's no cause for trouble. Sheriff Bentley knows that; he knows we're law-abiding folk and never gave him any cause for trouble. If we're carrying guns, it's not out of disrespect for the law; it's because a neighbor of ours was murdered just a few days ago."

"Tell you something, Gideon," Bentley said. "When a nigger gets too high, it makes trouble. The way you folks have it, that nigger was just driving along the road when someone up and shot him. My God, that don't make sense, Gideon, it don't make one bit of sense. How in hell's name do I know what he was up to? Give a nigger one inch and he'll take the shirt off your back."

"That's why we're here," Hugar agreed.

"Why are you here?" Gideon demanded.

"God damn you, we'll ask the questions!"

"Now take it easy, Jason," the sheriff said evenly. "Gideon's got a right to ask questions; we're on his property; that's a legal matter of law. But we got a right to ask questions too. We want to settle what we're here for quiet and peaceable. Yesterday afternoon, Gideon, three niggers come up to the back door of Clark Hasting's house. Clark's in the store; Sally and the little girl are there at home. Just as nice as pie, one of the niggers says, please, Miss Sally, we're a hungering, you got a little bite to spare. Well, you never known Clark to turn a nigger away, and Sally goes to fetch something, never thinking. Meanwhile, Clark's girl, nine years old, stands there, watching the niggers—"

At that point, Jeff, Trooper and Marion Jefferson came riding up in the chaise. Gideon was heartened when he saw them. Marion and Jeff got out; Trooper sat in the chaise, gripping his Spencer, the same one he had carried in the war, and said, in his slow, deep voice, "Take your finger off the trigger of that shotgun, Hugar."

The man's face reddened; a vein swelled out, a vertical band across his brow; his whole square body tightened.

"Take it off quick," Trooper said.

Bentley whispered, "Don't be a damn fool and do as he says." Abner Lait came riding up on his plough-horse, a shotgun over his shoulder. "Do as he says," Bentley told him.

Hugar's fingers unhooked themselves.

"Put that there gun at your feet," Trooper said. "You, too, sheriff."

"You can't talk—"

"At your feet," Trooper nodded.

They put the guns at their feet. Abner Lait joined the group around the gig. Frank Carson's wagon turned the corner of the road, up from the swamp. Hugar said:

"We got to remember some things, Lait."

"I got something to remember."

"The sheriff was telling us," Gideon said, "just why he's here." Gideon repeated what the sheriff had said. "Go on, sir," Gideon told him. "We want to hear the rest."

Frank Carson joined them. Bentley, watching them narrowly, continued, "The little girl stands there, watching them, and one of the niggers goes for her, rips her dress off. She began to scream, and Sally came running. One of the other niggers hits Sally. Sally crawls for a cabinet where Clark keeps his revolver, and then the niggers take to their heels."

"And how does that concern us?" Gideon asked.

"The niggers were recognized, and they all of them came from up here, at Carwell."

At first, there was dead silence. Then Abner Lait laughed. Then Jeff began, "Of all the insane—" "Keep quiet," Gideon said. "I'll do the talking."

And he asked Bentley, "What do you want?"

"We want them three niggers, Gideon."

"On what charge?"

"Assault and attempted rape."

"Who are these men you charge?" Gideon asked.

"Hannibal Washington, Andrew Sherman, and another nigger Sally says she seen in the store with Carwell niggers, but don't remember the name."

"All right," Gideon said. "We won't talk about your story; it doesn't concern me. But neither of the two men has been over to town for a week. All day yesterday, Hannibal Washington worked over by the schoolhouse, laying bricks. Andrew Sherman is ploughing and has twenty witnesses.

These men will bear me out. So there are your charges, sheriff. No one from Carwell was in town yesterday."

"We ain't taking nigger witness," Hugar said.

Gideon's mouth tightened. Abner Lait walked over to the gig, "I'm not a nigger, Hugar. Look close."

"We ain't taking your witness either."

"A long time ago I made up my mind to kill you, you dirty son of a bitch," Abner said quietly.

Bentley said, "That talk won't get us nowhere. We don't want trouble, Gideon."

"We don't want trouble either."

"But we aim to take those men back. They're going to get fair witness and fair trial."

"You have fair witness here," Gideon said.

"I'm going to make an arrest. Are you going to obstruct me?"

"Put it that way if you want to," Gideon nodded.

"I'm putting it that way. We came here peaceable on business of law and order. You surround us and offer us armed resistance. That's a God damned serious thing, Gideon."

"You're going back without those men," Gideon said. "If you want it, sheriff, you can have it. I say you're lying. I say no sane man could believe that cock and bull story you told. I say that."

"I hear you," the sheriff nodded. "I can hear a nigger five miles off. I can smell one. I'm going to have those men, Gideon, If I got to deputize every man in the county."

"Or outside the county," Gideon nodded. "Or every rotten scoundrel Hugar can lay hands on. Meanwhile, get out of Carwell, Bentley. You're standing on our land. Get to hell off it!"

The men stood in a close group, watching the gig as it drove back along the road. For a while there was silence. Then Abner Lait began to curse, softly, fluently, completely. Jeff said, "I wonder if you should have talked to him like that?"

"It don't matter," Frank Carson shrugged. "This was a long time coming and it ain't nothing a man says is going to change it."

"Every day I woke up this week, it was going to be like this," Gideon reflected. "A whole week, and every day you think about it. Every day, and then one morning it comes."

Standing around, subdued, quiet, not quite understanding why they had been dispossessed in the midst of a school day, the children watched the men enter the schoolhouse. A few of the older boys pushed in along with the men; they were not stopped. Half the men who sat down in the pews carried weapons of one sort or another; all of them moved slowly, the way men do when they can make no conciliation between their thoughts, their actions, and their hopes. Benjamin Winthrope stood at one side of the hall and watched them; he was both disturbed and frightened. He was a young man, Williams, '73; he came of a very average, religious New England family that traced their descent from the old governor, although they spelled their name differently; and coming from that sort of a family, complete within itself, the love he felt for his own humankind was more abstract than actual. It had taken a great strength of will, a constant struggle with himself to remain here among these—to him—strange, quiet, yet violent people. Now, watching them, he saw as well as they did that all was over. His job was done; he would go to the station and take a train, today, if possible.

Brother Peter opened the meeting by saying, "Brethren, we are gathered here today in fear and anger. God help us to choose the right way—and if we go and choose that way, God give us strength to bear with it. You going to talk, Gideon?"

Rising from where he sat, toward the back, Gideon answered, "This isn't a matter just for me alone. I can talk no better than anyone else. I know no more of what we should do than my neighbor does. The people can talk for themselves."

The heads turned to look at Gideon. He seemed older now than he ever had before. Hannibal Washington spoke up, "Maybe it's better you should talk for the people, Gideon. A man comes from us or he don't; you come from us, Gideon. You never gone away. You got your faults, God knows, but you walk low and humble, Gideon, God knows. Go on and talk."

"There isn't much to talk about," Gideon said. "You all know what happened. You know why, too. You know that if they take three of our people away and hang them, it would be only a beginning."

Andrew Sherman said tiredly, "I don't want to make no trouble for all, Gideon. Ain't we had enough trouble? Maybe they ain't going to do something so bad as hanging. Suppose I go in there to town and they look at me, and they say, no, that ain't the same nigger? How they going to say I'm the nigger did those things? I never been off the place yesterday or all the week before?"

"They'll hang you," Abner Lait said. "Just as sure as God, they'll hang you."

"They'll hang you," Gideon agreed. I'll make no decisions from here on, the decisions are up to you. After that, if you want me to lead, I will. But you decide. That story—well, they had to tell some story; they had to have some method that resembled legality. After all, it is only eight days they've had the power. Eight days are not enough time for them to shed all we've built in eight years."

"Well, what do we do, Gideon?" Frank Carson demanded.

"That's for you to decide. I think they'll be back tonight —if not tonight, tomorrow, but they'll be back, not two of them, but a good many more. Then they'll start the business of smashing us, and after a little while they won't feel any need for legal methods. As to what you can do, there are several things. You can stay in your homes and be murdered by twos and threes—not all of you, some may escape. You can run away, and there'll be a plantation somewhere you can hire on, for fatback and grits and a place to sleep, and if you keep your mouths shut, you can live that way. For the white men, it's a little different; perhaps they can join Jason Hugar, although I don't know if he'll have them—I guess it's not too different for the white men. Or else, you can stay together and fight!"

Jeff cried, "This is still the United States of America!

There is still law and there are still courts! My God, sir, do we have to destroy ourselves?"

"We don't have to," Gideon said. "I gave the other alternatives. I'm making no choices. For eight days there has been no law but the law of violence; the courts are not ours —and only because this is America do we have the strength to fight! Destruction? I don't know—when old Osawatomie Brown went into Harper's Ferry with nineteen men, he had less strength and less hope than we have, but he shook this nation—he woke it up, he made men see. I don't propose to fight to die; I want to fight to live. I want to fight so that this whole country will see what is happening here."

"There must be another way," Jeff said.

"What other way?"

"If you went back to Washington?"

"I tried there and I failed," Gideon said.

"If you tried again?"

"I would fail again, and it would be too late. Tomorrow will be too late."

Will Boone said, softly and lazily, "Suppose we reckon to fight, Gideon. I like to stand up for mine; that's a good way as I see things. But how? We ain't an army—three and half thousand acres, you take in all the places. That's a little thin, a little spread."

"I've thought of that," Gideon agreed. "God knows, I've been thinking of little else. If we fight, it means putting the women and children where they're safe, where they can be safe for a long while, long enough for this to get out, for this to burn. There's a place like that, big enough, easy to defend, nearby—I mean the old Carwell House. It stands on a hill, it commands the countryside—

"I've said enough," Gideon finished. "Decide for yourselves."

An hour later, they had decided; out of their strength and their weakness, their fear and anger, their hurt and pain and memory of their toil had come this, Abner Lait speaking after the welter of voices had quieted:

"We'll fight, Gideon. Do you stay with us?"

"If you want me?" Gideon said.

"We want you."

Gideon looked around the hall, and then he nodded. His steps dragged as he walked up to the front of the room. Brother Peter watched him, the old man's eyes full of pain. Gideon, glancing at his watch, said, "It is almost three o'clock now. Whatever we are going to do we should do before dark. I don't know if they'll come back tonight, perhaps not for several days. I suggest this—that we take our families up to the big house, that we take food and blankets. We can leave them there with a guard during the day while we work our places. At least, we'll know they're safe. We'll use the school bell for an alarm, but I would not use the schoolhouse—"

He turned to Benjamin Winthrope. "I don't know how you feel about this, Mr. Winthrope. Certainly this is not your concern. We shall have to discontinue the school for the time being."

Winthrope, rubbing his hands uneasily, answered, "I'm not an advocate of violence, Mr. Jackson. I don't approve of what you are doing, but it's not my affair. But you can't have the children run wild, all of them together in one place—"

"There's nothing else we can do."

Winthrope, resignedly, said, "I'll stay for a while until things are orderly. They're never orderly in the beginning."

"If you want to stay, we'd be thankful." He turned to the people, "Take whatever powder and shot you have up to the house. I would say take cornmeal, smoked meat—whatever you can move conveniently."

They left the schoolhouse the way they had come in, slowly, not talking much; each man gathered his children to himself as he walked or rode back to his house. Coming out, Trooper stopped Gideon and said:

"I ain't leaving my place."

"Why?"

The huge black man, standing inches higher than Gideon, inches broader, a great, slow mass of a man, shook his head. "I ain't leaving, Gideon."

"That's up to you," Gideon said.

Word by word, Trooper let it out. "I ain't like you, Gideon. When I'm a slave, that lash come down harder on me than anyone else, you big black bastard, you stupid black bastard, you god damn black bastard. All the time that. Mr. Dudley Carwell buy me at auction in Orleans. Pay a higher price any other man bring. Work me harder too. Work me morning, noon and night. Never see happy sunrise, never see happy nighttime; when there's whipping, old overseer say, whip that black bastard for example, won't hurt him none."

He pulled off his shirt. "Look at that back, Gideon!" Brother Peter and a few others had stopped to listen; they looked at the back that had whip scars all over it, like a moulded relief map.

"I ain't going off my place, Gideon. Me and my woman, we break our damn backs turning over that dirt. Got a piece of dirt's all my own. Got no master, got no overseer. Sometimes, I feel like kneeling me down and kissing that there earth, sure enough. Got a house my own; sit down there and woman brings me food. Ain't no slave shack, ain't no punishment cell—just my own house. I'm going to stay there, Gideon. Ain't nobody going to move me out of there."

"And your children?" Brother Peter asked.

"They going to stay. Ain't no harm going to come to them."

Eight years ago, Gideon would have stormed and pleaded; now he said, "All right, Trooper. If that's what you want, all right."

During all the long afternoon of that day, April eighteenth, the people of Carwell moved from their farms to the plantation house. Women filled wagons with bedding, pots, food, a few small, treasured household things, a calendar, a book or a Bible, a sewing basket, a plaster of paris figure, a bright Currier and Ives print. There was not much talk now about this thing, which they had talked about so much for weeks. Even the children, though filled with excitement by this one earth-shaking event in their simple, slow-moving lives, were more than ordinarily hushed. Tempers were short.

Men found themselves exploding over small and unimportant matters, a tool misplaced, a child underfoot; women became furious over nothing: while the great and single fact was accepted without comment, without tears. A family, loaded down in its wagon, drove slowly toward the hill, and waved at another family coming from another direction. One by one, the wagons converged on the house. When they were all there, the old, white, porticoed building gleamed all pink and golden in the setting sun.

Gideon took a few books, not many. Jeff took his instruments and some of the medicines he had bought in Charleston. They laid out the bedding on the big hay wagon, making poor Fred McHugh as comfortable as they could. They took all their arms, Gideon's army Spencer, Marcus' cavalry carbine, two shotguns, and a heavy, long-barreled Colt revolver that Gideon had bought in Washington the year before. They took Rachel's best pans and most of their household linen. Rachel had wanted to leave that behind, it was such fine white stuff; for years Gideon had been buying it, a little at a time, knowing how much she loved the feel of smooth white sheets and pillow cases: but Jeff said, "Take it all," offering no explanation.

Abner Lait said to Jimmy, his nineteen-year-old son, "What do you think? These ain't the times they were ten years ago. I'm stringing with Gideon because it's kind of become a habit. You don't have to."

A year before Gideon had helped Abner to buy an extra hundred-acre piece for Jimmy to move onto when he married. Now the boy reminded him.

"I know that. It's no skin off your back."

"I'll go along with you."

Abner nodded and laid an arm across the boy's shoulder. That was a rare show of affection. The boy shrugged it off and went into the house to help his mother.

Brother Peter and the Allenby boys were among the first to arrive at the big house. The course of years had not changed the outside too much, weathered it some, peeled off some of the paint. From a distance, the building had its old dignity and beauty, almost unimpaired; but when you came closer you saw that the windows were broken, the weeds grown higher, the doors hanging from their hinges. All of the furnishings had been sold at auction, but emptiness could not entirely displace the former grandeur. The big central staircase, with its mahogany banisters and oaken treads was if anything more impressive in the emptiness. The old hand-blocked wallpaper hung in leafs and shreds, but its color remained. The wonderfully-carved walnut dados seemed waiting, patiently, to be backed once more with cabinets, chairs, and sofas, and here and there the fine hardwood floors showed through the years' accumulation of dirt, dead leaves, and refuse brought in by the children who had played in the empty rooms.

Being encumbered by few possessions, Brother Peter had been able to make the change quickly. The three boys, who had been living with him since old Mr. Allenby died, came with him, and soon they were at work with brooms, cleaning the place. After a while, others joined them. The accumulated debris of a dozen years isn't quickly disposed of, but by the time the families were arriving in any numbers, a sort of neatness prevailed in the big house. Gideon took charge of the incoming folk. While there were more than twenty rooms, it would still mean a communal sort of life. The men would sleep in what had formerly been the main reception room. Keeping the families together as much as possible, he divided the women and small children among the many bedrooms. In some cases, such as that of Jake Sutter, where there was a grandmother, a wife, a sister and three daughters, he gave the family a room for itself. An overflow of the men would sleep in the dining room along with the teen-age boys; in the daytime, the room would be used for meals and as a schoolhouse. The food was put in the kitchen annex, and Gideon appointed a committee of women to apportion it and supervise the cooking. Another group of women set about cleaning the place. Men put paper patches over the broken windows, and Hannibal Washington and two others climbed down into the cistern and set about making it usable. Since the cistern was enclosed by the two back wings of the house, only a step from the kitchen door, Gideon saw no reason why it shouldn't be used to store all the water they needed, instead of relying on barrels in the house. It was clean by the time the sun set, and Hannibal Washington set a crew of boys to filling it from the well. Meanwhile, Gideon sent half a dozen wagons back for cordwood.

Some of the people, those who had small children, had brought cows with enough fodder to last them at least a few days. Since the Carwell barns and stables had been burned down long ago, Gideon put the cows and horses in the space between the wings, and made a fence for them out of the wagons.

It was amazing what had been accomplished by nightfall, and the very fact of that accomplishment cheered the people immensely. Except for Winthrope, there were no strangers here; those of the people who had not known each other from birth had at least been intimate for many years. Habits and mannerisms that would have been peculiar and annoying to others were not so to them. There was a novelty that buoyed them up in this being together, in sharing each other's problems, in being able to sit talking much later into the night than had been their habit. The old chandeliers had not been removed from the Carwell house; Gideon was wasteful of candles this night; he had two dozen put in each of the main chandeliers, and the bright glow that came sparkling through the cut glass gave a merry and cheerful atmosphere to the place.

Gideon broke down the men into committees. Ten would be sufficient to stay by the house, which meant, including the older boys, that a man need only give one day a week to this. They could not go very far into the future; if they did, it threw a pall of depression over them; they were content with tomorrow or the next day. A committee would see to the horses, another would be a sort of judicial board in the house itself. Things might go well tonight, but after a while this living together would get on people's nerves, and there would be squabbles and disputes to settle. There was much, too, that the children could do, a thousand small tasks which would keep them out of mischief.

Out of boxes and boards, Gideon had made himself a sort of table. Many of the people had brought chairs, a simple and needful thing for elementary comfort. When the confusion of the first meal cooked and served together in the house had passed, Gideon sat himself down to write a series of telegrams. He would send one to the editor of the New York *Herald;* Bennett had dispatched reporters through hell and high water before to get stories not half so good as the one that might presently unfold at Carwell. Another telegram to the president, another to the secretary of state, another to Frederick Douglass, the old and venerable Negro leader. One to Cardozo, describing the impending situation and make a last plea for unity and common action by every decent force in the South. In the message to Cardozo, he said, "I beg of you, Francis, to remember that we are not alone, that thousands of good and just men in the South, both black and white, can be inspired and united by the fact that here at Carwell, people have refused to accept tyranny and terror as the inevitable course of things." He sent a telegram to Ralph Waldo Emerson, that the old man lift his voice once more in the cause of justice. As each was written, he passed it among the men to read and comment on. And when he had finally finished, he took Marcus aside and told him:

"I want you to do this, son. It's important."

Marcus nodded.

"Go all the way to Columbia. I want you to go tonight, and you can be there when the Western Union office opens in the morning. Take the mare; Abner will let you use his saddle. Whatever happens, Marcus, boy, see that the wires are sent. Then get back here."

"I'll get back here," Marcus said.

Gideon walked outside with him before he left. Marcus wore high boots; he had the big Colt revolver in his jacket pocket with the telegrams. He had said his offhand goodbys, supremely assured of his own ability to do a thing. Now he was alive and eager with excitement; it was a fine moonlit night, a fine night for a ride to Columbia. The little mare could run like the wind; nothing would stop him, nothing could catch him, and in a few hours people all over the land would know what was happening at Carwell. Gideon watched him with pride; this was his son, this clean-limbed young man, unafraid, alive, proud—this was a testimony for what had been. The time to come would take care of itself. "You're not afraid?" he asked Marcus, and the boy just smiled. Jeff came out as he was mounting. "Good luck," Jeff said, squeezing the boy's thigh, smiling at him.

"Thank you, doctor," Marcus grinned, the same elusive note, part of sarcasm, part of respect in his voice. "I'll bring you back a box of pills." Then he was off, walking his horse down the hillside, past the decaying ruins that had been the slave cabins.

Shortly after that, Gideon lay down on his pallet in the reception room. It was strange to be lying there with the hoarse breathing and the restless movements of many men all around him. The silvery moonlight, streaming in through the tall windows, gave an added dream quality to the place. It took Gideon back to the time, so long ago now, when he had been in the army, stretching out for some tired bivouac, a long way from Carwell, a long way from young and lovely Rachel, a long way from the children he had left behind—because a time comes when a man does what he must. Thinking that way, of one thing and another that had happened long ago, Gideon fell asleep—to be awakened, how much later he did not know, by the sound of many shots echoing across the valley. Shots that went on intermittently until there was silence again.

Katie, Trooper's wife, would say nothing to him; she loved him and yet she feared him. He was bigger and stronger than any man at Carwell, yet he could be gentle as a woman; he could be moved to tears or to hot anger with equal ease. Katie put up with that; she had a good life with her man; she was small and plain, but Trooper was good to her, never sinned with other women, provided well, and had never raised a hand to her or the children. It was true that he had his ways; when he set his mind on something, that was that, and you could forget about it right there. When he said, no, he wasn't going to take a surname as everyone else was; Trooper was a name, a good enough name; it had always been his name; it would continue to be his name; when he said that, you just had to take it, and it was no use to argue with him. When he said he was going to stay, Katie accepted the fact. She told her two little girls, "We going to stay right here." Though her heart sank as she saw the families coming by on their way up to the plantation house, what could she do? And as night fell, and Trooper's little cabin appeared to sink into a well of lonesomeness, Katie became more and more terror-stricken, though she hid her feelings from her husband.

She didn't sleep at all that night. She lay awake and listening beside Trooper's inert body; he slept; he feared nothing. This was his, who could take it away? She lay there thinking of all the forces that would rear up, and as she lay there, as the minutes and hours passed by, she heard something.

She woke Trooper. "Listen!"

"What that?"

He listened and he heard the quick, even thud of hoofbeats. He climbed out of bed, pulled on his pants, located his Spencer in the moonlight that streamed into the room, and started out, barefooted.

"Where you going?" Katie whispered.

"Outside. You stay here!"

He went out and stood in front of the little house, gripping the rifle. Remembering that he had no cartridges, he went back and filled a pocket with them. The children stirred, and Trooper bent over them and soothed them. Katie watched him but said nothing. He went out of the house again and stood in the moonlight, listening, a giant of a man, bare from the waist up, the heavy, bulging muscles rippling with his every movement.

He heard the hoofbeats stop. He heard them pick up again from the direction of Gideon's house, and then grow softer as the pines swallowed the road. Then the road came over a bluff, bathed in moonlight, and there Trooper saw a body of men appear, at least thirty men bunched close together, all of them wearing white sheets and the pointed hoods of the Klan. He drew in his breath, cursed softly, but did not move. Then the road dipped out of sight again, and the hoofbeats stopped. That would be at Hannibal Washington's house. They were close enough now so that Trooper could hear the faint noise of their voices. The hoofbeats picked up again—his house was the next on the road. Trooper braced himself, feet apart, his chest swelling slightly.

In a little while, he saw them on the mottled, tree-shadowed road. His dog began to bark, a fine setter that charged fearlessly and stupidly into the mass of horses. They came on warily and slowly, walking their horses, and then dropping even that pace when they saw Trooper. They saw him like a strange, inhuman column of shiny black. They saw his waist high, level rifle. For a long moment, they paused, and then they came on, very slowly.

"What you want?" he asked, his deep voice rumbling with hate and anger. Katie came to the doorway; she saw the hooded men and began to sob hysterically.

A man in the lead said, "We want Hannibal Washington, Andrew Sherman, and you."

"You see me," Trooper said.

"Put down that gun!"

"You see me," Trooper repeated, his voice booming with hate now, like a resonant bass drum. "You on my land! God damn you sons of bitches, get off my land!"

The setter, taking the note from his master's voice, began to bark furiously, ripping at one of the horses. The horse reared. Someone said, "Quiet that god damn hound!" A revolver cracked, and the dog rolled over on its back, twisting from side to side. Trooper, his face contorted with rage, snapped up his rifle and fired. One of the hooded men became loose in his saddle, wavered, and then slipped to the ground, hanging by one foot from his stirrup. The horses stamped nervously. A half a dozen rifles cracked at once. The bullets were like hammers on Trooper's flesh, but he began to walk forward. The blood, in little rivulets, ran down Trooper's massive chest. His wife was screaming hysterically now. Someone yelled:

"Shoot the bastard!"

A rifle cracked again and Trooper staggered. The horses were milling around him now. He swung his rifle; the upraised arm to ward it off cracked like a dry twig. Trooper swung his rifle again, and the stock splintered on the man's collarbone, driving the broken bone deep into his chest. It was difficult to fire at him now without the danger of hitting each other. Trooper dragged a third man from his rearing horse, and shook the screaming wretch as a dog shakes a rat. Another man slipped off his horse, jammed a shotgun muzzle against Trooper's back, and fired. The giant body stiffened, then collapsed like an empty sack. The man he had just dragged from his horse lay on the ground, moaning with pain. The man with the broken arm and collarbone began to scream suddenly, wild, inhuman screams. They kept shooting into Trooper's inert body. They were all dismounting now. Katie ran from the house, trying to get to her husband. They caught her and tore off her thin nightdress. They got her down on the ground, clawing at her legs to pull them apart. Somehow, she twisted loose, and one of the hooded men, whimpering with excitement, brought down his rifle butt across her head. Her skull gave; suddenly, she was dead, her limbs without meaning or direction. A man yelled:

"You god damn crazy son of a bitch!"

They stood there, staring at the dead, naked body that had become so quickly and completely useless. They gathered around the man with the broken collarbone. The one Trooper had shot was dead. This one was dying; they stood there, watching him die, watching the blood well in a thick stream from a severed vein.

They turned toward the house; everything was so quiet now. One of them went to the barn and returned with a pitchfork full of hay, which he tossed into the open doorway. Someone else struck a match. They kept feeding hay to the blaze, and presently the whole front of the house was burning.

Then the children began to scream. Their fear, trapped inside of them until now, broke forth in the terrified wailing of those who fear without being able to know or understand the origins of their fear. The men stood around uneasily.

"Kids in there," someone said.

Someone else remarked, "Too damned many nigger kids anyway."

"Well, where in hell are these black bastards?"

"You ask me, they're all up at the old Carwell house."

The man who had spoken first said, "Harry, you ride back to town and ask Bentley where in hell's name is the bunch from Calhoun County? He was going to have two hundred men up here tonight. Well, where in hell are they?" And then he added, as an afterthought, "Tell him Matty Clark and Hep Lawson are dead."

Then he turned back to watch the burning house.

All of the men in the reception room were awakened by the shots. They crowded up to the windows to look across the moonlit hillside that seemed still to echo and re-echo with the sound. They ran with their rifles out onto the broad veranda, peering through the hazy and beautiful moonlit night. Women called down from upstairs, "What is it? What is it?" The children were awake and chattering excitedly.

A few of the men circled around the house, but found nothing.

Gideon's first thought had been of Marcus, but it was three o'clock in the morning now and he knew that Marcus was miles away. Standing out on the porch now, he said to Abner Lait, "Where do you think it came from?"

"Sounded like down in the valley where Trooper has his place."

They remembered Trooper now, and the men looked at one another. "Jesus God," Frank Carson said softly. Pointing, Hannibal Washington cried, "Look a there!"

There was a ruddiness in the night that grew and grew. It seemed to be a barn-fire at first, and then a tongue of flame licked up and they knew that something bigger than a stack of wood was burning. The glow reached up into the sky, until someone gave voice to what they had all been thinking,

"Trooper's house."

"His two kids—"

They started off the veranda with a rush, but Gideon called them back. "Don't loose your heads! For God's sake, don't lose your head! Stay here! Hannibal, could you slip down there and see what happened?"

Hannibal Washington nodded and darted away, a small, deft shadow of a man that disappeared in the moonlight. There was silence after he left, only some of the men watching Gideon.

"We stay together from here on," Gideon said. "You wanted me to lead you, then take my orders or find someone else."

"All right, Gideon," Abner said gently.

"James, Andrew, Ezra, each of you take one side of this place, stand out about thirty yards from the house and sing out if you hear or see anything."

The three men moved off. Some of the women came out onto the veranda and whispered to the men; they were sent back; they were told to get the children back to sleep. But there was no more sleep for anyone at Carwell that night. As time passed and nothing happened, the men broke into little groups, discussing and speculating on their situation in hoarse whispers. Some of them sat down on the broad steps of the house, and others leaned against the Doric columns that ranged up so majestically into the night. All of them kept scanning the hillside where Hannibal Washington had disappeared, and presently, about an hour after he had left, they saw a man moving.

"Hannibal?"

He came up panting, wet from head to foot with dew; he had to get his breath first, before he could tell them all he had seen.

"Where's the children?"

He shook his head. "Burned, I guess." He said, "I crawled as near as I could—I seen the bodies just as clear. I heard them talking."

"What did you hear?" Gideon asked dully.

"They're waiting for about two hundred men coming

from over in Calhoun County. The Klan branch south of here, maybe Georgia folk, I guess, are supposed to send some men up. They know we're here at the house."

A seventeen-year-old boy began to vomit; he hung over the veranda, retching constantly in a convulsive, aching rhythm. The glow was dying now, but a few of the men were straining their eyes in another direction. There, above the dark trees, a new spot of rosy red appeared; as it swelled, the men turned, one by one, to look at Abner Lait. He stood on the porch, his big red fists clenched, biting his lower lip until a trickle of blood ran down his chin. Then, though his long, sunburned face did not move, he began to cry, the tears welling out over his lean cheeks. He spoke in a whisper:

"The bastards—all I had, all I ever wanted to have, God damn them bastards, God damn them—a man works, builds, plans, dreams, God damn them—"

Hannibal Washington said, "Gideon, why don't we stop them before they burn every house on the place?"

"That's why they're burning the houses," Gideon nodded. "They want us to come out of here."

"I'm going down there," Abner Lait said.

"You're not. We let Trooper stay, and he's lying there dead now and his wife next to him."

"I'm going, Gideon."

Gideon's voice was level and cold. "You're not—"

There was something now. Ezra Golden sang out; they could hear the dull hoofbeats of many horses at a walk, and then through the haze loomed the ghostly outlines of the hooded men. They halted at a hundred and fifty yards, a mass of white-cloaked riders, more than twenty now, many more.

"Hello there!"

"What do you want?" Gideon called out. "Who are you?" The words floated through the night, rising, falling.

"You damn well know who we are, Jackson! We want those men!"

"It's no use to answer," Gideon said. "It's no use."

"We're coming up to get them, Jackson! We're going to get them or burn every house on the place!"

Gideon said sharply, "Spread out around the house! Keep down in the weeds! Don't fire until they're at fifty yards!" The men spread out, crouching down in the dry spring stems and shrubs. Those on the veranda lay at full length. Gideon, Abner and Brother Peter stood next to one of the columns. Gideon glanced at Abner; he was sighting on his rifle, a long, old, but accurate Sharps percussion gun. He stood as motionless as a rock, yet the tears still ran across his cheeks. "God forgive us," Brother Peter said, "God forgive us." Gideon lifted his Spencer and sighted; how long was it since he had looked across those sights at a man? In all the world there was nothing so insane, so unreasonable as killing; yet that was what made the ultimate right or wrong. The white line surged forward, a quick trot at first and then slower. At one hundred yards, Abner Lait's long rifle flashed and a man slumped from his horse. The men in white began to fire. At seventy-five yards, there was a crackle of answering shots from around the house, in spite of Gideon's warning. Another man fell from his horse; another screamed in pain. The white line stopped, hesitated, and then galloped away, fading into the moonlight.

The men from the veranda came forward slowly. Two of the hooded figures lay in the grass; two of the men from Carwell bent and removed their hoods. Both men were dead, strangers; no one at Carwell had ever seen their faces before.

In that first attack, no one at Carwell was hurt, but whatever small elation the people might have felt at that disappeared as the glow of new fires showed in the sky. One after another, houses and barns became pyres, each signalling the location of another man's ruin, another man's despair, another's agony. The women and children huddled together and watched. The sun rose, and still the houses burned, sending twisting flags of grey smoke upward.

The women cooked breakfast, and the people ate, but there was little talk and no laughter. Gideon's only consoling thought was that by now Marcus had sent off the telegrams.

Marcus had walked his horse down and taken a shortcut through the Carwell pastures, where in the old days the fine-bred saddle horses were kept. That way, he avoided the new road and the swamp causeway entirely, coming out on the main pike. The little mare picked up a smooth and distance-eating trot; she could keep that up for hours. The moonlit road was empty, on such a night as this, with the cool wind flowing past, a man could race to hell and back again. About eight miles from Carwell, at a time when he had pulled in his horse to rest her, Marcus heard the sound of many men riding. He dismounted, drawing the mare off the road into a clump of pine, whispering to her and stroking her soft nose. As they stood there, a group of mounted men came into view, about twenty in the white hoods of the Klan. Marcus waited until they were well out of sight and hearing; then he mounted and rode on again.

He was disturbed at first about the night riders. Obviously, they were bound for Carwell, and he wondered whether he shouldn't cut back, running the mare the way she was able to run, and warn the people. But then he reasoned that twenty men would be hardly enough to raid the big house, that his father would be on the alert, and that if he turned back he stood a good chance of being cornered and shot down. With that in mind, he pushed his horse on, leaning forward in the saddle, half dozing sometimes with the rush of the wind and the quick, gliding trot of the mare. The road slipped by underneath, and the hours passed. Young enough to forget quickly the situation at Carwell in the pleasure of his own mission, Marcus talked to the mare happily, "You wonderful horse, you sure enough beautiful little horse, you got a heart like a cannon blasting, you got a heart like a big sun rising—"

As the night sky turned gray with dawn, Marcus pulled the horse in to a walk. A while farther on, he turned off the road into a little meadow. The mare was breathing hard; they both needed rest. He was very tired now. Hitching the reins around his wrist, he lay down, only for a moment, only to catch his breath; certainly he couldn't really sleep here on the hard, damp ground. He closed his eyes for what seemed to be only a moment, and was awakened by the tugging of the reins. The hot sun was up now, and as he pushed himself up from the ground the mare came over and lowered her head for his caress. Glancing at his watch, he saw that it was past eight, that he had slept for an hour. He mounted and pushed on, and by a little after ten he rode into Columbia.

People glanced at him curiously as he rode through the outer residential streets. There was an air about the town, a mood, a warning. He went straight to the Western Union office, hitched his horse onto the rail outside and entered. The nap had not refreshed him a great deal; he was tired; he wanted to get this job done, get out of town, find a shaded place in a piney grove somewhere, and sleep. The pimple-faced boy was not there now, just the operator, a sullen, dark man of forty. He stared at Marcus for a moment before he got up and came to the counter.

"What do you want, boy?"

Marcus had the telegrams out in front of him. "Send all of these, please."

Just glancing at the sheets of paper, the operator said, "That's a lot of money, boy."

Marcus took out five ten dollar bills and laid them on the counter.

"That's a hell of a lot of money for a nigger to have."

Gideon had told Marcus, "Send the telegrams, I trust you." Now Marcus said, as ingratiatingly as he could, "I'm sending them for Representative Jackson. He gave me the money."

"Did he?"

Marcus said, "Please, mister, I tell you he did."

The operator began to read through the telegrams. Then he looked keenly at Marcus, at his dusty, mud-streaked clothes, then past him at the mare. Marcus put his hand in his jacket pocket, closing his fingers around the Colt. The operator read some more of the telegrams. Then he picked the lot up and said:

"All right, boy. I'll send them." He reached for the fifty dollars.

"Send them now, while I'm here," Marcus said.

An edge came into the man's voice. "Now look, boy—this sending telegrams takes time, a lot of time. I don't like to have niggers tell me how to do my business. You get out of here and don't worry about those telegrams."

"I paid you. Send them now," Marcus said.

"Get out!"

Marcus drew the Colt and let it lie on the counter, the muzzle a few inches from the man's stomach, his own body shielding the gun from anyone who might pass the shop or enter, his finger curled around the trigger. "Send them now," Marcus said. "Just sit down at your key and start sending."

The operator paled a little. His lower lip began to twitch. He started to say, haltingly, "Boy, this is a hell of a—"

"Start sending," Marcus said. "Don't try to make any trouble. I'll know what you're sending."

Keeping his eyes on Marcus, the operator walked over to his desk and sat down. He spread the telegrams and touched the key; then the key began it click, "attention central attention central Sumter street station columbia reporting nigger holdup in station wire railroad operator inform police attention—"

The operator kept sending the signal, over and over. He pretended that he had finished the first telegram, crumpled it into a basket, started on the second. The pimply-faced boy entered the store. Marcus glanced at him, motioned with the revolver, "Get behind there, over against the wall." The boy stood against the wall, mouth open, speechless. The operator's key clicked, "attention central i must keep sending—" He finished the third telegram and crumpled it into the basket. A middle aged business man entered the station. Marcus motioned with the revolver and he took his place alongside the boy. The operator dropped the fourth telegram into the basket. The key clicked on. The fifth and sixth telegram followed.

"That's all," the operator said hoarsely.

"Stay where you are," Marcus told them. He backed out. "Just stay where you are. Just don't move." He backed through the door into the street, still holding the revolver; then he heard the crack of a rifle, and together with the noise there was a smashing pain in his left arm, a red-hot hammer blow that left it hanging broken and useless. The pain was like nothing he had ever known; somehow, he kept on his feet, but he dropped the revolver. He staggered over to the mare, unhitched her, and tried to crawl into the saddle. Two men with rifles were running down the street. One of them stopped to take aim. This time the searing brand was in Marcus' thigh. Four more armed men darted around the opposite corner. People were running from every direction.

Marcus clawed onto the saddle. He got a leg over, telling the mare, "Run, baby, run." He lay across the saddle, and the mare started down the street with her smooth, gliding trot. Now the armed men stopped and began to shoot as if they were on a range. Rifle after rifle cracked, and the bullets ripped through Marcus. One caught the mare, and she stumbled and fell, pitching Marcus onto the earth. Neighing wildly, the mare gained her feet and raced off. The men approached Marcus slowly, still shooting, pausing every few steps to jam cartridges into their guns. Finally, they realized that he was dead. They walked close then, and one of them turned the boy over with his boot.

After the first breakfast at the plantation house, Gideon took Benjamin Winthrope aside and said, "Do you feel that you still want to stay here? They might let you go through."

"I've been thinking of that all night," Winthrope nodded. He was unshaven and haggard. "I'll stay, if you want me to. I can help you, I think."

"Thank you. I hope to God you don't regret it."

"I've given it some consideration," Winthrope said. "I try not to do things I'll later regret."

"If you could take the children upstairs and organize some sort of lessons?" Gideon said. "Brother Peter will help you. You know, it will be hard for them, cooped up here in the house all day. This sort of thing is terrible for children; they can't understand why. If you could, in very simple terms of course, make them understand why we are here and what we are doing, it would be a fine thing."

"I'll do my best," Winthrope said.

"Don't frighten them. Hold out hope to them. I think we have reason to hope."

Winthrope nodded and went to speak with Brother Peter. Most of the women were gathered in the dining room now. Gideon spoke to them, telling them simply and directly what their situation was.

"This is nothing we could have avoided," he said. "We must stand together. Trooper went his own way, and you know the result. Our only hope is to come through this together, to rebuild together, to make something enduring and fine that will be worth the price we are paying. I am full of hope. We are in a good place here. We have food for many days, plenty of water, medicine, and a doctor. Mr. Winthrope has agreed to remain with us and teach the children. I think that is very important; I think that lessons will go on and should go on, regardless of what happens. In a sense, we are a whole community here in this big house, and our great problem is whether we, the many families that we are, can live together for this time, however long or short, and solve the problems that arise. I think we can. In the past, we have met larger ones than face us now, and we have solved them together. We have here in the house more than two colored people for each white; I don't think that will be an obstacle. We have learned to live and work together, to respect each other. All that we have done has been based on the premise that in this state, where black and white live together, we must work together and build together. The men outside deny that fact. They have burned our houses to prove that they represent the right and justice. We have other ways to prove the justice of our contentions. We do not believe in terror, in murder, in destruction. We shall fight only in defense of our lives and our lands, and we will set an example to this nation of an orderly and disciplined and freedom-loving people.

"We made plans yesterday to go on working our land. For the time being, that is impossible. No one is to leave the house without permission. The men will have their tasks; in addition to seeing that the cistern is kept full, that the stock is cared for, and that there is sufficient firewood, they will guard this place. The administration of the house itself will be left to you, the women. You will apportion the food and be responsible for it. You will care for the sick and wounded, if there are wounded. You will do all the other many things that are part of running a house.

"Lastly, I beg of you not to despair. It may seem to us that we are alone here. We are not alone. We are part of this country and of all the many good people who make this nation. They will not abandon us."

All morning Gideon and others watched the small figures of men moving, in an out of the woods at the far edge of the fields. They remained out of rifle shot; they seemed to move aimlessly, without plan or order. A few still wore the white robes and hooded caps, but most had laid them aside. After last night, and from what they could see now, they estimated that there were at least two hundred and fifty men around the Carwell place. Today, at about eleven o'clock, those were joined by about fifty more men who came riding up the road from the south. Many of the newcomers rode around the house, looking curiously up at the hill where it stood.

The men and older boys had been divided into six groups, eight men in each group. The groups had captains, and each had a four hour sentry stand, two men to a side of the house. Gideon was in over-all command, under him Abner Lait and Hannibal Washington. Each group captain was a veteran soldier. Leslie Carson, who had been a trumpeter during the war and still had his battered army bugle was appointed to blow a short call for alarm. In the back of the house, between the wings, the wagons were tipped over on their faces, wheels in the air, to form a more effective barricade. A space was left to lead the stock in and out.

Gideon and Abner were standing on the veranda at about noon, when they noticed the man coming up the hill. He was on foot, and he carried a white pillowslip tied to a stick. About a hundred yards off, he halted and shouted:

"Hello there, Jackson! Can I come up?"

"It's Bentley," Abner Lait said.

Gideon told him, "Come along!"

A good many men and some of the women came out of the house; they made a compact group at one side of the veranda, staring at Bentley, their faces sullenly curious, as if arson and murder had given a new character to this man, something they had to understand. Bentley came up to the steps and sat down, bending one knee and folding an arm about it. There was no doubt about his courage; these were people whose houses he had burned, whose neighbors he had killed, but he had come up here alone and unarmed. He said to Gideon:

"Let's talk sense, plain and simple. We don't have to start a war, Gideon. I come up here to arrest a few men, and just look what's gone and happened."

"I know what's happened," Gideon said.

"All right, suppose you hand over those men."

"And then?" Gideon asked.

"Then we leave you alone," Bentley said.

"And then we go back to our homes, is that it? Or do we live in the fields like beasts? Or do we get out of Carwell?"

"Now look, Gideon," Bentley said easily, "you got no call to talk like that. You killed two men last night. I could have every last soul here at Carwell indicted. I'm willing to call that an accident. I'm willing to take those men and go away."

"And you needed three hundred to arrest them?"

Bentley made a deprecatory gesture. "The Klan is one thing, Gideon. I'm no Klansman, you know that. Jason Hugar's got his own row to hoe. You find a little excitement and the boys want to come along, and maybe they lose their heads a little. All right, that's done."

"And Trooper's two children were burned to death," Gideon said grimly.

"That was an accident. The boys lost their heads."

Will Boone, standing back on the veranda, said loud and clearly, "It's no use to talk. Why don't we shoot the son of a bitch, Gideon?"

Bentley just glanced at Boone. "I'll remember that, Will," he nodded.

"I'll tell you what I think," Gideon said. "I think you're alive at this moment, Bentley, because we are civilized and law abiding people. I think you knew that. It's a quality of your kind to have an instinctive if primitive understanding of what constitutes civilization. Do you follow me?"

"I follow you," Bentley said, smiling thinly.

"I want you to understand me. Do you know the rights of citizens of this state and this country, Bentley? I know them quite well; I helped to frame the Constitution of this state. You will not arrest any person in this house. On the other hand, we shall hold you and every one of your gang out there accountable. We shall hold you accountable for the murder of Trooper and his wife, for a piece of savagery that outdid most of your Klan's deeds, the burning of two small children alive. We shall hold you accountable for the sense-less, insane arson you have committed on the homes of a whole village of people. We shall hold you accountable for the death of Mrs. McHugh, for the assault and torture of Fred McHugh, for the murder of Zeke Hale, for the murder of Annie Fisher—for all the whippings and tortures and murders you have committed at Carwell. For all those things we hold you and your gang accountable, Bentley. We have been patient; we have been building a large and important thing, and we would not be turned from our course. We are going to continue building that thing. We are going to put an end, not only to you, but to all that you and your friends represent. That's what I have to say, and I speak for my people. Go back and tell that to your friends. Tell them that we will kill any man who approaches within rifle shot of this house. Tell them all of that."

"That's all you have to say, Jackson?" Bentley asked.

"That's all."

"Very well." The sheriff rose, dusted his pants, let his glance sweep across the faces of the people on the veranda, lingering on those that were white. Then he walked back down the hill.

Toward evening of that day, the first real attack came. Some two hundred of the Klansmen, unencumbered by their white robes now, began to crawl up the western face of the hill. They arranged the assault with care, choosing a time

when the blazing red sun of evening lay low on the horizon,
bathing the house with light and at the same time blinding
those who defended it. Gideon told off three companies to
take that side of the house, the side with the wings. They lay
behind the wagons and at windows. The remaining eighteen
men covered the other three sides. They set their rifles and
shaded their eyes as best they could. Upstairs, the women
and children were ordered to lie on the floor. The Klansmen came on slowly, trying not to show themselves, taking
advantage of every clump of weeds, every hummock.

"I wonder how many of them heroes was at Gettysburg?"
Frank Carson remarked, recalling how lines of men, in close
order and unafraid, had walked into a blazing hell.

At three hundred yards, Hannibal Washington, squinting
along his Spencer, wetting the sights with his thumb, tried
the first long shot. "Missed," he nodded. The Klansmen began to fire now. Their shots found the earth, or almost spent,
smacked into the wagons and the house. Marion Jefferson,
who had been lying rigid over a long, old squirrel gun, fired
and hit something. A man screamed with pain out there.
Others fired, slowly and carefully. At one hundred yards,
the Klansmen rose and attempted a charge. The sun was low
now, too low, its force spent, its melon-pink silhouetting the
charging, yelling men. The whole rear of the house, between
the two wings, blazed with rifle-fire. Within twenty yards,
the rush of the Klansmen broke and dissolved; at least a
dozen of them fell. The rest tumbled back down the hillside, a few limping, a few crawling.

"Hold fire!" Gideon shouted. "No more!"

The silence was painful now. Behind the barricade, someone moaned with pain, and someone else called for Jeff. The
space between the wings was in deep shadow. A man pressed
a hand over an arm that was spurting blood. The one who
was moaning, Lacy Douglass, had a smashed collarbone. Jeff,
tying a tourniquet on the arm, ordered, "Don't touch him.
Let him lie as he is." The men were standing, seeing what
damage had been wrought, staring down the hillside. Marion
Jefferson lay where he was, tight over his squirrel gun. When

Will Boone touched his shoulder, he rolled over. He had a hole between his eyes. A few of the men gathered around, standing quietly and looking at him. Out on the dusky hillside, a voice began to cry out spasmodically. Jeff, glancing up from the man whose shoulder had been broken, asked, "Why don't you do something? There's a wounded man out there." No one moved. Then Will Boone took off his jacket and covered Marion Jefferson's face. Gideon touched Hannibal Washington and said, "Take someone out there and bring in that man."

Hannibal took a step, then hesitated. "Let him lay," Abner Lait said.

"Go ahead," Gideon told them quietly.

Jeff had prepared a room as a hospital in advance. He had fitted it out with the best lamps available and had pressed Eva Carson and Hanna Washington into service as nurses. Now, with the lamps held close over him, he probed in the leg of the Klansman for a bullet. The man had been shot in two places, there and in the stomach; there was just a chance that he would live. Jeff found the lead slug and withdrew it. The man had a small red face and watery blue eyes, and what he was trying to say to Jeff was not too intelligible.

"Where are you from?" Jeff asked him. "What's your name?"

"Screven," he mumbled. "Screven, Screven—" But whether he meant that was his name or the name of a county in Georgia, Jeff didn't know.

Lacy Douglass was in torment, but there was nothing Jeff could do for him. The break was compounded; if he escaped blood-poisoning, he would have to lie recumbent and in one position for weeks. The other man had suffered only a flesh wound, and aside from the loss of some blood was not seriously injured.

As Jeff worked over the wounded men, he felt an increasing bitterness, an increasing frustration. This was Gideon's way, but it was insane. What came out of men fighting; what else but waste and death and ruin?

They laid Marion Jefferson out in one of the small rooms in back of the house, and there his wife and sister and children and old mother came to weep and lament. All through the house the people could hear their weeping. There, too, Brother Peter came to comfort them. He said to them the old words, "The Lord giveth, the Lord taketh away. Blessed be the name of the Lord."

But he could not answer why. His flock was not like the flock of other preachers; he had seen these people through all the stages of life, birth and childhood and youth and young manhood and maturity, and now he was seeing them in death, not death as it should come, gently, easily, naturally, a man or a woman giving out the soul-breath and lying down, but death that was smashing and terrible in its violence. He didn't understand. He had told Gideon once, "You like a little babe. All ready. Just fill you up, like bucket drawing water from the well. Just wait and see." That was what he had told Gideon once. But now he didn't know. Gideon had become hard and strange and certain in his course; when Gideon came here into this room and looked down at the dead man, not a muscle of his face had moved. He just stood there for about five minutes, staring at Marion Jefferson, and then he nodded and walked out. No word to Louise for her sorrow; no word to Brother Peter, no word to the children . . .

Gideon, Hannibal Washington, and Abner Lait stood on the veranda, talking about the things that had happened and the things that would happen, the things that had been done and the things that should be done. This was another night of moonlight, another night when the meadows and fields around the big house lay bathed in silver radiance. Down below them, just past the trees, they could see where the Klansmen had built fires. The fires ringed the house, but there were wide, dark spaces in between. All this early evening, Gideon had been thinking of Marcus. If everything had gone well, the boy should be back soon, unless he had stopped somewhere to sleep. He would not have much difficulty slipping past the Klansmen. Marcus was like a supple animal in the woods. Even if he had to leave the mare, he would easily come through to the house. But it would be more like him to dash through them and race up the slope. Gideon had warned the sentries. It made the inside of him go cold and sick and empty, just to think of anything happening to Marcus. He could never explain to anyone, not even to Rachel, how it was with him and Marcus, flesh of flesh, blood of blood; the most complete happiness he had ever known was to be with the boy, to hunt with him, to work with him, to sit and listen to the squalling of his accordion. With Jeff, it was different. He knew how different it was with Jeff.

Now Abner Lait was saying, "One dead ain't hopeless, Gideon, not against fourteen of them."

"One dead is the man of a family," Gideon said.

"It don't look like they'll attack again."

Hannibal Washington observed, "They stupid, but mark me, they going to learn. They frightened. They ain't got no guts to come into the place again, but maybe they bring up more men. They bring up six, seven hundred men, they find a way to do something, I swear."

"We were wrong on some matters," Gideon said. "It would be better if our men were upstairs, firing down. They couldn't take advantage of hummocks then. The women will be safer downstairs."

"I been figuring our shot," Hannibal said.

"I know."

Neither of them asked about Marcus, but Abner Lait said, "I stand a chance of getting through to Columbia, Gideon."

"We'll wait."

Abner Lait said, "I'm going to tell the men about the shot. Jesus God, they don't got to shoot unless they damn well see something to shoot at. Tonight they just shot off their guns like a pack of kids at a Fourth of July celebration."

"I want the dead buried tonight," Gideon said.

"Marion?"

"The others. I don't want the children to see it in the morning." And after a while, Gideon asked, "How many rounds have we, all told?"

"Ain't figuring shotgun shells?"

"For the rifles."

"About two thousand."

Gideon said, "Marcus will be back tonight, I know."

Later, Rachel came out on the porch where he was standing alone, and whispered, "Gideon?"

"Yes?"

She came over to him and pressed against his side. "Let me stay here, Gideon." He put his arm around her.

"Marcus will be back soon," he said.

"Why you sent him, Gideon?"

"Because I trust him the way I trust myself."

They stood there for a while, and then she asked, "Which way he come if he be coming, Gideon?"

"I don't know—whatever way is best."

"You think he'll come, Gideon?"

"I think so," he said.

"Whatever you say, Gideon. You say so, that way it comes."

He turned her around to him and said, "Rachel, honey, I love you."

She reached up to touch his face.

"Believe me, whatever happens, I always loved you. I became something I never wanted to become. The people needed someone, and I became what they needed, and when I became that, I turned into something strange to you. I couldn't help it; maybe if I were a better man, a stronger man—"

"You're a good man, Gideon," she whispered.

"I'm a makeshift. Maybe it's the strength of the people that they could take a thing like me and teach me what to do—and then I don't know. I don't know which way is best. Some day, there will be men who know, who understand why a thing like that out there should happen, who can work together, and plan, and build things that won't be burned down—"

"Gideon, child, honeychild," she told him, as she had in the old days.

Later on, she fell asleep, lying there in his arms on the porch. Gideon dozed a little, on and off. He was stiff when Hannibal Washington awakened him and said:

"It's come dawn, Gideon."

Then, like a cold, stabbing pain in his heart, it came to Gideon that Marcus would not return.

On that day, the second day, the Klansmen drew their line close. There were at least five or six hundred of them now, and they seemed to be better disciplined. They crawled within rifle range, dug holes in the ground, and kept up an intermittent, sniping fire. Two mules and a cow in the space behind the wagons were hit and had to be killed, but beyond that, not much damage was done. The women and children were brought down to the large reception hall, and the walls were buttressed with mattresses and planks. Gideon gave orders that no one should reply to the firing except Will Boone and Hannibal Washington, the two best shots. They climbed to the roof and lay there side by side, wetting their sights, hanging for as long as five minutes over a target, and then squeezing their triggers with infinite patience and care. Will Boone kept talking about his great-granddaddy, his great-granddaddy could bark a squirrel at a hundred yards, his great-granddaddy could do this and that, until finally, out of patience, Hannibal Washington demanded:

"Just who in hell is this great-granddaddy of yours?"

"Why you poor, dumb nigger, who in hell would he be with the name I got?"

But their sniping drew the concentrated attention of the Klansmen. Two or three hundred guns were turned on the roof-top. The bullets ripped through the base of the railing, sending splinters into their faces; about ten minutes of that before Hannibal Washington, sighing just a little, relaxed over his Spencer. Will Boone nudged him; then the white man began to curse, softly, steadily, firing while the rifle grew hot under his fingers. But in a little while his firing stopped too.

They buried their dead in the little compound where the cattle and horses and mules were. Curiously, no one cried now; the people watched with dry faces that were strangely old and hard; even the faces of the children were old. Brother Peter read from Psalms, "In my distress, I cried out unto the Lord, and he heard me." Gideon, watching, listening, tried to remember a time when there had been no Hannibal Washington, no small, gnome-like colored man, black as coal, gentle, wise, courageous, a man of great and incredible dignity, a man who could turn his hand to any trade, a man who was a repository for the misfortunes and complaints and problems of all the community. Now he lay in the warm Carolina earth, side by side with a white man whose great grandfather had been Daniel Boone.

All through the night, the firing continued, but at dawn it stopped. In the silence, the people ate their breakfast. In the silence, Benjamin Winthrope read the children *The Legend of Sleepy Hollow*. In the silence, Jeff stood over the little, red-faced Klansman and watched him die, never knowing his name, where he came from, or what strange pressures had driven him here.

In the silence, Bentley walked toward the house with a white flag, and called out, "Can I come up?"

There was no answer. He advanced slowly and stopped about fifty yards away, shouting out what he had to say. The Carwell folk had a doctor, Jeff Jackson. Old Doc Leed was drunk as a lord and had been for a week. They, the Klansmen, had wounded. They had a man whose leg was broken and swollen. The leg had to come off or the man would die. Would Jeff Jackson come down and treat their wounded? He had their word he would be allowed to return.

Abner Lait stared at Gideon, and Gideon, smiling bitterly, said, "You see, they understand us. They know us better than we know them."

Bentley walked away. Jeff came out on the veranda. "Did you hear that?" Gideon asked. Jeff nodded. Abner Lait said, "Let their Goddamned wounded die."

Frank Carson said, "I swear to God, the next time that son of a bitch walks up here, I'm going to plug him."

"I'm going down there," Jeff said.

Gideon grasped his arm, swung him around, and cried, "You poor damn fool! My own son, too! Can't I make you understand this? Can't I make you understand that we're not dealing with civilized men, that we're not dealing with an enemy as you comprehend an enemy? Those men down there want to destroy us! They're not human as we think of human folk! Their word means nothing! Good and bad, in their eyes, does not exist! You cannot reason with them; they've corrupted reason! It's because we've misjudged them, because we were such fools as to consider them bound by the rules that bind men, because we laid before them, on a silver platter, decency, right, and justice, that we're here today. That's why they are winning! That's why all over this southland of ours, good, decent men and women are cowed, divided, confused!"

"I'm going down there," Jeff said. "I took an oath, an oath to heal, an oath to put together the things men break—"

"No," Gideon said. "I've lost one son. But at least he understood. He knew what we fight."

"You'll have to kill me to keep me here," Jeff said quietly.

"So help me God—" Gideon began, and Abner Lait said, "Let him go, Gideon."

Jeff finished the amputation and they took away the moaning, half-conscious man. As Jeff wiped his hands, he said to the clump of curious men who had been watching:

"He'll need rest now. Nature has to take its course. When the dead tissue sloughs away, the sutures will come off easily. You test them by pulling gently, very gently, for it's painful. When the sutures come off, the basic healing is done. Any doctor can follow up the treatment—unless poisoning sets in. That's the main danger."

He was tired; a plank in a field under the hot sun is not a place to operate. He had treated a dozen wounded men. He was tired. "I'll go now," he said.

"Sir!"

He was bending over his bag, closing it; he glanced up at the man who had spoken, a broad-shouldered, sunburnt man whose hand rested on the butt of a revolver.

"I said I'll go now."

"Sir."

Jason Hugar, standing beside Sheriff Bentley, said, "You're a doctor, Jackson. That's something that happened. When a nigger becomes a doctor, it's the sort of God damned thing that makes this trouble we're having."

Jeff stared at him for a moment, then snapped shut his bag, picked it up, and started to walk away. The broad-shouldered man placed himself in Jeff's path.

"Sir," he said.

"What do you want?" Jeff asked.

"I want you to act as a God damned nigger should! Say *sir* when you talk to your betters!"

Jeff looked at the man, half in curiosity, half in wonder. A part of him was fear, a part was horror; but more than that was a logical curiosity that operated in spite of himself, a desire to rationalize this man in front of him with what Gideon·had said, with the whole insane pattern of what was happening at Carwell.

"You want me to say *sir*, is that it?"

"That's it."

"Sir," Jeff nodded, and added, "If you'll permit me to go, sir?"

Bentley laughed. Jason Hugar said, "You're not going, Jackson."

"What do you mean?"

"You're not going back, that's all."

Bentley interposed, "Tomorrow there won't be any need for you up there, Jackson. Better stay here."

Jeff watched them; still, fear was only a part of curiosity. The impossible did not occur in a scientific method. There was always a reason, always a cause. "I came here," he said, "because I felt it my duty to aid the hurt and the sick. Do you understand that? I came here because you asked me to come. As a doctor, I could not refuse. Can you, in all reason, demand that I stay here?"

The broad-shouldered man said, "*Sir*, you God damned nigger son of a bitch!"

Jeff shook his head. "I'm going." He pushed past the broad-shouldered man. That was all he knew, a memory that ceased to be a memory, an exploding crash that ceased as it came. He lay on the ground, his bag under him, and the broad-shouldered man said:

"That God damn nigger."

Rachel and Jenny sat with Ellen, but there was nothing they could say to her. Her blindness took in the whole world now; there was no edge to the darkness.

That night, Abner Lait told Gideon, "You know about Marcus."

"I know."

"Maybe he never sent the telegrams."

"Maybe he didn't," Gideon said. There comes a limit to hurt and a limit to pain.

"Somebody has to send them," Abner said evenly. "How in hell is anyone going to know that we're here? How in hell is anyone on this whole damned earth going to know what's happening here? Do we know what's happening anywhere else? They've sealed off this place; they've sealed it tighter than hell itself. Maybe everything in the South is sealed off that way. Maybe no one knows."

"Maybe," Gideon said.

"Write those telegrams again. I'll take them to Columbia and send them."

"And if they won't send them?"

"Then I'll take them clear to Washington."

"All right," Gideon said. "If you see it that way, all right."

Abner took the best horse, a fine, large bay that had belonged to Hannibal Washington. To do the thing on foot would be hopeless; the only way was to ride through them; it could be done.

It might have been done, but they shot down the horse

half a mile from the house, and Abner Lait lay under it with a broken leg. They took him out, held him upright for Jason Hugar to tell him:

"There's a special way for nigger lovers. Fred McHugh had a taste of it."

"Go to hell," Abner told him.

Abner Lait didn't speak again. They hanged him up by his hands and whipped him all through the night. Jason Hugar took a turn at the lash. "I'll make the son of a bitch talk," he said. But Abner Lait kept his lips closed. All through the following day, they let him hang there; but he was no longer conscious, no longer aware that his strength was part of the strength of many, no longer aware of the good fight that he had fought, of the good world of which he had seen a small piece, of the good comrades he had known.

Gideon watched them drag the howitzer into place the next day. It was emplaced a third of a mile away, and at first he had not known what it was. But the very fact that they had not fired on the house for almost twenty-four hours led him to expect something unusual. This was one of many possibilities. Frank Carson said:

"They must have got that from an arsenal somewhere."

"We're that important," Gideon said bitterly. There was nothing more beyond this. He was strangely calm as he told Benjamin Winthrope, "Take them all down to the cellar, all of them." You tried to put off the end; you continued to fight. You continued to hope; that was a process. Through all the terror, you realized that there was something beyond this, beyond the inevitable end; it gave you a link with others, with all the small, brave, frightened men who had held up their heads when the end was inevitable.

"It will be all right," Benjamin Winthrope said. "We'll sing. I'll keep them cheerful." He still wore his metal-rimmed spectacles.

"Thank you," Gideon said.

He stood on the veranda with Frank Carson, with Leslie Carson, with Ferdinand Lincoln, watching them try to find the range.

"They're no gunners," Leslie Carson said contemptuously.

The first shell burst a good hundred yards past the house and to one side. Four more shells burst wide of the house. Gideon called the men inside. They crouched behind the mattresses and planks, taking hopelessly long range shots at the gunners, careless of ammunition now, shooting because they had to strike back some way, had to resist. The first shell to strike the house burst on the floor above, showering them with plaster.

"Put up a white flag," Gideon cried. "Put it up, and we'll try to get the women and children out of here!"

Jake Sutter went out on the veranda with a white sheet. He stood there, waving it back and forth, while the Klansmen watched him and changed the angle of the howitzer, ever so slightly. The next shell burst square on the veranda, where he had been standing.

Brother Peter stood among the people, among the women and the young girls, the children and the boys who had just come into their troublesome and wonderful adolescence, among the girls whose fresh, firm new breasts stood like ripe apples under their frocks, among the grandmothers and the infants, among the suckling babes and the children who were just learning to mouth the mystery of words. He said to them, unafraid, "The Lord is my rock and my salvation, whom then shall I fear?"

The first shell burst overhead. Mr. Winthrope put his arms around the shoulders of a black boy and a little girl whose hair was like cornsilk.

"Of whom then shall I be afraid?" Brother Peter asked.

The people said, "Amen."

"The Lord is the strength of my life . . ."

Gideon's last memory was of the beginning, of how a people had been slaves, of how they had been bought and sold like cattle, of how their own condition had debased those other people whose skin was not black but who also worked with their hands, of how in this land there was little to hope for, of how in spite of that the people hoped.

Gideon Jackson's last memory as the shell struck, as the shell burst and caused his memory to cease being, was of the strength of these people in his land, the black and the white, the strength that had taken them through a long war, that had enabled them to build, out of the ruin, a promise for the future, a promise that was, in a sense, more wonderful than any the world had ever known. Of that strength, the strange yet simple ingredients were the people, his son, Marcus, his son, Jeff, his wife, Rachel, his daughter, Jenny, the old man who was called Brother Peter, the tall, red-headed white man, Abner Lait, the small and wizened black man, Hannibal Washington—there were so many of them, so many shades and colors, some strong, some weak, some wise, some foolish: yet together they made the whole of the thing that was the last memory of Gideon Jackson, the thing indefinable and unconquerable.

The men around the Carwell house, the men who hid their faces from the sun with white hoods, watched the old place burn. The wood was dry, and once the flame had started, nothing on earth could have put it out. All day long the house burned, and by nightfall, nothing was left except the seven tall chimneys that Hannibal Washington's father had built.

An Afterword

You may ask, and with justice, is there any truth in this tale? And if there is, why has it not been told before?

As to the first question, all the essentials of this story are true. There was not one Carwell in the south at that period, but a thousand, both larger and smaller. All that I have told about as being done at Carwell was duplicated in many other places. White men and black men lived together, worked together, and built together, much as I have described here. In many, many places, they died together, in defense of what they had built. There are enough sources for the person who cares to check on these facts. On the Ku Klux Conspiracy, there is the testimony taken by the Joint Select Committee to inquire into the condition of affairs in the late insurrectionary states, thirteen volumes of incredible material. There is the report of the Senate Committee detailed to inquire into the Mississippi elections of 1875, two volumes. There is Carl Schurz's report to Congress on Conditions in South Carolina, Georgia, etc. There is Hollowell's *Negro as a Soldier in the War of Rebellion*. There is *South Carolina During Reconstruction*, by Simkins and Woody. And that is only a beginning; there are the newspapers of the time; there are the Congressional debates: There are editorials, from both northern and southern papers, that showed complete awareness of the wholesale slaughter and destruction that was going on.

As for Gideon Jackson, he is a combination of several Negro statesmen of the time. All the things attributed to him were shared in good part by one or several of these men.

Carwell is an invented name. The people of Carwell, given names for this book, are taken from people who actually lived. Many of the other characters are real persons; some have been given fictional names.

The answer to the second question, why this has not been widely told before, is not complicated. When the eight-year period of Negro and white freedom and cooperation in the south was destroyed, it was destroyed completely. Not only were material things wiped out and people slain, but the very memory was expunged.

Powerful forces did not hold it to be a good thing for the American people to know that once there had been such an experiment—and that the experiment had worked. That the Negro had been given the right to exist in this nation as a free man, a man who stood on equal ground with his neighbor, that he had been given the right to work out his own destiny in conjunction with the southern poor whites, and that in an eight-year period of working out that destiny he had created a fine, a just, and a truly democratic civilization.